The Storm Dragon's Heart

STORM PHASE BOOK ONE

DAVID ALASTAIR HAYDEN

THE STORM DRAGON'S HEART

Storm Phase Book One

by David Alastair Hayden

Published by Typing Cat Press

Version 3.0 | September 2016

Cover illustration by Leos Ng "Okita"

Graphic Design by Pepper Thorn

Prologue

"I am a qengai...a spy...a warrior...a thief...an assassin."

The k'chasan girl lifted a sleeveless top off a pile of neatly folded clothing and slipped it over her head. Next came the matching charcoal shorts. She adjusted the skin-tight material so that it lay comfortably over her russet fur.

"I am devoted to Master Notasami's Sacred Codex."

Reluctantly, she stepped into a pair of thick canvas pants and cinched them tight. She hated the pants. Given her fur and the tropical rainforest she lived in, they were almost unbearably hot. But the pants protected her legs from brambles, rocks, and far more harmful things.

"I am willing to die for our cause."

She slid on her thick-soled sandals and wound the cross-gartered straps up her calves. Then, over the pants, she fastened on dark green shin and thigh guards made from hardened leather.

"I am the clouds and the wind."

She paused, savoring the feeling of one last cool breeze against her fur, before pulling on her long, canvas shirt and her padded leather breastplate.

"I am the rain and the hail."

With nimble fingers, she laced the hardened leather vambraces onto her forearms and wove her thick hair into a braid that circled her head like a crown. She pulled up the hood of her shirt, making sure her catlike ears retained their full range of motion, then wrapped the gauzy scarf around her lower face, so that only her amber eyes and the downy fur around them could be seen.

"I am the thunder and the lightning."

She tucked two sickle-shaped blades with long handles into the loops on her belt, strapped a sheathed knife onto each leg, and slid a set of throwing spikes into compartments hidden underneath the vambraces on her forearms.

"I am the storm."

Even though she had spent the last six years training in this uniform, she was already sweating. But a qengai ignored discomfort. All that mattered was the mission, the cause. She examined herself in a small, polished-bronze mirror, the most valuable thing she owned.

"And I am so not ready for this."

She sank onto the reed mat that served as a bed in her tiny, ramshackle cottage. Drawing a pebble from her pocket, she traced a finger across the name etched into it.

"It's just nerves. Everyone feels this way before their first mission...out in the world...all alone. I can do this." She clenched her fist around the smooth stone and nodded her head. "I *have* to do this: for myself, for my clan, and especially for my mother. I'll be fine. I've trained harder than anyone else. And I'm better than even some of the older, experienced boys."

Someone tapped on the door.

She kissed the stone and returned it to her pocket. Then she stood and looked at herself in the mirror again. "You've got this."

Elder Oreni, first-husband of their clan's leader, stood on the other side of the door, his expression sterner than usual. She didn't expect encouragement from him or anyone else in the village of Yasei-maka. Just because he was also her stepfather didn't mean that she got special treatment—exactly the opposite, in fact. "It's time to go. The Prophet is expecting you."

She nodded. "I'm ready."

"I took a chance on you, Iniru," her stepfather growled. "Don't make me regret it."

The Cavern of the Prophet lay deep within the heart of Yasei Forest, centered between the original nine qengai villages. The Prophet interpreted the inscriptions that magically appeared within the pages of their chapter of the Sacred Codex. After determining which qengai was called to serve and the nature of his or her mission, the Prophet would send a silver-beaked magpie to the appropriate village to summon the required qengai by shouting their name three times.

Only a few thin shafts of early morning sunlight managed to pierce the dense, evergreen canopy overhead, but it provided more than enough illumination for a k'chasan like Iniru to easily avoid fallen logs, stumps, thorn-tipped vines, and bogs. She darted from shadow to shadow, hurrying through the rainforest quietly and, as always, cautiously. The dangers so close to a village were few, but it was important for a qengai to maintain a constant state of heightened vigilance, even on her home turf.

Iniru's large, fur-tufted ears twitched back and forth, taking in all the sounds around her. Above her, loud birds in a myriad of bright hues cheeped, warbled, and sang. In the distance, monkeys howled and chattered. And among the foliage and ground debris, snakes slithered and all manner of insects and rodents crept and crawled.

The wind shifted. Iniru's nose crinkled. Somewhere close by lurked a panther, either perched in a tree or soundlessly stalking its prey. Iniru changed her route to lead her farther away from the cat. It wasn't likely to attack, unless threatened or starved, but it never hurt to be extra careful when dealing with them—especially today. She couldn't risk anything going wrong on her first and most important visit to the Cavern of the Prophet.

Besides, Iniru secretly didn't mind the delay changing her route would cause. It meant that for another precious few minutes, she was just a k'chasan girl, still training in the arts of subterfuge and combat, and not a full qengai burdened with the responsibility of a dangerous mission from the Sacred Codex.

The shadows lengthened as she slipped deeper into the forest. The birds and insects quieted. The vegetation changed.

Thick air—heavy with the cloying scents of fungus and rotting vegetation—invaded her nostrils and seeped through her clothes and into her fur. Despite the stifling atmosphere, she shivered.

The rainforest around her village had always seemed simultaneously ancient and new, with old trees and ferns dying and new ones sprouting up to replace them. But this part was different. Her mother had once said to her that walking into the heart of the forest was like stepping back in time, to a primordial forest that had once covered the entire continent of Okoro, long before k'chasans or any other peoples had come here. Iniru couldn't disagree.

The farther she went, the thicker the forest grew, closing in on her. Twisted, vine-wrapped firs of a type she'd never seen before leaned into one another. Red-striped bamboo stands grew so tightly together that they formed massive impenetrable barriers. At times, she was forced to climb over the bloated roots of towering magnolias, as if they were boulders on a mountain. Blue-tinged ferns with wide leaves lay amidst clusters of briars, their thorns dripping a strange sweet-scented ichor. And crimson flowers bobbed out from fungus clusters hanging off the sagging limbs of cypresses.

Shivering again, she suppressed her fear as she had been taught. Her pace slowed and every sense came alert. She crept forward, her eyes scanning the unnaturally dense vegetation on either side. A clear path had formed, leading her forward. That should have made her feel better. She had heard stories of interlopers being trapped by the forest until they starved to death. Even qengai would find their way blocked by an impenetrable wall of trees if they had not been called. No one could reach the Cavern of the Prophet without permission.

But it took all her willpower to force herself to keep going. As the canopy lowered and thickened to form a roof that choked out the already dim light, Iniru's hands started to tremble and her stomach twisted. The trees grew tighter and tighter together, interweaving their branches until she was walking down a living tunnel and even her sharp, k'chasan eyes could no longer see by the faint light that made its way in. By feel and instincts alone she advanced, picking her way carefully across the uneven floor of roots and earth.

Despite her training, her heartbeat raced as she imagined monsters lurking within the darkness. One legend said the forest had given birth here, that the goddess Ishiketa had emerged fully formed from this very tunnel. Another legend said the trees had been warped into this shape by the dark magic of a terrible monster. The great hero Akahiron had slain the beast eons ago but its twisted lair still remained. The elders dismissed all the stories except one: centuries ago, Master Jujuriki Notasami had meditated here for one hundred and forty-nine nights, recording his prophetic visions into the Sacred Codex. And only their Prophet, who lived out her entire life in the cavern, could decipher the strange glyphs of his transcriptions.

Thinking about the Prophet only increased her anxiety. Even the most hardened qengai master spoke of her in hushed tones edged in fear. Most people only mentioned the Prophet directly when she called someone to the cavern.

Iniru was on the verge of panicking, of breaking and running out, back toward the light and out into the fresh air beyond the heart of the forest. But then faint, flickering orange lights appeared ahead. Relief flooded through her, breaking her uncharacteristic paranoia. She took a deep breath, scoffed at herself, and tentatively walked into a huge cavern illuminated by a sparkling swarm of fireflies...and an expansive iron brazier filled with glowing, red-hot coals placed in the center.

"Hello?" she called.

At the sound of her voice, the fireflies stirred erratically for a few moments before settling back into their languid clouds.

Searching the circular cavern, she found a simple table, and three boxes—a large one filled with square sheets of paper, a medium one containing a number of charcoal sticks used for drawing, and a small one stuffed with an herbal, tea-like mixture. Beyond the table, a narrow passage led into a small room with a second, normal-sized brazier. Rows of boxes filled shelves that seemed to grow out of the walls, and what appeared to be two piles of bedding lay to one side.

"Greetings, Iniru of Yasei-maka," said a husky voice, behind her.

Iniru spun around, automatically raising her hands in a defensive position.

A stooped, white-furred k'chasan woman wearing only a short skirt stepped out from the shadows to Iniru's left. Chills pricked across Iniru's skin. She had examined the cavern carefully without seeing or smelling anyone. And if the woman had entered after her, surely Iniru would have heard some trace of sound.

Judging by the withered folds of her skin and her thinning fur, the Prophet was older than old. Trailing behind her was a girl several years younger than Iniru. She too had cloud-white fur and wore only a matching black loincloth split along the sides. Iniru had seen k'chasans with red-brown fur like her own or with paler browns, darker reds, and sable even. But she had never seen white fur before.

"I am the Prophet," the crone said.

Iniru removed the scarf from her face and bowed respectfully. "Hello...um...." Iniru frowned. "I'm sorry. No one told me how I should address you."

"It is of no matter," the Prophet said. "Let us begin."

"Oh...okay."

The Prophet gestured to a spot in front of the central iron brazier. "Kneel here."

As Iniru stepped that way, the girl smiled at her.

6

"And who are you?" Iniru asked.

The girl started to speak, but the Prophet interrupted her. "She is the Acolyte. Ignore her."

Iniru knelt before the brazier. Her knees settled into rounded indentations where thousands of knees had knelt before. This wasn't the only place to kneel. Eleven other pairs of indentations surrounded the brazier. Missions often required more than one qengai, so that didn't surprise Iniru.

"Are you prepared to serve the Sacred Codex?" the Prophet asked.

"I am ready."

The Prophet smiled, her bright-blue eyes disappearing into the folds of her skin and fur. "You are well-trained and determined, but you are not ready." She turned to the Acolyte. "They are never ready when they come here, because they are afraid—of their future, but more so of us. Do not doubt them, though. The ones like Iniru here will conquer their fear and serve." She waved the Acolyte closer. "Can you see the determination in her eyes? Can you feel the passion radiating from her soul?"

"I can," the girl said with a squeak.

The Prophet nodded. "In time, child, you will be able to sense her future as well."

Iniru gasped. "You can see my future?"

"I cannot *see* what will happen," the Prophet said. "But I can *feel* the possibilities that lie within your heart and mind."

Iniru studied the Prophet's ancient face shrewdly. She seemed calm, but her eyes glinted with fierce determination, her lips pressed firmly together, and her jaw was set. She looked as if she was prepared to do something terrible—if necessary.

"If you don't like what you...feel...you can reject me, can't you?"

"Yes."

Iniru breathed deep through her nostrils, blocking out the smoke from the burning coals in the brazier, the strong body odor of the Prophet and the Acolyte, and the pungent vegetative scents of the forest cavern.

She caught a faint but distinctive scent: acrid...cold...metallic.

"I didn't see you when I entered, but I thought for a moment that I had smelled steel," Iniru said. "And I was right. You have a dagger hidden somewhere, most likely strapped to your thigh and hidden underneath your skirt."

"You are well-trained, aren't you?" the Prophet said.

"I train all day, every day."

"I'm sure you do," the Prophet said. "Do you know what my dagger is for?"

Iniru nodded. No one had told her the consequences of being rejected but, she could guess. "Don't worry. If I don't deserve to be a qengai, then I will stand tall before you and allow you to plunge the dagger into my heart. I will make my mother proud. If I cannot do that with my life, then I can at least do it with my death."

The Prophet nodded appreciatively, then touched a fingertip to Iniru's forehead. "You will be important and accomplished..." she clenched her eyes shut "...but sorely tempted

7

to stray from the path and...in the end...you may fail as a qengai."

"I swear I won't fail. I will complete every mission assigned to me."

"That is not what I meant. And don't be daft. All qengai fail a mission at some point. Some even survive those failures."

"You mean you think I will abandon the path?" Iniru asked, her voice rising sharply.

The Prophet shrugged. "Now, let us begin."

Iniru leapt to her feet. "If you can sense that I'm going to be a failure, why haven't you drawn the dagger?" There was no fear in her anymore. She patted her chest. "Kill me now—the sooner the better."

"Stop being such a dramatic teenager and kneel back down."

Iniru hesitated.

"Kneel!"

Iniru did as commanded, albeit reluctantly.

"It is not my job to sense failure in you," the Prophet said.

"Then what's the point?"

"Child, tell her our responsibility."

"To sense evil," the Acolyte recited. "If there is evil in her heart now *and* evil in her future, we kill her—mercifully."

"Oh...I suppose that makes sense."

"Besides," the Prophet sighed deeply. "Truth be told, it is far more likely you will die before the thought of giving up ever occurs to you." A threatening tone entered the Prophet's voice. "Now, can we begin?"

Iniru nodded.

"Good."

The Acolyte handed the box of herbs to the Prophet. She removed a single pinch and returned the box to the child.

"Things will be different the next time you come here," the Prophet said. "I will give you a mission and a few words of encouragement, you will honor Master Notasami and the gods with a prayer, and then you will be on your way."

The Prophet tossed the herbs onto the hot coals. Purple flames flashed within the brazier and a thick, aromatic smoke billowed throughout the room. The firefly swarms zipped up to the ceiling, but as the smoke thinned out to a haze, they drifted back down.

"But this time," the Prophet said, "using methods handed down to us by Master Notasami, I will open your mind to the world of dreaming. There, what I felt before in your heart, you will see for yourself: glimpses of possibilities...scenes of what might happen...images that represent your destiny...should you stay true to yourself."

Iniru rubbed her swelling, smoke-irritated eyes. "So I will see my future?"

"In a manner of speaking," the Prophet said. "Many are the paths that lie ahead. The things you see might be specific, or they may be vague and open to interpretation. Or the visions might not mean anything to you...not yet, anyway."

"I only saw this cavern," the child said wistfully.

8

"It is true that a few souls will see only one thing, one future," the Prophet said. "For instance, when I ventured into the dreaming, I too saw this cavern and nothing else. This was the path of my heart, my only destiny. No matter what I did, I would always end up here."

Feeling dizzy and a little sick, as if she'd had too much wine, Iniru struggled to think. "So...so what's the point?"

"Perhaps knowing what lies ahead will bring you inner peace when things are darkest. Perhaps it will give you strength when you are weak." The Prophet shrugged. "Ultimately, only you can understand your heart's desire. Only you can embrace the possibilities you see today, or attempt to thwart a certain fate and forge for yourself a new destiny."

The Prophet shuffled to the table and picked up some items. "So the point is what you make of it."

She gave Iniru twelve small squares of parchment and a shard of charcoal. "The images you see will quickly fade from memory, as with scenes from a normal dream. But you can record the ones that resonate with you the most...if you like. Most qengai do."

"I'm not...I'm not an...artist," Iniru said drowsily. "I can't...draw anything."

The Prophet spoke a phrase Iniru didn't understand and tossed another pinch of herbs onto the hot coals. "The magic of the dreaming will guide your hand."

The Acolyte placed a small drafting table between Iniru and the brazier. "Here, everyone's an artist."

Iniru's normally erect shoulders slumped, and her mind went suddenly wonky. The room bobbed and spun, like a toy boat caught in rapids. She felt as if she might fall over and didn't see how she could possibly draw anything.

The Acolyte arranged the sheets of paper, adjusted the charcoal stick in Iniru's hand, and pulled the table closer.

"Don't let go of the charcoal." She patted Iniru on the back. "I'll be right behind you, and I won't let you fall over."

"How...how am I...supposed to...."

"It's so much easier if you stop fighting it," the child said as she placed her small hands on Iniru's back. "Let go."

Chanting arcane phrases, the Prophet paced the room, circling Iniru and the brazier. The fireflies descended and followed her, like a frothing stream of stars.

And then, spark-lit mists were all Iniru could see — erratic fireflies dancing in a dense morning fog. Images formed within the flickering mists and slowly came into focus. Iniru became vaguely aware of her hand moving in reality, the charcoal stick scratching against a square of paper.

She saw a boy, maybe the same age as her. He was baojendari—pale and tall and furless like all his kind, though he was especially lanky. She'd only met a few baojendari before. They had mocked her by saying her mother must have been a cat. It was a rude thing to say. But not surprising. It was the sort of thing you expected from them. The baojendari ruled Okoro, and most of them enjoyed lording themselves over the other races.

9

The boy's traveling clothes were gray and green; the breastplate he wore was burgundy. A sheathed sword hung from his hip. He had a small, round birthmark on his forehead. She sensed something powerful, a force that radiated out from him—fiery and intense, unlike anything she had ever before encountered. Then she saw it: an amber channeling stone dangling around his neck.

He was a wizard.

He stood at the end of a rope bridge, somewhere in the rainforest. Tears filled his striking blue eyes. Rage strained his face. Bodies lay all around him and along the bridge. His eyes locked onto her.

The vision shifted.

Again, the baojendari boy appeared. He had changed somehow. More than twice as much energy radiated from him—so much that her fur stood on end and her skin crawled. On his cheek there was now a cloud-shaped mark, pierced by a lightning bolt. What it was, she had no idea, but it worried her.

He reached a hand out toward her.

The vision shifted again.

Bundled in a coarse fur coat, Iniru stood on a windswept plain covered in snow and ice. Exhausted and frustrated, she argued with the boy. Over what, she had no idea. She couldn't hear anything in the visions.

After another shift, Iniru found herself standing in a lush courtyard. Horrified, she knelt beside the boy. Wounded, he lay still upon the ground, crimson blood and rose petals scattered around him.

The scenes then shifted into a rapid blur of adventures in exotic locales, where Iniru and the boy battled monstrous creatures beyond her imagination. The dream stopped suddenly. Iniru and the boy cowered as ahead of them rose up an enormous dragon—a dragon!—of deepest earth and darkest shadow.

And then she stood with the boy on a high cliff. A small, ragtag force gathered behind them. A vast army snaked through the valley below. She argued fiercely with the boy, until he seemed to give in. But there was an odd glint in his eyes that she didn't quite trust.

The visions picked up speed, racing by faster than her hand, or mind, could keep up. In every one, the baojendari boy was there. They shared bowls of tea and long sunsets. They laughed and kissed, argued and trained, and fought many desperate battles together. But the bowls of tea were the oddest, because they were always served by a flying, catlike creature whose presence irritated her.

The racing visions slammed to a halt and locked onto one that caught her breath. Again her hand flew into motion, the charcoal stick scratching across the paper. This was the only vision that hadn't included the baojendari boy. Iniru knelt across from a rune-carved, stone arch. She was alone in a forested land decorated with autumn leaves in all their colors. Day after day, she watched that lifeless arch. But she would never give up hope—just as she knew that he would never give up on finding a way to be with her again.

She woke suddenly—bewildered, the cavern spinning around her.

Gasping for air, she slumped over the table.

The Acolyte patted her back. "You did well."

"The arch in the autumn land...." she said. "Why wasn't he there? Where was he?"

"Where was who?" the Acolyte asked.

Iniru frowned. "I–I don't know."

"Here, drink this," the Prophet said. "It will clear your mind."

Iniru pulled herself up and took the bowl from the Prophet. She sipped the bitter tea and returned the bowl. After a few deep breaths, her thoughts cleared and the dizziness abated.

Twelve squares of parchment lay scattered across the table. On all but one, she had drawn a surprisingly accurate image of the baojendari boy, though the background scenery on each was sketched in crudely, probably because she hadn't had time to fill in all the details. On the exception, she had drawn herself kneeling alone across from the stone arch.

The visions slipped from her mind, falling rapidly away until all she had left were the pictures she'd drawn and a memory of the deep connection she had shared with the boy. It unnerved her to so quickly lose the memory of something so profound. No wonder the drawings were necessary.

"Why is he furless?" the Acolyte asked. "And what's wrong with his ears?"

Iniru stacked the pictures together. "He's baojendari."

"Oh," the girl said. "And he's the destiny you chose to focus on, huh?"

"Stop prying, child," the Prophet said.

Iniru sighed. "I didn't choose him. In every vision I saw, he was there. Except for one."

"I got this lousy cavern and you got a boy," the girl muttered. "That's hardly fair."

Iniru shrugged. Boys barely registered to her. She had relentlessly focused on one thing only: becoming the best qengai she could. All she was interested in was making her mother proud.

"What you just went through," the Prophet said, "is a sacred process. And it is to remain a secret—always. Speak of it to no one, not even your children, should you one day have any."

"I understand."

The Prophet gestured. "Follow me."

Iniru stood on wobbling legs and followed the Prophet and the Acolyte. They walked to the west side of the chamber and turned into a blind, narrow tunnel. Iniru glanced back toward the entrance.

"How could I have missed that?"

"It wasn't there," the Acolyte said. "It only appears when—"

"Hush, child."

A dank, winding tunnel that smelled of rotting leaves and upturned earth led them to a cramped chamber where, from a minuscule skylight above, a ray of sunshine struck a pedestal of interwoven roots and highlighted the enormous book that rested on top of it. Copper wire threaded through the book's ragged-edged pages and its worn, bamboo-plank cover.

Awestruck, Iniru stopped at the entrance and stared at what could only be her clan's chapter of the Sacred Codex of Master Notasami. The Prophet and the Acolyte entered the chamber and stood beside the pedestal.

Iniru dropped down to her knees and bowed low, touching her forehead to the earthen floor, while the Prophet and the Acolyte sang a long hymn honoring the Great Deities of the earth and sky, as well as the lesser gods known as the Shogakami.

"Rise and declare yourself," the Prophet said.

Iniru spoke her full name and recited the Vow of the Qengai, handed down by Master Notasami himself. Then, at the Prophet's invitation, she stepped up to the pedestal and gazed reverently at the Sacred Codex.

The Prophet flipped the book open about halfway, to a spot marked by a silk string. The right page was blank, while the left was filled with tiny, intricate glyphs that trailed along the page in narrow rows with barely any separation from one another. The glyphs in each row were either deep brown or yellow, with the yellow ones largely concentrated on the bottom of the page. A few brown rows were struck through by a crimson line that dripped ink like blood along its length.

"Each row describes a mission and names the qengai chosen to perform it." The Prophet pointed to the blank page. "When a new mission is required, a new line of writing will appear."

"So this is mine at the bottom?" Iniru asked.

The Prophet nodded. "The glyphs on your row are yellow, representing an ongoing mission. The missions described by the brown lines were completed successfully. The brown lines struck through in red..." she pointed to four lines near the top "...those are failed missions. If a qengai were to refuse a summons, then that yellow line would turn completely red." She gave Iniru a meaningful look. "That has happened only once in my lifetime."

Failing a mission was a shame that every qengai dreaded, because each failure added one or more lines to the codex, delaying the arrival of the Golden Age by months, maybe years. And it was always hard to face your clan and admit failure. But to refuse a summons...Iniru had seen the result firsthand. It had been....

Iniru clenched her fists and shook her head. She couldn't let her mind wander onto that subject. Nothing good would come of it. She had a job to do, and it was time to prove herself.

"So what now?" Iniru asked, excitement edging into her voice.

The Prophet reached out a folded slip of paper. "Here is your mission."

"I translated it myself!" the child said.

"I made sure she did it correctly," the Prophet said.

Heart thumping, Iniru took the paper. The missions of a qengai could range from spying or theft to scouting for an army or infiltrating a gang of thugs. But it could also, and often did, mean assassinating a target. Iniru, despite all her training, didn't want to kill anyone—especially if it wasn't in self-defense. Obviously, the day would come when the Sacred Codex would ask her to kill an unsuspecting victim—some threat to building their great new world. But she prayed that wouldn't be today, not on her first mission.

Iniru took a deep breath, steeled herself, and unfolded the paper. A grin tugged at her lips as she read the goal of the mission, its parameters, and the instructions for reaching the destination.

"Of course," she said. "Of course." She shook her head, laughing. "Well, he shouldn't be too hard to find."

"Why do you say that?" the Prophet asked.

Iniru pulled out the squares she had illustrated during the dream vision. "How could I miss him?"

"You don't know that it's the same baojendari boy," the Acolyte said.

"How could it be anyone else?"

Chapter One

"Haiyah!" yelled dozens of Chonda Clan warriors. Their wooden practice swords clacked together, thudded against metal shields, and clattered against the interlocking rings of their mail armor. "Haiyah!" Clack, thud, clatter.

The noise rose to the topmost level of an elegant granite tower—the home of Lord Kahenan, High Wizard of the Chonda. There, in his workshop, his fifteen-year-old grandson Turesobei chanted ancient words of power and in his mind pictured the runes for *darkest night* and *relentless fire*. Sparks danced about in the amber channeling stone that hung from his neck.

Slowly, as Turesobei concentrated, a ball of dark-fire formed over his sweating palm. Around the orb's black center crackled purple flames that burned hotter than any natural fire. But as long as Turesobei maintained his focus, the fire couldn't hurt him.

"Haiyah!" Clack, thud, clatter.

Beads of sweat popped out onto his face. His hands shook. His whole body trembled beneath his steel-gray outer robes. Across from him sat High Wizard Kahenan, bobbing his bald head and tugging at his braided white beard.

"Excellent," he said in a smooth, lilting voice. "Go on."

"Haiyah!" Clack, thud, clatter!

Turesobei tried to shut out the noise that blared through the open windows. He lifted his opposite hand and willed the ball of dark-fire to fly across the space between them. The orb rose and began to move.

"Haiyah!" Clack, thud, clatter!

Halfway, the orb began to bounce and weave. He couldn't control it much longer. Turesobei rushed the orb. But he overdid it. The orb struck his opposite palm so fast that he lost control and the dark-fire seared his skin.

"Kaiwen Earth-Mother!"

He drew his hand away, letting the spell drop entirely. The dark-fire orb sputtered and disappeared as it fell toward the floor.

Lord Kahenan scowled and offered no sympathy.

"Haiyah!" Clack, thud, clatter!

Tears welled in Turesobei's eyes. "By the gods, Grandfather! Tell them to practice somewhere else. The orchard isn't a training field. Kilono should know better."

He wouldn't have dared to address any other adult that way, but Kahenan insisted that he always speak freely. Kahenan thought such behavior befitting of a prince of the Chonda.

"But Sobei," he said, calling him by his familiar name. "I asked them to practice there. For your benefit."

Turesobei clutched his wrist as a giant, puckered blister rose on his palm. "What?!" he asked through gritted teeth. "Why would you do that?"

"Because the world does not know you need peace and quiet. And magic, I am afraid, must be worked in the world."

"Arrrgh! I give up. I don't even want to be a wizard."

Kahenan laughed. "What nonsense! Of course you do."

"No, I don't. No one ever asked me."

"No one asked me either, Sobei. But it is what you were born for, to succeed me as the High Wizard of the Chonda."

Turesobei blew on his burned palm. He could have soothed it with a minor healing spell, but he was too upset to even think of the proper words.

"You never tortured my father with all this training."

"He could not even summon a normal flame, much less dark-fire. That's why he's a knight of the clan. Now come, let me heal your hand so you can try again."

Turesobei stood. "I refuse."

"To have your palm healed?"

"No!" Turesobei stretched out his hand. "I refuse to try the spell again."

Kahenan grabbed Turesobei's forearm and studied the burn. "Ah, then you should have said so. A wizard should always say exactly and only what he means."

"You know what? You're an infuriating old man!"

Unmoved by Turesobei's insolence, Kahenan laughed and replied, "Old people are supposed to infuriate the young."

"Well then, you're the worst of them all."

With a twinkle in his eye, Kahenan replied, "That is because I am also your teacher. A good teacher always infuriates his students."

After his dramatic sigh turned into a wince of pain, Turesobei said, "Please, Grandfather, this is starting to hurt really bad."

Kahenan turned serious. His eyes fell into creased slits. With a voice that always reminded Turesobei of rushing water, Kahenan chanted. A tiny golden cloud condensed from the air and drifted down onto Turesobei's palm. The cloud felt like cool, dense fog on an autumn morning. Kahenan's tongue licked at the corner of his mouth as he focused the healing energies.

The blister disappeared and the skin healed. The pain faded to a dull ache, like a bruise. And it would feel like that for several days.

Kahenan stood and belted Yomifano, his legendary sword, to his waist. His emerald robe billowed out, and he drew his hands into its voluminous sleeves. "You may go now, but I expect you back early this evening."

"I already told you: I'm quitting."

"Yes, but I neglected to tell you that you cannot quit. I will never allow it, your parents will never allow it, and the King will never allow it. The clan's future depends on you."

"I'm not the only one here who can do magic," Turesobei said. There were other apprentices and four more wizards, too. But Kahenan spent very little time with them. All his efforts focused on Turesobei.

"None of them have even half your talent, Sobei. You know that. Besides, I have invested nine years of intensive training in you. I will be lucky if I live that many more. I cannot start over." Kahenan smiled warmly at Turesobei. "And I would also like for my grandson to succeed me, just as I followed my grandfather."

Turesobei muttered curses at his fate as Kahenan nodded toward the door. "Now, go. I have important rituals to conduct."

Turesobei became interested in his apprenticeship again. "Um ... perhaps I could stay, after all ... you may need my help."

"Well, I had intended for you to stay. However, I think your punishment for impudence — this time — will be to go away and leave me in peace."

Turesobei bowed sullenly then stalked toward the door. Outside, the soldiers continued to practice. "Haiyah!" Clack, thud, clatter!

"Oh, by the way, could you tell Arms Instructor Kilono to move elsewhere? All that noise is very distracting."

Turesobei clenched his fists, restrained a yell, and began to storm out of the tower.

"Sobei," Kahenan called.

He spun around. "What!?"

"You are forgetting your books."

When he'd arrived for his studies, Turesobei had placed his spell books on a table beneath the open east window. He stomped over, swept the books into his arms, and rushed out. But without realizing it, he took one book too many, a book that wasn't supposed to be there, a book that hadn't been there until a few moments ago. It was, in fact, a book unknown to Lord Kahenan or any other living wizard.

Awake for the first time in centuries, the arcane runes embossed on the cover shimmered beneath Turesobei's touch. If not for his anger, he might have felt this subtle pulse of magic.

Chapter Two

Just to spite his grandfather, Turesobei decided not to tell Arms Instructor Kilono to move away. But by the time he reached the steps of the Chonda Library, he turned around and went back. With gritted teeth, he delivered the message. Straight-faced Kilono let loose a sly smile and ordered his men to disperse.

Restraining his anger, Turesobei trudged back to the library to relax and read, but not to study magic like his grandfather would want. His martial arts lessons wouldn't begin until the afternoon, and his riding lessons were after that. This much free time was rare and he wanted to delve into some books on nature and history. No philosophy, no meta-physics, and no magic.

"Why me?" he muttered. He wanted to do something new and exciting. He was sick of being cooped up in the tower memorizing runes, reciting casting phrases, and reviewing volumes of energy theory. Wizardry was difficult, but only in a tedious, do-everything-precisely sort of way. Managing the energy flows and understanding the concepts had always been easy for him.

Though he didn't mind dabbling with magic, Turesobei wanted to be an explorer, like his father. Not a high wizard.

Not that he had a choice.

Not that anyone had ever asked him what he wanted.

His father got to roam all over Okoro. But Turesobei would be stuck here in the city of Ekaran for the rest of his life.

The Chonda Library consisted of a small but ornately decorated building with a three-tiered roof and a fenced-in garden out back. Turesobei removed his sandals and slid the paneled door aside. He was startled to find the Head Librarian standing in the doorway. She bowed and stepped aside so he could enter.

"Do you need help with anything today, my lord?" the librarian asked.

Bowing in respect for her position and age, he replied, "No, Head Librarian."

"Well, in that case, my lord, I am going off to run a few errands. If anyone needs me, tell them I will certainly return by the fourth gong. If not sooner."

She shuffled out and Turesobei closed the door behind her.

Inside, the library was filled with rows of wooden shelves that reached to the ceiling, and at various points there were tables with oil lamps and plush sitting mats. Turesobei thought about going outside but decided he shouldn't, in case anyone came in looking for the Head Librarian. So he went to the table farthest from the entrance, near the open back door.

Turesobei placed his books on the table and browsed the library shelves. He removed books with interesting titles, read a few snippets, and then put them back. He wandered until he found one he couldn't put down: *Legends of the Eastern Continent*. That was the land from which Turesobei's people, the baojendari, had originated.

Turesobei returned to his table and shoved his spell books aside. He noticed his channeling stone, his kavaru, was glowing.

He lifted the chain that held the stone around his neck.

"What's this?"

As soon as he looked into the kavaru, the light went away. This wasn't normal. The stone should never show any activity without him casting a spell or using some other wizard ability.

Was something wrong with it? Turesobei touched the stone to his forehead, matching it up to an unusually dark birthmark in the shape of a kavaru. This marked him as a baojendari noble, which meant his ancestry traced directly back to the ancient and magical Kaiaru race. Only people of the baojendari race could use the stones, and without such stones, wizards couldn't cast even the most basic of spells.

Turesobei's kavaru was the most powerful and most renowned in the clan, having originally belonged to the ancient Kaiaru hero Chonda Lu for whom his clan was named. The Kaiaru could be eternally reborn through the stones, but after three millennia and a score of rebirths, Chonda Lu had grown weary of life and released his body to death. His soul, however, would forever sleep within his kavaru. Kahenan should have inherited this stone from his own grandfather. But he had chosen a different stone and had always refused to explain why to Turesobei.

Out of the corner of his eye, Turesobei spotted a glimmer on the spine of one of his books. Except that wasn't one of his books.

Where had this fourth book come from?

He spread the books out in front of him but quickly tossed aside the three that were familiar to him. He closely examined the fourth. It was a tattered book, bound in leather and embossed with strange runes Turesobei couldn't read, though they did look familiar and were certainly of magical origin. The book was smaller than the others and it was bound unlike any book Turesobei had ever seen before, using wires instead of thread and a cover that seemed to be leather, though it was amber-colored and polished almost as smooth as glass.

Each time he touched it, the runes glowed with an amber cast.

The book must be one of Grandfather Kahenan's. But the table Turesobei had put his books on had been empty. And he would have noticed if his grandfather had put another one there. In fact, he didn't remember his grandfather getting up at all during the lesson.

Turesobei frowned. Was this a trick? Some kind of strange test his grandfather had devised? He really should take the book back to Kahenan, but it wouldn't be wise to interrupt him while he was conducting important rituals.

If his grandfather had given him the book, then he clearly didn't mind him using it. And if him finding it was an accident? Well, surely Kahenan wouldn't leave dangerous books lying around.

"So just what are you?" he asked the book.

Did it quiver in response?

There was nothing to do but open it. He flipped the cover open, and as it settled back, the pages stirred and rapidly flipped on their own.

Turesobei leaned back as the book rushed through page after page, all of them blank. When it reached the last page, the cover closed and with a muffled pop, the book exploded into a tiny cloud of swirling smoke.

The cloud churned for several moments, and then it started to draw in upon itself until at last it coalesced into the form of a strange little being only a foot tall.

The thing's skin was the color of amber, and the batwings it unfurled were a darker amber. Its big, round eyes bounced around, looking at everything in the library except Turesobei. It flicked a forked tongue across its tiny fangs. It flexed its clawed hands and swung its pronged tail.

Then it spoke in a faint, musty voice.

"Aha!" it said. "Free free free. Free at last."

Turesobei placed his palms on the table and leaned forward to get a better look. "What are you?!"

The creature looked at Turesobei. It narrowed its eyes and smiled.

"I'm a book, master."

"You are most certainly not a book. Are you a demon?"

"Ooh. Shadow or light?"

"Shadow," said Turesobei.

"No."

"Okay then, light?"

"No."

Turesobei had summoned and banished minor demons as part of his wizardry practice. He knew how to handle them. "I'm getting angry. Answer me precisely or I shall banish you."

With a stunned look on its face, the little creature blinked twice then recovered and bowed. "I'm a magical construct, master. A living metaphor. I am the essence and demon of the book you opened, which is a diary. Your diary, though you clearly don't remember."

Clearly.

"Did Lord Kahenan put you up to this?"

"No, no, master. Lord Kahenan would be very angry with me. If he knew I existed. Which he doesn't. I came back to you all on my own. Like I was supposed to. When I was supposed to ... I hope. I'm not early am I?"

"I ... I don't know. What's your name?"

"Lu Bei."

"How old are you, Lu Bei? When were you fashioned?"

"I am two thousand, four hundred and thirty-eight years old."

"Who made you?"

"Why, you did, master."

Turesobei sighed. "Don't play games with me."

The creature reached out and touched Turesobei's channeling stone. "I swear, master. You created me."

The kavaru vibrated and began to glow.

"Oh, you mean you were made using my stone."

"Yes, of course, master." The little creature sighed dramatically. "It is your stone, after all."

"Well, the stone first belonged to my ancestor, Chonda Lu."

"No, master, it belonged to—"

The strike of a gong sounded across Ekaran. Followed by a triple-tap to designate the exact time.

"Oh no!" Turesobei leapt to his feet. "I'm late for arms practice. Again!" Turesobei threw his books into a corner. He would have to come back for them later. "Lu Bei, you've got to go away. I cannot miss class again. I would be in so much trouble. Can you hide somewhere? Until I get back?"

"Of course, master. I can turn into a book again anytime you like. And if you stop focusing on me, I will return to book form anyway."

"Really?"

"Yes, master. I don't have enough energy to exist in this form independently."

"Then do it," Turesobei said. "Quick!"

There was a rush of air, a puff of smoke, and suddenly Lu Bei was gone. The diary lay on the table. Turesobei hid the book on one of the shelves and ran from the library.

Chapter Three

Putting the book and Lu Bei from his mind for now, Turesobei sprinted from the library toward the practice field. His black queue of hair fluttered behind him like a banner. His wide-legged pants ruffled noisily, and his sandals clapped across the gravel pathways that meandered throughout the inner city of Ekaran.

He would have to remove his outer robe for practice. The thigh-length, grey silk coat was tied in the front with eight knotted cords, so to save time he decided to pull it off over his head. That turned out to be a bad idea. Halfway off and covering his head, the coat got stuck. Still running, he squirmed and wriggled, but to no avail. He couldn't see a thing. Suddenly, a group of girls squealed. Feet scuffled away from him, and he skidded to a halt.

One girl clacked a fan shut and spat, "Watch where you're going!"

Turesobei knew that biting voice. He cringed. "Sorry, Awasa."

"Turesobei?"

The coat's ties finally slipped loose, and he pulled free. Beneath, he wore a simple cotton shirt suitable for martial arts practice. Turesobei grinned sheepishly at Awasa. The other girls backed away and snickered behind their painted fans. Awasa frowned at him, as usual, and tapped her foot with annoyance.

Awasa was a year younger than him, and quite beautiful, in the traditional, elegant way. She had large eyes, a round face, and high cheekbones. Her skin shone like yellow-tinted ivory. Today she wore a mint green outer robe with a pattern of white peonies. The silk robe beneath it was a light red like eastern wine. Silver pins and ribbons held her hair in a bun on the back of her head.

"You do realize you can untie your coat, right?"

"I was trying to save time," he replied. "I'm late for martial arts."

"Well, you are not getting there faster now, are you?"

"Er, I don't guess so."

"And you nearly ran into me."

"I am so very sorry, Awasa. I'll be more careful."

"Well, you should."

Turesobei grinned and fidgeted awkwardly. "Um, I was kind of hoping to talk to you. And I never seem to get a good chance." He blushed and found it hard to meet her gaze. "Do you, um ... Do you think next week, maybe ... the festival—"

"No."

"What?" he murmured stupidly.

"I said no. Since I'll have to spend most of my life with you I see no need to make it worse on myself by attending festivals with you now. I'm going with someone else."

Turesobei's mother and Awasa's parents, years ago, had arranged for their children to be married once Awasa turned eighteen, provided Turesobei passed his wizardry examinations, which no one doubted would happen. Turesobei thought the arrangement was splendid, but it didn't please Awasa in the least.

With a swift flick of her wrist Awasa unfolded her fan. "Come, girls. Turesobei needs his sword practice."

All of the girls snickered again and proudly marched off toward the gardens. Burning with shame, Turesobei sighed pitifully, then launched into a run. He was even later now.

On the practice field, nine boys followed Arms Instructor Kilono as he led them through the second of the three Crane Style fighting routines. The boys breathed deeply and eased smoothly from one pose to the next. The routine's sixteen movements imitated combat techniques, strengthened internal kenja, or life force, and increased balance and flexibility.

Turesobei removed his sandals and folded his outer coat. He knelt at the field's edge and waited for the routine's completion. Once they finished, Kilono ordered the boys into a line and stormed over to Turesobei, who bowed and touched his forehead to the ground in respect of the teacher he had wronged.

Arms Instructor Kilono yelled at Turesobei. "You're late again!"

"I am deeply sorry, master."

Kilono's eyes narrowed, and his face wrinkled from his second chin to his bald pate. His voice sounded like gravel poured into a wooden bucket. "Let me guess, the library again?"

"Yes, master. I was studying the—"

"I don't care what you were studying! There is a time for reading and a time for martial arts. This is the time for martial arts. You must learn to be aware of how much time has passed, no matter what you're doing."

"Yes, master. I will try to do better."

Kilono harrumphed deeply. "I will not tolerate tardiness from you any longer. What lessons do you have next?"

"Riding, master."

"After that, you will return here and repeat the Crane, Crow, and Sun Staff routines three times each. If you make any mistakes, you will repeat them all."

"I'm supposed to have dinner with Grandfather Kahenan after riding, master."

"Dinner is not my concern, and I will speak with Lord Kahenan."

Turesobei groaned. Grandfather Kahenan would let Kilono have his way then berate Turesobei for not being on time for his evening lesson.

"Now," ordered Kilono, "get up and join the others who were here on time, whose practice you have needlessly interrupted."

The other boys feared Kilono's reprimand too much to make a sound, but all of them laughed within. Turesobei could tell from their wide, sparkling eyes. They often laughed at his expense when they thought he wasn't looking. That had always been the way of things. Awasa and her companions had always mocked him, but they did so openly—something the boys couldn't afford to do to the future high wizard. Turesobei didn't really have any friends; unlike the other kids his age, he didn't really have any free time to spend on socializing.

Martial arts practice didn't enthuse Turesobei, anyway. He wasn't bad at fighting. In fact, he was talented. But he was behind the other boys his age. His wizardry studies denied him more than half the time they spent in martial arts lessons. And Kilono wouldn't let him practice with the younger boys, especially since he was tall for his age.

However, Turesobei did equal his peers in sword fighting, due to his longer reach and because Grandfather Kahenan insisted on him receiving extra sword practice. A wizard had to be able to wield a white-steel blade like Yomifano because only white-steel could slay demons and other spirit creatures.

After the long Crow routine of thirty-two movements to improve concentration and enhance the senses, Kilono directed them in attack and defense maneuvers, staff forms, and grappling. Turesobei took several scuffs and bruises from his more skilled opponents.

Kilono maliciously pointed out his every error, and with each mistake Turesobei lost more focus and did worse on the succeeding drills, earning more criticism. At last they reached sword fighting, but Turesobei was so rattled that he might as well have fought with both hands tied behind his back.

When practice finally ended, Turesobei was exhausted, but he had to rush straight to his riding lessons. And he would have more routines to do for Kilono afterward. Then Grandfather Kahenan would lecture him about his irresponsible behavior and assign him endless spell inscriptions. Worst of all, he feared he would miss dinner altogether.

As he sat in the stables, pulling on his riding boots, Turesobei's encounter with the strange, little creature from the book came rushing back to him. He had to figure it out as soon as possible. But how in all the seven worlds was he going to get back to the library before it closed?

Chapter Four

With a knotting, rumbling stomach, Turesobei ducked into the kitchen and stole a chunk of bread, a slice of cheese, and a drinking bowl of apple juice. He drank the juice in the kitchen and then crammed down the food as he hurried up the steps within his grand-father's tower. Running late already, he didn't have time for the library. He would have to either break in late tonight or go there first thing in the morning.

Turesobei stopped on the stair landing and composed himself in front of the sliding door that led into the top floor's single room. The painted scene on the rice paper panels depicted a goshawk taking flight from a mountain forest. The goshawk was the symbol of the Chonda Clan.

Tentatively, Turesobei slid open the door, bowed twice, and stepped into his grandfa-ther's open, circular workroom.

Kahenan sat cross-legged on a cushion in the room's center. His eyes were closed and his face held no expression, though he seemed peaceful and content. Another cushion lay five paces across from him.

Turesobei sat there in imitation and waited to be acknowledged. A cool breeze blew through the open windows. The leaves of the ferns and honeysuckle growing from giant pots rustled. The hanging bamboo chimes thunked and clattered. Scents of earth and leaves, jasmine incense and an early autumn night mingled in the room.

Turesobei stared at his grandfather for several minutes, but the old man didn't budge and Turesobei didn't dare speak.

"He knows I'm here," Turesobei said to himself, "and he's testing me."

Frogs began to croak in the lake below, and insects chirped and sang. After what seemed at least an hour, Turesobei grew tired of this game. He could have meditated, but he was exhausted, irritable, and far too distracted by thoughts about the Lu Bei book wait-ing for him in the library. It was all so difficult to believe and he had so many questions.

Kahenan, of course, wanted him to be patient and reflective. He was probably sup-posed to think about the mistakes he had made today, but right now he just didn't care about failing his grandfather or any of his other teachers. The only error that concerned him was having made a fool of himself in front of Awasa. Yet again.

If they would just give him some freedom...

Why did he always have to rush about to do everyone else's bidding? No one ever let him arrange his own schedule or do what he wanted for more than a few minutes each day. Even on festivals, he had to take part in boring rituals while other boys his age had time off.

He couldn't take it anymore. He had to get the book from the library, get some food, and rest. With a deep huff, Turesobei stood. "I've had enough. I'm tired, and I'm hungry. If you're not going to teach me, then I'm going home."

Lord Kahenan's eyes opened and anger blazed within them. His mouth tightened and his cheeks flushed. Thoroughly stunned by having riled his normally unflappable grandfather, Turesobei immediately sat back down and bowed his head. He cursed himself for being so impulsive.

"Sometimes you are an impudent fool!" Kahenan shouted. "Just because I have allowed you to speak your mind at ease with me, does not mean you are free to be disrespectful." He closed his eyes, and lines of strain creased his soft face. His chest heaved with labored breaths. "I would wonder what has gotten into you lately, Sobei, except that you are a teenage boy and angst and impertinence need no further excuse."

"I am sorry, Grandfather."

Kahenan's calm demeanor returned, though a little spark remained flickering within his eyes, waiting to be stirred again. "Perhaps you are, but I wish you could be sorry about things before you did them."

His grandfather relaxed and suddenly looked old and fatigued. "I have had a long day of difficult summonings and bindings. I am tired, and I thought that since you had a stressful day as well, that we could sit together and share some quiet meditation time. I see that I was wrong. Apparently you require no centering. Apparently your spirit feeds off insubordination and arrogance.

"Your mother has spoiled you, your father is never here to discipline you, and I am old and too lenient. Nevertheless, I know you have been taught better. No other child would dare to behave in such a way. Your attitude is simply not tolerable.

"You have been given a rare blessing to express yourself and treat your elders almost as equals. But you are taking advantage of this gift. Any other student I would have kicked out of here by now. Permanently."

Turesobei bowed and touched his head to the reed mats on the floor. "I am deeply sorry, Grandfather."

"You say that so much these days that I am not sure you mean it anymore. Go eat, get some rest, and come back here at first light to clean the entire workshop. Tomorrow I am going to work you until you know true fatigue in every possible way."

Turesobei walked to the door. He paused. Angry or not, Grandfather Kahenan always had one more thing to say when Turesobei reached the door. This time was no different.

"I received word from your father. The message came by pigeon this afternoon."

Chapter Five

Turesobei spun and excitement lifted his downcast features. "He's still alive!" His father was always in danger. "Will he get home in time for the festival?"

Turesobei's excitement seemed to lighten Grandfather Kahenan's mood a little. "He is doing well and riding fast. He should arrive tomorrow evening. But do not rejoice too much. If you do not accomplish all the tasks I set for you tomorrow, you will have little time for seeing him."

"I swear to do everything you ask."

"Then see that you get some rest. I am going to have to be harsh with you tomorrow."

Turesobei stared at his grandfather, debating what he should do about Lu Bei. He really should tell his grandfather, but for some reason, he couldn't bring himself to do so.

"Sobei, what is on your mind?"

"I need to get into the library. I left my spell books there this afternoon. By accident."

Grandfather Kahenan scowled. "Spell books should not be treated so lightly. If they fell into the wrong hands..."

"That's why I left them in the library. I figured they were safer there than on the practice field."

"I suppose..."

"So you will let me in?"

"No. You can get them in the morning. You are not going to be up studying tonight."

Biting his lip, Turesobei continued to stare at his grandfather.

"Something else on your mind, Sobei?"

"Well, it's about my kavaru. Why didn't you take it when your grandfather died?"

"A strange question at this hour. Can it not wait until another time?"

"It's just..." His mind raced, not wanting to reveal any secrets, and then he remembered: he did have a problem. "I've had strange dreams about my kavaru as of late." Which was true. He'd meant to bring this up weeks ago. Only he wasn't overly worried—dreams were dreams—and he hadn't had the chance.

"What kind of dreams?"

"Just ... strange. Not quite nightmares, but unsettling. I dream about the kavaru and about people I've never met before, but who I know intimately. And, in my dreams at least, I miss them terribly.

"It's probably nothing, though, right? My memories of the people fade like with any dream."

Kahenan walked to one of the windows and looked down on the lake. "It was not for me, that stone. Nor for anyone else but you."

"I know there aren't that many stones around any longer, but there were enough that I could have chosen. Why was I never given a choice like everyone else?" He'd had his stone since birth.

"The stone suited you. It was obvious. So I went ahead and gave it to you at birth. It is not unknown for a stone to pick a wielder. And I thought growing up with it would make you a better wizard.

"As for your dreams ... you will be fine. You spend a lot of time working with the stone, and you are nearly a man. You are bound to have such dreams. You are picking up echoes from past wielders of this kavaru. Do not fret over them.

"Now, is that all?"

"There is one other thing. Do you know if Chonda Lu had a fetch? Not a demon of light or shadow, but a spirit creature of some sort that served him. Perhaps one he would have made himself."

Kahenan stroked his beard thoughtfully. "No, I do not. Why do you ask?"

"I saw it in a book."

"Hmm. I have never read anything about it before. Did it describe the creature?"

"Very small with amber skin and batwings."

"I have never heard of such a creature. But you know, some of those old legends are full of fanciful details. Mind you do not put too much stock in them."

"Of course, Grandfather."

"Now away. Tomorrow we work."

"And see my dad."

"And see your father," said Kahenan. "But only if you work hard enough."

Having first made sure no one was anywhere within sight, Turesobei sprinted toward the bamboo wall. When he was only six paces from it, he chanted the command phrase for the *spell of prodigious leaping* and jumped upward. On a good day, he could have cleared a ten-foot wall.

But he was too tired for that. And the wall was higher than he had thought.

Thump!

He slammed into the wall hard, but before he fell, he threw a hand up and caught hold of the top. Aching and probably sporting a few new bruises, he climbed up and then dropped down into the garden of the locked but unguarded Clan Library.

Turesobei crept up to the back door and placed his hand against the lock. Forming the correct intent and the proper runic symbol in his mind, he whispered the *spell of unlock-*

ing. After a decisive click, he slid the wood paneled door open.

Intoning the *spell of the flickering flame* summoned a small, hovering sphere of fire. Turesobei set it to a strength no greater than a candle—not bright enough to draw attention and just enough to see where he was going. He could have cast the *spell of darksight,* but the only version he knew was of little use inside on a moonless night. In response to his spells, a barely noticeable mote of light appeared deep within his kavaru.

Turesobei made his way to the shelf and was relieved that the Head Librarian hadn't found his books. At a thought, the orange globe floated in closer. Shoving the other books aside, he picked up Lu Bei's diary.

The runes on the cover began to glow as Turesobei looked at them. His kavaru lit up as well. The book began to feel light and feathery.

"Not now, Lu Bei," Turesobei whispered. "We've got to get home first." The light began to fade and the book felt solid and heavy again. "And you have some explaining to do, little creature."

Suddenly the runes flared up again, then the book shivered and burst into a cloud of smoke.

"Master," a tinny voice croaked from within the cloud. "Watch out!"

At that moment, a withered hand grabbed Turesobei's shoulder.

Chapter Six

"Explaining to do, indeed," said a tired voice that Turesobei knew all too well.

As the hand released Turesobei's shoulder, Lu Bei coalesced from the energy cloud. Arms, claws, and wings flexed, and then ...

"Haiyah!" he squeaked, and he zipped past Turesobei.

Grandfather Kahenan instinctively reached up a hand to block the unexpected charge. Lu Bei crashed into Kahenan's hand, dug his claws in, and bit.

Kahenan swung his hand out, flinging Lu Bei away. "Off!"

Lu Bei flapped his wings, narrowly missed crashing into a bookcase, and circled to attack again. But even as Turesobei cried for Lu Bei to stop, a deep voice called out:

"Binding of my forefathers, take this demon now!"

Characters written on a bamboo spell strip in Grandfather Kahenan's other hand flared bright white momentarily and then disappeared.

Lu Bei was not a demon, but the bindings worked nonetheless, since he was a construct of sorcery. Streams of energy flew from the spell strip and wrapped around Lu Bei, physically binding him. Though he couldn't move his wings anymore, he yet floated, whether by a property of the binding spell or Lu Bei's nature, Turesobei didn't know.

"Sobei!" Kahenan roared, clutching his bleeding hand. "What is this thing?"

Turesobei met his grandfather's eyes and shivered. "A creature from a diary. Or rather it is the diary. It transforms from a book into this. Its name is Lu Bei. It says it was created ... well, it says it was created by me. But I think it means it was created with my kavaru. By Chonda Lu himself."

"How long have you had this book?"

"Since this morning."

"Where did you find it?"

"When I grabbed up my books in your workshop, it was mixed in with them. I didn't realize it was there until I reached the library. That was the first I saw it."

"You would not lie to me?"

"I swear it was with my books."

"True, true. Master speaks true!" Lu Bei said.

Kahenan pointed a finger at the fetch. "Quiet, you! I'll give you time enough to make your case soon." He turned back to Turesobei. "Why did you not tell me immediately?"

Turesobei shrugged. "I wanted to. I tried to. I just ... I don't know. I was angry and frustrated. And it seemed harmless."

"Often the most harmful things in a wizard's life are the ones that look the least harmful. Have I not taught you this?"

"Yes, Grandfather."

"Hmph. Not well enough it seems."

Grandfather Kahenan cast a spell and all the lanterns within the library blazed to life. He held his hand up to the light and frowned. The bleeding had stopped, though the punctures looked deep.

"How did you know I would be here?"

"I am not a fool, Turesobei. Why would you request that I open the library tonight, tired as you were, if you were not up to something? Besides, you were asking some rather strange questions."

"How did you get here so fast?"

"I am old, but not crippled, and you took forever with that leaping spell."

"You were watching?!"

Grandfather Kahenan ignored him and circled Lu Bei, examining him carefully. Kahenan's eyes were glowing white, which meant he was using his kenja sight to examine the energy that Lu Bei was made of. The technique would also show any spells that were active in the area.

After a few minutes, Kahenan's eyes returned to normal.

"Lu Bei, you will now answer the questions I ask of you."

"I obey only my master," Lu Bei snarled.

"Sobei?"

"Please, do as my grandfather requests, Lu Bei."

"I don't know..."

"That's an order," said Turesobei.

"Yes, but is it in your best interests?"

"Yes."

Kahenan fingered his white-steel sword, Yomifano. Lu Bei's eyes darted down to it. A white-steel sword could cut through and destroy a kenja being such as Lu Bei.

"It is in your best interests, that much is certain."

"Aha! Well then. Um ... what would you like to know?"

"Everything. Starting with your bite. Is it poisonous?"

"No."

"Who fashioned you?"

"Chonda Lu. The next answer is two thousand, four hundred thirty-eight years ago."

"How did you come here?"

"Well, I have always been here, in a pocket of the Shadowland that follows..."

The room went silent. Yet Lu Bei's lips were still moving. And Grandfather Kahenan was nodding in response to something Lu Bei had said.

Before he could mention the problem, Turesobei could suddenly hear again.

"Yes, he made me before he came here to Okoro," Lu Bei said. "I was to help him record everything he experienced. Obviously, it's easier if your diary can see and hear everything around you. Beyond that, he'd only need to tell me his thoughts and I could record them."

Turesobei knew what they were discussing. Chonda Lu, his long-lived Kaiaru ancestor, had been the first baojendari from the Eastern Continent to sail to Okoro. His arrival had unintentionally set the course that would lead the baojendari to invade and colonize Okoro.

Grandfather Kahenan's eyes were wide, his mouth was open. He stammered, "That ... that is amazingly clever. Do you still retain all this information?"

"Oh, yes, yes, of course. I remember everything master ever told me and everything I've ever seen or heard. That's my purpose. I am my master's second memory."

Grandfather Kahenan's smile creased his whole face. "The knowledge you must possess! We have only a simple account of that voyage."

"About forty-seven pages long, would you say?"

"Exactly. In terrible penmanship, I might add."

"Sorry, I wrote those for master. He was terribly busy and couldn't do it himself. I wrote a longer one, too. You must have lost it."

Kahenan shook his head as if he still couldn't quite believe what he was seeing or hearing. "It must have taken years for him to create you."

"One hundred and eighty-seven," Lu Bei said proudly. "Two hours each day." Even for a potentially eternal Kaiaru that was a long time.

"Astounding! The spells that must have gone into it, all that work and dedication..." Kahenan's eyes narrowed. "Why would he do this? No offense, but surely you must have served some additional purpose."

"Master enjoyed the effort in making a spirit construct, his own fetch. Not summoned, created. Then imbued with a personality he chose carefully. But you'd need master to explain the process to you. My memories begin when he first woke me, at the completion of all his long rituals."

Lu Bei looked at Turesobei who simply shrugged his shoulders.

"Will you tell me why else he made you? Why he needed everything to be recorded perfectly?"

"Oh yes, you see—"

Silence again. They were both still talking but Turesobei could hear none of it.

Turesobei interrupted them. "Grandfather, are you trying to keep me from hearing? Would you like for me to leave? It would make it easier."

Grandfather Kahenan turned to him. "You cannot hear what we have just said?"

"Not at all. I've been missing large parts of your conversation."

"Interesting. That explains why you did not react as I thought you might. But this is not surprising given—"

Silence again.

"You did not hear that, did you, Sobei?"

"No!" Turesobei said with exasperation.

"Alas," said Lu Bei. "It is not the time. I am early."

"Early?" Kahenan asked.

"Yes, when Chonda Lu decided to—"

Silence yet again for several minutes.

"Sorry, Sobei. I know you are frustrated but this is simply not something you are intended to hear at this time."

"Yeah, well this is worse than the 'I'll tell you when you're older' bit adults usually say."

"I am sorry. Oh, and Lu Bei, how careless of me." Grandfather Kahenan swiped his hand and the bindings around Lu Bei disappeared. The fetch fluttered down to the table.

"Truly amazing. No one could equal Chonda Lu. I wish I could cast a silence spell as effective as that."

Lu Bei began to talk but soon there was silence again. Turesobei ignored them because he had just noticed that there was light flickering within his kavaru.

He hadn't thought of that. The silencing spell had to originate from somewhere. He'd just assumed that it had to do with Lu Bei directly. But Lu Bei might not be able to cast spells, and his grandfather's sapphire stone was dark and cold.

Turesobei concentrated a moment and activated his kenja sight. He scanned the surrounding area, looking for a strong flow of energy. Lu Bei, being magical, obviously glowed. But none of his energy flowed toward Turesobei. The only other magic was the energy flowing from Turesobei's stone and enveloping him.

His own kavaru was creating the silence effect, and without his command or knowledge of it!

Turesobei tried to take the kavaru off, which he almost never did. He slept with it on, ate with it on, fought with it on. After all, a wizard would be nearly useless without it. He couldn't even remember the last time he hadn't worn it.

Turesobei grasped the chain and tugged. Or he intended to tug, but his hands wouldn't move the chain.

Clutching the kavaru, he grunted and strained, but he couldn't take it off. No matter how he tried, no matter how strongly he exerted his willpower, he could not bring himself to remove the stone.

He noticed then that Lu Bei and his grandfather were looking at him. Each said something to the other, but Turesobei couldn't hear them.

A thought occurred to him then. A ridiculous thought. Because it just could not be. There were no others in all Okoro. And yet ... little bits said over the years ... things only he could do, things maybe even his grandfather couldn't do...

"Lu Bei," Turesobei said. "Grandfather. Am I a..." Turesobei chuckled nervously. "This may sound silly, but I have to make sure. Am I a kai—"

The world darkened and bright specks floated in Turesobei's field of vision. "Am I ..." Weak and nauseous, he slumped toward the floor. "Must know if—"

Lu Bei was fluttering over him, tugging at his collar. "Master, master are you okay?"

Turesobei awoke; his head was fuzzy, ringing. "What happened?"

"You fainted," Grandfather Kahenan replied. "Likely from fatigue."

Turesobei sat up. "I was about to say something ... only now I can't remember what it was."

Kahenan chuckled. "You will find that a common occurrence when you are my age."

"It wasn't important, master."

Grandfather Kahenan reached a hand down and helped him up. "I will help you get home, Sobei."

"Lu Bei," Turesobei said. "Probably best if you turned back into a book now."

"Yes, master."

Moments later, the fetch was a diary again. The change made Kahenan's eyes dance. They left the library, and slowly Turesobei's strength returned, though he was more tired now than before.

"Keep Lu Bei out of sight," Grandfather Kahenan said as they neared Turesobei's house. "Especially do not let your mother see him in the house. Do not overuse him for now. He must take energy from you, or some other source you provide."

"How did he remain a fetch while I was passed out? He said I had to focus on the book to summon him and that he couldn't stay unless I was aware of him nearby."

"He will not fade instantly, and I doubt he had many minutes left before you woke up."

They reached the steps and Kahenan paused. "Tell your mother it is my fault you are late. And get some extra rest tonight. Show up an hour later than you normally would."

"I don't have to do the extra work tomorrow?" Turesobei said, with as much excitement as he could still manage.

Grandfather Kahenan laughed. "No, Sobei. You must still learn your lesson about being disrespectful. Just be thankful for the extra rest first. You will be up late again tomorrow, I fear."

Turesobei entered the house quietly, but before he could make it to his bedroom, his mother intercepted him.

"You're three hours late," she said with a slur. Her breath smelled faintly of wine and her hair was disheveled. "And I don't care if it's your fault or your grandfather's."

Turesobei groaned. She was going to use up his extra hour.

Chapter Seven

A hand gently shook Turesobei awake. He shoved it away and drifted off again, but the hand returned with a little more force. Turesobei opened an eye halfway and peered at his grandfather.

"What is it?" he grumbled.

"It is time for you to wake," Grandfather Kahenan said with a cheerful gleam.

Turesobei sat up and rubbed his eyes. As promised, his grandfather had worked him hard. He had inscribed practice spells until his hand cramped so badly that he couldn't flex his fingers anymore. Then, with drooping eyelids, he curled up beside the writing table and went to sleep. He had thought Kahenan would be angry about it.

A light wind blew in through the windows. Rain pattered outside, and thunder rumbled in the distance. Turesobei stretched his arms. "What time is it, Grandfather?"

"One hour until midnight. Your father has arrived."

"Where? When? Why didn't you wake me sooner?"

"Now is soon enough."

At that moment, the giant oak door at the bottom level of the tower creaked open, then slammed shut. The sound echoed up the staircase and into the workroom.

Turesobei paced, smoothed down his hair where it was slipping loose from its queue, and straightened his robes. Finally, he stood erect and tried for a proper, serious demeanor. He had not seen his father in nine months. He wanted to appear strong and mature to impress him.

Noboro's heavy footfalls reverberated with increasing intensity. He was a large man. Turesobei had inherited his height, though not his bulk. Instead, he was willowy like his mother, though he hoped that might change in time.

"He had best hurry up," Kahenan mumbled. "I have a ritual to finish." Though Noboro wandered all Okoro, he rarely moved in a hurry. Or perhaps because he was always moving at a steady pace, he never saw a need to rush.

"You're not scripting the howler summoning tonight are you?" Turesobei asked.

"Someone has need of it sooner than I had thought," Grandfather Kahenan said in his careful manner that always meant he was keeping a secret. "Besides, I had nothing else to do with you asleep and Noboro arriving late."

"I didn't mean to fall asleep."

"I know. You were exhausted. I hope you learned your lesson."

Turesobei was about to insist that he had when the door slid back and his father entered. Rain dripped from Noboro's battered cloak. His clothes, green cotton pants and a brown shirt, bore the stains and scars of long travel. He had removed his shoes at the main door. Weapon strikes had left deep scratches on his leather breastplate and forearm guards. A broadsword hung on his back. The giant curved blade rested in a battered leather sheath that seemed older than Noboro himself. A thin saber in a scabbard hung from his belt. This much smaller sword, named Sumada, was forged of precious white-steel.

Turesobei and Kahenan bowed, and with a sly grin Noboro returned the greeting.

"Father," Noboro said formally. "Turesobei. It warms my heart to see you both well." He scanned Turesobei. "You've grown. You'll be as tall as me soon." Noboro narrowed his eyes. "You are eating enough aren't you?"

"Oh, he does plenty of that," Grandfather Kahenan said. "He just takes after his mother a bit too much."

"Well, he does look more like her than me. And that, I think, is a good thing."

Turesobei was becoming embarrassed. "How was your expedition, Father?"

"Good, Sobei. Very good. I found an artifact that I have sought for a long time now. It was very difficult to track down and even worse to recover."

"What was it?"

Noboro scratched his cheek through his bushy, barely-kept beard. His father looked like a savage compared to all the refined clan nobles. "I think that I will have to tell you later."

"Please, Father. At least tell me how you came about finding it."

"Not tonight. I need to speak with your grandfather about some rather important matters. I'm not going to be here long, I'm afraid."

His voice cracking, Turesobei said, "You're staying through the festival though aren't you?"

He shook his head. "Sorry, Sobei."

"But you have to!"

"I would love to, but I truly can't stay, son. I need provisions and a few guards and then I'm off. I raced to get back here as soon as possible, and I must race back out again."

Turesobei's eyes filled with tears and he sighed. He didn't know why he had gotten his hopes up. It was always like this with his father. Something else was always more important than his family.

"Noboro," Grandfather Kahenan said, "I have a ritual sequence that I must finish now. It will take me about an hour."

"That's just as well. I need to take care of several matters and store..." He glanced suspiciously at Turesobei. "Something in the vault."

"Of course. Wait for me in the Dairen Pavilion."

"Why not in the tower? I should think it much more secure."

"After I finish this ritual, here will not be a good place. Your presence may disrupt the carefully balanced energies within the tower. Besides, I have demons here. Should any of them break loose, they would immediately rush to tell your enemies all the secrets they might have heard."

"Those aren't the real reasons, are they?" Noboro asked.

As Kahenan went back to his worktable he replied, "They could be."

Turesobei walked downstairs with his father.

"Are you coming home?" Turesobei asked, seemingly without interest.

Noboro slumped his broad shoulders. "I suppose I must, but not until morning. If your mother is up, tell her not to wait for me."

"Yes, father."

"It's good to see you, son."

Turesobei smiled meekly. "It's good to see you, too."

Turesobei trudged home and found that his mother, Wenari, had gone to sleep hours ago. He wasn't surprised. His parents' arranged marriage lacked anything resembling love or friendship. They had never grown close. Partly because Noboro traveled all the time. But Turesobei also suspected that Wenari didn't really like her rebellious husband and had expected greater things of him.

Turesobei often worried the same would happen to him. He tried to meet Awasa's expectations, but she refused to even think of him as a friend. She was only fourteen, of course, and she might change her mind yet. Turesobei certainly hoped so.

After rolling out his sleeping mat, Turesobei removed the new satchel from his back. The satchel was just big enough to carry a single large book and a set of basic writing implements. Kahenan had given it to him for carrying around Chonda Lu's diary. Kahenan thought it best that Lu Bei stay with Turesobei at all times.

Turesobei couldn't bring himself to go to bed. He was disappointed and restless. His father's return had been nothing like he had hoped. Noboro wasn't going to stay long, and he wasn't going to do anything special with either of his children. Turesobei had hoped his dad would teach him something about ... anything, really, and regale him with tales of his travels. Maybe Turesobei could even tell him what he had been learning, what he had accomplished in the last several months.

Turesobei pulled the book from the satchel and ran his hands along the cover. The runes shimmered but Lu Bei didn't appear. Turesobei had asked the fetch not to appear unless called for.

"Lu Bei," Turesobei whispered.

In a moment, the book transformed and Lu Bei wheeled around the room before landing on the sleeping mat.

"Did you need me, master?"

"I was just lonely. Wanted someone to talk to."

"Not a good night, then?"

"I've had better."

Lu Bei patted Turesobei on the hand. "I'm sorry, master."

36

In response, Turesobei tried to smile. "Can you hear what happens around you when you're a book?"

"Yes, unless you tell me not to. I can't see anything, of course. And as a book, I cannot talk back."

"Ah, that makes sense. I might need privacy or I might not want everything recorded."

Turesobei brought up what had happened that night.

"I think," squeaked Lu Bei, a little too loudly.

"Shh! You'll wake my mother."

"Sorry ... Anyway, I think it is wrong of them not to include master. You will be the next High Wizard. You should know the important things they're talking about!"

"I agree, but Father said no."

"And you're going to let that stop you?"

Turesobei stared at Lu Bei whose little face was set with a defiant scowl. "That would be wrong of me. There are rules against spying on others in the clan, even family."

"Those rules, master, should never apply to you."

Turesobei frowned at him. "You're a bad influence, Lu Bei."

"Yes, master."

"Do me a favor. Fly into the hallway and make sure my sister and mother are asleep. But stay out of sight. You can do that right?"

"As long as I don't stray more than about thirty paces from you, then yes, I can."

"Then do so."

With a feeling that he was going to regret his actions in a few hours, Turesobei donned his charcoal-gray rain cloak and grabbed his rainproof traveling boots. Then, with the all-clear signal from Lu Bei, he raced out into the rain-laced night with the tiny fetch fluttering alongside.

Chapter Eight

Staying just off the meandering stone paths, Turesobei padded through Inner Ekaran, the walled-off abode of the Chonda Clan nobility. Dense clouds covered the moons, and the rainfall had increased to a steady downpour.

Turesobei paused when he came within arrow-shot of the High Wizard's Tower, "Lu Bei, I think—"

"Shh!" Lu Bei muttered. "Someone's coming."

Turesobei dove behind a thicket of leafy shrubs. He tried to peer through the leaves and spindly trunks, but he couldn't see anything. Lu Bei, however, could crawl beneath the bush.

"I can see them," he whispered to Turesobei once he was hidden behind a rock on the other side.

"Who is it?" Turesobei replied in a voice so quiet it was almost silent.

Lu Bei had no trouble hearing it. He fluttered back and whispered in Turesobei's ear. "Just natives. Armed and on patrol."

By natives, he meant the zaboko, who were human like Turesobei. But compared to Turesobei's people, the zaboko were shorter and stockier, and their skin was a light grey, like rocks and rain clouds, rather than a pale cream. They were a strong people, far outnumbering the baojendari, but since they were not of Kaiaru descent, they were unable to wield kavaru stones, and thus unable to use magic. That was how Turesobei's race had conquered them.

As a noble, Turesobei could command any of the common zaboko guards, within reason, but it would be awkward. And it would likely get him caught once they reported to their superiors.

The guards drew parallel to his position, stopped, and looked around. After a few moments, one mumbled something to the other and they continued on.

Once they were out of sight, Turesobei let out a sigh.

"Are we allies with the natives now?" Lu Bei asked.

"I guess you wouldn't know, would you?"

Lu Bei shook his head. "Master ... put me away ... right after the invasion fleet set sail from Tengba Ren."

"Well, within a few generations, we conquered and enslaved most of the zaboko. By

38

we, I mean us baojendari as a whole. After we lost contact with Tengba Ren, the Chonda granted them limited, though not complete, freedom. In some places—"

"We lost contact with Tengba Ren?!"

"Keep it down. Yes, we've had no word from the mother country in over four centuries. We think—" Turesobei shook his head. "Look, I'll explain it all to you later. Now is not the time. We're almost there, so you'd better change back. If you're active, Grandfather will sense your presence."

Lu Bei landed in Turesobei's hands and transformed into the diary, which Turesobei then tucked into his satchel.

Turesobei circled the crescent lake beside the High Wizard's Tower, leapt over a wall using the *spell of prodigious leaping*, and landed in his grandfather's gardens. Turesobei could have cast the *spell of darksight* to aid him, but having played in these gardens daily all his life, he didn't need it. By memory, he dodged boulders, slipped between hedgerows, circumvented bamboo brakes, and leapt across narrow, artificial streams.

At last he reached the pavilion and hid within a stand of shrubs along the north wall. The Dairen Pavilion was an octagonal, wooden structure with a thatch roof and sliding outer walls bearing thick paper panels. Grandfather Kahenan liked to sit there with the doors pulled back and gaze out at the moons or the cherry orchard nearby. When the blossoms fell, he held a viewing party for all the top nobles. Anytime he needed to have a meeting of any sort, he went to the Dairen Pavilion. Kahenan liked to keep his tower off limits.

While he waited, Turesobei began to feel as if he were being watched. He glanced around, but didn't see anyone, not that he could see far. Tucking his kavaru under his robe, he cast the darksight spell and looked around again. Still nothing. His heartbeat quickened.

He uttered a chant and cast the *spell of auditory enhancement*, which he would likely need anyway in order to hear Noboro and Kahenan through the paper-paneled walls. These two spells were slight enough in power that his grandfather wasn't likely to sense them, unless he was on the lookout for magic.

Turesobei examined his surroundings carefully, but still detected nothing unusual. Something was wrong, though. He was tempted to call on Lu Bei, but he was convinced the strength of that magic would gain Kahenan's attention even if he wasn't trying to sense anything.

The rain continued to fall, and he grew cold and tired. He couldn't have managed all this if Kahenan hadn't let him sleep. He didn't want to risk getting spotted by moving around to warm himself, and the *spell of warming* was far too noticeable. He would just have to tough it out.

At last, his father approached the pavilion warily, with his hand on his sword. He wondered if his father sensed him watching. He was a canny and cautious man. Turesobei's sense of wrongness increased. With his spells still active—it took little energy to maintain these in particular—he scanned the garden again.

For a second he thought he saw something move within the upper branches of a nearby oak. But after a few minutes of watching, he decided it had only been a squirrel or a limb shaking off the rain. Still, the sense of danger remained, until Grandfather Kahenan arrived. And even then it only faded somewhat.

"What is it?" Kahenan said when he reached the pavilion door where Noboro stood watching the garden through the water that streamed from the roof.

"Someone is lurking within the garden."

"I did not see or hear anyone as I approached," Kahenan said confidently. "You are simply paranoid. Come, let us have tea where it is warm and dry. Light the lanterns."

The two men moved into the pavilion, shutting the door behind them. Turesobei edged closer to the wall but still stayed near enough to the shrubs that he would be partially hidden, even on a clear night. His father lit the lanterns within, and Turesobei watched their dark silhouettes through the paper panels.

"You would be paranoid, too, if you had been carrying that key for a month."

Kahenan hung an iron teapot over the hearth which was set into the floor in the pavilion's center. "Boro, I honestly never believed that you would find it. The zaboko take extreme care with their artifacts, especially those that are potentially dangerous."

"Well, they were careless enough with this one. People sometimes forget dangers that shouldn't be forgotten." Noboro knelt at the small table beside the hearth. "I wasn't the only person looking for it, either."

"That is not good news. But why so much interest in it now?"

"A book published in West Tagana three years ago, written by a man named Obu Sotenda. It stirred up a lot of new interest in the Storm Dragon legends. And then the key emerged for the first time in centuries. It had been lost in the vault of a West Taganan shrine, and the shrine closed."

Closing shrines wasn't uncommon. The zaboko were steadily moving away from their ancestral religions and following those of their baojendari conquerors instead.

"When the shrine's artifacts were being relocated, word got out from some of the laborers about the contents of the vault. I recognized it from a description that was circulating through the wine-houses. But, of course, I wasn't the only one."

Grandfather Kahenan knelt at the table and set down two cups. "So, are you off to open the vault now?"

"I am."

"I was afraid you would say that."

"I must."

"Well, if you must, take Sobei with you."

Turesobei's heart lurched with excitement but was crushed by the tone of his father's reply. "What? You've got to be joking!"

"No, I am not. The boy needs a break."

"Then give him one."

Kahenan placed tea leaves in both cups. "He needs to spend time with his father, too."

Noboro sighed. "But we're so different."

"Not as much as you think."

"The boy is so like his mother, and she grates on my nerves."

"I am not," Turesobei muttered to himself.

"He is young and headstrong," Kahenan said, "but teenagers are like that."

"He has more in common with you. Why don't you take him on a trip?"

"Because some of us have responsibilities to the clan, unless you've forgotten that I am the High Wizard and we are nearly at war with the Gawo Clan."

The Gawo were the nearest neighbors to the Chonda, and they had been warring with them off and on since before the baojendari left Tengba Ren to come to Okoro.

While Noboro stalked around shaking his head in frustration, Turesobei muttered a chant to himself, "Please take me with you. Please take me with you."

The water boiled and Kahenan slowly poured it into the cups. They sat in silence until Kahenan stirred his tea. "Son, do not let your relationship with him end up like ours. Sobei deserves better than that.

"I know he is different and not at all like a regular son, and that makes him strange to you. But he cannot help it. He is special and unique to the clan. Most parents would feel twice as blessed to have him."

Turesobei nearly bit off his tongue trying to keep quiet. Strange and not like a regular son? What the heck did that mean?!

"I know, I know. I do love him, you know."

Kahenan sipped his tea, released the long sigh he always made after the first sip, and then said, "I did wrong with you, Noboro. Do not repeat my mistakes. It is bad enough that you are never home. Did you not see how excited he was to see you and how crushed when you told him you were not staying?"

Noboro stared down into his cup. Turesobei could imagine his father's lips quavering with warring emotions and ideas. "It's going to be dangerous. Very dangerous. Probably deadly."

"He has to face danger eventually. He can handle himself. I am certain of that."

Noboro released a deep breath. "Will King Chonda allow it?"

"He will when I explain it to him. He trusts me."

"Well, his mother certainly won't like it."

"His mother does not like anything the two of us do. She will get over it. She needs to get used to Turesobei growing up. No son should be treated the way she treats him, and he is no ordinary boy."

"Fine then. I'll give it a try if you think that it's wise, but he'd best carry his own weight and not get me into more trouble."

Turesobei almost yelled out, "I won't!" But he managed not to.

"He is fifteen, not seven," Grandfather Kahenan said. "I have trained him for nine years now. He can take care of himself. He is a better student than I ever was, not as reckless either. Obviously, he is a far greater talent. And you are going to need someone who knows magic anyway."

Turesobei was astounded. He couldn't imagine his grandfather not being a better student than himself. Or obviously less talented! Kahenan rarely praised his abilities.

"If you say so," Noboro said. "I certainly didn't have your trust when I was fifteen."

"For good reason."

They stared at each other until Noboro laughed. "Hah! That's true enough!" After Grandfather Kahenan's laughter quieted, Noboro said, "It really is going to be dangerous. I'm being followed. But it's more than just another treasure hunter."

"Or a jealous husband?"

"Gods! I hope I haven't attracted another one of those."

Turesobei didn't know what to think about that. His head was already full of mysteries and revelations gathered over the last few minutes.

Kahenan tsked and shook his head. "Well, Sobei can take care of himself, like I said. Just take a couple of extra guards with you. He needs to face a little danger sometime or he will never be ready."

"You should know," Noboro said, "that I stole the key from a Keshuno spy who had stolen it from the new shrine. So I may have Keshuno agents after me as well as cultists. Perhaps a few treasure hunters, too. I came home for your advice and a dozen trustworthy soldiers."

The Keshuno were a dark-striped offshoot of the zaboko race. They were a proud and deadly people that everyone feared, even other zaboko. They possessed strange powers given them by their dragon goddess, Makazi Keshuno. Never subjugated, they lived in the harsh, mountainous rainforests of southern Okoro, a land to which few others had ever ventured. That the Keshuno were involved made Turesobei doubt, though only for a moment, whether he wanted to go.

"Ah." Grandfather Kahenan drained his cup and set it onto the table. For a few minutes he stroked his braided beard. "If you think that it is too risky for Turesobei to go, then perhaps another time. But I do think he can handle it. Even if there are Keshuno involved."

"No, you're right, I do need to spend some time with the boy. And I do need a wizard, someone I can trust, too. I was going to ask you who I should hire."

"Hire no wizard with this, Boro. I do not know a single wizard, even another from our own clan, that you could trust with such an object of power. And the clan certainly cannot spare the extras we have. Not right now."

Kahenan gathered the teacups, rinsed them, and put them away. "When you have the heart, what then?"

"I'll bring it back here and add it to our collection."

"The wisest course would be to simply keep the key here and guard it."

Noboro laughed gently. "You know I have to get into the vault and see the heart. I've worked on this for too long. Besides, it is better for us to guard it now that everyone is interested. Eventually someone who can open the vault without the key may find it.

Keshuno magic may open it where yours failed."

Grandfather Kahenan grunted irritably and stood. He moved to the other side of the room and Noboro followed him. Kahenan opened a chest on the floor and lifted something from it, perhaps a scroll. He handed it to Noboro and spoke, but Turesobei couldn't hear what his grandfather whispered. All he could hear now was the pouring rain. He crept around the edge of the building as quietly as he could, trying to get closer to them.

Turesobei turned the corner, and in between the pavilion and two large bushes he saw a shadow darker than the night. Thinking it might be a man, he decided to steal closer to get a better look.

Two steps later, his foot made a sloshing sound in the mud and the shadow turned toward him.

Chapter Nine

For a brief second Turesobei saw baojendari eyes and skin within a dark hood. The figure wore a black bodysuit like those worn by qengai assassins, an organization of ruthless paid killers who operated throughout Okoro.

A hand flashed toward him, and Turesobei's training kicked in. He immediately dove to the ground and a knife whistled through the air above him.

Turesobei rolled to his feet and drew the dagger he always kept in a sheathe on his belt. But before he could launch toward his attacker, something tiny and sharp struck him right over his collarbone and near to his neck.

The figure then turned and ran. Turesobei knew he had only a moment to decide what he must do. It might be the last moment of his life. A wave of vertigo and nausea swept through him. His limbs weakened. He shouted a warning as he slumped to the ground: "Spy!" he yelled. "Sound the alarms!"

With clumsy fingers, as if his hand had fallen asleep, he found the inch-long dart that had struck him. He hoped he had made his father and grandfather proud.

Turesobei jerked the dart free and released the enhanced-senses and darksight spells. As everything went dark around him, he calmly, if stutteringly, chanted the *spell of summer healing* over the wound. A stuttered spell was rarely successful, but he did the best he could.

His last sensations were of the comforting presence of his kavaru and the voices of a thousand forgotten friends.

Chapter Ten

Once again a hand shook him awake gently. Turesobei felt a cold, wet cloth being dabbed on his forehead. His head ached, and he felt cold and hot all at once, as if he had a fever. Probably he did. He lay within a pile of blankets on the pavilion floor. Grandfather Kahenan leaned over him and smiled.

"How do you feel?"

Turesobei stirred and pain shot through his chest, neck, and right shoulder. "Ow!"

"Sorry. I am afraid that was my doing. The anti-toxin spell is not pleasant. Of course, you should have died before I reached you. Did you cast a healing?"

"I managed a small one."

"Well, it must have slowed the poison enough, eh? As it was, I barely reached you in time. A bigger dose of poison would have killed you regardless. You gave us quite a scare. I trust you'll be more careful in the future. And that you'll refrain from spying on people as well."

Before Turesobei could apologize in shame, the two zaboko guards who were standing watch at the door stepped aside and Noboro walked in. He came over and patted Turesobei on the head. "You alright, son?"

Turesobei nodded. "There was a spy."

His father smiled. "Aye, we heard you right enough. I think everyone must have heard that yell."

"Oh." Turesobei blushed and turned his head away.

"But at least you did the right thing when you spotted the enemy. Otherwise, you would be dead and we would not know."

"Did you get him?" Turesobei said.

Noboro shook his head. "Slipped away. Whoever he was, he knew what he was doing."

Turesobei slumped his shoulders and sighed. "You're not going to take me now for sure, are you? It's too dangerous and I screwed up."

Noboro looked at Grandfather Kahenan, who nodded to him. Then Noboro said, "You can come."

"Really?" Turesobei said with as much excitement as he could manage. He lifted up to hug his father, but a wave of dizziness washed over him. He lay back down.

"I will allow it. You handled yourself well tonight, surviving an assassin's attack and sounding the alarm. Especially since Father tells me he had worked you hard all day."

Turesobei grasped his father's hand and squeezed. "Thank you, Father. I won't let you down."

"Of course you won't. You're a Chonda."

"There is one other matter, though," Grandfather Kahenan said. "If you wish to go, Sobei, you must first cast a few spells to my liking. A simple test."

Turesobei's heart fell. His grandfather's tests were anything but simple. He would have liked to complain that it wasn't fair, but he didn't have the strength for an argument. Besides, he knew it wouldn't do any good.

"Can you stand?" Noboro said.

"I don't think so."

Grandfather Kahenan called some servants in who had a stretcher with them. With their large hands and great strength, they loaded and carried him easily. "Thanks," he murmured.

"Come on," Noboro said. "Let's get you home for some rest. You're going to need it for those tests. And we're leaving in three days."

"Take tomorrow off, Sobei," Kahenan said. "But be here early the next day and prepared for your exam."

"I will," he said, and then he let himself drift off into sleep as he was carried home.

Chapter Eleven

Except for a couple of meals and assisted trips to the privy, Turesobei slept for thirty-six hours straight. When he awoke, he felt restored, though stiff and groggy. He sat up alone in his bedroom. He had hazy memories of Noboro, his mother Wenari, and Kahenan visiting him. And he remembered dreams about swarms of tiny creatures crawling and flying through the room, so he knew his thirteen-year-old sister Enashoma had kept watch over him, protective as always.

And he had the evidence to prove it: dozens of tiny origami creatures lay scattered about the room. Folding paper designs was Enashoma's special talent, taught to her by their grandmother, just before she had died. And by scribing on the pages a few strange sigils from a magic brush that had been handed down for generations, Enashoma could animate the ones shaped into animals. She claimed it was nothing more than a parlor trick, since the tiny creatures could only move around for a few minutes. But based on the way Kahenan praised Enashoma's efforts, Turesobei wondered if there was more to it.

Turesobei did his morning stretches then rolled up his bed mat and blanket. He dressed and went to the kitchen. He found his mother there. She was wearing an elegant, cream-colored silk dress and her hair was twisted around a wire frame with a curving wing on each side of her head. Though of average height, she seemed taller because of her forceful personality and her thin, willowy frame.

She stood prim and proper and thoroughly in charge as she directed the staff. Her every word served either bubbly praise or harsh scolding—the latter far more often. Of course, she didn't have to direct the servants. She did so only because she enjoyed it so much.

Turesobei stepped forward cautiously. "Good morning, Mother."

Wenari turned and frowned with worry. Turesobei cringed every time that expression twisted his mother's face. Everything worried her, at least everything that didn't annoy or offend her. Turesobei tried to pretend his mother wasn't as bad as his father made out, but he found it difficult.

Wenari rushed over and patted his head as if he were a small child. "Sweet Sobei, should you not rest a while longer?"

"No, Mother, I feel fine. Besides, I've got to pass some of Grandfather's tests before I can—"

"As for that," she announced, "I forbid you to go."

"What?!"

"You are simply too young, and it will be dangerous. Your father said so himself."

"Did he change his mind? Did he say I couldn't go?"

"No, but I make these decisions." She grabbed his arm. "Come, let's go sit in the garden. I'll have servants bring you breakfast there."

Turesobei allowed himself to be led along. The garden sounded pleasant, and his empty stomach was rumbling. While he had slept and recovered they had only brought him fruit and water.

They stopped at a tiny gazebo overlooking a koi pond. The two knelt down at a small table, facing each other. Turesobei decided he was not going to let her push him around like she usually did. He threw away traditional baojendari decorum altogether and said exactly what he wanted to say.

"I'm going whether you like it or not, Mother."

"Lord Kahenan told me you were becoming quite arrogant," Wenari said icily, "but I did not see it until just now."

"I'm not trying to be rude, Mother. This trip means a lot to me. I want to go and Grandfather said I could."

"Lord Kahenan is not in charge of you."

"But Father said I could go."

She chortled. "Hah! That man comes in for three days and thinks he can decide what's best for you? No, I do not think so."

"He has that right, you know. By law."

"Society may give him such rights, but I am in charge in this household. He forfeited that right long ago."

"He could take the matter to the King."

"Do you really think he cares that much? That he would go to all that trouble? Be honest with yourself, Sobei. He's only taking you because Lord Kahenan wants him to."

Turesobei frowned and bit off his reply as he saw servants approaching. The two zaboko girls, Imi and Shurada, were around his age. They usually spoke to him casually, but they would not do so in his mother's presence. They set the plates down, arranged the food, poured apple juice and water into the bowls, and then backed away.

"This is acceptable," Wenari said. "You may go."

"Thanks," Turesobei added. "It looks delicious."

The girls grinned slightly and bowed. His mother glowered at him. She didn't think servants should be treated politely. And she didn't like for him to converse with zaboko either, though that had never stopped him when she wasn't looking.

The food did look delicious: poached eggs, pickled vegetables, rice, spinach, and fruit. He dove in and ignored his mother for a while. Neither spoke while they ate, though Wenari merely picked at some fruit, since she had eaten breakfast earlier.

"As for your insolence," she proclaimed the moment he finished, "you are forgiven. Though I do not take kindly to being talked to in the manner you have chosen today."

"You're not going to punish me?"

"No. I talked with Lord Kahenan about it months ago, when you started becoming more difficult than usual. He says that it's natural."

"I don't get it. I'm allowed to speak my mind where others cannot, and no one else is allowed to behave the way I have today. Shoma certainly can't. You scold her for the slightest offense."

"No," Wenari said. "She cannot behave as you do."

"Because I'm a wizard?"

"No," she snapped. "It is because—" She hesitated. "Yes, it's because you are a wizard."

"You're lying. It's something else."

"No. It is not. And if you have further questions, talk to your grandfather."

Imi and Shurada returned and removed the empty plates. Then they brought out steaming bowls of green tea. As she bowed and withdrew, Shurada smiled at Turesobei, with a sparkle in her eyes. He was pretty sure she liked him, but he didn't have a clue what to think about that. Even among the Chonda, relationships between zaboko and baojendari were forbidden.

Turesobei sipped his tea. "Mother, this means everything to me. Please let me go."

"You are my only son. I will not lose you on some ridiculous expedition to only the gods know where."

"Please, mother. What can I do to change your mind?"

"Nothing."

"I have to grow up sometime."

"Not yet."

Turesobei sighed with frustration, held back a scream, and pleaded with her. "Can't you see that this may be my last chance to spend time with Father before I'm an adult? I never get to see him. I don't even really know him."

"You are not missing much, and it is not my fault."

"Yes, it is. At least partly." She winced and then narrowed her eyes with anger. "The two of you never get along and Father is always off doing this or that. I want to spend some time with him for a while. And I am coming back. Plus, you've got Enashoma here to keep you company."

She shook her head. "Sobei—"

"You're just being possessive and controlling. That's not fair to me."

She drew herself up straight, clenched her jaws, and crinkled her nose up into her eyes. If she hadn't been seething with anger, she would have looked ridiculous. But after a moment, her expression softened and she shook her head.

"I would let you go, Sobei, I really would. But I have a bad feeling about—"

Turesobei stood and interrupted her. She often used *intuitions* as excuses to make him and Enashoma do what she wanted. "I love you, Mother, but I'm going and that's all there is to it. I am the High Wizard's heir, you cannot restrain me."

He turned and headed back into the house to retrieve some of his things. He would sleep in the tower tonight.

"Sobei!" she yelled. "Sobei! I won't let you go! I'll tell Noboro not to let you!"

Turesobei kept walking.

"If you go, don't ever return to this household!"

"You look upset," Grandfather Kahenan said as soon as Turesobei trudged into the workroom.

Turesobei bowed to him as required. "I had a spat with Mother."

"Let me guess: she does not want you to go?"

"She forbade it."

"And you told her?"

"That I loved her but I'm going anyway."

Grandfather Kahenan smiled and put his hand on Turesobei's shoulder. "I am proud of you for standing up to her without compromising your love for her. And this is not unexpected. Your father and I figured this would happen."

"She said she'd tell him not to let me."

"Do not worry. He will let you if for no other reason than to spite your mother."

"Why are they like this?"

"Your parents were not a good match. That was King Ugara's fault; it is difficult to gauge a match when the children are only two years old. Your grandmother fought him on it, as best as she could. She didn't believe marriages should be arranged so early. Naturally the King got his way, and I had to step in and persuade him not to officially reprimand her."

"Why *do* we arrange marriages?"

"Because..." Grandfather Kahenan stared at the ceiling as if the answer might be hanging there. "You know, I am not sure why. We used to do it to solidify alliances. I suppose some clans still do. These days it seems to just be a tradition for the Chonda. At least we do it a few years later now than we used to. I think that helps, and you can thank your grandmother in your prayers for that."

"I'm afraid my intended doesn't like me much either."

"Well, hopefully that will change in time." Kahenan led him to the writing table. "Come, you need to get to work. How do you feel?"

"Perfectly fine, except that I'm upset."

"Well, take a while to cool off. Your test will not be easy."

"Grandfather, when I return, can I live with you?"

Kahenan chewed on his lip and stroked his beard. "Well, I guess that would be alright, but you would have to help out around here. You know, it might not be a bad thing. It would give me more opportunities for teaching you. But I doubt your mother would let you."

"She said I couldn't return home if I went off with Father."

"Ah. Well, we shall see. There is simply no telling what she will do when you return."

Turesobei sat cross-legged, placed his hands on his knees, and closed his eyes. He inhaled through his nose for five seconds then exhaled through his mouth for ten. Steadily, he increased the counts up to ten and twenty. He imagined himself breathing in the good kenja from his surroundings and pushing out the anger and worries from within his mind. Eventually he grew calm and focused.

"I'm ready, Grandfather."

Chapter Twelve

Kahenan pointed to the writing table. A dozen flat bamboo strips the width of three fingers and the length of a hand lay beside a pot of black ink mixed with minuscule particles of kenja-conducting dark iron. This metal had the opposite property to white-steel. While white steel could cut through kenja, dark iron could draw and channel it.

Turesobei sighed with relief. He possessed a steady hand and could script spells far better than he could cast them on the spot. They still needed activation commands and some manipulation, but most of the work was done by hand ahead of time. Of course, that made preparation essential, and the strips would only last a few months at best before the energies bound up within the runes would slowly start to fade.

Unfortunately, basic spells such as the *spell of the flickering flame* or the *spell of prodigious leaping* were too simple to script. Scripting was reserved, and was often a requirement, for more complicated spells.

"Before you script any spells, Sobei, you must perform a few without preparation. First, give me a flicker flame."

Turesobei chanted and a small globe of orange flame rose from his hand and hovered nearby.

"Excellent. Hold it and levitate a single bamboo strip."

Turesobei did so.

"Good. Now, activate your kenja-sight."

As his eyes glazed white, Turesobei found that his talent required far more concentration than normal, due to all the spells he had active, but he managed it.

"Excellent. I have placed a new, continuous and active spell within the room. Tell me where it is and describe its nature to me. Keep your spells going while you look."

Turesobei looked around, using his kenja-sight to see the flows of energy that permeate the world. Anything magical in origin would send out ripples like a stone thrown into a pond, except the waves were tinted according to the nature of the energy—red for fire, green for wood, yellow for earth, black for water, white for air, blue for metal. Natural, non-magical energy flows were transparent, like heat waves over a flame.

As Turesobei searched the shelves, the plants, and then the furniture, the spell strip drifted back down and the flicker flame globe dimmed. At the last moment, he noticed the spells weakening and brought them back to full strength.

A half hour passed and he began to tire. He started to panic, but then he reminded himself that this was not difficult. It only required patience and stamina. Taking deep breaths, he refocused and started searching again.

Almost immediately, he spotted a nuance he didn't remember having seen before. A miniscule wave of water energy pulsed from the clasp that held his grandfather's beard in its braid.

He pointed it out, and his grandfather exclaimed, "Excellent! Now, you will need to script eight spells."

Turesobei released his kenja-sight, the levitation, and the fire globe. He took a deep breath and let it out slowly with a tense sigh. This wasn't going to be easy.

"Three healing charms, a blinding strip, a demon banishment, a fog cloud, a fire beam, and a *spell of countering powerful spells.*"

"By the gods, Grandfather! Are you trying to kill me?"

"No," he said simply. "When you are finished, you can find me down at the pavilion. But do not wake me if I am napping."

Turesobei gulped and nodded. He might have to sleep through the entire trip after casting all those spells, especially if he ruined any of them. And he would have to be careful not to work himself until he passed out. Casting magic depleted one's inner kenja, and the more times it was depleted, the shorter one's lifespan would be. Passing out from casting was particularly dangerous because it meant that all of one's kenja had been drained away, at least for a moment.

Kahenan shuffled to the door. "Oh, one more thing. You may rest as often as you wish and join me for dinner if you like. However, you must finish all the spells by midnight."

Fortunately, kenja was at high tide because the dark moon Zhura was dominant in the sky, while the bright moon Avida, source of the ore from which white-steel was made, was absent. Turesobei dipped his brush into the inkpot and began scripting the first healing charm.

Every line in every character had to be perfect, without any stray marks. He drew the characters on the bamboo strip with his mind focused on summoning and binding the power that would pour out from the characters when the command was given. The other benefit to scripting spells was that when in danger, a sorcerer didn't have to drain himself in casting one or two spells. He invested most of the necessary energies ahead of time.

Turesobei labored without pause. He completely lost himself in his work and had no idea how much time passed. He forgot hunger, fatigue, worries, everything. He gave his entire being over to scripting the spells. When at last he finished the final spell, he plopped down onto the meditation cushions and fell asleep.

Grandfather Kahenan woke him some time later and handed him a steaming bowl of fried rice with crunchy greens mixed in. "You passed my test."

Turesobei smiled numbly and ate.

"You really should learn to pace yourself, though," he said with a mischievous smile. "You will not be young and vibrant forever."

53

Turesobei joined his sister and grandfather at the Dairen Pavilion for a quiet breakfast. Enashoma was sad he was leaving. He tried to reassure her, but it didn't do much good. Enashoma was almost a copy of their mother—looks, voice, and mannerisms—except that where Wenari was harsh and critical, Enashoma was sweet and caring. She was incredibly perceptive and Turesobei often thought that she might be smarter than him. Not that he would ever admit it to anyone, especially her.

Afterward, Turesobei ran off to say goodbye to Awasa before getting his gear packed and ready to go. He found her sitting beneath the shade of an oak. Her guardians were standing thirty paces away: a baojendari attendant named Marumi and a zaboko guard named Zaiporo who was Turesobei's age. Marumi liked Turesobei and never gave him any trouble. She was always kind enough to give them as much privacy as possible. Zaiporo had just begun his duties. Though he was too young for the role, it was traditional for his family to guard the members of Awasa's family, and his older brothers had all died.

Awasa was embroidering daisies onto a crimson sash. He approached nervously.

"Good morning, Awasa."

She shot him a look of contempt then looked back to her craftwork. "It was good." He admired her beauty and fidgeted while she ignored him. Finally she looked back up at him. "Well, what is it?"

"I'm off today." Awasa shrugged. "I'm setting off today on an expedition with my father."

"I know about your trip."

"I'm going to be gone for at least three months."

"So?"

"Well, I ... uh ... I thought you might miss me."

"Nope."

Turesobei grew exasperated. "Wakaro is wild and dangerous. I could get killed there."

"Why should I care?"

"Because you should! Because we're betrothed!"

A sly smile slid across her face. "We won't be if you get killed, though, will we?"

All his dreams of a parting kiss or hug or even a tender goodbye crashed around him. Turesobei stammered in frustration, blew out his breath with a *phew*, and turned to stamp away.

"By the way, Turesobei. Perhaps you should ride in the sun on the way there, you're looking pale."

"We're going by ship. And I look pale because I nearly died from poison a few days ago, and last night I scripted eight spells in a row."

"Okay. Whatever."

Turesobei began to stalk away but decided to give it one last try. "I'll send you a letter if I get the chance and tell you what I've seen."

"I won't read it," she said. "Goodbye now."

Sulking, Turesobei ambled back home to get a few more of his things he'd left the day before. He carefully avoided his mother, who was yelling at one of the servants. Enashoma was waiting for him in his room. She had promised to help him pack.

"What's wrong, Sobei?" Enashoma asked as she rolled up his spare clothes and placed them into his backpack. "If I were you, I'd be excited. I wish I could go."

Turesobei smiled dimly. "I wish you could too, Shoma. I'm just down because of Mother and—"

"Awasa again?"

He nodded. "She doesn't care that I'm going off and might get killed and never come back. She didn't even say goodbye."

Enashoma huffed and thrust a shirt down into Turesobei's backpack. Her eyes blazed a brighter green and her round cheeks turned red. "That little witch! I'll show her!"

"Oh, please don't. That would be embarrassing."

"Why?"

Turesobei shrugged helplessly. "Just because."

She eyed him dubiously.

"Promise you won't."

"Only if she doesn't cross my path anytime soon." Enashoma shoved another shirt into the backpack. "I don't know why you keep trying to befriend her."

"What choice do I have? Besides..." Turesobei struggled for the right words to express his complex feelings about Awasa, but he could never find them.

"I know. You like her but you don't know why. All the boys do. I don't understand it. She's pretty but that's about it. I told Mother so. I told her you deserved a better match."

"That won't get me anywhere. Mother thinks Awasa is wonderful, a goddess nearly."

"That's exactly what she said to me."

"Doesn't matter anyway. The King blessed the arrangement, and I think he would have picked Awasa himself if Mother hadn't."

Enashoma frowned and shook her head. "I'm so sorry, Sobei, but Awasa seems just like our mother. You may have to become like Father. I wouldn't blame you if you did."

"Maybe she'll change."

"Mother said I should try harder to be like Awasa so that I'll be more popular. That way I'll get a better marriage."

Turesobei hugged her. "Don't ever do that, Shoma. Promise me you won't."

She giggled. "No worries there. I couldn't care less what people think about me."

"You're lucky, you know, not having an intended anymore."

"That's an awful thing to say!"

"It's not our fault he died."

"Well, no. But it's still bad karma to say things like that." Enashoma finished packing his clothes. "Besides, Mother or King Ugara will find one for me sooner or later, and I won't get any say in it. You're the lucky one. You're going on an adventure. And everything will be better once you're back. You'll see."

"I don't know how you stay so positive."

"I take after Grandfather that way."

Turesobei shouldered his backpack. "That makes sense. Nothing ever rattles him. Come on, you can see me off."

"What about Mother?"

"If she wants to say goodbye, she'll come. If not, well, that's her loss."

Enashoma frowned but didn't argue. The two of them sneaked out of the house and ran to the tower where Kahenan and Noboro waited with a train of mounts and two dozen zaboko soldiers.

Chapter Thirteen

Packs of supplies weighted down all the denekon, but the reptilian mounts didn't seem to mind. As they waited for their riders, they scratched at the ground with their clawed feet and flicked long purple tongues across their thick snouts, moistening their nostrils. Though fully adult, they were young mounts with dark green scales. Not aging with autumn-hued scales, like those Turesobei had learned to ride on.

The Riding Master smiled at Turesobei, which was a first because he was usually irritated with him, and pointed to a mount in the midst of the line. Turesobei added the rest of his things to the saddle pack on the denekon. A double-lidded eye flicked back at him.

"Iyei," said the Riding Master, naming the denekon.

Turesobei leaned over and whispered in the beast's recessed ear, "Iyei, my friend, be well." By tradition, one always said this to a denekon before riding it, especially the first time. Why? Turesobei didn't know. He then rubbed the beast under its chin, where its large scales were softest, almost like leather. The denekon's eyelids drooped and it made a purring snort.

Turesobei went over to where his grandfather and father stood talking to one another in hushed tones.

Grandfather Kahenan held his white-steel longsword out toward Noboro. "Take Yomifano with you."

Noboro's eyes widened. "I couldn't!"

Kahenan shoved the curved sword into his hands. "I insist."

"But you may need it in defending the clan. It's too valuable."

Kahenan patted a scabbarded sword hanging from his sash. It was nearly identical to Yomifano except that it was only a third as long. "I have my short-sword. It will do in a pinch."

Noboro brushed his fingers along Yomifano's ornate wooden scabbard. "I couldn't take this sword from you. It's pure white-steel. The other is not." White-steel was so rare and precious that the clan had only four swords made purely of the metal. And that was three more than most clans had.

"Please, son. I wish I could go with you, but I cannot. This is the best I can do to protect you and Sobei."

Noboro sighed and bowed deeply. "I will guard it wisely and return it to you as soon as

I can." He took Yomifano and drew it. He angled the long-sword in the sunlight. The blade gleamed like steel except that it was white, almost like silvery bleached paper.

"Now," said Kahenan. "Give Sumada to Sobei."

Turesobei staggered back a step. "What?! Really?"

Noboro grinned. "A wizard does need a white-steel blade."

He handed it to Sobei who quickly fixed the scabbard to his belt and drew the blade. It was paler than regular steel but not nearly as white as Yomifano. Sumada, they thought, was half regular steel and half white-steel. It was hard to be sure. Though they had developed the techniques, the art of crafting white-steel items was lost to the baojendari.

"I will want it back when we return."

"Of course." Turesobei artfully slid the short blade back into its scabbard. "And I vow to do the blade honor while I wear it."

His Father clasped him on the shoulders. "I know you will."

Then Grandfather Kahenan hugged Turesobei. "Take care, Sobei. Do not summon any demons unless you are desperate. You are not ready for that without my supervision."

"Yes, Grandfather. I won't let you down either."

Kahenan winked at him. "You had best not."

Enashoma ran up and hugged Turesobei.

Turesobei lifted her, swung her around, and kissed her on the cheek. "Be good, Little Blossom."

She winced when he spoke her nickname. "You come back safely," she said. "And have fun."

"I promise, and I will write you if I get the chance."

Noboro hugged Enashoma and mounted his denekon. Turesobei followed his lead. "What's all this on my mount?" he asked, gesturing at the rather large packs strapped behind the end of the saddle.

"Your armor and weapons," Noboro said.

"Oh, of course," he said, blushing. He hadn't even thought to get them from the armory.

Grandfather Kahenan handed him a short bow and a quiver full of brightly fletched arrows. "They are all new. I purchased them for you yesterday."

Turesobei bowed his head. "Thank you, Grandfather. This is wonderful."

"You are quite welcome. Be sure to don your armor once you leave Chonda lands."

Noboro flicked his mount's reins. "Hai!" he called, and the group moved forward.

Turesobei waved to his grandfather and sister until they were out of sight. As they exited through the east gate and rode into Outer Ekaran, he thought for a moment that he saw Awasa watching from one of the high windows of her home. But he couldn't be sure. He shrugged and decided to leave her and all the weight of home behind.

Chapter Fourteen

After a half-day of riding, they reached Dakanuru, the primary Chonda port on the winding Taba River. There, they boarded a barge and traveled downriver toward Batsa, the capital city of Batsakun which occupies the northeast corner of Okoro.

After three days, they reached Batsa, purposefully arriving at night. Not wanting to be seen, they cut through poorly lit alleys and raced down lesser-known streets until they came upon the back of a small estate with an exquisite garden, a full stable, and a manse constructed in the old style—brightly colored tiles on the outer walls, a high-arched roof, and great oak doors painted vermilion.

Secret words were whispered over the wall. Moments later, the back gate creaked open and Turesobei rode in along with all the others.

"People will figure out I'm here," Noboro told the guards who met them. "But let's make it take as long as possible."

This was only Turesobei's second visit to this remote Chonda estate. Most of the family had little need for it. But its presence was necessary because as King of Ekaran Province, Chonda Ugara served as a member of the Ruling Council of Batsakun, which formulated many laws and elected the High King of Batsakun.

Here, Turesobei would spend the next several nights while his father acquired the ship and crew he needed for their expedition.

The next morning, after a much-deserved night of rest and a full breakfast, Turesobei searched the estate for his father. But he was nowhere to be seen. He did, however, spot Captain Fodoru preparing to ride out into the city.

Along the way to Batsa, Turesobei had gotten to know several of the zaboko soldiers with them rather well, especially their commander, whom he had known for years without ever spending more than a few minutes at a time in his company. Captain Fodoru had a sharp mind and an eloquent voice. He could recite entire volumes of poetry. Turesobei had marveled at this, but Fodoru had laughed and told him that the zaboko had always memorized poetry rather than publishing it in books.

Captain Fodoru worked directly with Turesobei's father and went on every expedition with him. The two could talk of their adventures for hours on end. But Turesobei didn't really know him because when they would return, Fodoru would say hello and then go to his home to spend time with his family, whom Turesobei suspected missed him as much as he and Enashoma missed Noboro.

"Captain Fodoru!" he cried as he ran toward the stables.

Fodoru paused and frowned. "Yes, my lord?"

"Do you know where my father is?"

"Yes, but you cannot go out into the city to see him. Sorry, my lord."

"How do you know that I can't?"

"Your father wouldn't allow it, my lord."

"Did he tell you this?"

"No, my lord," Fodoru said with a grin. "But it is what he would say, is it not?"

"You don't know that."

"After all these years I've been traveling with your father, danger after danger ... trust me. He would not let you out. Not on this trip. If you fell into enemy hands you would be a bargaining piece. Or dead."

Turesobei started to speak but Fodoru interrupted. "Don't make this harder on everyone, my lord, including yourself. Have I not accompanied your father for all your life? You know enough of me to know that I wouldn't mislead you."

"That's enough with the *my lord* stuff. You don't have to say it to Father, you don't have to say it to me."

Fodoru nodded sincerely. "Thank you for the honor."

"You really think it's that dangerous?"

"Your father and I have never before been in as much danger as we are in now. I'm shocked that he let you come along."

"I can take care of myself."

"Maybe you can. I heard about the assassin. Just be sure you don't think too highly of your skills. A bit of bad luck can take down even the best warrior."

Fodoru took up the reins of his denekon. "Sorry, but I have to leave now. Stay here. Don't try anything silly. Just be patient. You will have plenty of new sights and experiences to enjoy soon. I promise."

Returning to his room at the manse, Turesobei pulled the diary from his satchel and summoned Lu Bei. The fetch stretched, flew a circle around the room, and then sat on a table, dangling his feet over the edge.

"Well, master?" he asked. "What do you need?"

"Nothing really. I was just lonely. I can't leave the house until we're ready to set sail. And there's no one here except servants and the standard house guards."

The fetch pumped his fist high into the air. "Then we shall chat!"

"I'd like that," said Turesobei with a chuckle. "You know, I still don't know that much about you."

"Ask, and I shall make it known!"

"Alright. Let's get to business first. We could be facing danger, so what can you do? Do you have any special powers?"

"Like spells or tricks? No, master, I do not. I can remember everything you tell me. I have wings. And I have a nasty bite."

"Right. Yeah. I've seen that."

Lu Bei shrugged sheepishly. "It is all you gave me, master."

"It is all Chonda Lu gave you."

"Of course, master. You—" He spotted the scowl on Turesobei's face and flinched. "I mean, Chonda Lu thought it unwise to have his diary fighting in battles. But back then I could turn invisible for a short while. Well, not invisible but camouflaged so perfectly that I was practically invisible. I was like that up until you found me because of an old spell that I can't tell you about. Just sleeping and waiting for the spell to run out."

"Okay. I won't ask," Turesobei said. "So you can't turn invisible anymore?"

"No, master. You are not powerful enough for that. I can only draw enough energy to be as I am now. And only just. If you had me out during a fight, I'd only weaken you."

Lu Bei danced across the table and touched Turesobei's hand. "I am very sorry that I cannot defend you, master."

Moved by the concern on the fetch's little face, Turesobei patted him on the head. "I do not need a guardian. You will record all that is seen and heard, and I will be grateful."

"Thank you, master."

"You don't have to call me master."

"I am a summoning. It would be inappropriate for me to call you by your common name." He stood tall, at least as tall as he could, and placed his hands on his hips. "I will call you Turesobei only if you make me, but I won't like it."

"Okay, okay. I won't make you."

Lu Bei changed the subject. "So next we set sail, master? Through the reefs?"

The entire island of Okoro was surrounded by jutting rocks and reefs that extended out for over a hundred miles. Most sailors had never seen the open ocean that lay beyond the reefs. Ancient zaboko tales told of a time when the continent was many times larger, until earthquakes sank all the land except for what at that time was the central highland region. Many of the small, rocky outer islands and jutting rock formations were said to be former mountain peaks.

"I'm afraid so."

"I don't like the reefs. We barely made it through the first time. You said I should get to shore if possible, so someone might find the book someday."

"Lu Bei. You have to stop referring to me as if I'm Chonda Lu. I'm not. I'm not. I'm not. I just have his stone."

Lu Bei pointed at the stone. "But master, you—"

Turesobei woke up with Lu Bei patting him on the head.

61

"You all right, master?"

"I passed out again, didn't I?"

"Yes, master. There are things I cannot tell you. If I do you pass out."

Turesobei sighed as he sat up. "Let's not talk about them then, okay?"

"I will try, master. I will try. But it is very frustrating for me."

"So, what were we talking about?"

"You were telling me that we must sail through the reefs. And I told you Chonda Lu didn't think we would make it."

"Oh, right. I remember that part now. I'm a bit worried."

"We'll be fine, master."

"But I've never sailed before."

"Actually, master, you used to..."

"Yes?" Turesobei asked, his eyes narrowing.

"Er, I think you'll get used to it quickly, master."

When they finally left for the ship, Turesobei was wearing light armor: a breastplate and a helmet of green enameled leather along with padded sleeves and pants. As they traveled, he kept his hand close to Sumada since his father had warned him of potential danger. He had practiced with the blade daily and kept it polished religiously. As they went, he scanned the predawn streets with his kenja-sight but detected nothing unusual. He felt important, knowing that he could see dangers that no one else in their party could.

Even this early, people bustled along the city streets. Most headed in the same direction as they did, toward the docks, warehouses, and fisheries. Some were servants out on errands. Most were merchants opening their stalls along the edge of the streets. Several covered rickshaws rolled past, pulled by teenage zaboko boys with their skin tanned a dark grey. He imagined that beautiful princesses lurked within the veiled rickshaws and peered out at him with interest. But he knew the truth was likely far different, that these were probably aging baojendari bureaucrats on the way to their posts.

After presenting their passes, they passed through a well-guarded gate and entered the foul-smelling East Dock Ward. Here they no longer saw baojendari merchants with their expensive wares, accompanied by their zaboko laborers. Instead they saw zaboko beggars and prostitutes, sailors off duty, fishermen hauling in their catches, and a few well-dressed and armed baojendari who were obviously in charge. The streets were lined with brothels, wine-houses, and tall apartment buildings crammed with residents. The impoverished zaboko of the Dock Ward could leave it only if they had a pass allowing entry to another ward. Most of them did not and would be stuck here all their lives.

Turesobei found it hard not to feel guilty that he was born into the highest caste of Batsakun and had privileges most zaboko couldn't even dream of. Though it was obviously not his fault, he felt the heavy burden of it. That the Chonda treated the zaboko in their province as indentured peasants, while most other clans treated them as little more than slaves, did not make him feel much better about it.

As he was thinking of injustices and the history of the invasion, a sudden prick in his mind alerted him to danger. It was not unusual for him to get these, but it was not a reliable gift either. He glanced down the street to his right and spotted a group of riders racing toward them: a dozen zaboko warriors led by five baojendari.

They charged straight toward Turesobei, who was stuck in the middle of the formation.

Chapter Fifteen

Noboro wheeled his mount around, and the rest of his party followed. But before Noboro or any of the guards could move to shield Turesobei, the oncoming riders intercepted them.

"Chonda Noboro!" shouted the bulky baojendari riding in the front. He was a middle-aged man, like Turesobei's father, only with a stubby nose and a long, curling mustache.

Chonda swords were drawn.

The enemy reached for their hilts, but their leader held out his hand. In it was a thin wooden rod about three feet long.

"Steady, men," the man ordered. "Let's not take their blood unless we must. Easy though it might be."

Turesobei noticed then that golden maple leaves decorated the soldiers' shields and hauberks. A prominent one adorned the front of their leader's lacquered helmet.

The Gawo!

The leader's insignia marked him as a first-order knight, but Turesobei didn't know which one. He knew the names of most of the Gawo nobles, but he had seen very few of them, and then only in fleeting glimpses. No one considered it worthwhile to get a High Wizard started early on diplomacy.

"Sheathe your arms," Noboro ordered, and the Chonda obeyed, though some did so reluctantly. Turesobei had never thought to draw his blade. So much for his combat training.

The man eased his mount up beside Turesobei. Then he tapped his baton against Turesobei's breastplate, deliberately nudging the amber kavaru which he had unwisely left hanging outside his armor. Turesobei dropped his hand to the hilt of his sword and narrowed his eyes. It was an affront to touch a wizard's kavaru.

"Get away from him," said Noboro as he advanced through the gathered men to ride up to Turesobei's side.

"Or what?"

"By the gods, Jimusha, I would love an excuse to send your head to King Gawo in a basket."

"You would risk open warfare over me antagonizing your son a bit?"

"Yes, I would."

"You've no sense of humor," Jimusha said with a wry grin. He turned back to Turesobei, looking him over with a disapproving gaze. "He's not much to look at, is he? I doubt he has anything close to Lord Haisero's skill at magic."

Haisero was the counterpart to Turesobei, the High Wizard in Waiting for the Gawo. Turesobei had never seen him, but he was reputed to be very talented.

"Your nephew must be an impressive lad indeed, because I assure you Turesobei will be every bit the wizard his twice-great grandfather Denojei was."

This caused a lot of dark looks and sneers amongst the Gawo, for Turesobei's great-great-grandfather had led the Chonda to victory against their rivals when the Gawo were at the height of their power. Now that the balance was shifting back to the Gawo, they didn't wish to hear any such thing. For his part, Turesobei couldn't imagine achieving half of what his ancestor had accomplished.

"Pity Lord Haisero's not with us," said Jimusha, "or we could see a wizards' duel. You could prove your claim." Some of the Gawo party looked uneasy when he said this.

"According to our spies," Noboro replied, "your nephew is missing."

"Your spies," Jimusha snarled, "whoever they may be, know nothing. Haisero is away studying in retreat. He's learning advanced subjects you could never fathom."

"Alas, I'm sure I could not. Or else I would be the next High Wizard of the Chonda. Turesobei could master them easily, though, I'm certain."

"One day we shall see, Noboro. Perhaps on the day you and I draw swords against each other."

"May the day come soon. In the meantime, I will settle for killing the spies you keep sending after me."

"I have sent no spies to watch you," replied Jimusha with what appeared to be a genuinely surprised look on his face. "I have no interest in your expeditions. Never have."

"Well, the man trailing me last week was without doubt a Gawo. Maybe, Spymaster, you should keep better tabs on what your clan is up to."

The Gawo knight bristled but seemed suddenly distracted. "You should watch yourself, Noboro," he threatened, but without passion. "The world is dangerous, especially for a Chonda."

Jimusha wheeled his mount around and rode casually away, his guards following behind him. The Chonda watched them go, and when they were out of sight, Noboro leaned in close to Fodoru and whispered.

"Send word back to King Ugara. Tell him our spies are correct. Haisero is indeed missing."

Chapter Sixteen

Their ship, the *Little Goddess*, was a swift, medium-sized junk built for light shipping and rich passengers. It was just big enough to hold their soldiers, supplies, and mounts. After Turesobei stowed his gear in a passenger compartment the size of his bedroom closet at home, he joined his father on the deck and met the ship's captain, who was a free zaboko from the nation of Zangaiden. Tedeko wasn't what he expected. He wasn't old, fat, one-eyed, or grizzled at all. Instead, he was young, sharply dressed, and quite thin for a zaboko.

Captain Tedeko greeted him warmly and told him a boring story about how he had come to be owner and captain of the ship after saving a baojendari noble from drowning. The story should have been interesting, but Tedeko had no gift for storytelling and was quite monotone. Tedeko had good reason to be proud, though. Turesobei knew little about ships, but he knew this was a fine junk. Few zaboko commanded vessels, much less expensive ones such as this.

As soon as all the expedition's denekon and gear were loaded, the crew maneuvered the *Little Goddess* out into the harbor. Then Tedeko barked out orders and the zaboko crew raised the sails with a series of hand cranks. The ship eased out to the sea and within an hour caught a good northerly wind that rushed them along the coast. They kept sight of land and were wary of reefs and shoals, despite the ship's low draft.

Turesobei saw waves breaking against many reefs closer into shore and some farther out, but they didn't come close to any. Occasionally, he spotted rocks jutting ten or twenty feet out of the sea, but they steered far away from those since other rocks often lay nearby, hidden just below the surface.

Turesobei did quickly get used to sailing, as Lu Bei had predicted. So fast that he almost didn't notice that he was on the water, even when the boat was rocked by big waves. This impressed his father and many of the soldiers with them. Two of them, who had had no experience at sea, spent most of the first day vomiting over the rail.

On the third afternoon, as they rounded the Horn of Komo, they sat on the aft deck together and shared a bowl of eastern wine. The day was clear and bright. The Orichomo Mountains loomed in the distance like jagged rain clouds. The beaches on the shore looked barren and rocky with sparse vegetation beyond.

Noboro told Turesobei stories about the different ports he had been to. And he told Turesobei about nearly getting killed the first time he ventured into Batsa's streets by himself. As Turesobei laughed, Noboro sighed and shook his head.

"That first trip out on my own seems so long ago. I was young, impetuous, and hotheaded. I'm still amazed that I survived."

"You've never seemed ill-tempered to me," Turesobei said, not that he'd been around his father enough to really know.

"That's because I burned it all out when I was younger. What your mother didn't strip from my soul."

Turesobei winced. "You hate her don't you?"

Noboro frowned. "I don't hate her, Sobei. Hate is a strong and terrible thing. I've hated very few people in my life, even Jimusha, even most of those who've tried to kill me."

"How could you not hate someone like that?"

"Well, you must always ask yourself, 'Why is this person trying to kill me?' You need to understand why he's your enemy."

"So you can fix what angers him?"

"Yes perhaps, but also because it may not be personal, and hate will bring you to do things you'll regret."

"I don't understand. How could it not be personal?"

"Well, for example, in most wars, the conflict itself isn't personal between two soldiers. They are trying to kill each other because that's what they've been ordered to do."

"So some of the people who've tried to kill you were just doing their jobs?"

"Exactly. A man must fulfill his duties or lose his honor."

Turesobei eyed him critically. "And what about jealous husbands? Hated any of those for doing their duty in coming after you?"

Noboro glanced at him sharply then looked away in embarrassment. "No, I have not ... but you know, not all the women I've ... not all of them have been married."

"How many women have there been?" Turesobei asked.

Noboro's cheeks reddened. "Gods! What kind of question is that to ask your father?" Turesobei shrugged. "Well, if you must know, more than I can count. And I don't regret a single one."

Turesobei scowled at him but said nothing.

"You don't have to look at me like that," Noboro said.

"It's not fair to Mother."

"Oh come on! You have to be joking."

"I don't see anything funny about it."

Noboro eyed him carefully. "You mean you don't know about..."

"About what?" Turesobei asked when his father remained silent.

"Well, your mother has a lover, you know."

"What! Who?"

"I'm not telling you since she clearly doesn't want you to know. I can't believe she's kept it a secret that well."

Turesobei thought about some things Enashoma had said to him that he had disregarded as unimportant. She knew! He realized now that she had been trying to see if he also knew. But he hadn't. His little sister had figured it out, but he hadn't.

Turesobei stammered, "I just can't believe all this."

"I'm sorry, Sobei, but your mother and I don't like each other much, and that's no reason for us to keep each other from having some happiness in the world. You have to understand that the world of grown-ups is complex, and nothing is ever as simple as it should be. Studying to be a wizard takes up a lot of your time. And your mother is obviously good at sheltering you. I don't doubt that you haven't yet realized exactly what goes on within the palace walls, but you will one day soon."

Turesobei realized that he had known there was more going on without ever thinking about it. After a long while, he said, "I don't really want to go home after this is over."

"Of course not. No one wants to go home at the start of a journey. Only near the end."

"What about you, Father? Do you ever miss home?" Do you ever miss me and Enashoma was what he wanted to ask. He understood about Noboro avoiding Wenari. She was nearly impossible for Turesobei to live with, and he did love her.

"You ask hard questions, Sobei. And I wish I had a better answer for that one. I do miss it sometimes, but not a lot and not often. I miss you and Enashoma, and your grandfather. I was always closest to my mother, though, and I used to come home more when she was alive."

Turesobei nodded and watched the rise and swell of the sea. Noboro held the wine bowl out to him. "Do you want the rest?" Turesobei shook his head. He already felt flushed and a little dizzy.

"I'm sorry I haven't been a better father, Sobei. But I have my work, and your mother and grandfather take good care of you. I only married and had children because I was supposed to."

Noboro drained the wine bowl. "I'm going to do my best to make it up to you on this trip, though."

Turesobei smiled and was about to tell him he didn't hold his absences against him when a sailor interrupted them and told Noboro that the captain needed to see him.

They made a brief stop in the Zangaiden port of Changaku for supplies and then continued on their way. At first Turesobei enjoyed avoiding his normal routine, spending his days watching the sea and his nights, hidden in his compartment, chatting with Lu Bei, asking him all sorts of questions and sometimes getting a few answers. Grandfather Kahenan rarely gave him full days off. However, after five days, Turesobei grew bored and lethargic, so he began his martial arts practice again.

Noboro joined him on the deck and instructed him on the finer points of various movements. Turesobei was surprised to discover his father was a master at many of the routines. He thought he might even be better than Arms Instructor Kilono on a few. Turesobei guessed that his father had studied with and observed many teachers during his travels.

After another five days, Turesobei felt hollow and listless. He could no longer stand to avoid magic altogether. As he went through his meditations, he reveled in feeling the primal currents in the ocean's depths below them. He took out his spell strips and checked them for kenja leaks. Eventually he would need to boost them, but so far they had held properly. He summoned two flickering flame globes at once and skimmed the sea with them.

When he grew tired, he practiced his calligraphy in the old baojendari script and recited vocabulary from the ancient tongue. After he finished all that, he felt content again and wondered if he truly enjoyed wizardry or if he just didn't know how to live without it.

"Lu Bei," he asked the fetch late one night before retiring, "did Chonda Lu ever grow tired of magic?"

"Of course not, master. Magic was more than what he did. It was who he was."

The reef density increased. The ship slowed to navigate the treacherous waters and twice anchored at nightfall instead of continuing at half its normal speed. The weather had turned against them with strong westerly winds that required tedious tacking through the dangerous reef channels. This was the only safe and reliable way to sail around the continent of Okoro since the reefs extended so far out into the shallow ocean that surrounded them.

The western winds brought warmer weather, as well. On one particularly hot afternoon, Turesobei and Noboro practiced sword routines until sweat drenched them. The rhythm of the routines became a dance with the soles of their feet tapping the beats as they lunged, spun, thrust, backpedaled, and kicked.

Tap, thud, slash, swipe, thud, slash!

Neither wanted to end the dance of the long sword sequence, but a shout from the crow's nest interrupted them.

"Two sails on the horizon! Origin unknown!"

Chapter Seventeen

Sailors scrambled as Captain Tedeko shouted orders that Turesobei still didn't understand. He had only learned a little of the sailors' lingo. Other ships had passed them, but these were the first whose national origin wasn't clear. Captain Tedeko joined them at the port bow rail and aimed his telescope.

"What is it?" Noboro asked.

"I'm not sure," Tedeko said. "Maybe pirates. It's hard to tell whether they're pursuing us, but we'll know soon."

The two smaller ships were heading directly toward them. The *Little Goddess* was tacking into the wind the two new ships sailed with.

"We're going to turn north and see if they follow," Tedeko said. He shouted orders and the helmsman altered their course.

Immediately, the two ships adjusted to intercept them. At that time they raised their colors. Two flags, white with a single line of crimson across the center.

The color drained from Tedeko's face. "Captain Gaizanu," he said without expression.

Sailors gasped and murmured in fear. Turesobei's heart skipped a beat. He didn't know much of sailing, but everyone had heard of the sadistic pirate lord Gaizanu. It was said that men who were about to be captured would commit suicide rather than face Gaizanu's wicked tortures.

Noboro closed his eyes tight and grimaced, as if in pain. "Can you outrun him?"

"If we can outmaneuver him and get him heading into the wind with us," Captain Tedeko said, "then maybe. But they'll catch us when we stop tonight."

"But won't they get caught in the reefs in the dark?" Turesobei asked.

Tedeko shook his head. "They'll follow along the same path we took, knowing it's safe."

"I could cast a spell to summon a small cloud of fog behind us so they couldn't see," said Turesobei. "Would that help?"

"Could another wizard counter it?" the captain asked.

"Easily."

"It's no use to us then. Gaizanu is a sorcerer."

"Oh," said Turesobei. "I didn't know that."

"So what will we do?" Noboro asked.

"We'll just have to do our best with the lanterns and spotters and plow ahead. We don't fight them unless we must."

Turesobei turned to his father. "I could summon a couple of fire globes and have them hover over the sea ahead of the ship so it would be easier to see."

Noboro looked at the captain and raised an eyebrow. Tedeko nodded eagerly. "That would help."

Turesobei smiled, satisfied that he could help out in some way after all. "I'll be ready come night."

Tedeko consulted his charts. "The safest routes are due west but they are closed to us now. We have two northwestern routes on the charts that we can take early tomorrow morning. The safest and fastest path is not an option, though. And unfortunately the other is quite dangerous at speed."

"Why isn't the first an option?" Turesobei asked.

"Gitsukara. Reef Demons. They live between two large outcrops. A giant web stretches between the rocks and traps sailors as they come through. That's what I've heard anyway. I know this much for certain: no one goes through there."

"Would the pirates follow us through if we took that route?" Turesobei asked.

"They would have to be desperate."

"Everyone's afraid of that route," Noboro told him. "And everyone sailing through this region knows of it."

"You have Yomifano," Turesobei said to his father, "and I have your white-steel sword. We could fight our way through demons."

"But would that be better than fighting the pirates?" Noboro said. "We don't know how powerful these demons are."

Turesobei shrugged. "I'm not familiar with gitsukara, but I can try to banish them. It might work."

"I don't like it," Noboro said. "But if we have to..."

Captain Tedeko nodded. "Then we'll do what we must."

The *Little Goddess* had outmaneuvered the pirates, but her lead on them was dwindling rapidly. Turesobei stood in the ship's bow manipulating his two flame globes ahead of the spotters' lantern-light. He kept his focus by counting the sloshes of sea against the ship's keel. His father and Guard Captain Fodoru stood nearby watching quietly.

Captain Tedeko joined them. "We must fight either the pirates or the reef demons."

"It is your choice, captain," Noboro said. "Either way, you can count on us."

"We won't win if we fight the pirates. If the lookout has counted correctly, they outnumber us three to one. And my sailors are not hardened warriors."

"Then we risk the passage and see if the legends are true?" Noboro asked.

Tedeko sighed and with his fingers made the sign of the crescent to ward away evil. "If your son is up to the challenge..."

Chapter Eighteen

Turesobei drew a knife blade across his palm. He dipped one finger into the blood and then drew a series of runes onto Captain Fodoru's broadsword. To Turesobei's kenja-sight, the blood glowed with an eerie, pulsing cast. Blood magic provided strong energies, but its use held great risk. Turesobei chanted the proper words and completed the spell.

"What will this do?" Fodoru asked.

"It's a demon bane."

"Will my blade harm them like white-steel?"

"No, but they will feel more pain from it than normal."

Fodoru smiled weakly. "So it will anger them?"

"I intend for it to distract them. Could buy you some time if you're in danger."

Turesobei repeated the process on Captain Tedeko's saber. Then he placed demon wards on the armor of both men and that of the helmsman. Turesobei's armor of enameled leather had a permanent ward placed there by his grandfather before they had left. His father's armor had an identical spell that had been cast many years ago. The wards would fortify them against zhurakami magic and their physical attacks, but it wouldn't fully protect them by any means.

No one except Turesobei, Noboro, and Fodoru would stay on the foredeck as they approached the gitsukara.

Turesobei knelt and meditated as the *Little Goddess* eased into the wide channel that would lead them to the demon outcrops. Fog obscured much of their route. The helmsman steered by the sound of crashing waves more than by sight. Their ultimate destination he could see, however, as glowing gossamer strands slowly appeared ahead, like sapphire veins within the fog. Waves crashed against reefs and rocks and spindrift flew into their faces. A strange wind blew through the strands and whistled with a crooning *sweeeh*.

Turesobei wiped saltwater from his eyes and took deep breaths. His heart pounded. He was, he admitted, terrified. He was also afraid that he'd let everyone down. Forty-five people including his father and their Chonda guards depended on his skills in magic.

Lap, crash, *sweeeh*!

Turesobei let those sounds echo in his mind like a mantra as he opened his kenja-sight. The threads proved to be not entirely kenja as he had suspected, though they carried a strong taint of demon magic. He guessed they were more like spider silk than anything.

Lap, crash, *sweeeh!*

Turesobei spotted the gitsukara crouched in the center of the silken web. He had expected something like a spider. Instead he saw something as much like a squid or lobster, only larger than a man. A dozen tentacles emanated from a hard-shell body, and a pincer capped the end of each tentacle. Black eyes sat near a hooked beak. Thin spider legs held the body to the web.

"I-I see it," Turesobei stammered. "It's ugly and it has a lot of tentacles."

From mid-deck Captain Tedeko cursed. "I'd hoped the legends weren't true!"

"Just one gitsukara?" Noboro asked.

"That's all I—" Something moved out onto the web. "Wait, two more. They're smaller, though." Turesobei described them, cringing as he did so.

Lap, crash, *sweeeh!*

A screech pierced the fog, followed by a half-dozen lesser calls. Everyone clasped hands over their ears and fell to their knees as the noise deafened them.

"By the Earth-Mother!" Turesobei yelled, having seen more movement. "There are four more small ones now!"

The ship sailed to within thirty yards of the web. Turesobei glanced back and saw the helmsman had collapsed to his knees. They might soon crash into the rocks.

Turesobei struggled to his feet and drew the bamboo strip with the *spell of demon banishment.* He chanted and found that as he concentrated on the words, he could block out the effects of the screech.

Power lurched from his body. Kenja from the ocean, air, and even the reefs moved in tune with the energies propelled outward from within Turesobei and the spell strip. The banishment swept across the gitsukara. Immediately, the screeching stopped and the small ones withdrew to their rocks. The large one remained and tensed its body.

The demon opened its beak and projected silk webs toward the ship. The webs arced over the bow and struck Turesobei. He fell, wrapped in sticky webs that still trailed all the way back to the beast's maw.

The webs tightened and the gitsukara jerked him forward, sucking in the webs. Turesobei slid across the deck toward the bow. Noboro lunged forward and slashed through the webs with Yomifano. The demon snapped down on the loose webbing, severing it from its end, and then blasted another mouthful toward the ship.

Noboro swung Yomifano in a wide arc and cut through them just before they struck. "Captain Tedeko, guard the helmsman!"

Tedeko climbed the rear deck to shield his helmsman from danger. The ship closed to within ten yards.

Turesobei struggled but couldn't break free from the webs that were still wrapped around him. Fodoru hunched down and cut the webs off Turesobei while Noboro dodged another mouthful.

Turesobei stood and swept the stinging webs from his face and arms. He felt weak and nauseous. But he was lucky. If not for his armor's demon warding, the webbing could have leeched all the kenja from him within a few minutes.

He reached Sumada toward Fodoru. "Take it and give me yours."

"But—"

"I'll be too busy with spells."

Ignoring the law against a zaboko wielding a white-steel weapon, Fodoru took the blade. Then he gave Turesobei his broadsword.

The ship crashed into the webbing. The silken strands stretched and groaned but didn't tear. The ship slowed to a halt. The large gitsukara leapt onto the foredeck.

The smaller gitsukara started to crawl back onto the web, but Turesobei chanted an impromptu banishment and drove them back again. Fodoru stood nearby and shielded him. Noboro dodged another blast of webbing and waited to see what the beast would do next.

He didn't have to wait long. The gitsukara hissed and vaulted over them. While overhead, it spun around and slashed at them with its tentacles. One struck Turesobei in the back and knocked him down, though the claw didn't pierce his armor.

Noboro severed one tentacle, and it fell to the deck where it twitched for several moments before dissipating like smoke. But then another caught Noboro by the leg and lifted him into the air. He cursed and swatted wildly with Yomifano, but to no avail.

Fodoru rushed forward to save him, chopping through a tentacle as he went, but the moment he reached Noboro, a tentacle struck him in the neck. Fodoru fell and didn't move.

Turesobei rushed forward, sliding across the deck. Now that the creature was within range, he drew the fire-beam strip from his pouch and chanted the activation command. The red-gold beam shot forth from his hand with a crackling hiss. The blast seared across the creature's left flank and burned one eye shut.

The creature screeched in pain and dropped Noboro. Turesobei's father immediately jumped to his feet, dodged flailing tentacles, and plunged Yomifano deep into the creature's body. The gitsukara writhed and screamed.

Noboro jerked the blade free and stabbed the beast again. The gitsukara dimmed and turned hazy around the edges. Noboro struck again, and Turesobei, though weak and dizzy, chanted another banishment spell.

With a sucking gasp, the creature imploded. Like a cloud of smoke drawn into a pinhole, the gitsukara disappeared into the nether hell from which it had originated. The remaining gitsukara fled to the other side of their rocks.

Fodoru weakly rose to his feet. He felt at his neck and his hand returned with blood.

Noboro ran to him. "You all right?"

"Nothing serious," Fodoru said, wincing in pain. "At least I don't think so."

"We'd better cut the ship free before the others decide they can take us!" Captain Tedeko yelled.

Noboro ran to one side, Fodoru the other. With the white-steel blades the two easily cut through the webs holding the ship. As they did so, Turesobei collapsed to his knees.

"Sobei!" he heard his father yell as he slumped to the deck.

This wasn't good.

He wasn't injured, but the webs and his spell casting had drained his internal kenja down to a dangerous level.

Once again the ship lapped forward into the sea. Footsteps pounded across the deck. People spoke but he couldn't understand the words.

A hand touched Turesobei's arm as he passed into darkness.

Chapter Nineteen

Turesobei awoke to the din of a bustling street of haggling merchants, squawking chickens, rumbling denekon, and playing children. The scents of grilled meats and baking bread drifted through the bamboo slats of shuttered windows. Those scents mingled with the musty odor of the dingy, second story room. Only a little light filtered into the room, but it was enough to see that his accommodations were less than ideal.

Three more pallets lay near his, and Captain Fodoru sat on one of them meditating. A clay pitcher was placed on a shelf on the opposite side of the room along with what looked like hard biscuits and slices of apple.

Turesobei felt incredibly weak. The last thing he remembered was his father and Fodoru cutting the *Little Goddess* free from the gitsukara's webs. He tried to sit up, but couldn't manage it.

"Fodoru?" he called weakly.

The guard captain turned and smiled. A bandage was wrapped around his neck and shoulder. "You're awake at last. How do you feel?"

"Terrible ... thirsty."

"I bet you are." Fodoru brought a biscuit and a bowl of water to Turesobei. "Here, let me help you sit up." Fodoru lifted and turned Turesobei around so that he could lean back against the wall.

Turesobei drank and took a few bites out of the biscuit. His stomach couldn't tolerate more than that yet, so he set it aside.

"Where's everyone else?"

"Your father has gone to hire a local guide he knows. Some of the guards are with him, and the others are waiting outside this room." He grinned. "I'm stuck here with you because of my shoulder."

"How is it?"

"Getting better. The filthy beast had some sort of mild venom. The wound burns and itches like a giant mosquito bite. The healer said it would get better, though. You were the one we worried about. You've been out for five days."

Five days! No wonder he felt so stiff.

"I'll be all right," Turesobei said. "I just need to recover my spirit." If he was awake, the greatest danger was gone. Of course, he may have drained anywhere from several days to several years from his natural lifespan. "Where are we?"

"Nijona. It's a small coastal town in Wakaro."

"What about the ship?"

"Gone on to Dogo Daiyen. Captain Tedeko has a cargo to deliver. He's going to return here afterward and wait for us. Believe it nor not, but this is the best inn Nijona has to offer."

"It must not be very much of a town."

"Probably forty thousand people, actually, but they are not wealthy." Fodoru gave Turesobei an apple slice. "Try to eat some. It will make you stronger."

Turesobei managed to force it down then finished the bowl of water. "I'm going to rest some more now."

Fodoru helped him lie back down. "Of course. Noboro said we wouldn't leave until you were well enough."

"A few more days then," Turesobei murmured. "Tell him I'm sorry."

Two afternoons later, Fodoru left and Turesobei was at last in the room alone by himself.

"Lu Bei," he whispered.

A muffled pop emanated from his satchel, then out flew the amber, bat-winged fetch who immediately rushed to Turesobei and landed on the pallet beside him.

"Master, you shouldn't waste your energy on me!"

"Shh! There are guards outside. And don't worry about me, I'm almost well."

"I wish I could have done something, master."

"But you couldn't, and I made it here just fine. In fact, I'm glad I fought the demon."

Lu Bei's eyes went wide with expectation. "Why, master?"

"Because I've proven myself now. What test could Grandfather give me that would exceed that?"

"None, master. It was a great feat, and I'm certain you will accomplish many more like it in time. I'm certain that one day demons such as the gitsukara will prove to be of little challenge to you."

Turesobei chuckled. "I'm not so sure about that, little fetch. But I do feel that I'm up to the task now, that I can handle anything this expedition throws at me."

"But, master, we're still not entirely sure what we're questing for or what dangers could lie ahead."

"It doesn't matter," Turesobei proclaimed, no longer feeling hurt that his father wouldn't reveal to him exactly what they were doing or why. "Whatever it is, I can handle it."

The next day, Turesobei felt strong enough to ride. So with a pack train of denekon behind them, Noboro, Turesobei, and twenty-three guards led by Captain Fodoru exited Nijona. Urigi, a local zaboko tracker, rode in the front. Noboro had traveled this way before several times, but he insisted on having a guide who intimately knew the land, in case they ran into danger and were forced to take an alternate route.

People gathered to watch them pass. They wore ragged clothes, and their careworn faces were marred by downcast expressions. Turesobei didn't see any baojendari, but he did spot a few cloaked and hooded k'chasan traders. Though he'd never seen one before, he recognized them by the grey-brown fur on their hands and their graceful, catlike movements. K'chasans were the third major race on Okoro. They lived almost exclusively in the forests of the West.

Turesobei was scanning the crowd, trying to catch sight of an uncloaked k'chasan. But as his group neared the gate leading out of the walled town, Turesobei noticed someone following them intently. The thin zaboko boy had a strange, indescribable quality to his appearance. He looked exceedingly common and yet somehow familiar.

Their eyes met, and the boy sneered.

Chapter Twenty

Noboro called them to a halt and Turesobei turned to rein in his mount. When he looked back a moment later, the boy was gone. Suspicious, Turesobei activated his kenja-sight. He saw a trace of magic where the boy had stood and a strong flow of air energies that trailed back into the crowded street.

Turesobei warned Fodoru. "We're being followed."

Fodoru kept looking forward. "Where is he?"

"Gone now. Fled back into the crowd when he noticed that I had spotted him."

"You're certain he was spying on us?"

"Yes. He sneered at me."

"Hardly seems a good reason to suspect someone."

"He was also rather common looking, too common, and he was clouded in air kenja."

"Which means..."

"His appearance was an illusion."

The captain nodded thoughtfully and ordered two guards to watch the crowd, looking for suspicious people. The rest of them he put on alert. They had to wait to tell Noboro, who was busy meeting with the Wakaran guards who were manning the gate.

The eight zaboko soldiers wore ornate wooden armor and masks with terrible grimaces carved into them. A robed baojendari with a bald head and a long, white beard directed them. Dark skin circled his eyes, as if he hadn't slept in years. His mouth was twisted into a grin so terrible and depraved that it almost naturally matched the soldiers' masks.

"Watch yourself around these people," Fodoru whispered to Turesobei, with a glance toward the robed baojendari.

"A zealot?" Turesobei asked.

"Aye, the worst kind. An official Wakaran Inquisitor."

Turesobei knew about them from history lessons. They were the most devoted followers of Supreme Elder Jakawiju, who ruled Wakaro with a whimsical iron fist. He claimed to be an incarnation of the baojendari Supreme Celestial Emperor, and he wielded powerful magics and fanatical troops.

Decades ago he had led an uprising against the traditional baojendari clans ruling Wakaro. At first the zaboko loved him because he gave them greater freedoms. But soon, Jakawiju's economic restructuring brought devastation and starvation to all. Many people died, but he retained power through a devoted corps of young men brainwashed by his social programs and convinced of his godhood.

Noboro presented stamped papers, made explanations, and slipped the baojendari Inquisitor a long string of Taganan jade coins. The Inquisitor's men then conducted a routine search of their baggage and supplies. Finding no religious contraband, such as Shogakami texts or images, they allowed the group to go on.

Though they were respectful of the Great Deities, the Shogakami, and all the traditional festivals, the Chonda were not a religious people. So it immensely bothered Turesobei that a ruler would want to impose his religious ideas onto his people.

The more distance they put between themselves and the Wakaran Inquisitor, the better Turesobei felt.

The coastal lands in Wakaro looked no different from the wilder areas of Batsakun. However, as they moved inland over the next three days, this changed. They soon encountered large pockets of pristine forest and dozens of glittering lakes. They passed villages with less frequency and soon met a line of dense hills. When they reached the summit of this ridge, Turesobei gasped.

Beyond spread a valley of rainforest that stretched down to the distant Natsugami Mountains. A gleaming river wound through a deep gorge cut into the heart of the forest. Turesobei had no idea how they would cross the gorge. He guessed they would have to spend days, perhaps weeks, navigating around it.

By late afternoon, the terrain leading down to the rainforest had grown more rugged and intimidating. Noboro called for them to make camp early. He intended to rest thoroughly before entering the forest. Turesobei felt relieved. He had recovered much of his spirit, but he still tired easily. He also wasn't used to riding for such long periods. His thigh muscles had grown stiff and his bottom ached.

Later that evening, Turesobei and Noboro roasted pheasants over a fire. They sat away from the others so they could talk in private. For a long time they discussed geography, but finally Turesobei worked up the courage once again to ask his father about the purpose of their trip.

While sailing, he had asked twice without getting a response. His father just hadn't been prepared to tell him yet. Fodoru and four other guards who always traveled with Noboro knew exactly what was going on, though none of the others did.

"I guess I can tell you now. You deserve to know anyway." Noboro patted Turesobei on the shoulder. "I'm proud of you, son. The way you handled yourself on the ship against the gitsukara. I know I can trust you with anything. You're nearly a man now, even if you officially have three more years to go."

Turesobei beamed with pride. "Thank you, Father. I won't tell anyone what we're doing. I promise you can trust me."

"Well, it's a secret for good reason."

"When I was spying, I heard you say talking about a heart, a key, and cultists."

"The Storm Dragon's Heart. The heart of Naruwakiru."

Turesobei knew the legends. "But she's been dead for millennia."

"Yes, but her heart remains. Ten years ago, quite by accident, I discovered the secret vault where the heart is kept. I tried to get in, but failed. Then your grandfather tried magic, but that didn't work either. He gave up, but I didn't. Eventually I learned that zaboko priests had once kept a magical key to the vault."

"I heard you tell Grandfather about getting the key," Turesobei said. "What I don't understand is that if this heart is dangerous enough to keep locked away so well and for so long, why do you want it so badly?"

"If not me, someone else will get to it eventually. Better the Chonda than a clan like the Gawo. Besides, we don't know for sure that it's dangerous."

"The cult you were talking about must think that it's powerful."

"The Storm Dragon Cult. They claim to be descended from the original cult that worshiped Naruwakiru, before Tepebono slew her. Afterward they worshiped the heart, until Shogakami priests stole it from them and locked it away."

"Do you think that's true? That they are descendants of the original cult?"

"Maybe, but I doubt it. I think some crackpot discovered an old cult text and decided to resurrect the past for his own purposes."

"Do the cultists know where the vault is?"

"Apparently, because soon after I returned here, Obu Sotenda published his book and expanded the Storm Dragon Cult. I think they must have followed your grandfather and me to the vault, hoping that we would open it for them. I don't know how they found out about my discovery, though. I have no doubt that they're trying. That's why we have twenty-four guards with us."

Turesobei glanced around nervously. "I think we could've used more."

"This is all the clan could spare and all I could afford. Besides, with a much larger force we would have drawn far too much attention from the Wakaran government." Noboro smiled absently and stared into the fire. "It's going to be grand when we find that heart."

Turesobei eyed his impassioned father suspiciously. "You're obsessed with this thing aren't you?"

Noboro looked at him with surprise. "Well ... what's wrong with that?"

"Nothing, Father, except that your judgment may be a little clouded."

Noboro frowned. "You sound like your grandfather now."

"He's a wise man."

"But he doesn't understand this quest."

"Neither do I," said Turesobei. "I mean, I understand the things you're telling me, and they sound reasonable. But somehow this all seems ... hasty and ill-advised."

"But you don't understand either, Sobei. You and your grandfather didn't see it like I

81

did."

"You saw it? How?"

"Well, I first found the vault in the midst of a terrible storm."

"By accident, right?"

"It seems that way, though perhaps not. Certainly, I wasn't looking for it. I was looking for the ruins of an old shrine. Anyway, the storm was terrible and we couldn't find any shelter, until we at last stumbled upon the shrine. There was a tunnel in the back. We explored the tunnel during the storm and found the vault. When I touched the door..."

Noboro stared into the flames with wide eyes until Turesobei prompted him. "What happened?"

"I saw the heart, through the vault door, as if it were made of glass."

"Did the others see it?"

"No."

"What does it look like?"

"A jade orb with veins of crimson. It's just small enough that you can hold it in one hand. I swear I could feel it pulsing through the wall."

"So this vision is what drives your obsession?"

"There's more," he replied. "Every night in my dreams I see that orb locked within the vault and I know that I must recover it before anyone else. The dreams get stronger as I get closer to it. Those first nights ... it was like lying in bed with a lover but not being able to touch her or even speak to her."

Turesobei cringed. "This doesn't sound good, Father. Has it occurred to you that some arcane force might be manipulating you?"

Noboro nodded solemnly. "It has, but I couldn't live with myself if I didn't try. Besides, your grandfather thought the same and couldn't find any trace of a geas upon me. You can check yourself if you like."

"Why didn't Grandfather come with you this time?"

Noboro shrugged. "Well, he's not as able to withstand difficult journeys as he used to be. He also claimed he was too busy. I suspect there's something more, but that's all he would tell me. He has his reasons, I'm sure."

Grandfather Kahenan always had reasons, and he had a habit of not telling anyone what they were. He liked to let people figure things out on their own. Turesobei finished his dinner and began to contemplate all that his father had told him.

He was starting to understand why his grandfather had sent him along. Yes, he did need a break, and he did need to experience the world. But Kahenan wanted a wizard he trusted to accompany Noboro and watch over him. Yet what exactly did his grandfather expect him to do out here? Was there something more to it?

Chapter Twenty-One

The rainforest sang with the cries of a million birds, some brightly plumed, others darting shadows beneath the thick canopy. Their songs stopped only when it rained, which was at least once each day. And after each rain they chattered with greater fury as if making up for lost time. The rainforest sang other songs, too, with other voices. Wildcats caterwauled in the depths of night. Frogs croaked, monkeys screeched, leaves whispered, and insects buzzed.

Flies and mosquitoes plagued them. Clouds of gnats sometimes obscured their vision. One night, Turesobei slept beneath a curtain of vines and woke the next morning with a thin snake wrapped around his arm. He stared at it with wide-eyed terror and didn't budge a single muscle. With its tongue the snake kissed him twice on the nose before slithering away.

Noboro laughed afterward. "It wasn't poisonous."

"What if it had been?"

Noboro shrugged. "Good thing it wasn't, eh?"

Turesobei didn't think it was funny, and he chose his bed more carefully from then on. He began to learn from Noboro and Fodoru which snakes were venomous and which were harmless. Some that his father called constrictors were enormous and deadly without poison.

Beneath the shaded canopy, the weather remained mild. The wind only stirred the leaves at the top, so the air was humid and stale. Night came early and day arrived late. In some places, the forest grew so thick that they rode in perpetual twilight. Thankfully, the denekon deftly maneuvered through the rainforest, which was their natural habitat.

At last they reached the gorge. He hadn't seen a clear blue sky unfiltered in seven days, but with much relief, he saw one now.

With a thundering heart and a sense of vertigo, Turesobei carefully peered over the edge and gazed at the thin river far below. The sides of the gorge were scraggy and patched in moss. In several places, trees grew out from the cliff sides and bent upwards toward the light.

The journey so far had been arduous and grueling. More bug bites and scratches than he could count marked Turesobei's skin. Days of sweat and mud had dried on him. Leaves and bits of grass clung to his hair and his dirty, foul-smelling clothes. His muscles ached, and his mind was numb from the whole experience. And he knew they weren't even close to being finished. Many more difficult days lay ahead. The gorge marked only the halfway point of the rainforest, and they would have to cross all of it.

Their guide Urigi noticed his downcast expression and gave him a gap-toothed smile. His breath smelled of cheap wine. "Cheer up, lad. The bridge is only a day to the north."

"Who would build a bridge out here?"

"Many k'chasan tribes used to live in this region," Noboro answered.

"Did they leave when Jakawiju took over?"

"Most, like the ones who built the bridge, left way before then. But the remainder did leave when Jakawiju came to power."

"I saw a few k'chasan traders in the town."

Urigi nodded. "Aye, we've still got a few small clans left here and there. Still got one qengai-maka in these parts, too. That's a strange lot, I tell you."

"A qengai-maka?" Turesobei said with a worried voice. "An assassin village?"

"Aye, lad. But they don't bother anyone around here much. I wouldn't worry about them."

Turesobei relaxed a little, remembering that the qengai's code ultimately served the greater good even if their actions sometimes seemed wrong. Or at least they claimed to serve a good and noble purpose.

"I've never even met a k'chasan before."

"Really?" Urigi said, bewildered. "I can't imagine that."

"Not many k'chasans come east to Batsakun," Noboro explained.

"Well, perhaps you can remedy that, lad, when you return to town."

They rode again and followed the gorge northeast to the bridge. When they got there, Turesobei shook with fear. A bamboo-planked suspension bridge, perhaps three hundred paces long, stretched across the vast gorge. It was surprisingly wide, with room to fit five large denekon shoulder to shoulder. He wasn't even sure such a bridge was physically possible, much less when holding dozens of men and their mounts.

"Are you sure it's safe?" he asked his father.

"Of course."

Urigi chuckled with his hoarse laugh. "Can't know until we're across, can we? Ah, don't make such a face, lad. This bridge has been here for hundreds of years and she's got more life in her yet."

Turesobei found it hard to believe him as he watched the bridge gently sway under the power of a breeze that swept through the gorge. He had a terrible feeling he'd die if he crossed that bridge, but no one else looked afraid.

"Don't worry," Urigi said. "I may not understand this bridge, and people may no longer be able to duplicate the effort, but my ancestors knew what they were doing out here. Wouldn't be surprised if you found a bit of magic in those ropes and planks."

Most likely in the supports, Turesobei thought. But he didn't want to get close enough to the edge to examine them.

After a brief lunch, they rode out onto the bridge. The denekon claws clicked across the old planks. With their weight on it, the bridge bounced ominously, but the twined bamboo cables remained secure on their anchors, which rooted into stonework clearly shaped by zaboko hands. Turesobei rode with Fodoru near the end of the train. His father rode near the front with Urigi.

Crossing it was taking far too long. Vertigo plagued him, and his stomach churned. His knuckles turned white as he desperately clutched the denekon's reins. Ahead of him, Fodoru rode as if this were nothing more than a forest trail. Of course, Fodoru traveled to dangerous places with Noboro all the time.

Finally, to stay relaxed, Turesobei had to keep his eyes locked on the denekon ahead of him and recite a calming mantra.

This kept him settled until he heard the twanging of bowstrings and the first volley of arrows whistled through the air.

Half of the zaboko guards had reached the other end and were just beyond the bridge. They were waiting for the others while Urigi scouted ahead. Without warning, Urigi collapsed with an arrow protruding from his neck. Then a swarm of dark bolts with crimson fletching showered down onto the Chonda soldiers.

Chapter Twenty-Two

"Stay back!" Noboro yelled at Turesobei. He drew Yomifano and yelled a fierce battle cry, rallying his men. Turesobei watched in horror as six of the guards fell. His stomach rose into his throat. He had never seen men die in violence before. And he knew these men. He had been traveling with them for weeks now.

Camouflaged zaboko warriors wearing masks and armed with swords and axes poured from the trees beyond the gorge. Another volley of arrows streamed over them. Four more Chonda guards went down. One was crushed when his wounded mount fell and rolled onto him. They wouldn't be able to get off the bridge without fleeing back to the other side.

Before the ambushers reached the Chonda warriors, a final cloud of arrows rained down. Most thudded harmlessly into shields. One struck Noboro's denekon in the neck. The noble beast crumpled, but Noboro leapt clear, having to catch the bridge's rope railing to keep from falling off.

Captain Fodoru and the remaining guards raced forward and joined Noboro. As they rode, the bridge shook violently, and Turesobei hunkered down and clutched his mount's reins. Together on the bridge, Noboro and the Chonda guards stood bravely against the charging assassins, who outnumbered them two to one, not counting the archers hidden amongst the trees.

Turesobei waited on the bridge, forty paces away from the fighting. As the bridge stabilized, he fumbled into his spell-pouch. After a few moments he found what he was looking for. He held the spell-strip high and chanted the activation command.

A dense fog seeped up from beneath the bridge, near where his father was standing. The combatants ignored it at first, but as it grew thicker, the assassins paused. Noboro understood what was happening. Jumping into the saddle of a denekon whose rider had fallen, Noboro rallied his men again and backed them up along the bridge.

Arrows began falling onto the bridge beyond them, to ward them away. Two zipped right past Turesobei. He backed up his mount. The fog-shrouded assassins pressed on against Noboro and his guards, who at least had a chance of escaping now.

But a chant arose from the tree line. Energies stirred, and a strong wind howled through the gorge, assailing Turesobei's fog. He channeled more of his energy into the spell, trying to hold it. But the fog cloud weakened and was then dispersed.

Turesobei was stunned. Another sorcerer had countered him.

The assassins screamed, "Naruwakiru!"

They charged Noboro, Captain Fodoru, and the remaining soldiers.

Turesobei was fatigued. He could do no more magic. His inner kenja was nearly depleted, having not yet fully recovered from the fight against the gitsukara. He drew Sumada and prepared to charge in and fight alongside his father.

He prepared to die. He knew that would be the result.

His father fought free for a moment. A crimson smear covered half of Noboro's face. The blood was seeping from a wound near his scalp. He looked at Turesobei. Then he yelled in his most commanding voice.

"Get out of here!"

Turesobei paused, unsure of what he should do. Honor demanded that he fight with them. It also demanded that he obey his father.

"Go now!" yelled Noboro.

The intensity in Noboro's eyes, for that one moment before he rushed back in, swinging his sword against his enemies, forced Turesobei to obey. He didn't dare do anything else. Turesobei spun his mount around and rode as fast as he could.

The bridge jostled and swayed alarmingly as he thundered across it. His heart lurched every time he saw the gorge below.

Men screamed and died behind him. His father would soon be one of them.

For a moment, Turesobei heard a hum, almost a buzz.

Zwak!

An arrow struck the satchel on his back, pierced the diary, and punched through his armor. The razor-sharp arrowhead dug into his back, lodging only an inch from his spine.

For now, he felt only a dull ache.

He rode on with other arrows striking the bridge and whistling past him. Finally, the pain sharpened and raced across his back like pricking needles of flame. He winced and nearly passed out. His stomach knotted and his limbs began to tremble. He rode on, believing he could make it to the end. He was nearly halfway there now.

Suddenly, Iyei, his denekon, released a high-pitched roar and lurched out of control. The beast stumbled into the ropes that formed the side of the bridge. The crash propelled Turesobei from the saddle.

As he fell, Turesobei twisted and caught onto the edge of a bridge plank. He dangled over the steep gorge, trying to keep his grip. Blood seeped out onto the wood from a cut on one of his fingers. He looked for help, but the assassins were massed around the last two men standing.

Both of them were zaboko.

His heart sank.

A spatter of blood from the mouth of Iyei fell onto his face. The poor beast was dying, tangled in the ropes, with an arrow piercing its lungs.

Turesobei tried to reach up with his other arm, but that shoulder had gone numb from

87

the arrow wound. His fingers slipped a little. He tried to swing a leg up to the bridge. He couldn't get his foot up high enough, though, and as it swung back down, the momentum was too much and he lost his grip entirely.

Screaming, Turesobei plummeted down toward the glistening river seventy feet below, his fall slowed a fraction by a protective charm in his armor. He struck hard into the cold water.

Chapter Twenty-Three

He awoke deep down in a dark murk, surrounded by a cloud of bubbles. The swirling murk grew darker for a moment, but he fought off unconsciousness. Dazed and hurting, weighted down by his armor and sword, he panicked and flailed his arms. He struggled for breath, as if someone had punched him in the stomach. Waves of pain lanced outward from the arrow still jutting from his back.

He clawed his way to the surface and sucked in a painful gulp of air. But the river swallowed him again. He couldn't get his armor off. The arrow had pinned it to his back. And he refused to ditch Sumada. But he was tiring quickly. He wouldn't be able to make it much longer.

Suddenly a strong hand latched onto his right arm and plucked him out of the water. His savior heaved and dragged him up onto a bamboo raft.

"Got you!" said a deep, husky voice.

An aging zaboko man leaned over him. He had a wide face, wrinkled and sunburned from years of exposure. A scar underlined his right eye. He smiled a toothy grin and brushed the wet, clinging hair from Turesobei's face.

"You're going to be all right, young lord. You're quite lucky. The arrow isn't buried all that deep."

Turesobei mumbled weakly. He could barely open his jaw. "C-can you take it out?"

"Yes, my lord. No problem at all. I used to be a medic in the West Taganan Army." The old man bowed. "My name's Onudaka."

"Turesobei," he groaned.

"Well met then, my lord." Onudaka looked up toward the bridge. "I hope you didn't fall from up there." Turesobei nodded. "Well, you're certainly blessed by the gods to be alive."

Onudaka lifted a long wooden pole and thrust it down into the river. As Onudaka poled them to the riverbank, Turesobei remembered what was going on.

"I've got to get back up there ... and help my father. We were attacked ... they out-numbered us. I was hit and fell."

"I can't defeat a squad of warriors on my own, my lord. And you're not in any condition to fight them yourself."

"They may leave him ... could be wounded, dying."

"Then we'll get up there as soon as possible, but scaling that cliff won't be easy."

"No faster way?"

"Not that I know of, my lord."

Turesobei thrust his head back against the raft in disgust.

"You just rest," Onudaka said. "I'll get the arrow out of you and bind your wound."

Turesobei awoke. He lay naked beneath a blanket. A bandage was wrapped around his torso. He hurt badly, and a foul taste remained in his mouth from the medicines Onudaka had given him. The arrow was gone, though he didn't remember Onudaka taking it out. He did remember drinking a nasty concoction that had made him incredibly sleepy.

Onudaka sat with a small piece of stone in his hands that he was shaping into a figurine. Many zaboko possessed a natural talent that let them magically and smoothly, though slowly, shape stone using only their hands.

Onudaka looked up and smiled. Behind him lay an iron-shod quarterstaff, a rugged backpack, a leather breastplate, and a short bow.

"You were amazingly fortunate, young lord. Not everyone who plummets into a river with an arrow in their back has an old medic come across them."

"I don't feel lucky," Turesobei grumbled. Everything ached, and his jaw was so stiff and swollen that he could barely talk. "My father could be dead."

Lu Bei. The diary! The arrow had pierced it and then they had struck water. "Have you seen an old book, sir? It was in my satchel."

Onudaka grabbed the satchel and brought it to Turesobei. "To get the arrow out, I had to pull the book off it first."

Turesobei looked at the book. The pages were pierced, and soggy. The cover was warped. The book looked terrible. Worst of all, the runes didn't light up under his touch. He thought about trying to summon Lu Bei, but he couldn't do it with Onudaka here. And he probably didn't have enough internal kenja.

He suspected Lu Bei was gone anyhow. He couldn't imagine the fetch surviving that. For Lu Bei, an arrow through the diary was as good as an arrow through the chest.

"If you don't mind me asking," said Onudaka, "who is your father?"

"Chonda Noboro."

Onudaka frowned. "Ah, I thought that would be the case. Seems we have something in common. My family name is Obu."

Turesobei recognized the name instantly. "Sotenda?"

Onudaka nodded. "Yes, Obu Sotenda, leader of the Storm Dragon Cult, is my brother."

Chapter Twenty-Four

Turesobei reached for his sword.

"That's who attacked us," Turesobei growled. "I heard them cry out Naruwakiru's name when they charged." With a surge of strength, he rose to his knees. "I shouldn't have trusted you."

"Please, my lord, stay calm. I never said I was in league with them."

"You said he's your brother."

"Yes, but that doesn't mean we get along, does it?"

Turesobei glared at Onudaka suspiciously. "I guess not."

"As it is, he is only my half-brother, and he's mentally unstable. He's determined to recover the Storm Dragon's Heart no matter who he has to hurt in the process. From what I've heard, Sotenda has been obsessed with your father for some time now."

Turesobei thought of his father. "Does he see visions of it? Do dreams about it plague him?"

"Why, yes, my lord, I believe so."

Turesobei groaned. "It's the same for my father. I think the heart itself is calling them. Nothing good will come of that."

"No, I don't imagine so. There's got to be a good reason why it's locked up in a vault."

"I'm sorry I didn't trust you, Onudaka. Thank you for helping me."

"Nothing of it, my lord." The old man stood and stretched. "That's enough chatting for now. Let's get some food in you. Then you can rest some more."

Turesobei gritted his teeth. "I want to get back up to the bridge."

"I know, but you're in no condition to go yet. You're not even well enough for me to carry you up."

"You could do that?"

Onudaka chuckled. "Aye, young lord. You're tall but not so heavy. And I may be old but I'm still in good shape."

"Then we'll go up after I have a short rest."

"There's still your wound. These things take time to heal properly."

Turesobei grabbed the sealed leather pouch that lay with his clothes. "I can speed things up."

He pulled out one of his spell strips. Luckily, the seal had held and the ink hadn't smeared in the river. Onudaka eyed him curiously. Turesobei chanted and activated the strip. A warm, golden glow emanated from his kavaru and his hand. Slowly, the healing earth energies enveloped his arm, his shoulder, his torso, and his face. Torn muscles knitted back together. Pains dulled to aches. Skin healed over the wounds. The glow receded and then disappeared.

Onudaka whistled. "Wow! I saw your kavaru, of course, but I didn't know you were such a powerful wizard, my lord. You're so young."

Turesobei smiled wanly. "I've studied wizardry nearly all my life."

"It must be fabulous to wield magic! Useful too, I'd imagine."

"Useful, yes. But it's not exciting, not really. Most of the work is dull, and what isn't is too dangerous for me to use."

"Well, to someone who hasn't done magic all his life, it's quite interesting. Did you completely heal your injuries?"

"I sped up the natural healing process by about a week."

"If I'd had that ability, my job certainly would have been easier all these years."

Turesobei yawned. "Well, I'm afraid I couldn't have done much without you cleaning and binding the wound first. Healing an injury with magic will help you for a little while, but the magic won't hold without proper care."

Turesobei wanted to stay awake, to scale the cliff and check on his father, to try to summon Lu Bei. But he admitted to himself that he couldn't manage any of those things.

"I have to sleep now, Onudaka, but afterward, we will scale the cliff."

"As you wish, my lord."

Turesobei stretched out on the ground. "One more thing. Stop calling me *my lord*. Just my name is fine."

"Aye, lad. If that's what you wish."

The scent of catfish frying woke Turesobei. The morning sky had turned a bright blue, but it remained dark within the gorge. Turesobei devoured the breakfast awaiting him—fish, bread, and cheese—and thanked Onudaka. Then he demanded they scale the cliff despite any risk to himself. Onudaka reluctantly agreed.

The old man strapped climbing claws onto his hands and feet. A row of spikes jutted from his palms and toes. The spikes were attached to strips of wood held in place by leather wraps.

"In the old days," he said, "when us zaboko could meld with stone, we'd just sink our hands into the rock and climb mountains like they were giant mounds of rice. But long before your people arrived, we stopped living in tune with nature and lost most of our abilities."

"But the Keshuno didn't lose them."

Onudaka scowled and shook his head. "It's a high price they pay, too, serving Makazi

Keshuno. I'd not worship her for anything." He pulled a section of rope from his pack. "Now, you're going to climb onto my back and hold on. I'll tie a rope around us both, in case you slip."

"What about your supplies?"

"We're going to tie one end of a rope to my pack and carry the other end with us. When we get to the top, we'll pull the supplies up. Sound good to you?"

Turesobei nodded. "Let's go then."

Onudaka eyed the rock face near them carefully. He shook his head and moved to another section. Then he tsked and moved on again. This continued for nearly half an hour before he finally said, "Aha! Found it."

"Found what?"

"The best route up."

"How can you tell the difference?"

Onudaka winked. "Magic, lad, pure and simple." He laughed. "Truthfully, I happen to be something of a rock climber. I know what I'm doing and I've done it many times."

Turesobei climbed onto Onudaka's back. The old man casually stepped up to the wall, found a handhold, and lifted himself onto the rock face. Another handhold then a toehold followed. Onudaka's fat fingers would dig into a crevice and his palm spikes would jab into the rock. Then, he would lift them up easily before setting new holds.

"Are you sure I'm not too heavy?" Turesobei asked, even though Onudaka seemed to be breathing normally.

"I usually carry my pack when I climb. I think it weighs more than you."

"Oh." Turesobei looked down and saw that they had already climbed at least twenty feet up. "Are you trying to stop your brother before he gets the heart?"

"Something like that."

"How long have you followed him?"

"A year at least. Sotenda's not easy to track down. He keeps moving all the time, and I don't have much money for travel expenses. Once I found out where the vault is, I figured I would intercept him if I could. But I was delayed. It's not easy for a zaboko to leave his home in West Tagana and come up here."

"I didn't think of that," Turesobei said. "So you're not a freeman?"

"No."

"So you're a fugitive now."

"Well, yes, technically I am. But I doubt anyone's noticed. If you serve enough time in the army, you earn a little more freedom for yourself. I've a pass to work as a traveling merchant. No one will think much if I don't come home and report back to my ward chief. I'm not worth enough for anyone to track down, either. It happens sometimes. It's young men and farmers disappearing from their lands that concerns the lords most."

"I really don't know anything about how such things work. Many zaboko strive to reach our lands. None ever leave, though they can if they wish."

"Well, that's a tribute to the Chonda clan, then. My ruling clan wasn't so fair. I don't regret being gone, and now that I am, I don't plan on ever going back."

"You'd be welcome in our lands in Batsakun."

"Thanks, lad. I'll remember that."

Turesobei glanced down again, but then wished he hadn't. He found it easier to ignore the danger by chatting. "Onudaka, you said no one would miss you. Don't you have a family?"

"My parents are dead, and I never had time to start a family of my own. I was always on the move in the military."

"How long have you been out of service?"

"Just five years. I entered as soon as I was old enough and served thirty-five years."

"That's a long service!"

Onudaka laughed. "I never had much else to do, and I really am a pitiful merchant. I always liked helping wounded men, and I enjoyed staying on the move and always seeing new places. I guess I had a lot more freedom than most people like me ever get."

As they neared the top, Turesobei heard crows cawing. Some circled overhead. He feared the carnage that awaited them, but at the same time he became increasingly anxious to get there.

"It's not going to be pretty, lad. Death never is. I've seen more than a fair bit in my time, and I've always been horrified by what's left after a battle."

It had taken them two hours to scale the cliff. At last Onudaka locked his hands on the precipice and pulled them up. Turesobei quickly slid out from the rope tying him to Onudaka and ran toward the bridge. Onudaka called after him, but since he couldn't stop him, he secured the rope tied to his pack and followed.

They had climbed the southern face so they wouldn't have to cross the bridge. The Chonda dead lay scattered on the ground and bridge ahead. The cultists' bodies must have been taken away and buried, while the Chonda soldiers were left to rot.

Turesobei rushed toward the bridge, thinking of where he had last seen his father. He stopped, heart pounding, eyes wide.

It was not his father that he saw, but a k'chasan assassin heading toward him.

Chapter Twenty-Five

The assassin was a young k'chasan woman. Wide hips stretched out her grey bodysuit. A scarf covered her lower face, and a tight-fitting hood shaded her large amber eyes. She watched him carefully. Her stance conveyed quiet power, but Turesobei didn't fear her. She would pay for what her kind had done here.

Turesobei drew his father's white-steel saber and charged.

"Wait!" Onudaka called, but Turesobei ignored him.

He passed several bodies and leapt over one. Crows scattered into the air, cawing their curses at him. The assassin didn't budge. He watched for darts and throwing spikes, but she threw none. Turesobei reached her and swung with his sword.

The assassin sprang to the side and his blade whisked through empty air. He stumbled past her, and she kicked the back of his right knee. As he fell, she grasped his queue and jerked his head backward. As if from nowhere a sickle, made for combat and not farming, appeared within her hand. The crescent blade flashed in the daylight. His knees struck the ground and his neck lightly touched the inner curve of the blade.

"It was not wise to attack me," she said. Her voice was high, pleasing, and almost sweet. Not at all the voice an assassin should have.

Turesobei didn't dare move, but he did growl at her. "Murderer!"

"Hah!" was all she said in reply.

Onudaka plodded toward them with a heavy, rolling gait. Turesobei thought Onudaka would rush in to help, but the old medic stopped about ten feet away.

"He didn't mean any harm," Onudaka said, panting for breath.

"It doesn't seem that way to me."

"He's distraught. These are his people lying here."

"Ah," she said, "I suppose that does provide some excuse. He's lucky I didn't feel threatened or I might have killed him in self-defense."

She removed the blade and let go of his queue. He fell and smacked his injured jaw on the ground. "Ow!"

He climbed to his feet, wary of her. He backed away and held his blade at the ready. "Watch it, you."

The assassin narrowed her eyes and sighed. "You would have to be an impudent boy."

Turesobei's cheeks reddened. "I'm not impudent, and I'm not a boy either. You don't seem that old yourself."

"I'm an adult, and you are not."

"We really are sorry, my lady," Onudaka said.

She hung the combat sickle in a harness on her belt. "No harm, I suppose. And I've been sent here by my clan to help you."

"What!" Turesobei said as he lowered his sword. "You're a qengai?"

"Well, of course I am. Couldn't you tell?"

"No," he mumbled, but she ignored him.

"My clan's Codex assigned me to help an old man seeking his brother."

"That's me," Onudaka said.

"And a young man seeking his father and an ancient artifact."

Turesobei scowled. "I don't want your help, assassin."

Onudaka bowed. "We are vastly honored, my lady. And I will gladly accept any help you are willing to give."

"My name's Iniru."

"Obu Onudaka and this is Chonda Turesobei. He is not himself, right now, I'm afraid."

As soon as he heard the Chonda name, Turesobei remembered his father. Ignoring Iniru, he rushed about, scanning the bodies. He ran onto the bridge, barely noticing its sway, but he didn't see his father. He did, however, see Captain Fodoru.

Turesobei knelt beside the zaboko soldier. The face was swollen, discolored, and marred. Crows had pecked at his eyes and dug into his cheeks, exposing teeth and bone. A sword cut had bared flesh and bone from Fodoru's neck to his sternum. Another had nearly severed his right hand. Other cuts marked the body and sticky blood lay all around.

The stench of opened bowels and flesh already decaying in the heat overpowered Turesobei. The scent hung everywhere, but he hadn't noticed it until now. He turned and vomited out over the bridge. He looked down, and vertigo only made him feel worse.

Turesobei turned back toward Fodoru and tears streaked down his face. But he wiped them away and stood. Fodoru had fought and died proudly. He would not want Turesobei to cry over him.

Turesobei carefully left the bridge. His heart pounded, and bile rose into his throat. He checked everywhere. He saw all the bodies: men he had known for weeks, some for years, men he had chatted with only days ago.

"You are looking for your father?" Iniru asked.

"Yes," Turesobei grumbled.

"He's not here."

Chapter Twenty-Six

"Where's my father?" Turesobei asked. "What happened?"

"The assassins dragged away a baojendari who was alive and not their own, someone who kicked and fought against them."

"How do you know this?"

"I have been trained in the art of tracking. I was finishing my analysis of what happened when you arrived."

"I guess you'd know all about their tactics, wouldn't you?"

"Of course," she said, "though they're not highly skilled. Your father had knowledge they wanted, did he not?"

"Probably."

"So they would want to keep him alive, don't you think?"

Turesobei nodded. That made sense. The assassins obviously attacked them to get the vault key. But his father might also have important information the Storm Cult didn't possess.

To catch up to the assassins, they would need to get moving.

"They stole the denekon," Turesobei commented, noting only a few dead ones lying about, including his still tangled in the bridge ropes.

"Of course they stole the mounts."

Turesobei scowled and turned to Onudaka. "You trust this woman?"

"She's a qengai. If she wanted to kill us, she would have done so already."

Turesobei sighed and stalked toward the bridge, intent on retrieving his gear. Onudaka went to pull his pack of supplies up from the gorge. The assassin didn't seem to bother him. If anything, he seemed pleased that she was here.

Once on the bridge, with his adrenaline no longer pumping, Turesobei became afraid of its height and movements. He was taking light steps, but then the bridge began to jostle. Iniru was jogging toward him.

"What are you doing?" she said.

"Getting the packs off my denekon."

"Look, I'm sorry I gave you a hard time. And I'm sorry about your father. Honestly."

"Thanks," he muttered.

"I'm also sorry that I roughed you up back there."

"I could have hit you with magic," he replied sullenly.

She laughed so hard she bent over, clutching one of the guide ropes.

"Stop shaking the bridge!"

She chuckled and bounced up and down playfully. "Are you scared of heights?"

"This bridge worries me. It doesn't look secure."

She giggled like a girl. "Ah. Well, why don't you fix it with a bit of magic?"

"You know, I really am a wizard."

"I believe you. I can see the kavaru hanging from your neck. But if you're so skilled, why didn't you just blast me instead of charging in with your sword?"

"It's more complicated than that."

"I see," she said in a light, amused tone. She bounded ahead of him, hips swaying impertinently.

Iniru helped him remove the packs. "I am sorry," she said. "And I will help you rescue your father. I swear it on my honor."

Turesobei met her gaze and found it mesmerizing. He couldn't quite speak. He muttered a few unintelligible syllables and Iniru raised one of her thick eyebrows.

"Are you all right?"

"Er ... yes. It's just ... I've never met a k'chasan before."

"Are you serious?"

"I'm from Batsakun in the east. Not many of your people venture there."

She bowed. "Well, you've met one now. Iniru of Yasei-maka at your service."

Not knowing whether she was mocking him again, he said nothing in reply. After they removed everything valuable, she helped him untangle the denekon from the ropes. A third of the great beast hung out over the river, so they pushed and prodded until it fell.

That made the bridge swing in a great arc. Turesobei gasped and clutched at the ropes. Iniru didn't hold to anything. She laughed and easily balanced herself as the bridge swung back and forth.

"Come on," she said, grabbing him by the sleeve. "I'll help you back. There's nothing to it if you don't think about it being so high up. Just walk."

"And what?"

"And nothing. Just walk. That's all there really is to it."

Turesobei let her guide him from the bridge, hating her every step. He tried to tell himself that at least she had apologized, but his pride was wounded. When they reached solid ground, he sighed and knelt down, gasping for breath.

"You look terrible," she said.

"I was wounded in the battle, before I fell into the river."

"Then get some rest. I'll scout around and find their trail."

Turesobei watched her go and cursed. He hadn't expected anything like this. She was offering expert help, but he didn't want to trust her. And her golden eyes and graceful walk. Those haunted him so much that he nearly forgot about all the death that was surrounding him.

She returned a half-hour later. "I found their trail, but we need to move on. Trails age quickly and if it rains..."

Turesobei stood. "I have something more I must do first."

"If you wish to save your father, we must go quickly."

"She's right," said Onudaka.

Turesobei shook his head. "I have a duty to perform. I must honor those who fell here."

Onudaka patted him on the shoulder. "We don't have time to bury them, lad."

Turesobei inhaled a deep breath. "I know, but I can still see them honored."

Iniru cursed and stalked out toward the forest. "I'm going to take a nap. Wake me when you're done."

"Gods, but she's infuriating," Turesobei said to Onudaka.

"She's young and confident, and I think you may have gotten on her bad side when you attacked her."

"Well, it was an honest mistake."

"I know, lad. Now what are we doing?"

"The Chonda give metal amulets to each soldier. On one side is the Chonda Goshawk sigil; on the other is their name. I want to return these to their families. And if they have any personal effects with them like bracelets or talismans, I'll take those, too."

Onudaka stopped and Turesobei turned back toward him. He wasn't sure, but he thought he saw a gleam in the old man's eyes.

"You all right?"

"Fine, lad, quite fine." He smiled broadly. "Let's get to work."

They moved as fast as they could. Onudaka spoke the Shogakami Prayer for the Dead over each corpse and wished them a pleasant rebirth if they didn't reach Kaiwen Earth-Mother's paradise. Turesobei thanked each man for his service to the Chonda and promised to return their effects to their families back home. They finished by wrapping the effects within a torn shirt and putting them in Turesobei's pack.

"They deserved better."

"Aye, lad. Everyone deserves better, but life is rarely fair."

Chapter Twenty-Seven

Iniru darted silently through the forest ahead of Turesobei and Onudaka. They pushed through curtains of vines, groping bushes, and low-hanging limbs. They crossed fallen trees and small streams. And yet they followed a trail of sorts. They would've had to cut their way through otherwise.

By late afternoon, Turesobei felt like he was wading through mud. His leg muscles were stiff and exhausted. He stumbled over a tree root, fell, and scraped his knee on a rock.

"I can't go on any longer. I've got to rest."

This angered Iniru. Apparently, she didn't think an arrow wound was reason enough to stop so early.

Turesobei pulled his boots off and dipped his feet into a cool, shallow stream. He lay back against the forest turf with a deep sigh. Onudaka built a campfire just large enough to boil some water and heat their food rations.

Iniru removed her hood and scarf. Turesobei stared at her, upside down from where he lay. She had silky, red-brown fur and delicate, rounded features. He was stunned. He hadn't guessed she would be so ... gorgeous.

And young! She couldn't be much older than him.

Iniru began to strip off her charcoal bodysuit. Turesobei started to avert his eyes but then noticed she was wearing clothes underneath: a flimsy cotton top and scant shorts. It was hardly decent clothing. He really should have looked away.

He didn't, and then she noticed him staring.

Her eyes narrowed with suspicion. "What?"

"Nothing."

She leaned over him. Her nostrils flared. "Is there a problem?"

"Well, it's just that ... I've never seen..."

"A k'chasan before? You gave me that excuse already."

"You had the bodysuit on, and I couldn't even see your face. Just your eyes."

She lowered her face near to his. He could smell her warm breath. It was pleasant, like mint. "Got a good enough look now?"

"Er, yes, thank you."

"Hmm." She sat down nearby and dangled her feet into the stream.

Turesobei found he couldn't stop staring. He'd never seen quite so much of a girl before. He blurted out, "You're going to put on more clothes, aren't you?"

"Why would I do that? It's hot, and the bodysuit is for protection, not comfort. Besides, I don't have to worry about mosquitoes like you do. Fur is good that way."

"Well, it's just that ... it's not proper for a lady to wear so little."

Iniru laughed. "A lady? Well, I never thought someone would call me that. You really don't get out much, do you?"

Turesobei sulked. "I know how the world works."

"I'm not sure you do."

"How old are you anyway? You don't look much older than me."

"I turned fifteen two months ago," she said proudly.

"You're the same age as me!"

"And when will you be an adult?"

"When I turn eighteen."

"K'chasans become adults at fifteen."

"That's ridiculous!"

"Oh, really? My people thank you for pointing that out, your highness. Whatever would we have done without your expert baojendari knowledge?"

"I didn't mean it like that."

"Are you sure?"

"Of course. It's just that I've always thought..."

"That you wouldn't be a man until you were eighteen, even though you feel like you're one already. I've heard it all before from zaboko. They're just as bad that way. I've been making decisions for myself for years, and now I'm completely free to behave as I wish. I'm a woman now in every way. You'd be a man if you were a k'chasan, though it's clear your upbringing has left you far behind. You baojendari are just not in tune with nature."

Turesobei thought of a dozen mean retorts, but he ended up not saying anything and sulked throughout dinner.

That night, Turesobei tossed in his sleep, haunted by nightmares of his father weeping as he walked past the dead Chonda soldiers, of Iniru stalking toward him and laughing, of Lu Bei's pages crumbling into dust, of the dark trees overhead filled with millions of chirping insects waiting to devour his corpse.

At dawn, they returned to the trail. Turesobei felt stronger, even though his muscles were stiff and sore. The cultists probably had a substantial lead on them. Turesobei hoped their need for his father would last long enough to rescue him.

The three travelers spoke little. The forest sang to them, and they listened out for the discordant notes of enemies. Turesobei still needed frequent rest breaks, and at each stop, Iniru became agitated. On the fourth break, she moaned with disgust and Turesobei couldn't take it anymore.

"Why are you in such a hurry? It's my father who's been captured."

She stuck her face right up to his and scowled. He backed away but she followed him until he crashed into a tree.

"Who says I care?" she demanded. "Maybe I don't."

"Then why are you hurrying so much?"

"Perhaps because helping you is my job whether I like it or not."

"Well, I don't like it and I don't trust you either."

"I don't need you to trust me. What I need you to do is stop acting like a baby and follow my lead."

Onudaka stepped toward them. "I think we could all stand to be a little more civilized toward one another."

Turesobei ignored him. "I'm not a child!" he yelled at Iniru. "And you're not in charge of me!"

"Fine, but if your father dies before we get there, it's not my fault."

"I'm doing the best I can!"

"Well, it's not good enough."

"I'm not a qengai. I haven't trained for this sort of thing. I'm a wizard."

"And a spoiled brat."

"Arrrgh!" Turesobei shoved away from her. "I don't understand why you're so determined to help us anyway. Clearly you're too good for us."

"I have to help you because the Sacred Codex says I must."

Most k'chasan believed in the Sacred Codex, and Turesobei had been taught that the prophecies were true, at least in their most basic intents. However, he knew little about the specifics of how it all worked.

"Who cares? Ignore it."

"I can't. The prophecies within the Codex will bring about a golden age for Okoro. Its demands are more important than you or me. If it had said that I should kill you, you'd already be lying in a pool of blood."

He stormed out into the trees and sat down for a rest. "Stupid k'chasans!"

Half an hour passed and Turesobei's heart still thundered in his chest. Blood thumped in his temples. He couldn't meditate and only his legs were getting a rest.

"Let's go!" Iniru called out. "Only five hours of daylight left."

Turesobei groaned and rose to his feet.

Onudaka waved to him. "Come on, lad. We do need to move on."

He joined the old medic and they trudged onto the path. Iniru glanced at them, nodded, and ran ahead.

"Don't let her get to you, lad. She's just trying to do her job. She's young, and this is probably her first independent mission. For her to fail would be a huge dishonor to her clan."

"She's the most infuriating person I've ever met."

Onudaka smiled. "Women are like that. But I've found that the best are the ones that infuriate you the most."

"What does that mean?"

"Well, if they weren't worth being upset over, you'd just go away and ignore them, right? And if they don't frustrate you sometimes, then they don't have any spark to them."

"All the women in my life are frustrating."

"Then count yourself a lucky man."

"This coming from someone who never got married."

Onudaka patted him on the shoulder. "Lad, I've shared the company of a few ladies in my day. Trust me when I say that I know what I'm talking about."

"Perhaps we have different tastes."

Onudaka shrugged. "Perhaps."

"We do need Iniru's help, though, don't we?"

"Aye, lad. She knows more about this forest than we do, and she can fight better than both of us combined."

"Well, if we didn't need her, I'd tell her to shove off."

Onudaka bobbed his head. "Yep, I suppose you would." He grinned and began to softly whistle an old tune.

Chapter Twenty-Eight

Three days passed where it seemed they did nothing but march, eat, and sleep, with far too little of the last. Turesobei grew irritable from bug bites, fatigue, scrapes, and bruises, not to mention Iniru's commanding, know-it-all attitude. At dinner, no one spoke except Onudaka, who would entertain them with old songs and stories of various places he'd been, people he'd met, and battles he'd fought in. The stories, Turesobei enjoyed. Doubly so since Iniru kept silent throughout them.

Despite his distaste for her, Turesobei found himself stealing as many glances as possible at Iniru. He liked to watch her long, slender form as she crept through the forest ahead of them. At night, he enjoyed the glint of the campfire's light in her gleaming, amber eyes, their color almost perfectly matching that of his kavaru. He most relished the way she almost purred when she slept.

Whenever she started to notice him staring, he'd immediately flick his gaze away. If she noticed, she didn't say anything about it. He told himself his interest in her was only because she was exotic. If she were the twentieth k'chasan girl he'd ever met, he'd be no more interested in her than a rock.

Two more grueling days passed. The forest thinned, and the land rose. Though the underbrush hindered them less, walking became harder. Rocks and hills frequently slowed their progress. Iniru said they had gained ground but were still far behind.

Turesobei wanted to make an attempt at summoning Lu Bei. But Grandfather Kahenan had told him to keep the fetch a secret. Truthfully, he didn't care about Onudaka finding out. He just didn't want Iniru to know.

After a brief lunch, Turesobei stepped away from the others and into a hollow sheltered by maples adorned with bright autumn leaves. He sat cross-legged on a dry rock in the midst of a carpet of muddy turf. He drew in deep, languorous breaths and closed his eyes. He inhaled the forest's scents: loamy turf, decaying leaves, wet bark, and pine needles. His mind and body eased, his spirit strengthened.

He took out the battered diary and ran a hand across it.

Nothing.

He whispered, "Lu Bei. I summon thee."

One of the runes flickered, but only for a moment.

The only option left was to try to draw Lu Bei out the way a wizard might summon a demon from the Shadowland.

He began to whisper the *spell of lesser summonings* but the lightest, unnatural crinkling of leaves interrupted him. He opened his eyes and saw Iniru stepping into the hollow. Their eyes met for a moment, his blazing and hers surprised.

She dipped her head. "Sorry, I didn't mean to bother you."

"Did you need something?"

"I just wanted to make sure you were all right."

"You don't need to check up on me."

"Yes, I do. We all have to look out for one another. There are many dangers here, from cultists to poisonous snakes. All you had to do was tell us what you were doing and I would've left you alone."

"Well—" He choked back a smart reply. "I guess you're right. I'll do that next time."

"You know, your senses must be pretty sharp for you to have noticed me."

"I'm more sensitive while meditating." Or casting a spell.

She pointed to the rock he sat on. "May I join you?" He shrugged, and so she stepped over and sat beside him. "Do you always meditate cross-legged?"

"That's just my favorite way. My grandfather makes me meditate kneeling, walking, and standing."

"Hanging upside down?"

"What?! No. Why would that be necessary?"

She shrugged. "I haven't a clue, but I seem to be one up on you there. I've had to do it many times."

"Seriously? Upside down?"

She smiled—a beautiful thing that—and nodded. "Mostly kneeling, though. So, your grandfather instructs you in magic?"

"Yes. Grandfather Kahenan is the High Wizard of the Chonda."

"Will you be his successor?"

"Yes."

"Does the sword not bother your meditations?"

Turesobei followed her gaze down to his waist. For a moment he didn't understand what he was trying to ask.

"Not at all. And as long as I'm careful to keep it out of the way at the right times, the white-steel blade doesn't bother my spell casting either."

"May I see it?"

He eyed her suspiciously then shrugged. "Sure."

Turesobei handed over the scabbarded sword. She drew the blade and angled it in the sunlight. "I saw a ceremonial sword made of birch once. It looked a lot like this, only it wasn't metal. Does it have a name?"

"Sumada. It's my father's sword."

She handed it back to him. "If he's not a wizard, what does your father do?"

"Mostly he's an explorer. A treasure hunter really."

"So that's what got him into trouble out here?"

"Unfortunately. If this cult doesn't lead to his death, the artifact very well might. He's obsessed with it."

"Tell me about the artifact. Everything you know. If I'm going to help you, I need to know exactly what's going on."

"Your Sacred Codex didn't tell you?"

"The directives are clear and concise. The rest is vague at best."

"I'm not sure I can trust you."

She grabbed him by the upper arm. Her touch was strange. Not because she had small claws tucked into the fingertips or because her palm had thick pads. It was something else. He didn't understand what, but he liked the feeling.

"I'm not going to betray you. I'm here to help. I have sworn to faithfully serve the Sacred Codex."

He tried to avoid her gaze but couldn't. He nodded and she withdrew her hand. Then he recounted everything he knew about what was going on.

"Nothing good will come from that artifact," she said.

"That's what I've been saying, too. And we're not the only ones. Onudaka and my grandfather both agree. They are wise, experienced men. But no one can stop my father's ambition or that of the Storm Cult. And I'd rather us have it than them."

"I can agree with that. Maybe we can capture the key and destroy it so no one can get to the heart."

Turesobei placed Lu Bei's diary back into the satchel as Iniru stood.

"Your book," she said. "Is it important to you?"

"Yes, why?"

"Looks ruined."

"I can see that for myself."

"I can't help you with the hole in it or what looks like water damage, but I do know how to repair bindings. If you'd like some help with it, let me know. The pages will start falling out before long."

She reached out a hand to help him up. He accepted it gruffly, though he was faking the attitude this time to cover up that he really wanted to feel her touch again.

"Come on, we should keep moving. Perhaps we can stop all this nonsense and prevent anyone else from getting hurt."

Just as Turesobei stood, he saw a glimmer of something moving in the trees, far beyond the maples.

"Iniru," he whispered, "I think I just saw something."

"I heard it."

"I couldn't make out what it was." He activated his kenja-sight and gasped. "Iniru, the currents here are very disturbed now, but they weren't a few moments ago when I started my meditations."

A limb cracked and leaves rustled some way off. A faint howl, like wind through a chink in a barn wall, followed the rustlings. Iniru drew the two combat sickles from her sash and held one in each hand. She scanned the forest around them.

"We should get back to Onudaka."

Turesobei followed her back to the camp. Onudaka had somehow sensed the wrongness. He was standing with his quarterstaff in hand, wary of enemies.

"What is it?" he asked.

"Don't know," said Iniru.

Turesobei continued to scan around. "I see strong air energies, negatively aspected. Something's out there. A spirit creature of some sort."

"A demon?" Iniru asked.

"No, but whatever it is, I'm certain it's not friendly."

The noise continued and moved toward them, one tree at a time.

"It sounds like a wild animal," said Onudaka.

Turesobei drew Sumada. "Should we run?"

"We stand," Iniru whispered. "It's moving too fast for us to outrun it. Stay still and be quiet. Maybe it'll pass us by."

Leaves rustled in the tree above them, and a limb made a sharp creak as if something had fallen onto it. Indeed, something had. On the limb up above and just ahead of them sat a shimmering, translucent creature. It looked like a mountain gorilla composed of dense heat waves, or perhaps swirling mist.

The creature let out a piercing, mind-numbing scream and leapt toward them.

Chapter Twenty-Nine

"Get back!" Turesobei yelled.

Surprised by his sudden command, Onudaka and Iniru instinctively obeyed. Turesobei met the beast head-on, striking with Sumada. A normal sword would have passed through the creature as if it were made of water, causing pain but no damage. The white-steel sword met even less resistance. The blade ripped through the gorilla-spirit's torso, vibrating in tune with the sounds that seemed to compose the creature.

The beast was powerful. It flickered and dimmed but didn't die. The gorilla-spirit knocked Turesobei flat, expelled the air from his lungs with a *whoosh*, and nearly cracked his ribcage.

The beast howled so loudly that Turesobei could hear nothing else. Translucent fists beat at his head. He twisted and turned, just barely dodging the mighty blows that thudded into the earth. He would have been killed if the creature hadn't been dazed by pain.

Iniru leapt forward and smote the beast's side with her sickle. The blade whisked through the creature, causing little if any harm. But it did distract it long enough for Onudaka to pull Turesobei free. The gorilla-spirit bashed at Iniru, but she danced away from its fists. Turesobei jumped to his feet and lunged. He slashed the gorilla-spirit across its neck, severing its head.

A bellow erupted from the creature's neck. Turesobei's teeth and bones vibrated. His ears felt as if someone were shoving sticks into them. He dropped his sword, fell to his knees, and covered his ears. A tremendous boom knocked him flat, and a rush of released energies stormed through the forest.

Slowly, the echoes of the boom faded, leaving Turesobei with ringing ears and a pounding headache.

Onudaka and Iniru were both on the ground. Onudaka sat up, holding his head and grumbling. Iniru writhed and clutched at her tufted ears. Turesobei grabbed her by the arm and helped her up. She stumbled to her feet, whimpering. She looked woozy, and Turesobei thought she might faint any moment.

Turesobei looked around with his kenja-sight. The energies were returning to normal. "It's gone."

"What?" Onudaka said.

Iniru looked at him blankly. He noticed then a trickle of blood seeping from her left ear. He helped her sit down on a fallen tree. While doing so, Turesobei had to repeat himself three times, with increasing volume, before Onudaka could hear him. Iniru never did.

"I-I can't take another blast like that," Iniru said, far too loudly. "But more will be coming."

"What makes you say that?" Onudaka asked.

She shook her head in confusion.

"Why?" yelled Turesobei.

"Bogamaru Sengi," she said, reading his lips. "Don't know why they're after us, but they will come for us with greater force. And soon."

"Then we've got to do something about those screams," Turesobei said. "Onudaka, check on Iniru. Her ears are more sensitive than ours. She may have a busted eardrum."

"Gods, but I hope not."

Turesobei opened his pack and drew out the wax he used for sealing scrolls and letters. He weighed it in his hand and thought that he might just have enough.

"We've got to keep moving!" Iniru shouted.

Turesobei shook his head. Onudaka checked Iniru's ears carefully, muttering to himself. Turesobei summoned a small flame to one fingertip. He pinched off some of the wax and heated it. He let it cool until it could be shaped but wouldn't stick to his skin. He placed it in his ear and molded it into an earplug.

"Good idea," Onudaka said.

Turesobei finished the first set of earplugs and placed a simple sound-dampening spell on them.

"There's some damage to her ears for sure, lad, but it's hard to say how much. Her hearing may not ever be the same. But I'm not sure, because her ears are very different from ours."

While Turesobei made earplugs for everyone, Iniru loudly told them about the Bogamaru Sengi based on legends she'd heard growing up.

"Centuries ago, the King of Wakaro unjustly executed more than seventy elite warriors known as the Bogamaru Regiment. They were the most loyal of all his troops. But he killed them because he was afraid of their growing popularity and because he thought his wife had fallen in love with their sergeant.

"When the warriors were impaled, their death screams transformed into terrible spirit-beasts called sengi. Most formed into wolves, but others shaped into tigers, bears, and constrictors. The sergeant transformed into a giant condor.

"The Bogamaru Sengi ravaged the Wakaran capital, killed the King, and slaughtered thousands. Once they had slain all who had wronged them, some semblance of their honor and humanity returned and they regretted having harmed innocents.

"The Shogakami goddess Amasan, Lady of the Winds, persuaded them to retreat into the mountains. There, they moan and howl against the injustices done to them.

"But they shouldn't be this far down from the mountains," said Iniru in a quaking voice. "They've never left their home before."

"Well, I saw a taint of wizardry on that beast," Turesobei said. "I think it was bound or compelled by a wizard, probably the one working with the Storm Cult."

"They have a wizard?" Onudaka asked.

"I'm certain of it."

Onudaka cursed. "Can't you banish demons?"

"Only zhurakami from the Nether Hells or the Shadowland. Though similar in composition, these sengi aren't demons."

"And you can't bind them?"

"I could, but bindings require preparation and a lot of power."

As he walked over to Iniru, he drew a healing strip from his pouch. He hoped he'd have some downtime soon. He could certainly use more of these. In a situation like this, he was much too tired and tense to do the spell without having inscribed it already.

She gave him a puzzled, anxious look. He mouthed the words: *trust me.*

She nodded and Turesobei chanted the activation command. Yellow earth kenja rose from the ground, and viridian forest energies joined with it. The forest teemed with life forces that would boost the healing spell. He placed his hands on her ears, closed his eyes, and focused the healing energies. After a few minutes, the glow receded.

"Can you hear me?"

She beamed. "Fairly well. Not like normal, but I can hear you. The ringing is gone."

"You'll need time to fully recover. My hearing's just now turning normal. Just make sure you wear the earplugs."

Iniru smiled shyly and drew him into a quick hug. For a moment he knew of nothing in the world but her body pressed against his. She kissed him on the cheek. The fur of her short muzzle tickled lightly. Her lips were soft and smooth.

Turesobei blushed. "You're welcome, Iniru."

At that moment eerie howls sounded to the northwest. "There's nothing to do but press on," Turesobei said. "I'm not going back."

Onudaka nodded. "We're with you, lad."

"Maybe I underestimated you," Iniru said.

Turesobei smiled sheepishly. "I guess I do well under pressure."

"You didn't know that before now?"

Twilight approached. In a grove of tall trees set onto a distant hill, orange lights appeared. They didn't know the source, but the tracks of the cultists headed in that direction. The howls drew closer, so they maintained a steady, jogging pace. For a second, Turesobei thought he saw one of the Bogamaru Sengi soar through the sky overhead.

Turesobei stopped and leaned against a tree. "Hold up. I have to catch my breath."

Iniru stomped over to him. "We don't have time to stop!"

"I can't go on, and we're not going to outrun them."

"I've got to rest as well," Onudaka gasped. "I'm not as young as you two."

Iniru muttered a curse and paced around. After a few minutes, she said, "Ready yet?"

"Hold on, let me check the kenja currents to see where the beasts are." Turesobei scanned the forest with his kenja-sight. "They're trying to encircle us."

"I was afraid of that," Onudaka said.

Turesobei sighed and released his kenja-sight. "I guess the white-steel is making them wary. Otherwise, why not just attack us en masse?"

Iniru was looking at him strangely. "What?" he said accusingly.

"Don't get touchy," she said. "Your eyes glaze over white when you read the currents. Did you know that?"

"Yes. What about it?"

"It's creepy and unnatural."

"I'm glad you like it."

"There's hope for you," she said. "Come on, let's go."

She ran ahead to scout the way. Turesobei said to Onudaka, "Who put her in charge anyway?"

The old zaboko shrugged. "Best we listen to her. She knows what she's doing."

"We might as well rest and gather our strength. We're not going to escape them."

Iniru suddenly appeared at his side. He didn't know how she could move so fast and quietly. "I'm trying to find a defensible spot, you idiot. Now get moving!"

They reached a steep cliff, and Onudaka immediately spotted a cleft that led into a hollow about thirty paces across.

"This looks like a decent place to die," she said.

Turesobei gasped, "I'm glad ... you're so happy ... about it." He bent over and placed his hands on his knees, struggling for breath.

"Spare me the sarcasm," she said. "How close are they? Sounds like we got ahead of them."

"I don't know how we did it," Onudaka said. "They can move much faster than we can."

"I don't have the strength to open my sight," Turesobei said.

Iniru snapped at him. "Then keep your mouth closed and stand up straight. Bending over makes it harder to breathe properly."

Iniru sat down and leaned back against the rock. She pulled the scarf from her face and the hood from her head. For the first time, she appeared tired and winded. Turesobei couldn't imagine what sort of training she'd gone through to be in this good of shape.

"I knew there would be trouble with the sengi somewhere soon," she said. "Only I never imagined I'd be facing them."

"What do you mean?" Onudaka asked, dropping his heavy pack to partially block the cleft.

"Didn't you hear? Someone stole the shrine statue of the Bogamaru Regiment from the capital."

"Recently?" Turesobei asked.

"No, ten years ago, that's why I'm suddenly concerned now."

"I thought you didn't want to hear any sarcasm."

"I just don't want to hear it from you, baojendari. It was three months ago."

Turesobei bit back an angry reply. "The statue could be used to bind the sengi. That would make doing so much easier. Though I still can't imagine someone powerful enough to bind something like them. I'm pretty sure my grandfather couldn't do it."

"Is there a simpler way?" Iniru asked. "Some way to cut corners, perhaps? Maybe they didn't bind all the sengi."

Turesobei shrugged. "There are a lot of them after us, I know that. Based on my kenja-sight, I'd say at least a dozen. Possibly twice that."

Onudaka scratched through his grey beard. Suddenly, his large, charcoal eyes lit up. "Their leader! If they were anything like your legends, the Bogamaru would surely follow their sergeant even into the fires of Torment. What if he was the only one bound and the others simply followed him?"

"The statue actually depicts him," Iniru said.

"That's it!" Turesobei exclaimed. "And they may not be attacking us because they're awaiting his orders on how to deal with the sword. Iniru, tell me exactly what this statue looks like. Every detail you can remember."

After her description, Turesobei knelt and drew a ring of power around himself by tracing his finger through the muddy turf. He envisioned what the statue must look like and chanted the *spell of locating that which is hidden*. Ideally, a wizard would study firsthand an object he wished to pinpoint. Otherwise, he should have little chance of success. Nevertheless, Turesobei tried and was surprised when he picked up an energy trail.

He stood and gathered his resolve to move on. "I can find it, and it's not far away." He unbelted his father's white-steel sword and reached it out to Iniru. "Take it. I'm too weak to fight them. And I'm going to have to keep my kenja-sight going."

She frowned with suspicion. "Are you going to turn me in later for touching one of your sacred blades?"

"I'm not that kind of baojendari!"

Without apologizing, she took the blade. "Then let's go."

Onudaka took Turesobei's pack for him. Turesobei led them now, frequently adjusting his course so that they followed a winding trail through the forest, away from the cultists' tracks and the glowing trees. Twilight set upon them. Perhaps this was why the sengi had held off. In the dark, they would never be able to see the sengi coming.

"Why wouldn't they keep the statue at their base?" Iniru asked, after noting their course was moving farther away from the direction the cultists had taken.

Turesobei shrugged. "Maybe they're not going home. Maybe they can't keep it there for some reason. I have no idea."

"Are you sure your spell worked?"

"No way of knowing unless we find the statue."

Chapter Thirty

When the first Bogamaru Sengi attacked, it moved like lightning. A large, translucent wolf erupted from the trees and crashed into Onudaka. The two rolled across the ground.

Iniru leapt toward them and stabbed the white-steel sword into the wolf-sengi's back. The tip of the sword stopped just short of Onudaka's throat.

The beast howled in its death throes. Then, with a blast of sound, it perished. The earplugs saved their ears, but the blast still knocked them to the ground. They wasted no time in getting up and running again. Two more wolves charged them, and a bear rumbled after them, gaining fast.

"I think we're close!" Turesobei shouted.

Iniru slashed at the wolves, warding them away with the white-steel sword which they now feared. Howls and the pounding of paws came from close and far behind them.

Iniru slowed and turned toward the wolves and the bear. "You two go ahead! I'll hold them off as long as I can."

"No, Iniru!" Turesobei said.

"Get to the statue or we're all dead!"

Onudaka tugged his arm. "She knows what she's doing."

A giant, hazy condor swooped overhead, just above the treetops. Turesobei gritted his teeth and ran harder. Amazingly, Onudaka could keep up with him.

They raced into a clearing. In the center rose a jagged outcropping, about twenty feet high, with a flattened top. On its summit perched a statue about half Turesobei's height.

"That's it," he said. "At the top."

A feminine scream pierced through a host of roars and growls. Then came the death boom of another sengi.

"Iniru!" Turesobei shouted.

"Concentrate on this," Onudaka said. "It's the only way to save her."

"I can't climb it."

Onudaka dropped his pack and took out his climbing claws, which he hastily wrapped onto his hands. "Hop on my back. I'll get you up there."

Onudaka jumped up and caught onto a crevice with one hand. Turesobei leapt onto his back. They dangled for a moment, and then Onudaka jammed the claws of the other hand into the crevice. He lifted them up, eyed the rock ahead, picked another spot, and up they went.

Iniru rushed into the clearing with a tiger-sengi swatting at her back. She spun and slashed with Sumada. She scored the tiger across the nose and it backed off. She was bleeding. The left arm of her uniform was ripped open. Her facemask and half of her hood had been torn off. There was blood on her scalp, too.

As she put her back to the outcrop, over a dozen wolves, two tigers, and three bears entered the clearing. They were shimmering and barely visible in the twilight. If they charged all at once, some would surely die against Iniru, but not all of them. They would overwhelm her. Turesobei wanted to drop down and help, but he kept his resolve.

Onudaka slipped. For a moment they slid downward, but then he caught to something and they held on. Turesobei gripped Onudaka tighter and wished him onward. A bear-sengi tested Iniru's defenses. She held but only just.

A screeching cry echoed from above and the beasts began to advance in unison. Turesobei glanced up. A giant condor-sengi swept across Avida, the bright moon.

As soon as Onudaka gripped the top of the outcrop, Turesobei scrambled up his back and onto the outcrop's summit.

"Look out, lad!"

Turesobei dove toward the statue. The condor swooped by. Its razor-sharp talons slashed across Turesobei's right leg but weren't able to latch on. The expansive wings beat against the air as the beast cried with irritation at having missed its prey.

Iniru screamed below. Metal clanged against stone.

Turesobei leapt to his feet and grasped the head of the statue: a stern and honest-looking zaboko soldier in wicker armor, armed with a spear and a shield. A condor was emblazoned on the shield. The binding on the statue was powerful but faulty. It had been cast with dangerous blood magic, yet poorly drawn. Mistakes littered the blood runes drawn onto the stone. Whoever had bound this Bogamaru Sengi had tremendous talent, but not much more skill than Turesobei did. And this person was certainly more careless. There was already a weak spot in the binding on the statue. A normal zhurakami would have exploited such a chink to gain its freedom in a matter of days. But no doubt the Bogamaru thought differently than demons, having once lived as normal men.

Turesobei drew the spell-strip from his pouch and chanted the command, focusing on this vulnerability. The counter-spell erupted to life with a blaze of blue-white sparks. The spell was tearing and unraveling, faster than most bindings of this type, but not fast enough.

The condor wheeled about in the air and plunged downward.

Turesobei had to do something, and fast. With sweaty palms he streaked his hand across the statue, smudging the blood runes.

The condor pulled up from its dive, flashed across the outcrop, and flew off into the forest.

Turesobei looked about. Where was Onudaka? Why wasn't he up here with him? What about Iniru? He didn't hear any sounds from down below, from the sengi or his companions.

Turesobei rushed to the edge of the outcrop. "Iniru! Onudaka!"

"We're here," the zaboko medic called out.

Below him, the qengai girl was lying motionless at the base of the outcrop. Onudaka was standing guard over her. Seven of the Bogamaru Sengi were warily backing away from them.

"Is she..."

"Alive?" said Onudaka. "Yes. And I think her injuries are relatively mild."

"What about you? Are you okay?"

"Just some scrapes and bruises. I'll manage."

Leaves rustled and wings flapped. The translucent condor reemerged from the forest, flew to the outcrop, and landed beside Turesobei.

"We are not your enemies," Turesobei stated swiftly.

"Yes, I know," the condor said in a distant voice. "You freed me, and by extension, my companions. For my fate is theirs." The accent was thick, the language ancient and difficult for Turesobei to understand. "We hadn't known we were bound, though I remember when it happened, almost a month ago."

"Who bound you?"

"A pale-skin sorcerer like you. I don't know his name. He sent us here to defend the approach to a citadel further up into the mountains. We followed blindly." The condor's eyes narrowed. "I shall have my revenge upon him."

An idea struck Turesobei. "Would you help me rescue my father? I believe he is being kept in the citadel, which belongs to a group known as the Storm Cult. Have you heard of them before? The wizard who did this is apparently one of them."

"I have not heard of this cult," said the condor, "but I think any object related to Naruwakiru should be left alone."

"I agree, but reason couldn't stop my father from seeking it any more than it could stop the Storm Cult."

"We will help you," the condor said. "But we cannot help for long. We have other responsibilities. Before Zhura Dark Moon is born anew in four days, we must return to our home high in the mountains. Long have we guarded a fragile breeding ground for condors. Their revenant enemies rise with each new Zhura, and if we are not there, the condors will perish."

"We shall move fast, then."

"Also, you must vow that if we do not reach him, you will avenge us upon this wizard. He dared much to mislead and bind us."

"I understand," said Turesobei. "And I swear that I shall avenge the wrong done to you, sir..."

"Condor. That is the name I go by now."

"Chonda Turesobei," he replied, holding out his hand.

Condor bent his head and touched his beak to Turesobei's hand. "The vow is accepted, Chonda Turesobei."

Turesobei glanced down the outcrop. "Sorry, but I must go down and make sure my friends are okay."

"We are sorry," Condor said. "We did not mean to harm any of you."

A lump of guilt caught in Turesobei's throat. "And I am sorry that we ... killed ... some of you."

Condor shook his head. "Do not be sorry. I was a fool to be tricked and bound in this manner. Besides, oblivion is not so bad. It is a welcome release from this half-life we've been punished with."

"I could give all of you that release," he said, quaking in dread from his own words.

"Thank you, my new friend. It is a kind and honorable offer. But it would not be acceptable. We have sworn to guard Amasan's children in the mountains. That is our punishment for taking vengeance beyond what was our right to give. We will continue that mission as promised, until the end of forever or until the goddess returns and releases us."

While the sengi kept guard on the outskirts of the clearing, Turesobei helped Onudaka tend to Iniru, who woke for just long enough to drink an herbal potion and some water. He couldn't cast another healing on her yet. A second one within twenty-four hours never helped and sometimes made matters worse.

Onudaka and Turesobei tended each others' wounds then made camp beneath the outcrop. They slept without a watch, allowing the Bogamaru Sengi to guard them.

When Turesobei awoke several hours after dawn, he cast healing spells onto Onudaka and Iniru. She was now half recovered, and Onudaka was nearly well. Iniru was grateful to Turesobei for half a day before she started snapping and complaining at him. He sighed and endured it all patiently. In a way it was almost like being at home.

"How far is it to the citadel?" Turesobei asked Condor.

"A full day's walk for you."

Turesobei wanted to march off immediately. He trembled as he restrained himself from declaring that he would set out on his own. It felt like he was giving up, but he had to do this right. It wouldn't help his father for him to rush in and botch a rescue attempt.

"In that case, we should rest another night before pressing on," Turesobei said in a shaky, unsure murmur. "We are in no condition to fight at the moment. Is that all right?"

"Yes."

"Promise you won't attack the citadel without us."

"You have my word," Condor said, and then he returned to the skies, where he circled overhead most of the day and night, watching for enemies.

Onudaka and Iniru ate and went to sleep early, curled up near the small fire they'd built at the base of the outcrop. Turesobei didn't join them. Though dismayed and anxious to try to rescue his dad, he was going to take this opportunity to at last check up on poor Lu Bei, though he feared the little fetch, like his dad, was probably lost forever.

Chapter Thirty-One

Sixty paces, a boulder, and a stand of trees separated Turesobei from the others, but he was still within the area guarded by the Bogamaru Sengi. He took the diary from his satchel. The runes still didn't glimmer under his touch. It felt lifeless and his kenja-sight showed only faint traces of energy. He thumbed through the diary carefully. The hole ripped through the middle was unchanged, and spots of blue mildew had begun to stain the pages.

He called to Lu Bei, but there was no response. He focused his full intent and called again. Sparks glinted within his amber kavaru, and for a moment he thought he heard the rustling of a page. But nothing happened. He would have to try the *spell of lesser summoning*.

The spell was intended for conjuring minor spirits from the Shadowland or nature spirits from nearby. Though normally difficult, the spell should prove relatively easy because he knew Lu Bei's name and had personally interacted with him. Also, Lu Bei would not be trying to resist the summoning as a lesser demon or nature spirit would.

Turesobei cleared the ground of debris. He drew runes into the earth with a pointed stick, surrounding the book in complex symbols. He chanted for an hour and then spoke the command phrase.

His kavaru flared to life. Matching amber energy glowed around the book. There was a puff of smoke, and Lu Bei appeared!

But with a hole in his chest, a torn wing, and blue splotches all over his body. His face was contorted by pain. His voice was harsh, cracking.

"Master, you must—"

The fetch turned back into smoke.

Turesobei repeated the command and Lu Bei reappeared.

"The pain!" he cried. "Master, you must—"

And he was gone again. With more force, Turesobei repeated the command a third time. "Lu Bei, I summon thee!"

The fetch flickered back and was clearly stronger this time.

Lu Bei spoke quickly. "Master, you must heed what I say. I know you won't hear what I'm about to tell you, but maybe you will remember when it is time. It's the best I can do." He bowed his head low. "I have failed my mission, master. I am sorry."

"Lu Bei, it's all right. I don't—"

"Shh! I must say this before I shift back." Lu Bei took a deep ragged breath and went on. "The day we anticipated is not yet. Our calculations were off. Years will pass before ... But I see what must be more clearly now. You will reach a ... then you must ... Chonda Lu..."

Turesobei had begun to black out, missing long parts of what Lu Bei was telling him. He tried to focus on what was said, but as before, there were certain things Turesobei couldn't hear when Lu Bei said them, no matter how much Turesobei tried.

A few minutes passed while Turesobei only barely remained conscious. But then it was over. He was fully awake and could focus again. Lu Bei was touching his arm. Tears flowed from his large, black eyes. He was gritting his teeth and fangs.

"Please, master, end the pain. It's worse in this form, but even as a book it's unbearable. Take up the sword. Do what must be done. But remember me always, and yourself when it is time."

Lu Bei began to shift, bowing as he did so, and turned into a cloud of smoke. Turesobei uttered the command again, with as much power as he could. There was a single flicker of Lu Bei, then smoke, and then the damaged diary lying still, nearly lifeless.

Turesobei placed a hand on the cover of the book. After a few quiet moments, when it seemed not even the forest made any sound, he stood, tears rolling down his cheeks. He drew the white-steel sword. Sumada gleamed under the light of Avida, almost as brightly as it would in daylight.

Turesobei hovered over the book, sword drawn back, ready to strike. One clean cut would destroy the book, sever the magic, and end Lu Bei's suffering. He flexed his muscles. Moments passed, but he did nothing. His courage had failed.

He lingered, trying hard to steel himself to do what he knew he must, for Lu Bei's sake. He flexed his muscles again but then released them.

"Is there something wrong?" said a voice behind him.

Turesobei spun. "Condor! I didn't hear you."

Condor was sitting on a boulder behind him. "My apologies. I spotted you as I kept watch from above and landed to see what you were doing. I hope I have not offended you."

"Not at all," Turesobei said. Though he was actually offended that his privacy had been interrupted, he was also glad to have a diversion. "How long have you been here?"

"Since before you summoned the little demon," said Condor. "But I promise that your secrets will be safe with me."

Turesobei picked up the diary and held it firmly, wishing he could think of any way to recover Lu Bei.

"You are not ready to end it," said Condor.

"But he's suffering."

"Yes, I know. But this diary, it is linked to you and your kavaru."

Turesobei nodded. "My ancestor, Chonda Lu, made Lu Bei, using this kavaru."

"Maybe you cannot dispatch him for a reason. Maybe your kavaru does not want this to happen."

"Maybe..."

"Reflect on it. Decide what to do after we have dealt with the cultists. Once you've rescued your father, your emotions and thoughts will be clear. Maybe a solution will come to you. Maybe you will then have the resolve to go through with it. Taking the life of someone dear to you, even to end their suffering, is not an easy thing to do."

It was early in the evening two days later when they reached the Storm Cult's citadel. Turesobei was anxious—about Lu Bei, about his father, about Iniru's condition. She said she was okay but he wasn't sure she was telling the truth. She had obviously recovered, but how much? Onudaka had said he was fine as well. Turesobei didn't think the old medic would lie.

The three of them hid in a thicket of shrubs at the tree line four hundred paces away and observed the citadel, while the Bogamaru Sengi scouted the surrounding area.

The citadel sat on a hill cleared of vegetation except for a stand of pines at its summit. A high, wooden stockade with a single gate surrounded the pines. Four small platforms clung to the pine trunks, high above the citadel's interior. Lanterns, carried by masked assassins, danced among the tree limbs and within the citadel.

"We must strike tonight," Iniru whispered intensely.

"Won't be simple," replied Onudaka.

"No, it won't," Turesobei said. "But it's not going to get any easier if we wait. And they could kill my dad at any time. We've got to go. We've got to get him out of there!"

Chapter Thirty-Two

Turesobei and his allies met in a secluded grove a league away from the Storm Cult's citadel. It was nearly midnight.

"I don't think the sorcerer is here," Condor said. He was perched on a fallen tree while the other sengi roamed out of sight. "Our vengeance shall be unfulfilled."

"Are you sure?" Turesobei asked in surprise. "What about my father? If they took him away, then there's no need for us to have come here."

"I cannot say whether your father is here. My connection was only to the sorcerer, and though I have been trying since we arrived, I don't sense his presence. I flew far around here, but couldn't detect him. He must have left at least a day before we arrived."

"In that case, I must try to locate my father with magic."

He then went off by himself, and with considerable determination and focus, conducted the *spell of locating that which is hidden*. It was far easier to find the aura of someone he loved than to pinpoint a statue he'd never seen. But that didn't make it easy, and the spell wouldn't work from much further out than he was now.

An hour later, he returned to his companions and announced with relief, "He's there, and he's alive, though I don't know what condition he might be in."

"Excellent," Iniru said. "Now we need a plan of attack. Turesobei, is there any sort of magic that you can do to help us?"

"I can give you and Onudaka darksight, but without preparation and working under pressure, mostly all I can manage are simple conjurations like fire-globes or limited manipulations of elements like fog and rain. I can cast spells to help me jump higher, run faster, be less noticeable. That sort of thing. Not much I can do to help all of us together. And anything else requires a lot of personal energy and will weaken me."

"We can't wait for something grand," Iniru said with annoyance. "The longer your father is there, the more danger he's in." She turned to Condor. "Could you carry me while flying?"

"Normally, we are only solid the moment we strike. To remain solid longer weakens us. But I can manage it for a little while without too much trouble. Why?"

"I need you to drop me onto one of the platforms. We have to take out their spotters first. Even if they don't see us approaching, we can't let them rain arrows down on us once we attack. We're vulnerable and they might have white-steel to use against you."

"I doubt they would," said Turesobei. "Not many white-steel arrowheads out there, even with diluted alloys. Very expensive and potentially wasteful."

"Yes, but you never know," said Iniru. "Even just one or two of them could be devastating. But most of all, if we don't hit them by surprise, I'm afraid of what they might do to your father."

"All right then, what about the other platforms?"

"I will take one," Condor said. "Panther and Black Bear can take out the other two, though they'll have to penetrate the interior of the citadel and climb up unnoticed to do so."

Onudaka began to stretch his limbs. His joints creaked like rusty cogs. "Shouldn't be too hard tonight."

There were no moons out and a thick fog had already begun to roll down from the mountains.

"How will Panther and Black Bear get inside?" Iniru asked. "The walls seem too high and sheer for them to climb."

Condor called out and Black Bear leapt into the grove, flying well over twelve feet into the air. He went far higher and farther than any normal, wingless animal could go.

"Wow!" Turesobei exclaimed. "Why didn't you do that against us?"

"That would not have been honorable," Black Bear growled. "Against an honorable foe we fight only as would the forms that we are in."

"But these are not honorable opponents we face tonight," Condor said in a chilling voice. "These men will pay for having misused the Bogamaru. We will use our every capability to exact our revenge. We cannot kill the sorcerer, but we can ruin his cult and his base."

"What about Onudaka and me?" asked Turesobei.

"You can rush in after the wolves attack and secure your father," Iniru said. "You'll need to go right on in to make sure they don't kill him as soon as they're under attack."

"That's a lot of ground to cover," Onudaka commented.

"You two can ride on the backs of Grizzly and Brother Grizzly," said Condor. "They're fat and slow as far as spirit-bears go, but they'll get you there."

"They were fat and slow as humans, too," said Black Bear with a hoarse laugh.

Condor seemed to smile, if any expression a giant, translucent bird of prey had could be called a smile. For a rare moment, Condor's past humanity had shown through.

"You'll have to be careful not to attack my father," Turesobei said.

"He will smell like you and his presence will remind us of yours," Condor said. "There is no risk of us harming him. You have my word."

They waited until two hours past midnight. The sentries on duty had served three hours of what Iniru believed was a four-hour shift. After a deep breath she knelt and Condor grasped the back of her bodysuit with his talons. Turesobei could barely see the sengi, even with the *spell of darksight*, which he had cast on himself, Iniru, and Onudaka.

"Remember," she said, "someone will have to count out the time. I can't risk waking them all up by signaling you."

Turesobei stepped up to her and put a hand on her arm. "Be careful."

Her eyes glinted with amusement. "I've trained my whole life for this. If I can't do it without getting killed, then I've wasted the last fifteen years."

"Well ... um..."

She smirked and drew her grey silk scarf across her lower face. "Perhaps I should tell you to be careful."

"Thanks," he responded meekly.

"Let's go," she said.

Condor beat his great wings and took off. Iniru seemed to be flying through the air as she dangled from his talons. It was a strange sight. Turesobei sighed with worry. Both for her and himself. He'd never imagined he'd be doing anything like this. The expedition had proven exceedingly dangerous and far more of a learning experience than Grandfather Kahenan had anticipated.

"How are you holding up, lad?"

"I'll be all right, Onudaka."

The big zaboko patted him on the back. "Call me Daka, lad."

"You can call me Sobei if you like."

"Be brave, then, young Sobei. We'll make it through and get your father out. I can't see us failing. Iniru's help alone is worth a thousand jade per week."

"A thousand!"

"Probably more. Plus we've got powerful spirit allies and a wizard."

"I'm not much of a wizard. I feel useless."

Onudaka chuckled. "More useful than me, lad, more than me. Without your skills, we'd all be dead now and the sengi would still be bound."

The grizzlies rumbled forward. "Get ready," Brother Grizzly muttered.

Turesobei followed Onudaka's lead and climbed onto the back of Brother Grizzly.

"Keep that sword away from me," he growled.

Turesobei had strapped the scabbarded white-steel sword onto his back, anticipating this. "It's as far away as I can get it. Can you feel it?"

"Like a sunburn."

"Really?" The wizard's apprentice in him took over for a moment. "Is it stronger now that I'm sitting on you or was it worse when you stood next to me."

"I don't really want to talk about it."

Turesobei sighed with disappointment. "Sorry."

The bear apparently noticed his dashed curiosity and said grudgingly, "It's better now that you're blocking it."

"Thanks. Knowing that may come in handy in the future."

"Just be sure you use it against some Zhura demons and not any more of us."

Turesobei bowed his head with regret and grew silent. Onudaka said a few words of greeting to Grizzly and massaged him along the scruff of his neck as a gesture of friendship. Whether they could feel it or not, the gesture seemed appreciated, judging from the peaceful, rumbling growl Grizzly emitted. Turesobei copied the action and achieved the same result.

The wolf-sengi gathered along the tree line, pacing and baring their teeth in anticipation of the battle to come. Turesobei squinted at the citadel but couldn't see much of anything. Fog had descended down to the battlements of the stockade. That would cover them from sight most of the way once Iniru, Condor, Panther, and Black Bear took out the archers and sentries on the platforms.

"Brother Grizzly," said Turesobei, "what do you do in your spare time?"

"We guard a colony of special condors. And we meditate."

"That's all?"

"Well, when we must, we howl the rage that made us what we are. We try to hold that in, though. We try to still ourselves into silence. The more we do that, the closer we come to the human existence that made us."

"But wouldn't that mean death?"

"Stillness is a peaceful oblivion. A ceasing of the sounds of anguish that created us."

"Have any of you achieved this stillness?"

"Aye. Brother Hawk and Thirty-two Wolf have gone on into the silence of death. Their energies are returned to the cycle of life."

"Have you come close?"

"I will be one of the last, I'm sure."

Constrictor, who served as their lookout, hissed, "The count is up. It's time to move forward."

"Hold tight," Brother Grizzly warned Turesobei.

The wolves marched out onto the barren hill, heading toward the citadel. Slinking close to the ground, they spread out into a staggered line. They moved at a steady pace, not too slow but not so fast as to be more noticeable either. To Turesobei with his frayed nerves, it felt as if it took them an hour to reach the walls rather than a minute.

Despite his darksight spell, he lost sight of their barely luminescent forms until he saw them leap over the walls. The screams of dying men followed. The grizzlies surged forward and bounded up the hill. They had gone last so Turesobei and Onudaka wouldn't be spotted floating in the air.

Turesobei would never forget this ride. Brother Grizzly's gait was quite unlike the lumber of a denekon. He could feel every ripple of the bear's cold muscles.

Screams of despair overpowered the sounds of men fighting. Most had probably realized they couldn't stop the beasts that attacked them. Some would have demon-warding talismans. One or two might even have a peach-wood dagger. The properties of peach-wood caused spirits twice as much pain as a normal steel weapon but no permanent damage. The talismans, those few that worked and weren't fakes, would make it harder for the sengi to focus on those wearing them, but not impossible. The warding talisman on Turesobei's armor hadn't significantly distracted them.

The bears neared the stockade. "The gate doesn't look strong to me," Grizzly called out. "Through it or over?"

"I'm not sure I can make the jump!" bellowed Brother Grizzly.

"Through it then. You two will want to hold on tight or jump off."

"We'll drop off," Turesobei muttered quickly.

"Then go now!"

Turesobei slid off Brother Grizzly's back and plopped onto the ground. Onudaka joined him. The two bears crashed through the gate. Without pausing they rampaged through the citadel, joining the chaos already under way.

"Do you know where your father is, lad?"

"When I cast the spell I sensed that he was somewhere near the center."

Onudaka took the staff from his back. "Then let's get moving."

They ran into the citadel. Turesobei paused, horrified by the mangled corpses strewn across the grounds. At least two dozen cultists lay scattered about. Some wore no armor and had obviously just woken up and charged out when the alarm was signaled.

Snarls and fighting continued and Turesobei realized there were far more cultists here than he had expected. He trudged forward until he stood beside a zaboko with his arm torn off and wide gashes across his face. Bile rose into Turesobei's throat.

Onudaka tugged at his sleeve. "Your father, lad. Gather yourself."

Turesobei shook himself from the haze and rushed toward the crude barracks and other buildings in the citadel's center. He hoped he could get his father out. He hoped Iniru was all right.

Upon nearing a fight between a squad of soldiers and two wolf-sengi, they ducked into an alleyway between the barracks. Onudaka pointed out a tiny building like a squat outhouse stuck onto the side of the central building, which appeared to be a meetinghouse.

"There! That looks like a prisoner box."

Two guards still stood, cringing beside the small door. They had held their posts and gone unmolested by the sengi so far. The alleyway partially secluded them from the rest of the citadel.

Turesobei drew his sword and followed behind Onudaka as he charged in. The old medic met the first cultist, blocked a sword-strike, and cracked the man's skull with his staff. As that one fell, the other attacked. Onudaka blocked and countered. The cultist dodged, feinted, and attacked unsuccessfully.

With adrenaline pounding through his veins, Turesobei lunged in and thrust. His sword cut the cultist across the arm. The wound was enough to distract him for a moment. Onudaka then thudded him beneath the chin with the end of his staff. The cultist fell back and slumped down next to his comrade.

Onudaka dragged the bodies out of the way. Turesobei went to the door and cursed as he saw the iron lock.

"Out of the way, lad."

Onudaka got a running start and shouldered into the door of the prison box. The pine planks shattered. Onudaka lost his balance and crashed inside with a loud oomph.

"You all right?" Turesobei asked as he crawled in through the gaping hole.

Onudaka sat up, rubbing his shoulder. Splinters and dust clung to his hair. "Fine, lad."

Then Turesobei looked up at the far wall and gasped.

Chapter Thirty-Three

Noboro hung from the wall—his arms and legs chained tightly and splayed out. Lash marks scarred his body along with ample bruises. He was filthy, ragged, and naked. But he was alive, and with a resolute spark in his eyes.

Turesobei hugged him by the waist. "Father!"

A strained, distant voice responded, "Sobei, you're alive. My prayers are answered."

"This is Onudaka, Father. He saved my life. He's a medic. He's going to help get you out of here."

"My best ... to you, sir." Noboro coughed. "My limbs are weak. I'm afraid ... someone must carry me."

Turesobei drew a healing strip from his pouch. "I can fix some of your weakness and injury. Enough that we can get you to safety."

"What's going on out there? It's sounds ... like you summoned a horde of demons."

"It's a long story, my lord," Onudaka said. "But a horde of demons isn't far from the mark. Your son has earned us sengi as allies."

"The Bogamaru Sengi?"

"Aye. You should be quite proud of him."

Noboro smiled. "I am." His eyes then focused on Turesobei. "There's much ... I must tell you, but we've ... got to get out of here first."

"The sengi should have this wrapped up soon," said Onudaka. "The cultists don't seem to have any weapons that can hurt them."

"Sotenda and the sorcerer ... they're not here?"

"No," Turesobei replied.

His father's face took on a frantic expression. "Then you're too late. They've gone on with the key. We have little time left."

"Try to relax, Father." Turesobei activated the healing strip. A warm glow of yellow earth energies filled the little hut, sealing Noboro's scrapes and revitalizing his haggard body.

Onudaka gave the chains one hard tug and then cursed with frustration. "I can't break them loose."

"They're secured ... to iron posts inside the timbers," Noboro said.

Without another moment wasted, Turesobei summoned a dark-fire globe and settled it onto the links holding Noboro's arms. His father cringed from the heat but said nothing in complaint. That he trusted his son made Turesobei feel proud. After the metal links softened a bit, Onudaka yanked again and broke the chain. They repeated the process on the chains binding his other three limbs.

Freed, Noboro stood and walked a few shaky steps. Then he took Turesobei up into a giant hug. Tears rolled from his father's eyes.

"They bound and tortured me," Noboro said. "Got everything out of me. Used magic ... along with pain. I couldn't resist."

"Do you know who this sorcerer is?" Turesobei asked.

"He sounded familiar. His accent was that of a Batsan baojendari, and he's young. But that's all I could tell. He wore a mask when he interrogated me. I never heard his name."

"Can you walk?" Onudaka asked.

Noboro nodded his head. "I can make it. Come, we must head out immediately."

"Father, you should rest first."

"We have no time. Sotenda is already on his way to the vault. He has the Storm Key, and I told him how to use it. We must hurry."

Turesobei looked to Onudaka for help, but the old man merely shrugged. Both of them knew Noboro couldn't be convinced otherwise, and they both knew that he could be right, that if they didn't move quickly a powerful artifact would fall into the wrong hands.

They met no resistance outside as they moved through the citadel grounds. Fighting continued in pockets here and there, but most of it seemed over already. Noboro leaned on Onudaka for support while Turesobei led the way with his sword drawn. He saw no sign of Iniru and was deeply worried about her.

They rounded up four frightened denekon from a stable and coaxed them outside, but just barely. They walked them out through the gate and halfway down the hill. They thought they were safe.

Four cultists emerged from the trees at a run, spotted them, and drew to a halt. Turesobei assumed it was a scouting party out on patrol that must have rushed back as soon as they heard fighting.

Three of the scouts drew swords and charged uphill. The fourth—with an arrow nocked to his bowstring already—drew, aimed, and released.

Somehow unable to move, Turesobei watched in disbelief as the arrow sped toward him. Then suddenly, Noboro lunged forward and knocked him aside.

With a horrid, wet thunk, the arrow struck Noboro. It punched all the way through his torso. The silver tip of the arrowhead poked out from his bare back.

Noboro collapsed and began coughing blood. An odd wheezing sound issued from the wound.

"No!" Turesobei screamed. "Father, no!"

He dropped his sword and clutched at his father's body. Hazy eyes looked up at him. Onudaka leapt ahead of them. "Sobei! We're in danger."

But Turesobei ignored him ... until Noboro said, "Save yourself."

Turesobei picked up the sword and faced the enemy.

The archer drew another arrow, but then he fell, clawing at his throat. Onudaka took a cut on the forearm, but he maintained his composure and defended himself admirably, backpedaling and holding off the three cultists that were attacking him. Turesobei joined in, but his attacks gained them nothing, except to ease the pressure on Onudaka.

Unexpectedly, one of the cultists arched backward and spat blood onto Onudaka. The man fell. An arrow was lodged in the back of his neck. As the other two glanced at their fallen comrade, Onudaka clocked one on the side of the head.

A predatory cry and the flapping of wings sped toward them. The talons of Condor scraped across the face of the remaining cultist, and Onudaka finished him off as he fell writhing.

Turesobei glanced to the tree line and saw Iniru with the archer's bow in hand. She was running toward them. He had no idea how she'd gotten out into the forest.

Turesobei rushed back to Noboro with Onudaka following behind. Blood stained his father's pale skin. The arrow had pierced a lung.

"Father!"

"Sobei, I'm ... not going ... to make it..."

Turesobei fumbled at his pouch. Tears welled in his eyes. "I can heal you."

"The wound's ... too bad. And we both know ... you can't make it work ... twice ... in one day."

Turesobei drew his father's head into his lap and stroked his forehead. "Onudaka, can't you do something?"

The zaboko medic shook his head. "I'm sorry. The wound is too bad. Even if you could heal him again, I don't think I could save him."

Turesobei looked at Condor who had landed beside them. The sengi swiftly replied to his pleading gaze, "I'm only a killer, Chonda Turesobei. I cannot heal your father."

Noboro clutched Turesobei's hand. He coughed up blood, swallowed, and then spoke. His voice grew strong for a moment. His eyes blazed with passion. "Sobei, you must recover Yomifano ... for Lord Kahenan. I promised Father ... I'd bring it back. And you must get the Storm Key before ... the cult can steal the heart."

"I swear I will do as you ask."

Noboro reached up a hand and touched Turesobei's cheek. With his bloody fingertips he drew the sigil of the Chonda Goshawk, the clan's sacred symbol. His touch felt like a burning brand on Turesobei's skin.

Power resided in that blood as well as in the oath Turesobei swore: "I swear by all the gods and powers in the world that I will restore Yomifano, avenge your death, and retrieve the Storm Dragon's Heart from the cultists."

The sigil burned hotter on his skin. For a moment, it glowed softly. He saw it reflected in his father's eyes and on Onudaka's surprised face.

Noboro smiled weakly and grabbed the back of Turesobei's head. Turesobei leaned in so he could hear his father's fading whispers. "Remember our journey here ... martial arts on the ship's deck. Good wine ... good times. You had a decent father ... at least for a few days ... remember me for that..."

Chonda Noboro's voice trailed his spirit into the realm of death. Turesobei cried out. Condor screeched with him, their grief resonating into one force.

Iniru knelt beside Turesobei and gently put a hand on his shoulder. "I'm sorry," she said. "I got to them as quickly as I could."

"I'm sorry that I could do nothing for him," said Onudaka. "I'll pray for his spirit, though, if you'd like."

Turesobei said nothing. He merely clung to his father's body, wilted, and cried. The *Sigil of the Chonda Goshawk* burned on his cheek, and the tears that touched it did not streak the blood, but simply rolled across as if it were a tattoo.

Chapter Thirty-Four

Turesobei knelt beside Noboro and chanted the *ritual of preservation*. He fixed his mind on this task and nothing else, shutting out his grief, almost entirely. His grandfather would have been proud of his focus. Iniru and Onudaka helped the sengi check all the buildings for Storm Cultists, and then slept in Sotenda's house within the citadel while the sengi kept watch. Two hours after dawn, Onudaka came to Turesobei as he was completing the ritual.

"Lad, you need to get some rest."

"I can't. We must move on today." Turesobei stood and rubbed at his eyes. "Can you help me?"

"Of course, lad."

With quiet reverence, they wrapped Noboro in silk sheets from Sotenda's bedroom. Then they placed him within the house's small wine cellar. Only when they were finished did Onudaka say:

"Lad, why are you doing this? We could give him a good burial here."

Turesobei shook his head. "When I'm finished with the Storm Cult, I intend to take him home and give him a proper Chonda funeral."

Iniru locked the cellar door behind them. "That's not very practical."

"I don't care!" Turesobei snapped. "I'm going to do it and if you don't like it, then just stay out of my way."

She started to snap back but restrained herself and turned to Onudaka. "We should replenish our supplies here before leaving. Do you know how to ride?"

"I can't fight from a mount or do anything fancy like that, but I can move along well enough."

"In that case we'll take seven mounts with us, one for supplies and a spare for each of us. Do you have any problems with that, Turesobei?"

"Whatever you think best." He met her fierce eyes. "You know what you're doing."

Her expression softened. "I found a map to the shrine where the heart is. There's a shorter, alternate route we could take, a mountain road that leads to a Moshingan monastery and then to the Storm Dragon Shrine. No one takes that road anymore, though. Sotenda's notes say that it's haunted."

"How much time would it save us?" Onudaka asked.

"Probably two days out of five. But I'm not sure about the danger."

"I'm not afraid of ghosts," Turesobei said. "I've dared one haunted route already. Another means nothing to me. Any demon that gets in my way can taste white-steel."

Iniru nodded. "All right then."

As soon as she agreed with him, the fire in his spirit drained away. He slumped back against the wall, and his eyelids drooped. "Wake me up when you have everything ready to go."

Three hours later, they were ready to ride out from the Storm Cult Citadel. The Bogamaru Sengi gathered before them: rows of regal, translucent beasts. All at once, they bowed elegantly, and Turesobei, Iniru, and Onudaka returned the gesture.

Condor approached. "Chonda Turesobei, will you uphold your vow to us?"

"I will see your vengeance paid."

"That is good," Condor said.

A long, thin snake-sengi emerged from the weeds and rose up before Turesobei. He had not seen this one before.

"Greetings, Chonda Turesobei," the snake hissed.

"Hello, honored sengi."

"This is Racer," said Condor. "For these many years he has been our advance scout. But he kills no longer and he fights no longer. Not even under the Storm Cult's spell would he act aggressively."

"I am prepared to move on," said Racer. "I am prepared to embrace silence."

"My best to you, then," said Turesobei, trying to figure out why this was supposed to be important to him. He was grieving and worried and so tired he could barely think.

"I have a proposition for you," said Racer. "When I give myself to the Void, I will release the energies that make up this form. Those energies can be given to you."

"But what would I do with..." Turesobei's mind awoke with purpose. "The diary!"

"Yes," said Condor. "Your friend Lu Bei. Would that be enough power to restore your little friend?"

"Perhaps..."

"I was preparing to withdraw when we were bound," said Racer. "If in my ceasing I could help someone else in some way, any way, that would be all the better."

"What are they talking about?" asked Iniru. "What friend?"

"You will see," said Turesobei with hope. "I must prepare the ritual."

"We don't have long, lad," said Onudaka.

"I know, but this is extremely important. And it will only take an hour."

The sengi, along with Iniru and Onudaka, gathered in a circle around Turesobei, who had spent most of the last hour chanting and drawing sigils in the dust. Racer was coiled in the midst of these sigils.

"Are you ready?" he asked the snake.

Racer looked to all the sengi and bowed his head. "My friends ... I hope you all find peace as I have. You will always be my brothers." He bobbed his head. "I am ready now, Chonda Turesobei."

Turesobei placed the book before Racer. He wasn't sure how the energies would be released, and the sengi were no help in this regard. They knew nothing of wizardry. He assumed air kenja would be the predominant form released and had prepared thusly.

Racer threaded the hole in the book, coiled around the book many times, and then clasped his tail with his own mouth. He closed his eyes. Moments passed, then minutes. Silence. No one spoke nor moved. And then there was a flash of light and a soft, almost inaudible moan, then silence again.

The sigils flared to life, one by one.

Racer glowed and then disappeared.

The book's ruined pages turned crisp and clean. The cover mended. The runes on the cover sparkled with an amber glow. And then the book burst into smoke. Onudaka and Iniru gasped as the smoke coalesced into a small creature.

Turesobei was struck in the chest. Iniru surged forward, blade in hand, but Onudaka held her back.

"Wait, lass."

Turesobei fell back onto the ground with a foot-high creature latched onto his chest. It had amber skin, large black eyes, tiny fangs, and a spiked tail. Its bat-wings fluttered as if it were a butterfly.

"Lu Bei!" Turesobei said.

"My lord, you have restored me." Lu Bei stood up and looked down into his face. "I didn't think it possible. Thank you, thank you." His eyes began to well with tears. "Oh, master, you have suffered so. Whatever can I do to aid you?"

"You are returned, Lu Bei. That is enough."

Lu Bei's expression turned to concern. He reached out a hand and touched the crimson Goshawk sigil on Turesobei's face. "Master, this—"

"I know. We can discuss it later. Now is not the time." Turesobei sat up and turned to his friends. "Onudaka, Iniru, I'd like for you to meet my diary. I'd like for you to meet Lu Bei."

Lu Bei bowed to them. "Greetings, friends of my master."

Iniru eyed him warily. "You trust this creature?"

"Yes, but please keep his existence a secret. No one is supposed to know about him."

"We will keep the secret," said Onudaka. "Lu Bei, I am pleased to meet you."

Iniru grunted and backed away.

Minutes later, they had said their goodbyes and made their last preparations. Lu Bei had personally thanked each sengi for Racer's help. It was the best he could do, since Racer was gone.

Along with Onudaka, Iniru, and Lu Bei, Turesobei bowed before the sengi. "Thank you for the help you gave in rescuing my father."

"Keep your promise to us," said Condor, "and fare well."

The sengi all bowed again and then silently ran, flew, and slithered out into the forest. Their hazy forms disappeared amongst the vegetation.

"Their presence was almost like a dream," Onudaka said. "I never thought to see anything like that in my life. Up until now, I don't think I'd seen more than a dozen spirits total."

"It was amazing," Iniru said. She eyed Lu Bei. "I've seen so many things I never thought to see. I'm not sure what to make of it all."

Turesobei climbed into his saddle, and Lu Bei sat on his shoulder. The fetch didn't want to be a book again just yet.

Turesobei flicked the reins. "Let's get moving."

Chapter Thirty-Five

Just before nightfall, they turned off the cultists' well-worn path to the Storm Dragon Shrine and headed up the mountain on an old, cobbled road that somehow remained clear of the forest's undergrowth, as if it were kept up by gardeners.

"Why is this road out here?" Turesobei asked.

"There were once many thriving villages in this area," Iniru replied. "Some of the roads have been lost in floods, overtaken by vegetation, or destroyed by earthquakes. This one is in the best shape of any that I've ever seen."

Onudaka shook his head in amazement. "In Tagana, almost everywhere you go you will find villages and people. A road like this would never become abandoned, and the forests are never this thick anywhere because we've cut all the trees down. It's one of the reasons you don't see many spirits there anymore."

"Tagana was only wilderness when I first came to Okoro with master," said Lu Bei. He hadn't yet returned to book form, which was fine with Turesobei. He could spare the energy for now, since it didn't take much with Lu Bei sitting still and riding with him.

"I thought Turesobei was your master," said Iniru.

"He is."

"So he's your current master. And your original master was..."

"Chonda Lu, founder of the Chonda Clan created me. And he has always been—"

"Lu Bei," interrupted Turesobei, "gets really confused when talking about his master. My kavaru was original to Chonda Lu, and it was used to create Lu Bei. So he calls who-ever wears it his master."

"Well," said Lu Bei, "that's not—"

"It's accurate enough," snapped Turesobei.

Iniru raised an eyebrow but said nothing.

They stopped only for a brief meal and to make camp at midnight. Turesobei had drowsed in the saddle for much of the time. A stone marker lay nearby. Presumably the glyphs on it named the mountain or the monastery, but none of them could read the an-cient zaboko runes. Lu Bei claimed he could read many of the old zaboko scripts, but he couldn't puzzle out any of this one.

Turesobei returned Lu Bei to book form, ate quickly, and prepared for bed. Onudaka and Iniru tried to make small talk with him, but he ignored them. He had nothing to say to them. He hated the world and everything in it. He hated the ones who'd taken his father from him.

Iniru approached him with a small, wet cloth in hand. She lifted it up toward his cheek. "Let me clean the blood off."

He slapped her hand away. "No."

"There's no reason to leave it."

"It reminds me of the vow I made."

"Fine." She turned and stamped away.

In the morning, while gathering brushwood for a fire, Onudaka discovered a small stone shrine hidden just off from the road within a growth of kudzu. He cleared the vines away to reveal a granite arch that rose only four feet. Beneath it was a zaboko statue with large onyx eyes. The figure was seated with his legs crossed in the lotus position.

"Lord Moshinga," Turesobei murmured.

Onudaka nodded. "Help me clear the rest of this out."

Iniru put her hands on her hips and frowned. "We don't have time for that."

"Aye, lass, we do. If this is a haunted mountain, then we'd be fools not to honor the gods before ascending."

Iniru rolled her eyes and looked to Turesobei. His first impulse was to agree with her. But then he thought of the hauntings and a lesson his grandfather had given him about spirits and deities.

"Many people," Grandfather Kahenan had said, "think that they have encountered ghosts or demons when they have merely angered otherwise benign spirits. Always treat spirits with the same respect you would your elders."

Thinking of his grandfather made his heart lurch. He missed the old man more than he'd ever thought possible, and yet he didn't really want to see him again. He didn't want to break his heart and tell him that his son had died.

"No," Turesobei said to Iniru, "as much as we're in a hurry, I think it would be best to honor Lord Moshinga and ask for his blessing and his permission to go on."

"Lord Moshinga departed with the other Shogakami centuries ago," Iniru argued. "I don't think he cares."

"But the mountain spirits must still honor him," Onudaka said. "If we don't do the same, we may offend them."

"I agree," Turesobei said.

Iniru sighed with frustration, pouted, then grumbled while she used her sickle-bladed kama to chop away kudzu. Turesobei pulled weeds. Onudaka swept and dusted. Beneath all the mess, they discovered an intricately sculpted statue standing on a black and white mosaic. With water from a nearby spring they scrubbed the shrine clean.

When they finished, it was nearly noon. Onudaka pulled three sticks of incense from his pack. "This is all I have, I'm afraid."

They knelt together, each with a smoldering stick of jasmine incense. They bowed three times and spoke the Shogakami Prayer to the Great Deities. Then they asked for Moshinga's blessing and permission to travel the mountain road. Finally, they placed what little fruit they could spare before the statue and bowed three more times.

Nothing unusual happened the rest of that day or the next. Though they struggled going uphill, they still moved much faster than they would have if they were cutting through the dense rainforest. The road was clear, and the denekon made good speed.

At dusk on the third day, they reached the monastery. Its condition wasn't as bad as they had expected. The grounds were clean and the gardens maintained. Statues yet stood, though they were worn by time. Some walls had crumbled, but the stones had been piled up in an orderly fashion nearby. The main temple hall was open to the elements in the front, but the architecture within remained intact.

"Someone must live here," Onudaka said.

"Aye," said Iniru, "be wary."

As they rode in closer, they spotted the monastery's caretakers. A group of dusty, redbrown mountain spirits knelt before the main hall and bowed serenely to them. They stood only four feet high, and their bodies appeared jagged and hard, as if someone had carved them from stone. Onudaka, Turesobei, and Iniru climbed down from their saddles and returned the bow.

The spirits grinned sprightly, waved, and then scampered off with surprising speed and agility.

Onudaka scratched his head. "Bless me, but that was odd. And I think we know now who cares for the place."

"And likely who haunts the mountain," Turesobei said, eyeing Iniru.

She bowed her head apologetically. "Forgive me, Onudaka."

"Think nothing of it, lass. I wasn't sure it would get us anywhere to worship at the shrine. Just thought it was proper."

Inside, they found out exactly how good a decision it was. The mountain spirits had stacked fallen limbs for a campfire. There was a store of fresh fruits from the forest, root vegetables, fodder for the denekon, three barrels of water, and a bundle of precious cinnamon sticks.

Turesobei slapped Onudaka on the back. "I think you were really on to something, Onudaka."

"We owe our thanks to the spirits."

"Indeed. We are fortunate."

"Let's hope our luck continues," Iniru said.

As they rested and ate, Turesobei summoned Lu Bei, who darted about searching the temple.

"What are you up to?" Iniru asked.

"You don't like me, do you?" Lu Bei said, frowning.

"I like you just fine. The problem is that I don't trust you."

"Why?"

"Because you are strange and magical. Because you've been listening all this time but were hiding."

"I couldn't manifest. I was nearly dead."

"Still, I don't like secrets and you reek of them."

Lu Bei stuck out his chest and his tongue. "I don't like you either."

"Lu Bei," said Turesobei, hoping to change the mood, "could you tell us the story of Naruwakiru? Perhaps you know a different version than we do."

"Of course, master." The amber fetch flicked one nasty look at Iniru then fluttered down and landed on top of a water barrel. He settled his wings, loosened his neck, and took a deep breath.

"Millennia ago, long before the baojendari came to Okoro, the wrathful storm dragon Naruwakiru terrorized the land. She was the fiercest of all the storm spirits, who have an-gry dispositions anyway, and jealousy of her half-sister, Lady Amasan, had corrupted her. When her wicked priests forged a heart of jade for her using sinister blood rituals, Naruwakiru bound herself to it and carried it in her chest. With it, her power tripled. She captured her sister and imprisoned Amasan within her belly. After that, anyone who would harm Naruwakiru risked harming Lady Amasan. The other Shogakami were not willing to take such a risk.

"But the zaboko hero Tepebono was not afraid of Naruwakiru. He was a temple guard, devoted to protecting Amasan and her priestesses. But more than that, he would do anything to free his lover, the Lady Amasan herself. After—"

"A mortal?" interjected Iniru. "You think Lady Amasan had a mortal lover?"

"In those days, such things happened. Greater and even lesser spirit beings would sometimes take mortals as lovers and companions."

"I've not heard of such," Iniru snorted. "How can we believe this?"

"I have not heard such tales, either," Onudaka added, quietly and respectfully. "But maybe we have missed them."

"I am retelling only what my master learned when he came to this land," Lu Bei said proudly. "I cannot verify the accuracy, but my tales were heard centuries before you were born."

Turesobei gritted his teeth and glared at Iniru. "Go on, Lu Bei. Ignore our doubting companion."

"Hmph!" puffed Lu Bei. "Only because master wishes it. Now where was I? Oh, yes, after a desperate battle fought at the summit of one of Okoro's tallest mountains, Tepebono smote Naruwakiru and cast her down. How he defeated her is a mystery that even legends have not sought to answer.

"But when Naruwakiru died, the energies released ravaged Okoro as if a dozen hurricanes had struck the island at once. Lady Amasan broke free without harm, just in time to save Tepebono from the fierce storms that were pounding the mountain.

"The jade heart fell into the hands of Naruwakiru's remaining priests, who hoped to use it to resurrect Naruwakiru, but the Shogakami priesthood seized the artifact from them and locked it away. It held too much power, power that anyone could abuse, whether they brought Naruwakiru back to life or not."

Lu Bei sighed. "That is, I am afraid, all that I know."

"Other than the bit about Amasan and Tepebono being lovers, it is no different from our k'chasan tales," said Iniru, "if a little more stale in its telling."

Lu Bei snapped his wings out. "I am a diary, not a storyteller!"

"Enough," said Turesobei. "Enough. The two of you will stop bickering at once. Lu Bei, I think it's time for both of us to get some rest."

After another day of riding, they reached the bottom of the mountain and found an identical shrine to the first. They cleaned the shrine and worshiped again.

"Isn't it odd," said Iniru, "that the spirits don't maintain these shrines as well?"

"They'll be overgrown again within a week," Onudaka said. "And I think maybe they leave them like this as a test. We didn't have any hauntings the whole way through, did we?"

Following the map they'd seized from the citadel, they rode through the forest again and ascended another mountain, but on a faint, narrow trail this time. The forest thinned as they went, and they frequently encountered boulders and scree. Twice they sighted rams munching on bits of grass growing between rocks.

By midmorning, Turesobei was starting to feel desperate. "If we don't catch up to them today, I think we should ride through the dark tonight. I need to reach the Storm Dragon's Heart before—"

Suddenly the earth was spinning about him, and strange waves of kenja passed through his body. His vision darkened, and in the midst of the blackness, there glowed an orb of deep green jade with crimson veins running across it. A forking web of lightning spread through the blackness beyond it, revealing dense thunderclouds and a coiling, winged outline. The Storm Dragon's Heart called to him and it felt as if the very pulse of Naruwakiru flowed through him.

Then his cheek began to burn hot as the *Sigil of the Chonda Goshawk* flared to life.

Chapter Thirty-Six

Someone touched him and the vision faded. Turesobei looked up into Onudaka's concerned face. "You all right, lad?"

"We must ride. Swiftly!"

"The glyph on your cheek was glowing," Iniru said.

He didn't like her accusatory tone. "There's no harm in it." He picked up the reins of his denekon. "They're nearing the heart. I think they may have opened the vault already. It's calling to me. It wants me to hurry."

Before the others could voice their concerns, Turesobei urged his denekon into a full sprint. In a mad frenzy, Turesobei raced toward the Storm Dragon's Heart. But after a few minutes, Iniru caught up to him and he slowed a little.

"Are you mad?" she yelled.

"Possibly."

"A little more caution would be wise."

"No time for that!"

"You're certain?"

"I've never been more certain of anything."

"Why does the heart call to you and not us?"

"I don't know."

Iniru cursed and started to ride ahead, but Turesobei overtook her. "Let me lead. I can feel the way now better than you can see it."

"Fine, but you know the denekon can't keep this speed for more than a few minutes. We'll have to slow them to a jog."

With a desolate sigh, he nodded and pulled up on the reins.

An hour later, they spotted the trail leading up to the Storm Cult Shrine. Just outside the cultists had built a corral, and their denekon grazed there, cropping at sprigs of mountain grass. Two sentries stood guard nearby. One ran toward the shrine yelling a warning, but before he could shout more than three words, Iniru zipped an arrow into the base of his skull.

The other sentry nocked an arrow and drew back on his bow. Iniru loaded and aimed much faster, so that they were both ready at the same moment. They released in unison. His arrow whistled over her head. Hers slammed into his throat.

"They'll know we're coming," she said as they leapt off their mounts.

Turesobei shrugged, not caring so long as he reached the Storm Dragon's Heart quickly. He started forward, but Iniru grabbed him by the collar and yanked him back.

"Listen to me," she said, but he was struggling to break free so hard that she could barely hold him much less talk to him.

Onudaka grabbed him around the waist and lifted him off the ground. Iniru put her face right up to his.

"Put me down!"

"Not until she's spoken, lad."

"We do this my way," Iniru growled. "I'm trained for this. You're not. You follow me and do exactly what I say. If you've got ideas, you tell me and we all work together."

His nostrils flared, and he cursed at her. Instantly, she reared back and slapped him. His cheek and mouth stung. Blood trickled from a busted lip.

"Ow! What in the—"

Turesobei shook his head.

He still felt the call for the heart, the desire and urgency, but not as strongly as he had a few moments earlier. He took several deep breaths.

"Better?" she asked. He nodded. "Good. You'll do what I say? Cause you know I'm here to help you. That's my job. Let me do what I've come here to do."

"I-I'm sorry. I don't know what's happening in my head. But I can control it now."

Onudaka sat him down. They exchanged apologies.

"If they're alerted," Iniru said, "then they're not coming out. It may be that, since they weren't expecting danger, they're all too far within to have heard us."

Iniru crept up to the shrine's entrance, a stone gateway carved into the mountain. Like many ancient zaboko buildings, the shrine had been excavated and shaped out of existing rock. Outside the entrance, crumbling statues, a fountain, an altar, and other structures remained. Turesobei knew from his father that the tunnel went deep into the mountain.

Iniru checked the tunnel, then she motioned for Onudaka and Turesobei to join her. The passageway was dark, lit only by a few widely spaced hanging lanterns. Iniru set her bow and quiver down near the entrance. She wouldn't need the bow's range inside. Turesobei suspected she had a dozen weapons more suitable for this, hidden somewhere within all the secret pockets and folds of her bodysuit.

Smaller tunnels and rooms branched off in many different directions. Reaching the vault would be easy, though. They had only to follow the lanterns and the mass of footprints in the dust.

At last the tunnel opened to a massive, dome-shaped cavern. The floor was twenty feet lower than the tunnel, and a staircase led down to it. Iniru, Turesobei, and Onudaka paused and crouched down into the shadows at the top of the staircase.

"The vault is open," whispered Turesobei.

Opposite them, at the top of another staircase, was an arched portal with a massive stone door that had been pushed part of the way open. Zaboko runes decorated the top of the arch. Carved into the door was an imprint where a thin triangle of the appropriate material and bearing certain runes could be placed to make the door open.

In between this second staircase and the first milled two dozen cultists. The scarves they wore to cover their faces in battle hung loosely from their necks. Leather breastplates, thigh guards, and vambraces served as their armor. Broadswords hung from their belts, and a few carried spears.

Iniru sighed. "We can't take out that many on our own, and I don't see any way past them. Perhaps we can wait and steal the heart from them later."

"No," Turesobei said, "we must get it now. If we wait, they might learn how to use it. We don't really know how it works. Might not take long for them to figure it out."

"What if they already know, lad?"

"Then we're in trouble."

Turesobei steeled his nerves and drew his sword. He fumbled his other hand into his spell-pouch. Iniru placed a hand on his cheek and pulled his face around so that she could look him in the eyes. "We cannot fight them all. Are you insane?"

"I'm a wizard."

"So? What can you do against so many?"

"Blind them." He drew a spell-strip from the pouch at his belt.

"What about their wizard?"

"He's not out here, so he must be in the vault."

"Well, how are you going to stop him?"

Turesobei shrugged. "I'll figure something out. No, don't argue. I'm going on with or without you. Now, shield your eyes and get ready to charge them. We'll make a break for the vault and get the heart. We're going to have to face the guards no matter how we do it, so we might as well face them now."

"How long will the blinding last?" Onudaka asked.

"Maybe a minute, depending on how it strikes them."

Iniru groaned and looked to Onudaka. "First we take out any missed by it, then the rest."

"Keep your eyes closed until my signal."

Turesobei stood and walked down the stairs toward the cultists. A few spotted him and murmurs arose.

"I am afraid," he announced, "that you all must die."

Chapter Thirty-Seven

"Get him," snarled a cultist.

Swords rasped as they slid from their sheaths. The men surged forward.

Turesobei continued down the steps, and when the men were all looking at him and were only a dozen paces away, he held out his hand and shouted the activation command.

A blazing white light burst out and blinded nearly all of them. Only a few blinked as it went off. As soon as the burst ended, he sprinted toward the opposite staircase.

Tears streamed from the cultists' eyes. Some backed away, while others grasped at their eyes and stumbled about. Only a half-dozen or so had the sense to hold their weapons up and listen for attackers.

"Attack now!" Turesobei yelled to his companions.

As Turesobei shouldered through the mass of cultists, knocking some aside, he slashed left and right with his sword, scoring a number of light wounds. He attacked just to get them out of the way.

One of the cultists who hadn't been blinded rushed toward him and tried to block his way. But two of Iniru's steel throwing spikes thudded into the man's chest and he dropped his sword. Turesobei shoved him down and crossed the chamber.

He glanced back to his companions as he reached the staircase. Onudaka barreled into three cultists, knocking them down with his staff. Iniru moved in, deftly slashing with her sickle, spilling blood everywhere she went. A cold shudder ran down Turesobei's spine as he realized how deadly she was. And killing, as far as he could tell, didn't seem to bother her. Turesobei actually worried about the men he had just cut.

He raced up the steps to the landing and saw a flash like lightning in the darkness ahead. Turesobei entered a chamber less than half the size of the last, noting the old zaboko runes that adorned the rust-colored walls throughout, runes that had held enough power to keep Grandfather Kahenan from forcing his way into the chamber.

Turesobei glanced at the partially open door and saw the same runes on its inside. If Sotenda and his wizard had left the key in place, he could have simply closed the door and locked them within, but they hadn't been that foolish.

The heart called to him. This was how his father must have felt. Was his father's blood sigil giving him this desire to seize the heart, or had the heart decided to call to him as well? And why did the vision come to some and not others?

In the chamber, two men stood beside a pedestal. One was a nazaboko, a man of half-baojendari and half-zaboko parentage. He had pale skin of a slight grey cast and a medium body frame. Turesobei knew this was Onudaka's brother, because Sotenda resembled Onudaka, only he was much younger. The other man was a baojendari in his late teens. Turesobei recognized him immediately, having seen him at a festival at Noda Blossom Shrine once before.

Gawo Haisero, his counterpart in the rival Gawo Clan.

Both of them looked straight at him. Sotenda held a curved dagger in one hand, a short sword in the other. Yomifano in its scabbard hung from Haisero's waist, but in his hands he held the pulsing heart of Naruwakiru. Their eyes met for the second time since Turesobei has arrived in Wakaro. Haisero was the one he'd seen disguised in Nijona.

Haisero sneered at him and lifted the orb. Turesobei ran forward as Haisero's brow furrowed in concentration. With a crackling burst followed by a boom that shook the whole mountain, a jagged bolt of lightning flew from the orb.

Instinctively, Turesobei struck out with the white-steel sword. The lightning bolt struck the blade, forked in two, and blasted the wall to each side of the vault door.

As the lightning diverted around Turesobei, some of the current on one side smashed into his body and flung him aside. For a moment he blacked out, but then he pulled himself together and tried to stand. His limbs wouldn't obey him. His skin was blistered, and a solid ache dug deep into his bones.

Haisero stalked toward him, but Sotenda grabbed him by the shoulder. "Let's get out of here, Sero!"

"What do we have to fear now that we've got the heart?"

"Much," Sotenda said desperately. Horror gripped his face. "Look at your hand!"

Turesobei followed their gaze and saw the wizard's blistered hand. The energies around the heart were beginning to flicker and surge randomly. Haisero didn't have a firm control of it.

Haisero yelled, "I can't even feel the burns!"

"Your nerves must have been numbed by it," said Sotenda. "We need to study the orb more before we use it. It's one thing to read the sacred texts, another to actually use the techniques."

Haisero glanced back to Turesobei, but Sotenda kept pulling him. "He's not worth it. I promise. I don't even think he can move."

Haisero grinned wickedly and waved to Turesobei. He and Sotenda approached the stairs.

"I could lock him in," Haisero said.

"The door's too heavy to—" Sotenda paused a moment then yelled, "Onudaka! I knew you'd try to ruin my life again!"

The old medic's voice boomed within the other chamber. "You'll pay for what you've done, Sotenda!"

"Not today, brother. Not today!"

A glittering spark struck Haisero in the shoulder. "Ugh!" He stumbled backward. A steel spike was glistening amidst the blood pouring from his shoulder.

Sotenda pulled Haisero away from the doorway. A desperate look gleamed in his eyes. "They've taken out most of our warriors and we can't fight a qengai right now. Summon a small thundercloud. Nothing more. Don't overdo it!"

The young wizard looked dazed as he plucked the steel spike from his shoulder. Nevertheless, he held up the jade heart and chanted. From out of nowhere gale force winds appeared and howled within the larger chamber. Lightning flashed along the ceiling, and moisture condensed from the air and rained down. Cultists screamed and Iniru called Turesobei's name.

With feeling and strength returning to his limbs, Turesobei climbed to his feet, intending to sneak up behind Haisero, but he had to lean against the wall just to walk. Turesobei reached the steps and could see his enemies advancing through the chamber. Onudaka was fighting the winds to reach Sotenda, only he could barely move forward. Iniru was plastered against a wall, face first, struggling to turn around. Sotenda and the sorcerer walked through unaffected. The storm swirled around them, and everywhere they stepped, the storm disappeared. It was as if a miniature hurricane occupied the chamber, and its empty eye followed those who had summoned it.

The two men were laughing. "We can kill them easily," Haisero said, moving toward Onudaka. "They can't fight the winds."

Sotenda stared at his half-brother with a mixture of anger and fear.

Chanting, Turesobei gathered as much of the loose storm energy scattered throughout the room as he could. Using this immense amount of available power, he was able to easily summon a small globe of dark-fire. He flung it out toward Haisero, and the black-flamed globe pierced the storm with no difficulty. Haisero was unprepared to defend himself from the attack. The globe struck him on the side of his face and splattered. The flames went out instantly, but their damage was done. Haisero collapsed, wailing and clutching at his ruined face.

The Storm Dragon's Heart fell from his hand and thunked onto the floor. The storm surged instead of ceasing as Turesobei had hoped. Sotenda grabbed the orb before it could roll away and grimaced as it blistered his hands. The storm's eye began to shrink. Sotenda chanted desperately but couldn't bring the storm under control.

He reached down and lifted Haisero by the arm. The wizard was crying pitifully, muttering, "I'll kill him for that. I'll make him pay!"

Haisero took the orb, turned his remaining, unharmed eye toward Turesobei, and glared. He lifted the orb, but then staggered and nearly collapsed again.

Sotenda drew him by the arm, yelling, "We've got to get out of here! We can kill them later."

Haisero and Sotenda fled up the stairs and out of the temple. The storm slowly faded. As soon as possible, Iniru was on her feet running toward the stairs after them, but then she spotted Turesobei slumped back against the vault door, unable to move on.

"Go on!" he yelled.

She glanced to Onudaka. The old man had sat up, clutching at his head. He was bleeding profusely.

The five remaining cultists began to stand and retrieve their weapons. Iniru had no choice but to stay and defend her injured companions. Turesobei watched in a haze as she downed three of the cultists before the last two fled.

Sotenda probably had a ten-minute lead by now, if he wasn't lying in wait for them. Turesobei doubted that he was. His injury was pretty bad. If anything, he was resting. Unfortunately, Iniru was the only one in any condition to pursue them.

Iniru checked on Onudaka and helped him tear a strip of cloth from the pants leg of a cultist to use as a bandage. His injury wasn't bad, just a scalp wound from where he had struck his head on a rock when the stronger winds had cast him down.

"Not sure I can walk, busted ankle, but I'm all right. Check on the lad."

Iniru bounded up the stairs and crouched beside Turesobei. "You look terrible. What happened to you?"

"Struck by lightning ... they know how to use the orb."

"Really? I hadn't noticed."

He tried to rise. "They're getting away."

She placed a hand on his chest and shoved him back down. "You're scorched and battered. Onudaka is bleeding and can't walk. I have two small cuts and a dozen bruises of my own. We have to rest."

"I've got to get Yomifano and the heart. Haisero's wounded."

"Who?"

"The sorcerer. I know who he is."

"He may be wounded, but he's still conscious and he has the orb. Sotenda isn't hurt and Onudaka claims his brother is quite a swordsman."

"But—"

"We'll get them later."

Turesobei looked into her eyes and prepared his argument. But before he could speak she grabbed his hand and looked deep into his eyes. "We'll get the heart and the sword. I swear I'll do everything I can to help you. But we can't go after them now. They'd just use the orb against us. You know that."

Her eyes melted his resolve. He gave in and slumped back against the wall.

Chapter Thirty-Eight

Turesobei awoke with a start and saw Iniru bandaging Onudaka's ankle. He stumbled over and sat beside them. Iniru tried to smile.

"It's a good thing we didn't follow them. I interrogated one of the men that we'd only knocked out—"

"Wait," he said in confusion. "How long was I asleep?"

Onudaka grinned. "About two hours, lad."

"No wonder I'm so stiff. Go on."

"Well, I found out that they had twelve of their best woodsmen stationed along the trail most people would have taken to get up here. Sotenda and Haisero almost certainly rode straight to them for help."

"Do you think they'll come back here with them?"

"I doubt it, though we'll have to watch out just in case. I think they'll head back to their citadel. Once they find it in ruins, who knows? They may decide to flee elsewhere."

"You sure they aren't waiting right outside with the orb?"

"They're not. I checked. I think their injuries are bad enough that they don't want to risk facing us or using the orb again until they've mastered it."

"So you know this wizard, lad?"

"I do," said Turesobei. He told them all he knew about Gawo Haisero, which wasn't a lot. "He's arrogant. And obviously he's talented. But I don't know why he'd be in this cult and not at home, unless he's securing the heart for the Gawo."

"I can understand how it would help the Gawo," Iniru said, "but how would the Storm Cult benefit from them in return?"

"Sotenda is a visionary and a leader," Onudaka said, "but he has always lacked resources for his plans. So maybe that's it. But I really can't begin to guess exactly what his ultimate plans may be. They might not have anything to do with his professed religion."

"You didn't tell us your brother was a nazaboko," said Turesobei. "I'm starting to think that the heart only calls to baojendari blood, though I don't know why it would, since we came here long after Naruwakiru."

"I'm sorry I didn't tell you about my brother," Onudaka said. "Yes, his mother was baojendari."

Turesobei raised his eyebrows. Normally, nazaboko were created specifically to be servants to their baojendari masters and were placed above all zaboko. It was a practice many clans like the Gawo used. The Chonda had never used nor condoned the practice.

"His mother ran off with my much older father. It was quite a scandal. Sotenda grew up hating them both and blaming them for all the problems in his life. That's why he killed them."

"What?!" Turesobei and Iniru both exclaimed.

"Afterward I put him into a special home for disturbed people, run by Shogakami priests in a rural, outlaw village. He was addle-witted at the time. I had hoped he could get over his problems. But he still holds my sending him there against me. He was a teenager then and stayed there for nearly ten years. It didn't fix him, though. I mean, he's more stable now, but he has greater delusions.

"He started reading ancient histories and fell in love with Naruwakiru. That's what got this all started. I knew when he got out that he was organizing a rebirth of the Storm Cult, but I thought as long as he just dug up old sites and worshiped the Storm Dragon he couldn't really hurt anyone. Then he did start hurting people. His cult is nothing but a band of thugs, thieves, and out-of-work soldiers. I suppose some may be true believers in this nonsense, but who knows, eh?"

Iniru took some rations out of her pack and passed them around. She had also retrieved their canteens. "Our denekon are well," she said. "Those two didn't waste much time getting away."

"Well, Haisero can't control the heart yet, and it's hurting him. We both injured him, too. Pretty badly. Maybe that will keep them off us for a while. Of course, he could come back for revenge."

"Well, Sotenda's scared of me at least," said Onudaka. "He always has been. I'm sure he could beat me in a fair fight, but I don't think he knows it deep down. Somehow he still thinks of me as his much older, much bigger brother."

Onudaka shook his head. "I wish I could've helped my father more in raising him, but he and his new wife had to flee up into the mountains to escape the baojendari authorities ... and to escape zaboko persecution, as well. I knew how to get there, but I rarely had enough leave time to make the trip, and when I did have leave, I wasn't supposed to go anywhere but my home ward in Nobashiki."

After they finished eating, Turesobei remembered something Iniru had said. "What did you do with the soldiers you interrogated? I don't see them anywhere." He thought of the bodies in the chamber, of how coldly she could kill in battle. "You didn't kill them did you?"

Her eyes paled and she looked away.

"I-I didn't mean to hurt your feelings or anything, but ... I just didn't know. And when you're fighting ..."

"What?"

"Well, how can you kill people like that? You're so efficient and it doesn't seem to bother you at all. I worry about every sword strike I make."

"First of all, worrying about killing someone with every attack is ludicrous and will just get you killed. I promise you that your enemy isn't worried about hurting you.

"As for me killing..." She shrugged. "It's what I do. What I've trained for all my life. I simply enter another state of mind and do it."

"That sounds dangerous ... sinister."

"It would be if I killed out of self-interest or for the wrong reason. But against those cultists, what choice did I have? If I didn't kill them, they would kill me. And if we don't succeed, they will kill others. It's not a perfect world, Sobei. Sometimes we do what we must, that's all."

She looked tough, but he thought some of it was just an act. But he didn't know her or any other k'chasans well enough to read their expressions well, so he couldn't be sure. She was a new qengai, just barely an adult, and these cultists and the ones at the citadel were probably the first men she'd ever killed. What must she really be feeling and thinking?

He pondered this while they tended their injuries, released the cultists' denekon into the wild, and mounted their own. He ultimately decided that he just didn't know her well enough to even guess what was in her mind.

"So what did you do with the ones you interrogated?"

Onudaka cringed and Iniru replied coldly, "I broke their wrists and sent them out into the forest without food or clothing. It was better than they deserved."

They took shelter in a cave in the hills, a place where they could hide for a night or two and recover. Turesobei worried that Haisero would return to the citadel and find his father's body in the cellar, but there was nothing he could do about it. And even if they did find it, why would Haisero mess with the body?

They rested all that day and the next before returning to the citadel. Along the way they spent the night at the Moshingan monastery, and again the mountain spirits left them food, brushwood, and cinnamon. A large pot of cinnamon-flavored tea restored some of their spirit. Turesobei had grown up with the finest spices available, but he was certain that he'd never tasted cinnamon this good before.

When they finally reached the ruined citadel, Iniru sneaked in and checked the place out. No one was there anymore, but she concluded that two days ago, Sotenda, Haisero, and their woodsmen had ridden in and stayed for a night. Noboro's body was unharmed in the cellar, just as they'd left it. As Turesobei looked at his father, the blood on his cheek burned, along with the shame he felt. He had failed to achieve anything he'd vowed to his father.

He went to Iniru who was washing her uniform in a nearby stream. "Can you clean the blood sigil off my face for me?"

"You can't do it yourself?"

"I can't bring myself to."

"Ugh. You know, you really could use a bath. You smell foul."

"Thanks. I want to clean this off first, though. I know it doesn't make sense, really, but if I bathed, I might wash it off by accident. Removing it has to be intentional."

Iniru dipped a cloth in the water and rubbed at his face. After a few minutes of scrubbing, she frowned.

"What?"

"Nothing." She retrieved a tiny bar of soap from her pack and washed his face again. She looked worried. "Umm ... Turesobei, it — it's not coming off. I mean, I got the blood off, but there's a crimson stain beneath. The lines are sharp and crisp. It looks like a tattoo."

Turesobei peered at his reflection in the water and saw a perfect Chonda Goshawk sigil on the side of his face. "I've been marked by blood magic. Because of my vow."

"Will it come off?"

"Not until my vow is complete."

"I'm sorry."

"Don't worry about it. I won't."

She looked at him with doubt, but then shrugged. "Why don't we bathe?"

"That sounds like a good idea."

She pulled off the cotton shirt she wore under her uniform.

Turesobei stared dumbstruck for a second, then his face turned so red that the tattoo almost disappeared. He spun around. "Iniru! What are you doing?"

She put a hand on his shoulder. He was quite uncomfortable with her touching him right then. "I thought we were going to bathe."

"Well, obviously not at the same time and in the same place."

"Why not?"

"Because, because it's..."

"Not proper?"

"For one thing."

"There are other reasons?"

"Well, I mean ... you're a girl."

"Really?"

"And I'm a boy."

"I had noticed."

"And ... and..."

Iniru laughed and playfully slapped him on the backside. "You baojendari are such prudes, and no fun at all. What's a little nudity among friends? We are friends, aren't we?"

"Yes, I guess so, but we're not—"

"You'd better go on, Turesobei. Before you say something you'll regret."

Turesobei nodded and started climbing the hill. He heard her slip out of her shorts behind him and step into the water. He couldn't help himself. For a moment, he turned and looked. She had soft fur, nicely muscled legs, round hips, and...

He had to get out of there. So he turned and ran.

Chapter Thirty-Nine

That night, while eating bowls of rice and freshly roasted game Iniru had caught, they discussed what to do next. They had already agreed that until they had rested sufficiently, rushing after Sotenda and Haisero was futile.

"Where do you think they're headed?" Onudaka asked.

"Back to the Gawo, I'd guess," said Turesobei. "Unless you think Sotenda will head back to Tagana instead."

"No," Onudaka said. "Even West Tagana is too restrictive on the freedoms of nazaboko. Unless he's willing to live in the mountains and foster his cult there. But he won't. He has developed a taste for finer things. And unless I misread them, I think maybe my brother has finally found someone on his level. Someone who fulfills a need he has. I think maybe he respects and perhaps worships Haisero."

"Even though he's at least ten years older?"

"Probably fifteen."

"They may be lovers," Iniru said.

Onudaka and Turesobei both cringed slightly.

"What? I know it happens in your society."

Onudaka nodded. "You're right, of course. We just don't talk about it openly."

"That's because you don't practice it openly either. The more fault yours."

"Well, they may only be lovers in spirit rather than in body," Onudaka said. "That would be my guess."

"In either case," said Turesobei, "I'm going to take my father home and then get help in pursuing them. My family could be in great danger from that heart. The two of you are more than welcome to come with me if you wish."

"If you don't mind, I will," said Iniru. "I must see this to the end."

"Me too," said Onudaka. "I feel responsible for the damage Sotenda causes. Besides, I'd like to see this progressive land ruled by the Chonda. I need somewhere to retire to."

On the trek out of the rainforest, Turesobei felt as if his entire being had been dulled. When they reached the bridge, they found bones bleaching in the sun, picked clean by animals and insects, washed by the frequent rains. They said prayers and moved on.

Turesobei rode across the bridge without looking down. His fear had drained away completely. He said little to the others and remained deep within his thoughts, mostly memories of his father. Sometimes he thought about the Storm Dragon's Heart and his vow. As little as possible he thought about the crimson sigil tattooed onto his cheek.

Noboro's body lay strapped to a stretcher that they had fixed onto a denekon's saddle. Knowing he carried his father home didn't improve his mood. He would often stare at the preserved body and imagine his father in life, how he had talked and smiled along the trip. He had come so close to having a relationship with the mysterious man he'd always admired from afar.

Turesobei's heart was heavy, and the only things that lightened it were Onudaka's stories, Lu Bei's fluttering antics, and Iniru. Not anything she did or said but just her presence—all grace, beauty, and power. No one had ever fired his senses the way she did. Of course, they still bickered. Occasionally she picked at him. A few times she was actually playful and friendly, but that would usually end with her being annoyed by something he did or said or by some baojendari mannerism or cultural belief that she found ridiculous or insulting.

And she was always bickering with Lu Bei. So much that he started summoning Lu Bei only when Iniru was sleeping or too busy to talk. He didn't understand why they couldn't trust one another and get along.

After an arduous journey, they at last reached Nijona. The *Little Goddess* hadn't returned to port yet, so they rented a room in the same sleazy hotel as before. Turesobei strengthened the preservation spell on his father's body and went out the next day and purchased a wooden coffin.

He spent most of his time sleeping and preparing a few emergency spell-strips while Lu Bei watched and occasionally clucked his tongue when he thought Turesobei wasn't doing one just so. It was annoying. Mostly because Lu Bei was usually correct.

"I could hardly tell you how to do a spell," he squeaked apologetically when Turesobei suggested he should script one instead. "I'm not a grimoire, much less a wizard. But I've seen so many spells written and performed." He shrugged. "I guess I've just developed a knack for knowing when the marks and gestures aren't perfect."

While Onudaka kept watch for their ship, Iniru investigated the town, looking for signs of Sotenda and Haisero. Eventually, she got the information they needed.

"The cultists sailed east on a small ship three days ago. If your ship's as good as you say, and it arrives soon, then we might catch up to them."

But that didn't work out because a storm delayed the *Little Goddess*, and four more days passed before she arrived.

Iniru sent word to her family that she was continuing onward. She didn't seem worried about them missing her. In fact, she didn't seem to miss them herself, but Turesobei thought that maybe she was hiding it.

Captain Tedeko was surprised to see Turesobei alone, and he clearly didn't trust Iniru and Onudaka. So Turesobei told Tedeko the entire tale of what had happened. Afterward, the captain apologized and said a prayer for Noboro.

"I'm sorry, my lord. I know how you feel. My father was a sailor, lost at sea and never returned."

"Did you know him well?"

"Not really. He traveled all the time just like your father."

Turesobei sighed. "It doesn't seem fair. I was just getting to know him."

"Aye, my lord. It seems that's always the way of it. It hurt me when my father died, mostly for the loss of what I could never have. But my mother and grandmother, they knew him, and it hurt them far more."

Turesobei thought of how crushed Grandfather Kahenan would be, though he didn't think Kahenan would be surprised. He must have prepared himself for something like this years ago. Enashoma would certainly be sad, though not greatly. She knew Noboro far less than even Turesobei did. How would his mother react, though? What would she do? His parents had never been close, but they'd had children together. There must have been some bond between them, however tenuous.

Captain Tedeko provisioned the ship, and they set sail. Turesobei felt glad to be out on the sea with Wakaro behind him. He never wanted to see that land again.

After another full day of rest, he was strong enough to become bored and restless. Since there was little else to do, he began to practice martial arts forms on the deck. Iniru joined him. Though critical of his every movement, her opinions proved insightful. And he could tell she was making an effort to keep her tone gentle.

"After the Crane Stance," she said, demonstrating the technique, "when you go into the Downward Snake, you want to lower your arm a little more with a loose wrist. Carry the arc further, then rise up slowly, smoothly, before striking downward fast. But not too fast. Maintain focus and control."

"That's not quite how my arms instructor does it. He keeps it all at the same speed."

"Well, then he's wasting striking power. Trust me. I've studied all my life with an emphasis on strength and speed. Your instructor follows the formalized method. Nice for nobles getting exercise I suppose, but not the best if you want to fight and win."

Turesobei's first impulse was to defend his arms instructor, but as the words went through his mind, he realized how ridiculous that would be. She was a qengai. Since she would often have to fight alone, her life depended on these techniques even more than a baojendari warrior's. He also thought about how she'd told him he mustn't worry about hurting his enemy or he'd get himself killed. He suspected that he'd be facing more dangers soon.

Turesobei swallowed his pride and looked her in the eyes. Deep, round, and amber with those exotic slitted pupils. He lost himself in her gaze. She was so alluring that his chest constricted.

"Well, don't just gawk at me," she snapped.

He shook himself from the daze and stammered, "I-I ... well ... teach me."

"What?"

"Teach me how to fight! I want to know how you do it. I want to be like you. You barely break a sweat taking out zaboko cultists twice your age. And you're so graceful and beautiful, even when you're fighting, or when you're just walking. I saw some k'chasans out in the street when we returned, and none of them moved the way you do. You're sinuous and..."

He shrugged, having said all the words he could think of to describe her. For once, Iniru looked taken aback. He thought that if a k'chasan could be seen blushing, that she was.

She took up one of his hands in both of hers. Her lips parted and she whispered, "Thank you." He thought her eyes were actually watering a bit. "That's the kindest thing ... I'm honored."

He didn't know what had made it so kind, but he smiled and said, "You're welcome."

Their smiles met. He imagined that streams of kenja connected their souls. Then suddenly, her expression hardened and she dropped his hand. "All right, then. Let's see all the fighting forms you know. I want to examine your sword techniques, too. Then I'll correct you. Once we get that out of the way, I'll show you some exercises you're not likely to learn anywhere else."

"Are they qengai secrets?"

"Nearly, since most everyone else has forgotten them."

"Are there secret qengai exercises and techniques?"

"Of course, stupid. You know, to be a wizard, you can ask some obvious questions."

"A bad habit. I ask things before I can think about them. Iniru, can you teach me any secret techniques?"

"No."

He sighed. "Oh, sorry. Obviously you can't. How else would they remain secrets?"

She said demurely, "Well, I could teach them to you if you met one of two conditions."

"Like what?"

"First, if you became a qengai."

"That's not likely."

"No, it's not. You'd have to train for many years and I don't think you have the temperament for it."

"What's the other way?"

"To become k'chasan, in a qengai family, of course. All k'chasans within a qengai maka are entrusted with secrets if they take and keep certain basic vows."

He knew that a maka was sort of like a family or clan—or was it a village?—but he wasn't sure exactly how it worked. He just knew it was different.

Turesobei laughed. "Well, I could certainly never become k'chasan, since I've already been born baojendari."

She scowled. "You baojendari are obsessed with birth and lineage. Being k'chasan isn't about having fur and tufted ears. K'chasan is our culture, our heritage, and our family connections more so than what we were born looking like."

"I don't understand how that makes a difference."

"If you became a seiwei—"

"A what?"

"A k'chasan mate or companion."

"Oh, right."

"You don't know how it works, do you?"

"Not really."

"A k'chasan's siwo or sawa becomes k'chasan, regardless of race. A siwo is a mate. A sawa is like a close friend, a pledged lifelong companion to you and any other seiwei you have."

"Oh, well I guess I'll never learn any secrets, since there's no chance I'll ever be either one of those."

Iniru's eyes narrowed. Her jaw clenched. Her nostrils flared. Turesobei stepped back in response. She stammered, "You ... you stupid boy! Go to blazes!"

She stomped away.

What had he said? "Iniru! I'm sorry." She turned and glowered at him. "I'm sorry for whatever it was I did."

Her eyes widened and then she huffed and stormed away.

"What about my lessons?" he called out.

"Tomorrow!" she yelled.

Iniru skipped dinner, and Onudaka asked Turesobei what was wrong. Except for a little stretching and basic staff practice, Onudaka had done nothing but rest and work on shaping the amulet he always carried with him. Turesobei explained what had happened to him, and the old man shook his head.

"You need me to explain that to you? I thought you were a wizard."

"Why does everyone always say that?" he replied in frustration. "Just because I'm smart and know how to cast spells doesn't mean I understand everything. And I'm especially dumb when it comes to girls."

"I can see that. And I'm of a mind not to tell you. Best that you think on what she said and figure it out for yourself. Me telling you won't help you learn how to manage it."

"Do you think I should apologize?"

Onudaka scratched through his newly trimmed grey beard. "I haven't a clue. I've never had many long relationships, and things like that vary from person to person. You're on your own, I'm afraid."

He decided not to apologize, not today anyway. Once angry, Iniru was also irrational. He stayed up gazing at Avida the Bright Moon as he rose over the sea. Repeatedly, Turesobei thought about his conversation with Iniru, until he finally gave up.

A while later the obvious conclusion struck him.

A seiwei? Him? And with her?

That was too fabulous to be true! She was everything he could ever desire. She was already a woman even.

But did she desire him as a mate or as a friendly companion? He had no idea. It didn't ultimately matter, though. His family would never allow him to do something like that.

Chapter Forty

The next day, after a terse breakfast, Turesobei met Iniru on the deck for arms practice. He apologized and tried to express his doubts and feelings to her. She interrupted him and said sternly, "I'm sorry about yesterday. I didn't mean it. I was being silly. Come on, let's get to work."

"Really, Iniru, I didn't mean to—"

"I said don't worry about. The moment's gone. It didn't mean anything."

Iniru instructed him as promised, and the lesson was every bit as brutal as he had feared it would be. He wondered if she was exacting revenge on him. Fortunately, he learned a lot. More than he would've gotten from three months of martial arts lessons at home. That made not being able to walk that night much more tolerable.

"Lu Bei, was Chonda Lu ... How was he when it came to..."

The little fetch fluttered down from the rigging over Turesobei's head and landed on the edge of the ship where he tottered for a moment. Turesobei stretched out and caught him.

"Don't fall in! I don't want your pages getting wet again."

"No worry, master. No worry. Water can't usually harm me, in either form. It was only the arrow wound that made me vulnerable."

"You know, now that you mention it, I'd have thought only white-steel could truly harm you."

"White-steel would destroy me quick and for certain, but I'm not a true spirit. I'm a construct. It's different. You'd know if ... never mind."

"What?"

Lu Bei shook his head. "It's one of those things I can't tell you. So, what was it that you wanted to ask me, master? How was Chonda Lu with..."

"Well, women."

Lu Bei giggled and his cheeks turned a dark amber. "It would not be proper for me to give details to you, master. Suffice it to say that he had no problems."

"Well, I'm afraid that I do."

"Why would you say that, master?"

"Iniru. She's angry at me. I said the wrong—"

Lu Bei placed his hands on his hips. "I'll not advise you when it comes to her, not unless you order me to. I don't like her."

Turesobei sighed. "Could you at least try to get along with her?"

"Not unless she apologizes and says that she'll trust me. Maybe then."

A week passed as favorable winds sailed them with speed toward Batsa. They saw neither pirates nor cultists and Iniru drilled Turesobei in martial arts lessons daily. Afterward, Onudaka taught them both first aid and healing. Iniru knew much of the theory already but lacked his vast experience with actual cases. Turesobei knew almost none of it and was glad for the instruction. When they were alone, Lu Bei would regale him with bits of history no one else knew, though he rarely answered Turesobei's questions and avoided a large range of areas, especially those involving Chonda Lu. He also refused to impart any knowledge of wizardry.

After dinner, when darkness settled over the ship, Iniru would sit with Turesobei on the foredeck and talk. Mostly they discussed martial arts and wizardry. A few times they spoke about their lives at home. Slowly, she seemed to forget she was angry with him.

"Iniru," he said one night as they sat watching Avida's light ripple across the sea. "Are you old enough to marry?"

"Yes," she said dubiously. "I *am* an adult, you know."

"Do you have any companions?"

She motioned toward her head. "Do you see any earrings?"

"Well, no." He scowled in confusion. "Wait ... what does that have to do with anything?"

Iniru groaned in frustration. "In my culture, you can always tell when someone has a mate or a companion, a siwo or a sawa, by the earrings they wear. If I had a siwo, I would be wearing a hoop earring on my right ear, and if I had any sawa, they would be represented by triangular studs on the left ear."

"Oh. So why don't you have any sawa already?"

"I just don't, okay?"

"Okay ... but I still don't understand how —"

"Don't baojendari have friends? Don't some couples among you enjoy spending a lot of time together? Do you not help each other when there are problems? This is just like that, only we seal our friendships as well as our marriages with vows and signs."

Turesobei thought of how his parents related to one another. "Seems like there would be a lot of problems between that many people bonded together. What if your mate has a companion that you don't like, you know?"

"That rarely happens to start with, though problems do occur sometimes. This system has been a part of our culture for thousands of years. We're used to it. And if someone wants out, they're free to end their vows at any time."

"Really?"

"Of course. Why stay together and make each other miserable if it doesn't work? Mistakes happen. That's part of the beauty of the seiwei relationship, of having pledged friends as well as a mate. For instance, if you don't get along with the father of your child and he leaves, you still have other dedicated companions to help you along."

"Must be nice. If that's how it worked for us, Awasa could leave me right away and I would be—"

Her ears pricked up. "Who?"

Turesobei blushed and cursed to himself. He'd made a mistake, but then it wasn't really a mistake, because he was going to have to explain that eventually. "My intended."

Her eyes scalded him. "You're engaged to have a siwo ... I mean a wife?"

"Yes, but don't look at me like that. It wasn't my choice. My mother arranged it when I was only three years old, and King Ugara approved it."

"Do you like this Awasa?"

Turesobei shrugged. "I guess so. At least in some ways. She's beautiful, but she's also stuck-up and infuriating. But in other ways, I hate her."

"Well, I'm glad to know this. You should've said so earlier."

"I don't like to talk about it. My parents' marriage was arranged by the king and they didn't like each other. It was a mess."

"Well, seiwei families aren't perfect either," Iniru said monotonously as if she were trying to pretend she wasn't upset. "People are people, after all."

"I guess I might like it if my sister could be my sawa. She's a great friend, and we've always connected well. A sibling could be a companion, right?"

"Of course." She smiled a little and he relaxed.

"Do you have siblings?" he asked.

"Twelve of them. I'm not close with any of them, though. I'm the youngest by five years."

"Wow! What about close friends?"

"I have some good friends, but we're not close enough to be sawa. Don't really see each other that much."

Turesobei sighed and glanced at Iniru furtively. "I wish that you and I could—"

Iniru put a finger to his lips and shook her head. "Don't say that. You know it could never happen. You're a High Wizard in Waiting and you have a fiancée. Besides, why would I want you?"

Iniru stood and walked back to the cabins. Her hips swayed enticingly as she went. Turesobei sighed and watched the moonlight reflecting on the undulating waves. He listened to the whistling of the night breeze through the sail battens. He felt the thump of sailors treading the deck. So many new ideas and emotions swirled through him. He couldn't focus on any single one, so he just let them flow through until his melancholy turned to fatigue and led him to bed.

Without a hitch they sailed into Batsa. Turesobei met the Chonda retainers at the house in the city and saw that Captain Tedeko was paid well, including a hazard bonus due to the pirates. The captain was grateful and wished him the best. They stayed in Batsa only a single night, long enough for Iniru to extract information on the docks. She found out that Haisero and Sotenda had indeed reached Batsa, but getting word on where they went next would've taken time, since Batsa was a city of a million people. So they paid for passage on a barge that transported them toward the Chonda lands.

Once they reached the river port of Dakanuru, they requisitioned mounts and an escort of Chonda soldiers, who all eyed Iniru nervously but quickly warmed up to Onudaka.

As they approached Ekaran, Turesobei reassured his friends. "We are not like other baojendari. I promise. Ask any of these men here. We don't make nazaboko, and we don't oppress our people."

"My lord speaks true," said the zaboko captain who led their escort. "I was lucky to be born here."

"You're still rich nobles," Iniru said.

"Well, I can't change how the world works. If we gave away our power and wealth, other baojendari would come and take it from whomever we'd given it to. That's why we try to do our best."

"I'll believe it when I see it," she said.

"Aye, lad," said Onudaka. "Being from the south, I can't imagine a whole clan as liberal-minded as yourself."

Chapter Forty-One

A messenger had carried word of Turesobei's return ahead, so when they rode into Ekaran, a crowd gathered around them. Zaboko families drew near, hoping for news about their sons and fathers who had guarded the expedition. Lord Kahenan, Wenari, and Enashoma stood among a number of cousins and friends to Noboro. Even elderly King Chonda Ugara and his son Prince Chien waited there with their bodyguards.

With a stern face, Turesobei dismounted. He kowtowed before King Ugara, touching his forehead to the ground. He barely knew the old man, even though he was the High Wizard in Waiting. Perhaps Ugara figured he'd die before Turesobei rose to the position. Ugara's heir Chien was friendly toward Turesobei and had always treated him like an adult. One day, they would be working together.

The king stepped forward. "Rise, son of Noboro, and tell me what has happened."

Turesobei motioned, and a squad of soldiers brought forward Noboro's coffin. They set it down respectfully and Turesobei lifted the lid. "My lord, Chonda Noboro, son of High Wizard Kahenan, returns to Ekaran with his body in my care, his soul in the hands of the Great Deities, his spirit in the abode of our ancestors."

With the ritual words spoken, he added, "He died to save me. Our expedition failed. All except me were lost."

At that, zaboko family members cried out and wept. Some withdrew. Others crowded closer to learn more, but the king's guard ushered them away with promises of soon being told everything they wanted to know.

King Ugara looked down on Noboro. "You have done well with this preservation, Turesobei. A proper funeral will be arranged immediately." His sharp eyes focused on Turesobei. "Now tell me, who are these two people with you? Are they friends to the Chonda?"

"They are, your majesty. Obu Onudaka is a retired medic from the army of West Tagana. Iniru of Yasei-maka is a qengai who has sworn to aid me. Both saved my life more than once. Both helped me to strike down most of those who killed my father and our guards. Two enemies yet remain, but we will get them."

King Ugara raised an eyebrow at Turesobei then turned and nodded to Iniru and Onudaka. "The two of you may rise. You are welcomed to Ekaran as guests of the Chonda." Ugara put his fingers on Turesobei's cheek. "What is this mark you bear?"

Grandfather Kahenan stepped up beside the king. Ugara looked at him questioningly and Kahenan replied before Turesobei could.

"Blood magic, my lord."

"I made a vow, that I would return Yomifano to Grandfather and take the Storm Dragon's Heart. Father drew the Chonda Goshawk on my face with his own blood when I made the vow. It didn't wash off afterward. I failed my vow, and so the mark remains."

Grandfather Kahenan's face creased into a frowning web of wrinkles. Ugara observed this expression and made a vague guttural noise.

"Why have you not completed this vow, Turesobei?" asked the king.

"I tried to, with help from Onudaka and Iniru. We defeated many Storm Cultists, but by using the power of Naruwakiru's heart, the cult leaders escaped."

"Who are these leaders?"

"Obu Sotenda, Onudaka's wayward brother. A murderer and a bandit. A nazaboko. He is their high priest. The sorcerer who wields the heart is Gawo Haisero."

King Ugara clenched his jaw, and his eyes fell into narrow slits. "Where have these two gone?"

"To the lands of the Gawo, my lord. That's our guess. We know they sailed into Batsa."

Ugara looked meaningfully at Grandfather Kahenan then said, "There is certainly much for us to discuss later." He motioned with his hand. "Take the body home and let the family mourn. Turesobei, I will see you in my garden for tea later this afternoon. You will fully brief me then. In the meantime, do not speak to anyone else of what happened."

"Yes, your majesty."

Grandfather Kahenan led a silent procession bearing Noboro's body. The home they carried him into wasn't really his. It was Wenari's, but it was as much of a home as he had anywhere. Once the body was placed on a bier in the main room, Grandfather Kahenan recited the Chonda Prayer for the Dead, followed by an invocation calling down the blessings of the Great Deities. Iniru and Onudaka stood against the back wall as far out of the way as possible.

As soon as the ritual was done, Enashoma ran forward and nearly tackled Turesobei. Tears streamed down her cheeks. "I feared for you the whole time. I had nightmares once you were gone, and I just knew something terrible had happened."

"It's all right," he said hugging her close. "I'm home now, and Father died doing what he loved most."

Enashoma backed away and Kahenan swept him up into a hug of his own. Tears now filled Turesobei's eyes. "I failed you, Grandfather. I lost the sword."

"We will get it back. Do not worry. Besides, I never placed it in your keeping."

"But I made a vow to father—"

"I am aware of that, and it was a foolish gesture for both of you. The magic that marks you is powerful. Noboro had the power of our family, he just never could focus it, at least not until death eased him, apparently." Kahenan sighed. "No good will come of it, but we

162

will do our best to manage what has happened. I am sure you acquitted yourself well."

Turesobei tried to smile, but couldn't. "I learned more from you than I thought. I did well, actually."

"Of course you did. I would not have sent you along had I expected otherwise."

Turesobei looked to his mother. Wenari hadn't greeted him. This surprised him, despite the argument they'd had before he had left. She wasn't paying him any attention, though. She stood over Noboro. Her lips and hands trembled ever so slightly. She wiped a few tears from her cheeks and sighed. Turesobei had no idea what was going through her mind. He stood beside her and took one of her hands in his.

"Mother?"

She looked at him and smiled weakly. Then she kissed him on the cheek and drew him into a hug. "I am proud of you, Sobei. Thank you for bringing him back. My heart will rest better having seen him. I always assumed that he would disappear one day and we'd never see him again, never knowing what had happened. This way is better."

Turesobei looked at her in confusion. She noted the expression and said mildly, "I know what you're thinking. No, we didn't love each other. But we cared in our own way. And we had children together. He was a fine man, and it's a shame that death has taken him so early."

"Aye," said Kahenan as he gazed down upon his son's peaceful face. "He was a fine Chonda. He had the adventurous spirit that so often runs in our clan, and he fed that fire well. It has burned out now, but brightly it burned in his time. We will not forget. My heart is heavy, but I knew for many years this day would come. I am just thankful that his mother went before him."

Lord Kahenan turned to Turesobei. "Go get cleaned up so that we can meet with the king for tea. It is important that we know all that has transpired."

Enashoma had recovered quickly from the shock of Noboro's demise, having always been prepared for him not to come home from an expedition, and not really having known him anyway. Enashoma grasped Iniru's hand. A strange k'chasan and a frightening qengai she might be, but Enashoma didn't mind. She trusted any friend of Turesobei. "You can come with me. We'll get you cleaned up. I'm certain King Ugara will want to meet with you, too."

Kahenan smiled as Iniru was dragged away. "Onudaka, if you will follow me, I will show you to my tower. You can refresh yourself there."

Onudaka bowed. "Thank you, my lord."

Imi and Shurada poured hot water into a stone bathtub set into the floor. They stood there shyly, waiting to attend Turesobei. They well knew that wasn't necessary. He blushed rather furiously as he said. "I'm not getting in until the two of you leave!"

Both of them giggled, and Shurada said playfully, "We've seen you bathe before."

"You have not!" Laughter again as they backed away. Shurada, he noticed, was blushing. His eyes widened. "When?" More laugher. "Tell me!" Both shook their heads and he was halfway tempted to order them, but he couldn't. He would never do that to them. It was bad enough they waited on him and had to suffer his mother. He wouldn't demean them by treating them as if they were anything other than friends helping him out.

Perhaps Shurada sensed this temptation to boss them because she said suddenly, almost in a whisper, "You really should be careful where you bathe. Some places in this town have peepholes."

With that said, the two of them dashed away. He glanced around suspiciously, wondering if there were peepholes anywhere within his bath chamber. He had stone walls all around him except for windows at the top along the two outside walls. He couldn't see anything. He'd bathed in other places. In Kahenan's tower, though a peephole there was impossible. And the training barracks where the other boys in training bathed after practice sometimes. That was the most likely place, he decided.

Turesobei relaxed and stripped. Then he slid into the lilac-scented water. After a few minutes of soaking and breathing in the rising steam, he scrubbed himself off. Then he rested the back of his neck on the edge of the tub and dozed for a while. He woke up and noticed the water was tepid. He ducked his head under and scrubbed. When he came back up, he noticed bits of dust and trash floating in the water. He'd thought he'd cleaned his hair out well several times already, but apparently not. He was perfectly clean now, though, for the first time since he'd left.

Imi and Shurada had also left apple juice and rice cakes out for him. He ate them lying on his sleeping pallet while his body dried. Afternoon sunlight filtered in through the paper-paneled window above him and illuminated his room. Just having the familiar setting around him gave him comfort. He enjoyed his wall-scrolls depicting heroic battles in old Tengba Ren, sorcerous triumphs of his ancestors, and illustrations of the seven planets of the solar system.

After dozing again, he saw the sun descending and knew he should go check on Iniru before they had to meet the king. Languidly, he got up, summoned Lu Bei so he would have someone to chat with for distraction, and then dressed in formal robes. They were a silvery grey, almost a copy of his normal apprentice uniform except for a crimson sash and a Chonda Goshawk carrying a wizard's scroll on the left breast. They were finer made, too. He had only two nicer robes, which were for even more formal occasions.

"Lu Bei, return to your book form. You're coming with me. I may need you."

"Of course, master. Best to always have me around, I should think."

Turesobei dropped by Enashoma's room and tapped on the sliding door. He heard laughing inside so he tapped harder. "Come in," his sister called, and he entered cautiously. As soon as they were in sight, he stopped in mid-step and his jaw dropped.

"Well, what do you think?" asked Iniru, and she spun around to show off her borrowed outfit.

"It's ... it's great."

The two girls exchanged smiles and Turesobei began to fear for his sanity. They were getting along far too well, far too quickly.

"It's one of Mother's old riding outfits," said Enashoma. "Iniru refused to wear proper robes."

"K'chasans never dress like that," Iniru said sternly. "Besides, this is far richer clothing than any I've ever worn before."

The outfit was stunning on her, though it was not as tight as her qengai uniform. The pants were a soft doeskin and the top was silk with loose arms. It made her look dignified. The rust-colored silk brought out the reddish highlights in her grey-brown fur and reflected brightly off the amber in her eyes. Her mahogany mane, which had grown out some over the last two weeks, hung loose, curling back about her ears. Usually she kept it pinned in the back.

Turesobei said timidly, "It really does look good on you."

She smiled girlishly and stared at the floor. "Thanks, Turesobei."

Enashoma's smile vanished, and she chastised Turesobei. "You've been friends with her for how long now and you haven't told her she could call you Sobei?"

"Er, well, it just never came up."

"Call him Sobei," Enashoma said to Iniru. "And if you're a friend of his, you're a friend of mine, so you can call me Shoma."

Iniru laughed. "My pleasure, Shoma. You can call me Niru if you like. And if he wants, tell your brother he's welcome to call me that as well."

Turesobei blushed. He stared at her deeply and said softly, "Niru."

"Sobei," she replied.

Out of the corner of his eye, he saw Enashoma raise an eyebrow. She was quick-witted and it didn't take much for her to figure things out. Or make assumptions that weren't quite right.

"Well," he said quickly, "why don't I show you around? We've got about an hour before we have to meet King Ugara for tea. Shoma, would you like to join us?"

"I think I would." As they left the room, she whispered in his ear. "Are you going to take her to meet Awasa?"

"I don't think that's a good idea. "

"Well, promise I can be there if you do."

He scowled at her, and she giggled furiously.

Chapter Forty-Two

Fully armored guards led Turesobei, Iniru, and Onudaka into King Ugara's formal gardens. Both his companions were amazed by the artificial ponds, streams, and waterfalls spaced throughout the area of carefully tended shrubs, vines, and trees. Four shrines to the Great Deities sat tucked away in four different bamboo thickets. A vermilion gate stood over the start to each path. A gazebo on an island in the middle pond was the main attraction, and they knelt beside a table there and waited for the interview.

After a few minutes, King Ugara arrived along with Lord Kahenan in his official role as High Wizard. Ugara wore a formal silk robe of crimson with a silver goshawk emblazoned on the back. His inner robes were black and white. Kahenan wore his emerald surcoat over a grey robe not unlike the one Turesobei was wearing. Swords hung from the waists of both men. Turesobei and his companions had entered unarmed, as required when entering the king's presence, though he suspected Iniru had at least one weapon hidden somewhere.

No one else joined them, though guards stood all around the garden's edge. King Ugara had heightened the palace's security and put the entire town on watch for Haisero and Sotenda. Once everyone had exchanged formal bows and greetings, servants brought steaming bowls of green tea flavored with jasmine blossoms. Iniru seemed dubious about being served by others. Onudaka was downright frightened. He had never been treated this way in his life.

King Ugara noticed how daintily Iniru sipped at her bowl of tea and how Onudaka was afraid to touch the biscuits they had brought. He smiled warmly, "We do not concern ourselves overmuch with manners here. We expect our guests to eat and converse in whatever manner they are accustomed."

Onudaka blushed and half-bowed. "Thank you, your majesty."

"Think nothing of it. Now, on to business. Turesobei, why don't you tell us what happened? From the very beginning, please."

"About the trip as well, or just what happened to Father?"

"Everything," said Grandfather Kahenan. "Something unimportant to you may be important to us."

"Besides," said King Ugara as he slurped unceremoniously at his tea, "I like travel stories. I don't get to travel myself anymore."

Turesobei thought of the adventurous Chonda spirit and decided Chonda Lu's descendants carried his legacy well.

Before he could begin telling an accurate description of the journey, though, there was another matter, something King Ugara knew nothing about. "Grandfather, Lu Bei..."

"Ah, yes," said Lord Kahenan. "I don't think you need trouble the king about him..."

"Perhaps I should be the one to decide that, old friend," King Ugara said. "Who is this Lu Bei?"

"A pet of Turesobei's," Lord Kahenan began. "A most unusual construct of sorcery. Very difficult magic that Turesobei was able to achieve using the text from an old book he found. He quite surprised me with it."

Fumbling, Turesobei added to the lie, "The creature turned out to be a little help to us along the way, your majesty. Nothing of great importance, though."

"I see," said the king. "Go on then."

Turesobei began with his description of arriving in Batsa and then of boarding the *Little Goddess*. He told of sailing and getting to know his father better, which made Kahenan smile. He told of the pirates and their decision to sail through the demon-haunted pass, and he didn't leave out a single detail of the fight.

"And I swear that it's all true."

"Sobei!" Kahenan exclaimed, beaming with pleasure, "you did exceptionally well. I am heartened that I made you prepare a demon-banishment beforehand. I almost did not."

"I'm grateful, Grandfather. In fact, I used nearly all the spells you had me script in advance."

"Then you learned an essential lesson about preparation and survival. It is the most important lesson a wizard should learn beyond the basic techniques of casting."

King Ugara seemed delighted with the story as well. "The future of the Chonda is well in hand. Our next High Wizard will certainly exceed our current's considerable capabilities."

Turesobei blushed, even more so when Kahenan said, "You are right, of course, your majesty. I could not have managed what Sobei did when I was his age. I am hard on him, but it is only because he is obviously far more talented than anyone else."

To spare himself further embarrassment, Turesobei returned to his story and told of waking up in Wakaro and resting before their departure. He covered in detail how he'd spotted someone following them and how the Storm Cult had ambushed them. "I was unconscious when I hit the water, so my body was relaxed. I probably would've drowned after that if not for Onudaka."

Onudaka shook his head. "It was sheer luck, my lords. Nothing grand on my part. He fell right near me. I plucked him out and tended his arrow wound. Nothing to it. Something I've done a thousand times."

"Then Onudaka helped me back up the cliff."

"I was tracking down my brother, Sotenda, to stop him if I could."

"That was when they met me," Iniru said.

"Your Sacred Codex sent you to help them?" King Ugara asked.

"Yes, your majesty. To help a young baojendari rescue his father, to help an old zaboko medic oppose his brother, and to aid them against the Storm Cult. That was the directive I was given."

"And you think this mission is not yet complete?"

"The leaders of the cult remain. Besides, Turesobei and Onudaka are friends, and I won't desert them until I've seen them through this."

"That is well," said the king.

"You believe in the Sacred Codex, your majesty?" Iniru asked.

"I have never seen reason not to."

"And you also trust that I'm telling you the truth."

"Is there a reason I should not trust you?"

"No, your majesty, none at all."

"Good. So what happened next?"

Turesobei drew in a deep breath and continued. "We closed on the cultists' citadel, but we encountered their guardians, the Bogamaru Sengi."

Grandfather Kahenan's eyes drew wide. "How on earth did Haisero bind them? He is only an apprentice. I could not manage such a feat after a year of preparation."

"He used crude blood magic and he stole the Bogamaru Regiment Statue to do it."

"That is still quite a feat."

"The spell was messy. I broke it easily. He is talented, though. Strong but not diligent, I would say. I fear he intended to use the sengi as an army against his enemies."

Turesobei went over how they befriended the sengi and got their help in attacking the citadel. With tears in his eyes, he struggled through how his father had died to save him.

"He loved you more than he desired the heart," Kahenan said solemnly. "He was a good man, though misguided."

Then they told all the rest about how they had assaulted the cultists at the vault and barely escaped alive.

"At least you wounded the bastard," King Ugara growled. "This is just what we need, the Gawo wielding a super-weapon." He shook his head. "Well, I am very impressed with you, Turesobei. I may have more questions for you later. But for now, I need to think on all of this and speak with my advisors."

"What should I do now, my lord?" Turesobei said. "I want to continue after Haisero."

Grandfather Kahenan said, "You are going to rest and then I am going to examine this mark on your cheek. As for chasing after the enemy, I do not know what task I might give you. You are, after all, only an apprentice. We have trained wizards and soldiers to deal with such problems."

"But this is my problem! It's my vow that must be fulfilled. You can't tell me I'm not going to help, that I can't finish what I started!"

"I will tell you whatever I wish, and you will obey!"

Turesobei looked to the king with desperation, finding no help at all. "You will do,"

Ugara said with a frown, "as your master desires. For now, just be patient. We have to sort this matter out. Divinations should be made, plans drawn up. If Haisero is with the Gawo now, we cannot simply charge after him. That could easily start a war. Rest for now and we will decide your role in this. I promise that we will give you as large a role as we think is appropriate."

"What about my friends, my lord?"

"They are free to do as they wish as long as they act responsibly and realize that an action against the Gawo by them could bring war on us."

King Ugara stood and nodded to them. All of them bowed low. Grandfather Kahenan rose and the two men departed. Once they were gone, Turesobei cursed. "It's not fair at all."

Onudaka patted him on the arm. "It'll work out. Be patient."

"Aye," said Iniru. Her expression showed that she felt sorry for Turesobei. She was probably sorry that he was just a boy. It was clearer now more than ever that in the eyes of his people he was not yet a man. It was probably clear in her eyes now, too.

"We need rest," she said, "and after your father's funeral, I can start scouting around and see what I can find out. If I don't want to be seen, no Gawo will detect me. Your family will come around, I think. Especially since that tattoo is not likely to come off unless you play a part in avenging your father's death."

Turesobei nodded, but sulked nonetheless. He didn't have her optimism; he knew how the clan worked. Adolescents were simply not allowed dangerous missions. They had made one exception for him already and it had nearly gotten him killed. They couldn't risk losing their next high wizard.

The traditional baojendari funeral for Noboro began just before dark on the next evening. Baojendari guests wearing stark white robes and crimson ribbons massed within the funeral garden. Behind them stood a few dozen zaboko wearing white robes, those few who cared to see off a baojendari adventurer who'd led zaboko guards to their deaths in a faraway land.

Dark clouds gathered on the horizon, forming what they expected to be a typical rainstorm. Colored paper lanterns hung in the trees all around. Their flames flickered as the lights swayed in the mountain-descending breeze. Noboro's body, draped in a red shroud, lay atop a wooden platform. In the tower's center were mounds of brushwood, straw, and cedar branches. Surrounding the tower, Shogakami priests in robes of autumn gold chanted prayers for the dead to the beat of thunderous drums.

The drum rhythms picked up, and a sword dance began. The dancers whirled. Their flowing ribbons snapped behind them as they danced. Twirl and stomp, snap and glide. And after several minutes they finished with one great stomp.

King Ugara stood and gave a speech. He praised Noboro's accomplishments and wished him well on his journey through the afterlife.

Turesobei shed no tears during the funeral, though others who had known his father did. All his grieving was done. The funeral, in fact, brought him relief. He was happy that his father had received the proper rites after he'd worked so hard to see him back home. The journey to and from Wakaro was complete, even if Yomifano and the Storm Dragon's Heart remained with Gawo Haisero.

High Wizard Kahenan stepped forward with a flaming brand. "And now," he announced, "I shall send this man of the Chonda, my son, into those realms walked only by the dead. We wish him well."

Kahenan placed the torch into the kindling beneath the tower and stepped back. A choir of young maidens sang a mournful chantey, followed by a rousing victory anthem sung by a group of young warriors. The Shogakami priests said their final prayers to the Shogakami and the Great Deities. Then the ritual was done.

Most people stood and watched the fire burn. Very few left. Funerals such as this didn't happen often. Noboro was a knight of the clan and the son of the High Wizard, and therefore ranked high among the nobility. No expense had been spared. But soon, clouds covered the sky above so that the grey column of smoke looked like a pillar supporting them. A strong breeze began, and tiny drops of rain pelted the earth. The rain couldn't stop the cremation, though. The body and the wood had been soaked with oil.

As the rain fell harder, people began to depart. Turesobei stood beside Enashoma and Wenari. Nearby Kahenan, King Ugara, and Prince Chien were sheltered under a set of umbrellas. According to tradition, neither the king nor the prince could leave until the body had burned entirely. Servants brought the rest of the family umbrellas, and Turesobei invited Iniru and Onudaka to join them. Neither spoke, but simply stayed nearby to give Turesobei comfort.

Wenari cried gentle tears. Enashoma snuggled up against Turesobei. He put his arm around her and hugged her warm body. Out of the corner of his eye he saw Awasa and her parents departing the funeral.

Peals of thunder rolled across the distant hills like drums of the gods. The rain fell harder, pouring down across them, washing away their grief. The pyre burned and the ashes of Chonda Noboro washed into the ground while his essence rose into the dark sky. His body returned to the earth, and his soul began its journey into the mysterious lands of death.

Chapter Forty-Three

Turesobei sat across from his grandfather in the tower workroom.

"Now," said Lord Kahenan. "Tell me what you had to leave out for the king. What part did the fetch play in all this?"

"Why didn't you tell him the truth about Lu Bei?"

Kahenan smiled slightly. "Our king has many responsibilities. It is not always best to trouble him with complicated matters of wizardry that do not directly affect the welfare of the people or his duties as a ruler. I did not think it was worth the effort to explain it all to him. Not at this time."

"Lu Bei ... he didn't really play a major part in it, though he assisted along the way. Certainly made me feel better to have him along. But through a significant portion of the trip, he was injured. When we were ambushed ... an arrow that would have struck me struck the book instead and nearly destroyed him."

Kahenan seemed disturbed but said nothing.

"Luckily I was able to revive him with help from the Bogamaru Sengi." Turesobei went on to describe the procedure in detail.

"Again, I am proud of your efforts. It seems you have paid far more attention than I thought all these years. I fear what would have become of our future if the fetch had perished."

"You really think that he's that important?"

"An object of Chonda Lu's returning from the past? This has happened for a purpose. I have no doubt of the diary's importance. Besides, I know things you cannot."

"And you're not mad at me?"

"Why should I be?"

"The diary was nearly destroyed."

His grandfather smiled. "I am merely thankful to have you back. I could have lost you as well. Artifacts, no matter how powerful, are not as important as people."

The rainstorm that began during the funeral worsened into a torrential thunderstorm. Hail, lightning, and gale-force winds pelted Ekaran and all the lands of the Chonda. The storm's brutality waxed and waned, but the dark roiling clouds never moved away. It was as if a small hurricane had been anchored to Batsakun.

Gusting winds ripped tiles from rooftops. Limbs fell onto houses. Trees were uproot-ed. Glass windows shattered. Paper windows tore. Low-lying places flooded. Many zaboko near rivers and lakes had to abandon their homes. Word filtered in that the Taba River had swallowed the docks at Dakanuru, and dozens of boats had sunk. Thousands of people lost homes. Dozens lost their lives.

During the first day, Turesobei ran outside during an ebb in the storm, accompanied by Iniru and Onudaka. He carried a pack over his shoulder and kept the hood of his oiled rain cloak tightly pulled over his face. He walked behind Onudaka to keep out of some of the wind, but one gust still knocked him over.

Drenched despite the cloak, he banged on the door of a quaint, three-story townhouse. It was typical of most of the zaboko houses in Ekaran. A lean zaboko woman opened the door and stared at him with surprise. No one else was out. And no baojendari noble had likely ever come to her house before. She clearly recognized who he was, though.

She bowed. "Can I help you, my lord?"

"Can you please let us in? The weather's terrible."

"Of course, my lord, of course. Please forgive me." She led them in to a sparsely deco-rated main room. Several children were running about playing, but they stopped dead in their tracks and backed away when Turesobei and his companions entered. An older woman, a grandmother he assumed, and two older daughters came into the room and bowed down low.

Turesobei removed his coat and hung it on a hook on the back of the door. He intro-duced his companions and accepted the woman's offer for tea. One of the daughters scur-ried off after it immediately.

"You are Fodoru Rimei, correct?"

"I am," said the woman, forlornly. She glanced at him miserably. "You were there when my husband..."

"I was." Turesobei waited until the daughter returned and asked her to sit and not get anything else. "Is this all of your immediate family?"

"All that live here in Ekaran right now."

"Captain Fodoru, your husband, served with my father many years. I know that must have been hard on all of you."

"He was a wandering man," she said, staring off toward the corner. "I guess I'm a loner. Our arrangement worked for us. But I'll still miss him." She shook her head. Tears had welled in her eyes. "Gods, I knew this would happen someday. I only hoped all the chil-dren would be older."

Turesobei reached into his pack and drew out a bundle of items. He stepped forward, half-bowed, and reached the packet to her. She gazed at in wonder. "These are the items he carried with him. I couldn't bring home anyone but my father. But I made sure to bring home the effects of every man that served with him."

With surprise she unwrapped the packet and found a scarf that Fodoru had always

172

worn around his neck, his Chonda insignia, a medal of merit he'd won in training, and a carving of a small bear that he'd attached to the inside of his breastplate, over the heart. Rimei drew this last object into her hands, kissed it, then held it against her cheek. She sobbed.

The grandmother spoke. "You have brought fulfillment to my daughter. We are indebted to you, my lord."

"Fodoru was a good traveling companion. I didn't know him long, but in that time I learned many things from him. He saved my life, and who knows how many times he and my father probably saved each other's lives."

"Tell me how it happened."

Turesobei drew in a deep breath and told her as much of the story as he could. King Ugara and Grandfather Kahenan had told him not to give out details about the Storm Dragon's Heart.

Onudaka said, "I know it's hard, madam. I was a medic in the army for many years. I've seen so many die, most with far less dignity than your husband received. I could tell from his wounds that he fought and died well. And Turesobei here has done more than any lord I've heard tell of to bring these items back to you."

"Thank you," she said to him. She turned to Turesobei. "I'll always be grateful to you, my lord."

"That's not quite all of it," he said. He drew out a pouch filled with a hundred coins and a bank note for three thousand jade.

"That's a small fortune, my lord! I can't accept that kind of money."

"Wasn't my decision," he replied with a smile. "My father arranged it with Fodoru years ago to take care of you if something ever happened to him."

She looked at in wonderment, all of them did. But she couldn't seem to find anything to say.

"Will it be enough?" Turesobei asked.

She chuckled a bit. "Aye, my lord. It should clothe my grandchildren."

"Good. If it's not, just send word to me and I'll see what I can do for you. In fact, if you ever need anything, just come to me. Who's your warder?" The warders were baojendari in charge of each section of the town and were the immediate administrators of zaboko affairs. It was a throwback to the overseers in the days of slavery.

She named the man and Turesobei said, "I'll talk with him and see that you are treated fairly. I'll tell him how you came about the money, too, so he won't be suspicious."

"Thank you, my lord. He's a fair man, to be sure, but he isn't a trusting one."

"If you ever have trouble with him, just send a note to me and I'll see that the problem gets fixed."

She thanked them profusely and they finished drinking their tea. She showed them to the door. "I would talk longer, but I have other families that I must visit."

When they reached the next home, Iniru pulled him back for a second. He could barely see her face through the driving rain. "You're a good man," she said.

"Are you sure I'm not a boy?"

"No boy would do this. Nor most men, either, for that matter."

While Turesobei and Enashoma watched, Iniru sharpened all twenty weapons she carried with her: the two sickles, sixteen steel throwing spikes and stars, and two stilettos. Then she started pacing Turesobei's room and glancing toward the window. Rain and wind lashed against the closed bamboo shutters and the glass pane. Lightning flashed, thunder boomed. Every so often hail would pelt the tile roof.

"You might as well relax."

Iniru stopped and scowled at him. "It's not going to stop. You know this is Haisero's doing."

Turesobei shrugged. "Maybe he's only worsening an existing storm."

"I doubt it."

"He couldn't have mastered the heart that quickly."

"You told me he was talented and that they talked about a text that told them how to use it. They've had it for weeks now. We also know that Haisero doesn't mind taking risks with magic."

"Well, when we meet with Grandfather Kahenan this afternoon, we'll find out for sure."

"Is Onudaka going with us?"

"He said he wouldn't unless we needed him. He plans to keep helping the medics. A lot of injured people are coming in."

"I don't suppose Grandfather would let me come?" Enashoma asked.

"You can try if you like, but he'll probably just kick you out."

"Hmm," she said, scratching her cheek and staring at Iniru, "I think I'll try anyway."

Iniru paced again. "Sobei, have you not tried yourself to use magic to determine the origin of the storm?"

"Have you seen me try? Honestly, I've barely been awake when you're not around."

Glancing toward the door with a mischievous look on her face, she said with a snicker, "I had thought you might be sneaking off to visit your intended when I wasn't around."

"Yeah right," Turesobei said. "Like I'd do that."

A high-pitched voice from the doorway said, "Ahem."

It figured that Awasa would be determined enough to go through the storm if she wanted. She strolled into the room with her attendant Marumi and her young guard Zaiporo in tow. Zaiporo hung back at the doorway, looking uncomfortable. She wore an elegant silk dress with elaborate floral patterns. At one time, the dress might have stunned Turesobei. Now, it only seemed pointless and confining. Not surprisingly, mud stained the bottom.

Iniru and Awasa stared at each other. "So," Awasa said haughtily, "this is the k'chasan

174

tramp you've been hanging around with. She's hardly human."

Iniru's eyes flared, but Turesobei responded first. He stalked toward her. "You take that back! She is not a tramp, she's my friend. And she's a better human than you'll ever be."

"My mother may seek to annul our engagement. I hope she does. You being around such people ... It's distasteful."

"Fine by me. That would be a relief."

"I suppose you're going to run off to the forest with her afterward."

"I'd rather do that than marry you. But Iniru and I are not like that."

"Why should I believe you? You clearly can't be trusted anymore."

"Awasa," Enashoma said, "be reasonable. If Sobei says it's not like that, then you know it's not. He never lies."

Awasa glowered at Enashoma then turned back to Turesobei. "I didn't receive a letter from you."

"You said you wouldn't read any if I sent them."

"I wouldn't have, but you still should have sent one. It was the proper thing to do. It would have shown that you are still devoted to me. That you are not off with this tramp doing gods—"

"That's enough," Iniru said. "Go be jealous somewhere else."

"Or what?"

Iniru drew one of her blades. "Or I cut your throat."

"You wouldn't dare."

Marumi gasped and backed up against the wall. With a hand on the hilt of his sword, Zaiporo stepped forward and placed himself between Iniru and Awasa.

"I could escape them easily. And Turesobei would be welcome to come join me. I'd rather marry him than let him suffer a lifetime with you."

Awasa fumed and looked as if she might scream at any moment. Iniru put an arm around Turesobei. "Don't you have games to go play, little girl?"

"You're not much older than me," Awasa spat.

"Among my people I'm an adult already. I am free to marry. I could take Sobei," she emphasized his casual name which Awasa didn't use, "as my siwo, as my mate, right now."

"He's betrothed to me!"

"So? What do I care? Your mother's arrangements don't matter to my people."

Awasa looked as if she would slap Iniru but then clearly thought better of it. She closed on Turesobei. Oddly, their faces had never been so close before. "Turesobei, I don't expect you to be tricked by her deceitful nature."

He shrugged helplessly. "Well, she is nicer to me than you are. A lot more interesting, too."

Awasa slapped Turesobei hard across the cheek. Iniru's arm swept forward, but Enashoma caught her wrist and held her back. "It's not worth it," she said.

Awasa stared at him angrily. Tears welled in her eyes. Then she spun around and stormed out with her shaken handmaidens in tow.

Enashoma released Iniru's wrist. "Sorry I stopped you."

"No, you were right." Iniru eyed her closely.

"What is it?"

"You have amazing reflexes."

"Thanks."

"You could be a qengai, you know."

Enashoma blushed and smiled. "Really?"

"Definitely. That is, with about ten years of intense training."

Enashoma's face fell. "Oh."

Iniru patted her on the head and was about to say something further when Turesobei moaned. "Thanks for your concern."

Both turned to look at him. He was holding a hand to his lip to stop the bleeding.

Iniru looked at him and tsked. "It's just a busted lip from a dainty little girl."

"Well, it still hurts."

"I've seen you suffer worse. That's just your pride that's stinging."

Enashoma got a hand cloth and dipped it in water. She dabbed the blood away and made him hold the cloth against his lip. Then she traced the tattoo with her finger.

"Stop that!"

"It worries me."

"It's my vow. It doesn't concern you."

"Fine," Enashoma huffed. She stamped over to the cushions in the corner and plopped down.

"You do have a way with women," Iniru teased.

"I've noticed," he mumbled. "Niru, what you said about running off—"

"Don't get your hopes up. I was just trying to give her a good scare. She really likes you, you know."

"Whatever."

"It's true. Trust me, I can tell. But she thinks she owns you. That's your biggest problem. She's a bit high-strung, but maybe if you keep growing a backbone you can cure her of that."

"How?"

"Stop looking at her like a lost puppy for one thing. She's too used to being adored."

Turesobei shook his head and sat down near Enashoma. "It doesn't matter. I'm tired of her anyway. She's boring and she's the most irritating female on all the Earth."

"Not me?" Iniru asked.

"You're irritating in a different way."

"I see. What about Shoma?"

"Yeah, Sobei, what about me?"

"You've never irritated me that much and you know it."

"I'm going to have give you pointers, Shoma."

Enashoma grinned mischievously. "I'd like that a lot."

Turesobei moaned. "You two will be the death of me."

"Nonsense," Iniru said. "Awasa's more likely to kill you."

Chapter Forty-Four

Grandfather Kahenan hadn't been out in the storm, but Turesobei would have thought that he'd sat out in it for hours judging from the mood he was in when they arrived at his tower. He opened the door for them, frowned at Enashoma, grunted, and motioned for them to follow him up into the workroom.

"This is where you work?" Iniru whispered to Turesobei as she looked around. Enashoma was doing the same. She had only been up this high in the tower a few times before.

"I practically live here, and I'm thinking about moving in. One day, this will be my tower. If I don't—" He glanced at Kahenan and hushed.

"It's nice here," Iniru said. "Though it reeks of magic."

"Well, what did you expect?" He paused. "Wait, how do you know it reeks of magic?"

"I can sense kenja disturbances and gatherings."

"You didn't tell me that!"

"You didn't ask."

"Oh. Well, thanks for telling me."

"Thought you should know."

They entered the workroom and Iniru looked around appreciatively at all the books, scrolls, tables, wall charts, and diagrams. Turesobei knew it was a lot to take in all at once. It was a cozy room, with its bamboo floor, cushions, teak tables, hanging vines trailing from pots near the ceiling, trees and shrubs, painted screens.

"Did the storm let up?" Iniru asked.

The storm was beating against the shutters but not as loudly as at Turesobei's home.

"No," Kahenan said. "I think it is getting worse, actually. The tower is shielded by various charms. Come, sit down."

He offered them cold tea, which they declined.

"So," Turesobei said, "is the heart causing this storm?"

"You know that it is. Use your brain, Sobei."

Turesobei was stunned for a moment, and then he dipped his head and apologized.

"No, no. I am sorry for snapping at you. I am under a lot of stress right now. And I'm tired. I was up all night working location spells and conducting divinations."

"Why didn't you call me in? I am your apprentice."

"I called in Yurika, Etera, and Nokusada for help. You needed rest."

"The other wizards in the clan," Turesobei explained to Iniru. He frowned and said to Kahenan, "I still could have helped."

"Oh, you are going to help all right. That is why you are here now. The others are resting. I used them for what best suited their talents. Now I am going to use you for what you do best."

"Scripting?"

"Indeed."

"I could help locate the heart if you haven't yet. I've seen it. I've felt its power."

"So have I, Sobei. Or did you think that when I went out there with your father that it did not call to me, too?"

Turesobei's eyes widened. "That's why you didn't go! It's been calling to you all this time. Like with me and father!"

Kahenan sighed. "Yes, though it seems I can control the impulses better. I suppose due to years of meditation."

"Why did you send me if you knew it would call to me?"

"Your father needed a wizard. He also needed with him someone he cared about deeply, a strong blood tie to hold him back from giving in completely to the heart. It is a powerful artifact, and I am not sure of all it can do. I fear that it could possess a man entirely."

"Then that could have happened to me."

"Indeed. But if anyone among us could withstand the heart, it is you, Sobei."

"Me? But you are far more powerful than I am, master."

Kahenan chuckled. "Knowledgeable? For now. But more powerful? Hardly, and I am old, too. That heart would burn through what life force I have left rather quickly. Too much power for an old man like me. And I do not have the natural strength of will that you do. I have boosted mine through years of study and meditation, but an old man has less to live for and is more likely to give up."

Turesobei thought on what his grandfather said, but he didn't really believe him. "I don't think my will is that strong."

"It is," Iniru said. "You don't always use it, but when you're in danger, it kicks in."

"I agree," said Enashoma who'd been so quiet that Turesobei had forgotten her. "When you want something enough, it's impossible to distract you."

"They are correct," Kahenan said. "Your will is like iron. And your aspect is the opposite to that of the Storm Dragon's Heart. Your power is calm and centered, yet no less persistent."

"I don't feel that way."

"That is because you are a teenager. Your emotions rage and your identity wavers. This is natural."

"Couldn't it respond to that?"

"Perhaps. All of this is a risk, Sobei. I am certain of very little."

"We should never have freed the heart."

179

"The heart wanted to be free, and I think its power has been growing over the years. It would have found someone else to free it eventually. Better now when we can try to keep it in check. At least that was my plan. I told King Ugara to send more people with Noboro, but he did not believe me."

"I guess he does now," Iniru said.

"All too well. And I fear the heart must be with the Gawo."

"You can't detect it?" Turesobei said.

"Not at all. I have tried but the storm is so filled with kenja that my location spells have been ineffective. It is almost as if the heart, when it summons a storm, expands into the storm itself. But we will find it. We must, for King Ugara is going to gather the clan to ride against the Gawo."

"Out in the storm?"

"What other choice do we have? They will not expect us and they cannot see us coming."

"An army might could make it through the storm," Iniru said, "but it would be hard and many lives would be lost along the way."

"Yes, and we must hope that when they see us coming that Haisero cannot focus the heart's power against us without releasing the storm."

"So if all this is planned," Turesobei said, "what am I here for?"

"To scribe spells of protection against the storm's elements."

"How many?"

"As many as you can."

"I've never done one before."

"I will show you. I am going to make more powerful ones to give the commanders, myself, King Ugara, Iniru, Onudaka, and you."

"Why us? Are we going to go with the army?"

"I do not want you to, but I fear you must. If we capture the heart, you must take it, Sobei."

"Why not someone who isn't a wizard, who won't be tempted to use it?"

"Because I think that Naruwakiru's heart will kill anyone who touches it who has not been called by it."

"And you wouldn't dare risk it?"

"It would corrupt me or kill me, I am certain. You are the one destined to take the heart. I have known this since the moment it first called to me. You are the only one who could have the talent and willpower to wield it safely."

"Should I go and scout ahead?" Iniru asked.

"No. We have scouts who know the Gawo out already."

"I am certain that—"

"You are better than them? I have no doubt. But I need you to stay by Sobei's side, if you do not mind. I need you to protect him. In some ways he is powerful, in others he is quite vulnerable. And tonight, Shoma, I want you to stay here with them as well."

Her face lit up with a broad smile. "Of course, Grandfather. What should I do?"

"Help Turesobei with whatever he asks. He must work hard, and if he overextends himself, you must care for him."

"What will you be doing?" Enashoma asked.

"After I show Turesobei the spell and see that he is doing it right, I am going to sleep for a long time."

"When is the army moving out?" Turesobei asked.

"Two days. They are preparing already." Kahenan stood and yawned. "Now, let's get to work."

The *spell of storm guarding* was more intricate than most of the spells Turesobei knew already. It required several complex runes because it needed to guard against rain, hail, wind, and lightning. Obviously the spell couldn't fully protect anyone, but it could greatly improve their chances of surviving something like a nearby lightning strike, maybe even a small direct one. Of course, those Kahenan had drawn gave far more protection because his skill was greater.

When Turesobei had adequately drawn two, he took a break and ate dinner. Kahenan looked over them and pronounced them effective, if not perfect. "Good for first tries. Now, I am off to bed. When I wake I must work on a shielding charm that can dampen the storm in a small location."

"Is that possible, master?"

"I think so, but I am not certain. If it works, it will not work for long. I have not the power to fully counter Naruwakiru's heart."

"I can't imagine how Tepebono slew her in the first place if that's just her heart."

"Tepebono was much like you, I think. Besides, love motivated him, and that is the most powerful force in the world."

During his breaks, Turesobei chatted with Enashoma and Iniru. Enashoma marked sheets of paper with their grandmother's magic brush and folded them into origami cranes and bats. She would then send the little paper creatures flying around the room. This entertainment wasn't really aimed at Turesobei, who had seen it dozens of times, but at Iniru. Her delight in it irritated Turesobei for reasons he didn't understand, but couldn't control, either.

After Enashoma went to bed, Turesobei brought Lu Bei out. The fetch fluttered about, bickered with Iniru, and told Turesobei when he made scribing mistakes. Turesobei was somewhat relieved that he didn't have the strength to keep Lu Bei in his fetch form for long.

It was late when Turesobei collapsed. He'd finished nine spells and could do no more. The last thing he saw was Iniru's smiling face, and his dreams that night were good despite the storm.

Chapter Forty-Five

During a lull in the storm's strength, Turesobei, Iniru, and Onudaka rode out with Grandfather Kahenan onto the military training grounds. Onudaka had joined Iniru as one of Turesobei's personal bodyguards. Being that important bothered Turesobei, though he knew he should get used to it. When he was High Wizard, he'd have bodyguards every time he left Ekaran.

Kahenan dismounted and paced twenty yards ahead. Using an iron rod engraved with runes, he drew a pentagram in the mud. At each of the star's five points he carved a light-ning bolt sigil. Kahenan backed away and then crooned a complex incantation.

A jagged bolt of lightning struck down from the roiling black clouds above. Runes along the rod blared to life, glowing blue-silver then yellow-white. Lightning fired back in-to the clouds with an upstroke, back down, and then up again. With his kenja-sight Turesobei's trained eye could follow the strikes, despite their speed.

The connection ended with successive thunderclaps that shook the ground like an earthquake. Some of the denekon reared and panicked. Iniru cringed and clasped her hands over her ears. The iron shaft glowed white from the heat, but the runes held and the rod didn't melt. The lightning's power was contained. The hairs along Turesobei's arms stood out, though not so much as Iniru's fur. All of them stared dumfounded.

Kahenan stumbled and Turesobei sprinted his denekon forward.

"I stored the energies," Kahenan said, gasping for breath as he leaned against Tureso-bei. "You remember what happened ... last time I developed my own spell?"

Turesobei shared a cautious smile with his master. Kahenan was well noted for his ability to perfect the spells of others, but he wasn't good at designing his own. The last time he had created a spell, the parchment he'd scribed it onto had burst into flames and sprayed ash into his face.

"Niru!" Turesobei shouted. "Ride in and tell them we're ready!"

Iniru returned moments later. "They're coming."

"Are you sure you shouldn't rest first, master?"

"The rod won't hold the lightning long, Sobei. You know that. Stop worrying about me. If it kills me ... well, I am old. It happens."

Wearing thick gloves, Kahenan retrieved the iron rod and chanted. Slowly, a clear bubble formed around the rod and expanded to cover him. Within the bubble, rain fell and winds blew but with half as much strength as without. Kahenan continued to chant, with increasing intensity, as he used the captured energy.

With pride, Turesobei guessed that only a dozen wizards in Okoro could likely pull off such a grueling and complicated spell. He knew that it was far beyond him. Of course, with his age, Kahenan would need days, maybe even weeks of rest after this.

The storm-shield bubble expanded to cover Turesobei and his companions. As it passed over them, the only noticeable effects were a slight tingling across their skin followed by a decrease in wind and rainfall.

"It's just a summer rainstorm now," Iniru commented.

"Aye," said Onudaka, "I've marched through plenty of these in my lifetime. No big concern for a military unit. At least not as long as the bubble holds."

That was Turesobei's biggest worry. It was also his duty in this mission. He had to prevent any other wizard from countering the bubble. To that end, two of the three adult Chonda wizards would be going along to help him.

Three rolling blasts from a trumpet heralded the attack force, and two hundred of the Chonda's best cavalry rode out into the storm-shield, which had expanded to its full diameter of one hundred paces. Armor and weaponry jingled and clattered under the soldiers' rain cloaks. Banners had been forsaken due to the winds. Only the trumpets would signal orders. Zaboko made up two-thirds of the force and some served as sergeants and captains. Even among the Chonda, all the higher-ranking officers were baojendari, and those officers had the best equipment available.

Hopefully the small strike force was large enough to make a solid surprise attack on the Gawo. They were leaving behind the mass of footmen and archers who composed the bulk of the Chonda army. Without denekon, moving through the storm would prove difficult, if not impossible.

Kahenan ceased his chanting, nodded appreciatively, and grinned weakly. "I did it well, Sobei."

"That you did, Grandfather. I wasn't sure you could pull it off."

Kahenan smirked at him. "Thanks for the confidence. I would like to see you try it." Kahenan put his hand on Turesobei's denekon and said, "Be careful. Watch for counterspells. Maintain the shield."

"I will."

"And be..." Kahenan started to swoon and Turesobei caught him. "Be very ... cautious ... with the heart."

"I will. Now you need rest. Captain Eibana!"

The grim and silent baojendari captain of Kahenan's guardsmen hurried forward with two zaboko guards. "We'll get him back home, my lord."

"See that servants are called to see to him, since I cannot."

"Not necessary," Kahenan complained as the captain lifted him into his mount's saddle.

Turesobei and Captain Eibana ignored him. "Captain, tell Enashoma to help you see

183

to him. Also, my mother's servants Shurada and Imi are trustworthy and may assist her if needed."

"Yes, my lord."

Kahenan was escorted away, and Turesobei hoped he would be all right. The column of troops gathered and Turesobei took up the lightning rod. The storm-shield bubble would go wherever he went.

Three trumpet blasts signaled them onward.

Turesobei, Iniru, and Onudaka rode near the center beside Prince Chien, who tugged at his mustache thoughtfully and said little. Iniru stayed close beside Turesobei at all times. She undertook her role as Turesobei's bodyguard earnestly, but he could tell that she would rather be out scouting for the enemy.

So far, none of the Chonda scouts had returned with word of the enemy. That wasn't a good sign, but they hoped it was only because the weather had slowed them down.

Prince Chien at last dropped his hand from his long, luxurious mustache and looked over at Turesobei. "This shield is quite impressive."

"It is, my lord. Hopefully I'll be able to wield such power when my time comes."

"According to the High Wizard, you shall far exceed him."

"He's being too generous, my lord."

"I daresay a grandfather is often biased about his grandchildren, but in this case I think he is correct. I expect you will accomplish great things for the Chonda."

Turesobei noticed out of the corner of his eye that Iniru had fixed him with a piercing gaze. He muttered, "I'll do my best, Prince Chien."

"I know you will. I am quite proud of you, Turesobei, for how you brought your father home and handled yourself when many would have lost hope. I will have no fear about the position of High Wizard when I become king."

Turesobei dipped his head with embarrassment. "Thank you, my lord."

"Watch yourself in the battle and call me if you are in danger."

"Yes, my lord."

Chien nodded and rode forward to speak with his officers. Turesobei turned to Iniru. "What?"

"I didn't say anything."

"You were thinking something and eyeing me awfully hard."

"Nothing."

"Tell me!"

She shrugged. "The clan's future seems very dependent on you."

"I am the High Wizard's heir."

"But you say you don't want to be."

"I don't."

"I'm not so sure from the way you act. You are proud to serve. You want to do your best for the clan."

"Well, of course. What's wrong with that?"

184

"Nothing. I do the same for my clan. And I take my responsibilities seriously, too."

"I always do my best, but that doesn't mean that I want this role."

"You've got it anyway, though."

"Niru, I really would rather run off with you than get stuck here forever. With Awasa on top of everything else."

"You'd just slow me down. Besides, you like her."

"I do not! And you could use a wizard."

"Not one whose back I have to guard all the time." She kept her voice even but Turesobei thought he saw sadness in her eyes. "And I've seen the way you look at her. You love her."

I love you just as much, he thought. *And I like you more.* But he couldn't bring himself to say it. He muttered incoherent words and looked away.

She snatched up her reins and huffed, "You're safe enough right now, so I'm going to scout around the edges. I'll be back."

When she had ridden off, Turesobei turned to Onudaka. "What am I supposed to say to her?"

"I don't know, lad. Maybe it would help if you told her how you feel."

"But she must know already."

"Do you know how she feels?"

"Kind of, I think. I mean sometimes, yeah, I know what she feels, but other times I don't know."

"That's because she's not sure. There are many walls between you, and you both have strong ties to different places, different clans. Neither of you could know what the other really feels without saying so. And if she hears you, maybe she'll better know her own heart."

"You think so?"

"Maybe."

"She does like me though, doesn't she? I mean sometimes she resents me and gets irritated, but she does like me, right?"

"I'm sure she must. You know, perhaps it would be best if the two of you just tried to enjoy your time together and didn't worry about the future. Don't let the threat of the sun setting keep you from walking in the daylight."

Chapter Forty-Six

Instead of thinking about Iniru and Awasa, Turesobei actually spent most of the ride contemplating his revenge against Haisero. The mark on his cheek burned strongly, reminding him of his duty. He also thought about the Storm Dragon's Heart and wondered why it couldn't simply be taken up by a net and not touched by anyone. Then it could be dumped out into the sea. He hadn't gathered the nerve to ask his grandfather. In part, he feared that the orb was affecting Kahenan without his knowing.

He also feared the same thing was happening to him. He believed the orb didn't control his actions, that it only called to him. But maybe it had gotten to him already and he just didn't know it. He didn't think so, but his only evidence to that effect was his desire to destroy it.

He looked to Onudaka riding beside him. "What are you going to do when you reach Sotenda?"

"Stop this madness if I can."

"You don't intend to kill him, do you?"

"Not unless I must, lad. Not unless I must."

The Chonda strike force stopped when it became too dark to ride and camped on a rocky, wooded hill. Rising waters had overtaken many valleys and low-lying areas, destroying bridges and roads, so they had traveled rough, high ground all the way.

Turesobei helped Onudaka pitch the tent they were going to share, then he ate with everyone else in the expansive galley tent. Few spoke. The weather held their spirits down.

As they walked back toward their tent, Iniru grabbed Turesobei by the arm. She had her hood and facemask pulled down and was smiling sweetly. Or mischievously. It was hard to tell sometimes.

"I'm not sleepy yet," she said, "are you?"

"Tired," he said yawning, "but not sleepy."

"Good." She pulled him toward her tent. "Let's talk for a while."

"Well, um..." He looked to Onudaka.

"Hold on," the old man said. He ducked into the tent and reappeared a moment later with a bundle. He chucked the bundle and Turesobei caught it.

"This is my blanket."

"Aye, lad."

Onudaka tossed him his backpack next. "There. Now I can sleep in peace and snore as loud as I want."

"But I—"

Onudaka waved him on. "Go stay with Iniru. Have fun."

"Er, is that all right, Niru? If I stay with you tonight?"

"Of course. Provided you don't snore."

"Have you ever heard me snore before?"

She laughed. "Come on. I don't want to sleep in a two-man army tent all by myself."

Turesobei hunched down and went into Iniru's tent as if he were entering another world. As if he were walking into Awasa's bedchamber. But except for Iniru's backpack, it was no different from his own tent. And why should it seem strange? They had slept beside each other in the rainforest without a tent. Was it that no one could see what they did within? Or that their feelings for each other had grown stronger?

The tent reached high enough that he could stand if he stooped over. In all, there was plenty of room for him and Iniru, since the tent was made large enough to accommodate two grown men and their gear.

As she lit the lantern, he asked, "So what did you want to talk about?"

"Nothing special."

"Oh," he said, disappointed. He spread out his blanket then tucked his backpack away. As he dug out his spare, dry clothes, he recognized the clinks of metal behind him that signaled Iniru was removing weapons from her bodysuit. Then he heard her strip from the bodysuit, unlashing ties and unwinding sashes.

"Was there something you wanted to talk about, Sobei?"

"Well, I—" He turned and looked at her, but to his dismay she wasn't wearing anything. He rapidly spun away. "Uh, n-no, I ... uh ... I don't guess so."

"You sure?" she asked as if nothing had happened.

"I'm sure. Niru, you aren't ... you aren't intending to sleep ... naked ... are you?"

"Hmm," she said with half a giggle. She rubbed her hands across his shoulders. He could feel the heat of her body so close to him. "Do you want me to?"

"No!"

"Oh, so you don't find me appealing?"

"No! I mean, yes! It's just ... I mean ... you're not being fair to me!"

She stood and laughed. He heard her rumble through her backpack and then a few moments later she said, "You can turn around now."

He did so and found that she had dressed in a dry pair of the shorts and shirt which she usually wore beneath her uniform.

"I assume you plan to get out of your own wet clothes. Doesn't look like your rain cloak is perfect either."

"Well, yeah, I guess so. Turn around, though, ok?"

"All right."

Turesobei turned his back to her and stripped.

"Lovely!" she said.

Turesobei's cheeks reddened and goosebumps swept across his body. He whirled around. "What!?"

Iniru was lying on her stomach, propped up on her elbows, chin cupped in her hands. "Oh, very nice! Thanks for giving me a full demonstration."

Clasping his hands over his privates, he said, "You promised to turn around!"

"I did. All the way around in fact."

He pulled on his pants. "You are the most infuriating woman ever!"

"Aha! At last, I'm back on top. I knew that little over-dressed strumpet couldn't beat me for long."

Turesobei cursed, mumbled, and sagged down onto his blanket. "I really don't know how to deal with you. I give up."

She put one of her hands on one of his. "Don't do that. It really wouldn't be any fun. And I promise that you really do like it."

He didn't draw his hand away. "Are all k'chasans like you?"

"Are all baojendari like you?"

"Are you all so lacking in manners?"

"Not at all. I'm somewhat unique in that fashion."

"Oh."

"We are less prudish than you baojendari. But most aren't as bad as me." She was still holding his hand. "You know, I just tease you because I like you."

"I know." He drew his hand away. "Niru, am I just a boy to you?"

"Sometimes. But most males act like boys for a long time after they've supposedly become men. Women do the same thing, though in different ways."

"You and I, we're very different."

"Obviously. You hadn't noticed?" He shot her a harsh look, and she replied, "Does it bother you?"

"Well, I mean the future..."

"We can't do anything about that can we?"

"No." He sighed deeply. "No, and I don't want it to ruin our time together."

"Good, then don't let it."

Turesobei began to shiver despite his dry clothes.

"Are you cold, Sobei?"

"A little. I wish I had fur."

"Yes, it is rather useful sometimes."

Iniru scooted over and lay against his side. She pulled her blanket over them. Timidly, they smiled at one another. Then they stared quietly at the flickering lantern. Rain pattered outside the tent. Wind tugged at the canvas. Thunder boomed loudly. Outside

Kahenan's shield, harsher winds howled and lightning popped.

"Sobei, are you going to kiss me?"

"Huh?" He turned his head and stared into her face, only inches away from his.

"I've been waiting."

"I-I didn't know that."

"You do want to kiss me, don't you?"

"Of course. I just ... I just didn't know you wanted to kiss me."

"Did I not make that clear?"

"Well, I guess you probably did. I mean ... I am clueless, you know."

"You have kissed a girl before, haven't you?"

"Honestly? No. Have you?"

"Kissed a girl? Once."

Turesobei's cheeks flushed. "No, I meant kissed a boy!"

"That too."

"Oh."

Turesobei found himself utterly lost in the moment as if he had fallen into a dream while awake. He stared at the lantern again. Moments passed and then he heard Iniru clear her throat.

"You're still waiting aren't you?"

"Yep."

Turesobei drew in a deep breath and steeled his courage. But then her padded hands grasped him by the cheeks. She turned his head into hers. She smiled into his eyes and drew him in for a kiss.

Their lips met. Softly once. Twice. Then the kiss deepened. Somehow, Turesobei knew how all of this worked, though he'd never actually thought about it. He guessed it was instinct. They sat halfway up and snuggled up to one another.

Iniru woke Turesobei softly. He had fallen asleep curled up beside her. She was standing over him, still in her casual clothes. When had she gotten up? Or had she ever gone to sleep?

The lantern still burned, flickering on its lowest setting. Her eyes were filled with intent.

"Two scouts have returned. I just heard them speak with the sentries. They're going to wake Prince Chien."

"We really shouldn't go unless we're summoned."

"So? Who cares? Let's sneak out and listen."

"I'll just get in the way. You go and then come back and tell me what they said."

She donned her bodysuit with amazing speed. Then she was out of the tent and into the rain. Turesobei put on his armor and cloak and packed his gear just in case. He was groggy and yet infused with desire. There was so much more to experience with her. And so much more he wanted to do again.

Iniru rushed back into the tent. "The scouts had trouble getting back because of the weather. The Gawo lands are under the storm, too. Which means either Haisero has lost control of the Storm Dragon's Heart or he isn't helping his clan."

"King Gawo is aggressive and paranoid. He would've moved against us quickly if he even suspected we were guilty of causing the storms. But he didn't, which means they probably know what's going on and who's using the heart."

"Well, Prince Chien is going to return home in the morning, and the scouts will be sent back out to learn more. Your people are going to rethink their strategy. The prince is considering sending a delegation to King Gawo."

"King Gawo won't talk, even if he does know something."

"Then let's go out and search for the heart ourselves. If you get close, the heart might call to you through the storm's interference. Your grandfather is never going to locate it. And they're just going to get better at using the heart. At this rate, your clan will be battered into submission within a month."

"Prince Chien would never let me go."

"Then let's make a break for it now."

"We can't do that!"

"Why not?"

"Because..."

"Turesobei, be your own man. Make your own decisions. You know they can't stop this. But maybe you and I can if we act now."

Turesobei worried about how his grandfather and King Ugara would react if he went out on his own. But then he thought of his vow to his father. The sigil grew hotter. He touched it and knew what he would do.

"As soon as the coast is clear, get the mounts and bring them up behind the tent. I'll gather our things."

Iniru pressed up to him and kissed him. "This is the right thing, I know it."

"Me, too. But I don't know how we'll make it through the storm. The wind and debris alone could kill us."

"We'll manage," she said. "Trust me."

Chapter Forty-Seven

The wind and rain lashed Turesobei as he clung precariously to a suddenly new cliff side. One hand grasped a jutting rock. The other held tightly to an exposed root.

"Niru!" he screamed. "I thought I could trust you!"

Iniru peeked over the edge. "It's not my fault you can't watch where you're going!"

"The ledge fell out from under me! You should've picked a better path!"

Iniru disappeared. Turesobei glanced at the raging river forty feet below. It used to be a pleasant mountain stream. The ground had fallen out from under him only minutes before. By luck alone he had caught the tangle of exposed roots and spared himself from his denekon's fate. She had already floated downstream. The fall onto the rocks in the river below had killed her.

Turesobei's grip on the rock slipped away and six inches of root ripped free from the cliff. His weight bounced and another foot of root tore loose. If his weight bounced again...

"Hurry up!" he yelled as he frantically kicked his feet. His left foot struck a rock. He leaned all his weight onto it, hoping. The rock held. He didn't bounce. And the root held as well. For now. The tiny threads coming off the main root were starting to break.

Niru reappeared with a rope and began to lower it. "This was the only path available without going too far out of the way."

Turesobei grabbed the rope. "Out of the way doesn't sound so bad."

"Hindsight. Now climb. Quickly! The tree I anchored the line to could fall over any minute."

Turesobei reached the precipice of the newly made cliff, scrambled up onto the ledge, and noted with horror how far over the anchoring tree had begun to lean.

"Thanks, Niru." He tried to kiss her, but she pulled him away from the ledge. "Go!"

Iniru untied the rope and joined him. The wind blew sheets of rain into their faces. Twice, lightning bolts had nearly struck them. Both were bruised from hailstones. The sky was lighter outside now, not pitch dark any longer, and they guessed it was three hours past dawn.

Turesobei climbed into the saddle behind Iniru.

"Which way now?" she asked.

Turesobei closed his eyes and thought intently on the Storm Dragon's Heart ... nothing.

Mostly he had been guiding them with intuition. Vague impressions of the heart's location came and went. Sometimes, he thought it was calling to him softly.

"I can't tell," he said.

"Think harder then."

"How?"

"I don't know. You're the wizard! Maybe if you called to it?"

He called to it aloud, using Naruwakiru's name.

He got a slight pulse. He tried again ... Nothing.

"That almost worked," he said.

"Keep trying, then. What direction should I take in the meantime?"

He'd already established that the heart and Haisero were moving. "Keep going the same way as before. Maybe when we get closer I'll get another read on it."

An hour later, he still couldn't get a lead and both of them were shivering from being wet and tired. Iniru had a cut on her cheek where a piece of debris, kicked up by the wind, had struck her. Turesobei was becoming frustrated, and the tattoo on his cheek burned and itched.

"Naruwakiru," he thought, trying to project his thoughts toward the heart. "What do you want with me?"

Nothing.

"If you want me, you'd better tell me where you are."

He got a flash of the heart within his head. For a moment, he even saw Haisero and Sotenda riding together. Then it was gone.

"Naruwakiru," he thought again intently. "I want your power coursing through me. Let me carry you. They are not worthy, but I will be. Give me the chance to prove it."

The sensation returned to him, a feeling of direction and distance, stronger this time. He pointed. "That way, Niru. I've got it. It's not much further. I convinced the heart to give me a shot."

"You what?"

"I'll explain later."

She eyed him with suspicion but said nothing. He tried not to think about it. He tried hard to mean everything he'd said in case the heart could read his thoughts and would realize that he didn't really want its power to influence him.

For three hours, they rode through the raging storm. All the while, the Storm Dragon's Heart called louder and louder to Turesobei. He did not mention this to Iniru. He only told her that he could hear it and they were going the right direction. And then they knew for certain, because they spotted a protected path through the storm—a long tunnel that behaved like a perfect version of Kahenan's storm-shield.

The tunnel stretched out farther than they could see. Going one way, the tunnel ascended into the highlands. The other way penetrated Gawo Province and headed toward their capital. Iniru and Turesobei scanned for enemies but saw none within the tunnel. They rode up to it. Turesobei examined it with his kenja-sight.

"Looks safe. The energies are just holding back the elements."

Iniru picked up a rock and tossed it. The rock went through the side of the tunnel and landed inside, unharmed. "You can never be too sure."

They rode inside, feeling only a tingle of energy as they passed through. The tunnel widened to about thirty feet and seemed from within as if it were made of glass. Rain pattered onto the top and rolled down the sides. Wind and lightning were absent. The thunder was reduced to a distant rumbling. They were relieved to be free of the wind and rain.

"Why a tunnel?" Iniru said. "Before they just created an eye around themselves."

Turesobei shrugged. "I'm sure they have reasons." He pointed toward the Gawo Province. "The heart lies that way."

An hour later, all their enemies came into view: Haisero, Sotenda, and twenty hooded cultists were meeting with two dozen Gawo soldiers. The two sides were approaching each other warily when Iniru spotted them.

"King Gawo," Turesobei said. "I recognize his bulk and his ornate crimson armor. We've got to get in closer and find out what they're saying."

"Follow my lead, then."

They tied their denekon to a tree. The poor beast looked happy to be out of the weather and resting at last. Turesobei cast the *spell of auditory enhancement* on himself and Iniru so they wouldn't have to get too close. Then they crept forward and hid amongst several thick bushes.

King Gawo sat on a fine but aging mount. Heavy rolls of fat jiggled beneath his chin and in various places were stuffed into his armor. Two grey-robed sorcerers lurked to one side. To the other sat their High Wizard, Gawo Yureigu. He was a short, skeletal man with sunken eyes and a scar across his mouth. Gawo's elite nazaboko guards, the most fearsome of his murderous troops, surrounded them all.

"Haisero!" boomed King Gawo with his jowls swaying. "I insist that you stop this madness!"

Haisero motioned, and a crackling wall of lightning formed between the two parties. He dismissed the lightning and shouted, "I could destroy you all with ease!"

King Gawo belted out, "Then do so and be done with it!"

"Not until you have all bent your knees to me." Haisero held up the heart and gestured toward High Wizard Yureigu. "Especially that pig!"

Yureigu scowled but said nothing. King Gawo spat, "We will not bow to you, Haisero."

"You will, King Gawo, unless my demands are met!"

"Son," called out Yureigu, "listen to reason. This is fruitless."

"I've had it with your reason, Father. All you've done for years is order me about. You lashed me when I didn't do the lessons the way you wanted. And when I succeeded, you punished me for not doing better. You asked the impossible and demeaned me in every way. And all the while you were holding me back. You knew I was talented, and you held me back so I wouldn't surpass you."

"I did no such thing! I was molding you to be the best ever."

"I have been ready for three years. I'm nineteen now and you still treat me as an apprentice."

Turesobei thought of how Kahenan taught him and how he sometimes felt constrained and treated like a child. But he always knew that Kahenan was being fair and had his best interests in mind. He certainly hoped he wasn't as pompous and arrogant as Haisero when frustrated.

"You are a journeyman sorcerer," Yureigu said. "You cannot do everything."

"But I can, Father! Look at the orb!" Sparks of lightning shot forth from the Storm Dragon's Heart and arced into the sky. "I control the heart of Naruwakiru. I control the very storm that ravages our land and the Chonda's. I can stop it and punish only the Chonda, but you'll have to make me the High Wizard and my friend Sotenda must become the heir to the kingdom!"

"This is ridiculous!" countered King Gawo. "And who is this ruffian anyway?"

"I am the High Priest of Naruwakiru!" announced Sotenda.

"He is a great man and my dearest friend," said Haisero. "He is the only one who has understood me, the only one who has comforted me and helped me develop my true talents."

"This charlatan is using you," Yureigu said. "He has turned you against us."

"He has allowed me to wield the sacred power!"

"Any two-bit sorcerer could do what you are doing, son. Look at you. Your face is scarred, and so are your arms. The heart is consuming you."

"I gained those scars when I first wielded the orb, but I know all the rituals now." A maddened look took over Haisero's eyes. "I have been chosen to wield the heart. No one else. And I won't bear your presence any longer. I do not have to. You have hurt me for the last time!"

Haisero lifted the orb, but Sotenda rushed forward and grasped his arm. He pulled him close and whispered to him. After a few moments, Haisero relaxed.

"If you will not meet our demands," Sotenda announced, "then you must pay our ransom. Otherwise, we will destroy you."

"What ransom?" King Gawo said.

"One hundred thousand jade, fifty denekon, all the white-steel you have, and those lives Haisero wishes ended."

"My father, my mother, and my siblings!" Haisero screamed. "Give them to me! I will sear their bodies with the goddess' sky-fire!"

Haisero cackled and twitched until Sotenda calmed him again. The orb was killing Haisero, starting with his mind. And Grandfather wanted Turesobei to take it!

Sotenda gestured toward the Gawo with his sword. "If you do not meet these demands, we will destroy all your holdings. You have three days."

Chapter Forty-Eight

Iniru leapt up and tugged Turesobei with her. "Back to the denekon! I have a plan."

As they mounted, Turesobei glanced back. Haisero held the heart aloft and shouted. The storm tunnel collapsed past him, stranding King Gawo and his men in the raging storm. Laughter rang out from the cultists as Iniru urged their denekon into a sprint.

"Keep an eye on them," she said.

"We're going down their tunnel?"

"It must lead to their base, don't you think?"

"Yeah. Ride fast, though. We can't let them spot us."

Soon, the cultists were out of sight.

"Niru, what are we going to do when we get there?"

"Wait until we have a chance to steal the heart. We can't fight them all at once."

The denekon began to foam around the mouth, and their bodies heaved with deep breaths. Turesobei and Iniru slowed them to a jog, the medium pace for a denekon, because denekon could only hold to a sprint for a few minutes at best.

An hour passed, and with his kenja-sight Turesobei caught a slight glimpse of the heart's aura. "They're getting close."

"How fast are they going?"

"A jog, I would guess."

"This mount can't keep going. We're going to have to abandon the tunnel."

She urged the poor denekon into one last sprint, which turned out to be slower than a normal jog. They left the tunnel and rode into the forested hills. They dismounted and peered out, through the storm, at their enemies from behind a bush-covered outcropping.

Suddenly, the cultists sprinted toward the spot where Turesobei and Iniru had exited. As they moved, the tunnel closed behind them. The cultists roamed about looking at tracks. They discussed something amongst themselves, but after a few minutes they began to move on.

Haisero hesitated, and then he called out a command.

The storm's intensity doubled, as if a full hurricane lay overhead. A relentless gale forced Turesobei and Iniru to crawl along the ground, holding their heads down to keep debris out of their faces. Lightning increased with bolts randomly striking all around them. Twice Turesobei felt electric currents run through the ground beneath them. The enchantments Kahenan had placed in their armor protected them from harm.

Drenched by the downpour and bruised by hail and flying debris, they inched forward. At times they pulled each other along. Turesobei led them, trusting to his sense of where the heart lay.

A towering water oak moaned and creaked beside them. Iniru climbed to her feet and dragged Turesobei with her. "Run!"

They ran with the wind at their backs. The tree crashed down behind them. The topmost of its limbs struck and knocked them down, but they suffered only a few more scratches and bruises.

"We've got to keep moving!" Iniru yelled over the wind.

"I can't take much more!"

"No choice!"

"We should at least find shelter and rest!"

"Only if we have to! Otherwise, Haisero will get away from us!"

Turesobei lay panting, ready to give up, but Iniru pressed her face against his and kissed him. That gave him the strength to go on. If he gave up, she would be lost, too. They crawled onward, and at last they reached the shore of a swollen, thrashing lake.

The wind switched directions again and now blew water from the lake along with sand from the shore into their faces. Turesobei held an arm across his face and looked at the lake as best as he could.

"The heart's on the opposite shore!"

"Are you sure?"

"Look closely. It's not storming on the other side."

"We'll have to find a way around."

"It's calling to me stronger now."

"Are you sure it's safe for you to go to it?"

"The alternative is to die in this storm."

"Well," she said, "which way should we go, left or right?"

"Neither."

"Then how do you plan to get there?"

"Through the lake," he said.

"Are you mad?"

"It's the fastest way."

"With all this lightning, we'll get electrocuted if we go into the water."

"We'll have to take that chance. The armor will help protect us."

"But there's no way we can swim that far in this weather!"

"We're not going to swim it," Turesobei said. "We're going to walk across the bottom."

"Magic? Are you strong enough for something like that?"

"Grandfather taught me the ritual when I was a child, when I first learned to swim. I haven't done it in years, though." He took a deep breath and thought about all the steps the ritual required. "I'll need to rest for a little while, and I'll need some shelter. Some place where I can scribe the runes."

Lightning struck a tree nearby. With a loud crack, the oak split down the middle. The peal of thunder nearly threw them to the ground.

"Gods!" Iniru cursed. She tugged Turesobei down into a safe crouch, further away from the water's edge. "You can't just cast the spell now?"

"No. It's a ritual. It takes time."

Iniru sighed. "The hill we passed a half-hour ago. There are some outcroppings at the top. Perhaps we'll find a cave there. The lightning may be worse, though."

"Just do your best."

"Sobei, it might take less time just to go around the lake."

"We need to go through the lake. I'm sure of it. I've been here before. Two creeks flow into the lake on one side. We'd have to cross them, and there's a swamp to the other side. Besides, if we come through the water, we can sneak into their camp. They'd never expect that."

Iniru nodded. "Well, at least you're beginning to think like a qengai. But be careful. If you black out while casting, we can't rest out here for days."

"Don't worry," Turesobei said darkly, "I'm using blood magic for this spell. If I pass out, I'm sure it will kill me. I see that look in your eyes. Don't even start with me. I've made my decision."

Chapter Forty-Nine

The water was dark and murky, as if the black clouds above had bled onto the earth. Weighted down by their gear, Turesobei and Iniru trudged across the lake bottom like clunky marionettes being walked across a stage. Muck stirred with every step as they crossed land that had once lain far outside the lake's edge.

The *ritual of watery life* gave them air to breathe, taken from the water itself, but it did not grant them sight through the darkness. They couldn't see more than five feet ahead, and even the *spell of darksight* couldn't penetrate the lake's murkiness. A rope tied around their waists kept them together. Turesobei just had to trust the call of the Storm Dragon's Heart to lead him in the right direction.

Waves chopped on the surface above, illuminated by lightning flashes. Muted rumblings of thunder reverberated within the depths. So far, lightning hadn't struck the lake, but it was only a matter of time, so they went as fast as they could. Turesobei had no idea how deep the charge from a strike might travel, and he didn't care to find out.

The frequency of drowned plants decreased as they descended into a depression lined with slimy tendrils growing from a thicker muck of leaves and decay. They had reached the lake proper, as it had been before the storm caused so much flooding.

"We're maybe a third of the way across," Turesobei said. His words sounded normal to him.

"You sure the spell will last long enough?" Iniru said. To Turesobei, it sounded as if she were speaking into a giant, wobbling vase.

"Of course," Turesobei lied. He couldn't be sure how effective the ritual had been, cast through tremendous fatigue and performed in a shallow, waterlogged cave. He'd done the best he could, though.

A strangely garbled, high-pitched voice, almost a wail, called out, "This is our lake!"

"What?" asked Iniru.

"Our lake," the voice said again.

"Some type of nadaji," said Turesobei. "A water spirit. I can think of nothing else."

"Sobei! I felt something stirring past me. It wasn't a fish."

They glanced around fearfully but saw nothing.

"Our lake!" the voice wailed.

"We are sorry to intrude!" Turesobei called out. "We seek only to cross to the other side. We are trying to stop the storms! I promise we will not harm anything within your lake."

A terrible green face appeared in the murk before them. Turesobei and Iniru both gasped, sending a mass of bubbles toward the surface, and stumbled backward.

"A shaidera," Turesobei muttered.

Shaidera were the dreaded, tyrannical queens who ruled many nadaji colonies. This one looked angrier than those depicted in the bestiaries Turesobei had studied. A green-blue luminescence highlighted the lines of the shaidera's distorted, half-human and half-fish face. Large fins fanned out from the sides of her head. Air bubbled out from gills at her neck. The nadaji queen wore only a necklace of shells. Except on her smooth, pink breasts and stomach, scales covered her body. She had a tapered body as tall as Turesobei with a sinuous, eel's tail twice that length. Her flesh beneath the scales, like that of all proper nadaji, was made of compressed water but within that water was muck from the lake bottom and luminescent algae.

A score of transparent, algae-stained nadaji gathered behind the shaidera, and schools of large carp massed behind Turesobei and Iniru.

Turesobei made a half-bow. "We are sorry, dear queen, for intruding on your territory. We just need to get across to the other side, so we can stop the storm that rages above and floods our lands."

"My domain is growing," she said. "Why should I wish for the flooding to stop?"

Turesobei glanced fearfully at Iniru then continued. "Well, the waters would not be stirred so much. And the lightning—"

"None of that bothers us below, in the deep. Your sword, that bothers us. You must remove it and yourselves at once. Return from whence you came!"

Turesobei dropped a hand to the hilt of Sumada, his father's white-steel blade which Kahenan had insisted he carry on this trip, though he'd given it back to him as a replacement for Yomifano.

"I would not harm you with it."

"But you would stop the expansion of our domain," she hissed.

"The expansion is not right. It's not natural. You would not ultimately profit from it."

"I will decide what benefits me, not you, foreigner."

"Please let us pass," said Iniru. "We must to save our people."

"I care not."

Turesobei had tired of this. The water breathing spell wouldn't last forever. Taking care not to pierce the energies of the spell surrounding him and Iniru, he drew the white-steel blade and leapt forward. Faster than he could move, the shaidera darted out of reach. But he kept the blade drawn and held it forward.

"You will let us pass or I will destroy you."

"You may try!" she said. "But you will fail!"

Turesobei swung the sword in a wide arc and stopped it, just barely, before he cut into his spell. Water spirits fled in all directions, though some surrounded their queen.

"I see that you've had few dealings with people, but that is no excuse. We are not here to harm you. People are destroying our land and changing yours. Soon everything will be different. Other lakes will join this one, and other queens will compete with your power. Your lake may even grow into a new sea and touch powers far beyond you. I know this, for I have encountered spirits greater than you."

Turesobei was not sure of this last, but there was no reason to let the shaidera know otherwise. The queen didn't reply, and the other nadaji remained silent.

"Come," Turesobei said to Iniru. He moved forward carefully with the sword still drawn. Spirits parted from his path, but the queen didn't move. Fish gathered around her.

Turesobei hesitated no longer. "Donusai arukai!" he yelled, calling out the command of a binding spell. He placed only a slight burst of kenja within the binding spell. Not so much that it would weaken him or could work. A natural spirit like these was ten times more difficult to bind than a shadowy Zhura demon. However, the spell worked in the manner he had intended. The queen fled in fear, though the fish stayed behind to exact her revenge.

"What did you do?" Iniru asked.

"I threatened her with a binding." And she was too ignorant of people to know it couldn't work. "We must hurry."

They half-ran and half-swam along the bottom, swinging their weapons to cut through the schools of carp and catfish that charged and battered them. They got ahead of the larger fish and reached a precipice where the lake bottom plummeted down.

"We have to swim now," Turesobei said.

Iniru cut the straps to her pack. "We'll have to go without our supplies. Keep only what you must."

With fish swarming about and banging into them, they abandoned their non-essential gear. Then they swam out, still weighted by their light armor but not so much that they immediately sank into the depths.

Turesobei kept up an awareness of the energy currents, which was tiring with his other spell going and with the storm above. It was good that he did, though, for as they neared the old lakeshore on the opposite side, the nadaji began to stream toward them.

"She's decided I'm too weak to bind her. I think they'll try to rush us. You go ahead of me, and I'll try to ward them off with the sword."

Iniru let slack into the rope, many feet of it, and swam ahead until he couldn't see her. She was a much faster swimmer than he was.

The first nadaji reached him and Turesobei knew he couldn't hold back any longer. He felt sorry for them, for their queen had led them to this. Most water spirits were peaceful. Only the shaidera carried such venom in their hearts.

The sword swept through the first ones rushing him. There were bubbles and an increase of muck as if the bottom had been stirred and then those spirits were gone.

But more charged, and so he swung and slashed, destroying dozens. One reached him at last. A solidified hand of water punched him hard in the stomach and he recoiled, gasping out bubbles. More charged him, and the queen rose into view behind them carrying a spear.

The rope jerked taut, and he was pulled backward with speed. The spirits rushed toward him, and he continued to strike out with the sword. At last his feet brushed against the bottom, and he turned and ran up onto the shore. Iniru pulled him with the rope that she had wound once around a tree on the bank.

There was no wind above, not even a slight breeze. Overhead, the sky wasn't dark but a light grey and no rain fell on them. They had reached the eye of the storm.

The shaidera rose onto the surface. They saw her, illuminated by a lightning strike. She threw the javelin of petrified oak, and before Turesobei could get away, it struck him in the chest and knocked him to the ground. He felt Iniru tugging at him. He stumbled. And then he felt nothing at all.

Chapter Fifty

Turesobei groaned as he awoke. He opened his eyes and saw, dimly, Iniru hunched over him. "Unnh, where are we?"

Iniru slapped him on the back of the head. "Shh!"

"Ouch!" he whispered. He looked around, but except for a shaft of moonlight he couldn't see much of anything. Wherever they were, it was dank and dark like a cave, and wooden crates were piled in front of them.

"We're in the storm's eye," Iniru whispered. "On the other side of the lake."

"I remember that much."

"The shaidera threw her javelin and struck you in the chest, right side, almost at your shoulder. You passed out." She reached the javelin out to him. "I saved it, thought you might need it. In case it had a curse on it."

Turesobei took the four-foot spear in his hand, a slender, jagged piece of petrified wood. It was tainted with the shaidera's power. On it she had placed an enchantment of poison, from which his grandfather's armor charms had protected him. He knew it had worked because he was still alive.

"You hold onto it for now, Iniru. It's magic, and it might come in handy sometime."

She nodded and set it down beside her. "I dragged your heavy, unconscious body from the shore into this cave. The cultists seem to keep their extra supplies here."

"It doesn't hurt as much as I'd expect."

"Your armor spared you a worse wound."

His reinforced leather armor was piled up beside him. A thick bandage was wrapped around his chest. "This is near where the arrow struck me before, on the bridge in Wakaro. An unlucky spot for me, I guess. How long has it been?"

"You were out for four hours. It's about midnight now."

"Have you scouted their camp yet?"

"No."

"Do you think we'll be safe for the night?"

"I think so. You could probably rest all day tomorrow. It's dark here in the back, and they have a lot of supplies put away. No guards outside it, either. It's the perfect place to hide."

"Then I'm going back to sleep. You check everything out. I'll rest and then keep watch while you sleep in the morning."

Iniru bent down and kissed him on the lips. Then she ruffled a hand through his hair and said, "Rest well. I'll wake you after dawn."

Dawn's light filtered in through the mouth of the cave. Turesobei, however, lay within the shadows of the wall of stacked crates. The sound of Iniru climbing over the boxes woke him, though in truth there was little sound to be heard. He must have been close to waking already.

"How did you get me over those?" he whispered to her.

"Not easily, and when I tossed you over, you hit with a rather loud thud."

"That didn't wake me?"

"Not at all."

He drew her into an embrace. "You were cutting things a little close with the sun rising, don't you think?"

"I know what I'm doing."

"I'm not questioning your methods, just trying to understand them."

"I saw the heart tonight."

Turesobei sat up so quickly that his head spun and his vision darkened for a few moments. The pain in his chest helped to keep him awake, though. "Could we get to it?"

"I think so. I might have myself, but I was afraid to take it, after what your grandfather said."

"I'm not sure that it wouldn't be safer for you to take it instead of me, but I guess we will have to trust Grandfather."

"We can get past the guards at night. These cultists are different from the others. More devoted, I think, but with far less military training."

"What about Sotenda? Onudaka says he's a formidable swordsman."

"Sotenda doesn't sleep near Haisero. Probably because Haisero tosses with nightmares, moaning and wailing."

"Where does he keep the heart?"

"Cradled in his arms. I saw it ... through a thin paper window." She looked away and drew in a deep breath. "It was pulsing and glowing with crimson light." She took his hand. "Sobei, I was afraid of it. I don't think I could have taken it from him. And I don't want you to have to touch it either."

"It will be all right," he said meekly.

"You don't sound certain."

"I'm not, but I am trying to be positive. I have to trust Grandfather Kahenan. He knows about things like this better than I do."

"But the heart predates your people coming here by millennia. He can't really know what it might do."

Turesobei shrugged. "Even if it kills me, it's best for us to get it out of Haisero's hands. Besides, even though it affects him, it hasn't killed him yet."

Iniru pulled two packets from her uniform and handed one to Turesobei. He unwrapped the coarse cloth and found dried fruit and meat within it.

"Rations I stole from one of the crates."

They ate and then Iniru laid down. "Keep watch and wake me at sundown. Then I want you take a nap before we go after the heart."

"You have a plan?"

"Of course."

Iniru closed her eyes and was asleep within moments. Turesobei rose and stretched carefully. He practiced deep breathing exercises and tried to meditate, hoping he could recover enough kenja to handle the cultists. But he grew unsettled, instead of peaceful and contemplative. Thoughts about the heart kept penetrating his mind.

He moved as far away from Iniru as possible, given their surroundings, and pulled the diary from his backpack. He swished his hand across the cover and whispered, "Lu Bei!"

Amber sparks glinted within his kavaru and along the runes on the book's cover. The fetch appeared and immediately flew into Turesobei's arms.

"Master! Are you all right?"

"I'm fine, I'm fine. You know that."

"I heard her say it."

"Lu Bei, you can trust her. You need to trust her. She's now my..."

"What, master?"

"She ... she means a lot to me. Try to get along with her, okay?"

"Yes, master."

"Say, the other night. You weren't listening when Iniru and I—"

Lu Bei threw out his hands and shook his head. "No, master. No, no. When you are with a lady friend, I do not eavesdrop unless requested. Just like you told me to—"

"You mean Chonda Lu told you to do that?"

"Of course, master."

"Lu Bei, what do you think about the Storm Dragon's Heart? Do you think it's having an effect on me? Did Chonda Lu ever go through anything like this?"

"Never anything quite the same as this."

The fetch touched Turesobei's head and then his kavaru. He stared into his eyes for sometime after that and frowned.

"It is affecting you, master. It is hard for me to tell how much. I'm closely linked to you, but I am not a wizard."

A small, clawed hand touched the crimson goshawk sigil on Turesobei's cheek.

"And you are influenced by this as well. I cannot tell which is affecting you more. Their purpose seems the same. I know you cannot avoid it, master, but I fear what it might do to you."

Turesobei and Iniru crept out of the cave where the cultists stored their excess supplies. Above them, stars glittered in a clear, moonless sky seen through the eye of the still-raging storm. Sotenda's followers had seized four A-frame cabins and a manse that were the vacation homes of baojendari nobles from the Gawo Clan. The buildings sat along a sheer bluff with their back porches facing the flooded lake. Twelve cultists stood guard along the building fronts, but only two at the manse kept watch along the backside. To the north, in the direction of the cave, the bluff sloped down to a boggy shoreline.

Keeping out of sight, Turesobei and Iniru moved away from the camp down to the lakeshore. As they waded in, Turesobei feared the shaidera would come after them, but she didn't. After a few minutes of wading and then swimming alongside the cliff, they reached the path of natural handholds Iniru had found before and began to climb.

Turesobei had more trouble climbing than Iniru, who used her claws and wasn't wounded. Several times, his wet hands and feet slipped, but only one at a time, and thankfully the rocks protruded enough that he managed to keep his grip. Pain coursed through his chest and into his shoulder, but the closer he came to the heart, the more enlivened and determined he became.

Once atop the bluff, Iniru led Turesobei through the shadows toward the back of the manse. Before, she had simply peeked into Haisero's room through a tiny window near the ceiling. This time, they would have to deal with two guards and infiltrate the house.

"Wait here," Iniru whispered into Turesobei's ear when they were within a stone's throw of the guards.

She darted ahead, and somehow he lost sight of her until she was right upon the enemy. Within three heartbeats, she had silently knocked out both cultists.

After pulling the bodies out of sight, they passed through the unlocked back door and tiptoed into a dark room filled with weapons and supplies. A sliding door on the room's opposite side led to a lantern-lit hallway. Seeing and hearing no one moving about, they inched forward with their weapons drawn.

Halfway down the sparse hallway, Iniru stopped and touched an elegant, paper-paneled door painted with a rustic mountain landscape. Turesobei nodded and then tensed as she slid the partition back. Turesobei had known before looking that the heart lay within this room. He had felt the heat of its presence, as if he were walking toward an invisible bonfire.

Against the far wall, Haisero lay curled up on a plush sleeping mat, snoring heavily, with sweat beading on his forehead. The maniac clutched the jade orb to his chest as if it were his own heart. The heart's pulsing veins cast the room in a sinister, crimson glow.

With his kenja-sight opened, Turesobei saw the vibrant currents of energy that pierced the room and wrapped like threads of yarn around the orb. It glowed so brightly that he raised his hands and shaded his eyes. He also spotted the ward spell that Iniru had instinctively sensed earlier with her qengai training. If anyone came within ten feet of

Haisero, the spell would wake Haisero and immobilize the intruder.

Iniru drew out the small blowgun she had already loaded with a poisoned dart. She inhaled deeply and then puffed. With only a light scraping sound, the dart rocketed forth and stabbed into Haisero's neck. Haisero stirred and swatted at the tiny dart, but he didn't wake up.

Now it was Turesobei's turn. He drew out a spell-strip and chanted as quietly as he could, his phrases merely a whisper as he strained to break the ward spell. For all his arrogance and lack of precision in casting, Haisero had a talent for binding raw power into his spells. Turesobei broke out into a sweat as he forced kenja away from the orb and into his counter-spell. He thought of his grandfather urging him to greater concentration and effort, and with Kahenan's clear voice echoing in his mind, he at last disabled Haisero's spell.

"Got it," he whispered to Iniru, gasping for breath.

They crept forward. Turesobei wondered if he should kill Haisero as honor demanded. He knew someone must, but he just couldn't bring himself to do it.

Iniru might have other ideas, though. The dart's poison wasn't lethal. He had convinced her that killing Haisero while he was still in contact with the heart was dangerous. The sudden shock of Haisero's death might cause the heart to do any number of things. Of course, she would probably kill him as soon as the heart was safely away. Turesobei could almost read the lethal thoughts that coiled in her mind. And he wouldn't try to stop her.

Turesobei reached down for the orb, but sensing its powerful malice, he hesitated. Visible tendrils of storm kenja spread like static electricity to his fingertips. He inhaled once and steeled his courage. Then he swiftly took the Storm Dragon's Heart in both hands and wrenched it out of Haisero arms.

Power burned through him.

His blood turned to falling rain. His heartbeat became thunder. His thoughts lightning. His body was ... immense and weightless, expanding rapidly ... full of anger.

Turesobei was cloud and storm, power and willfulness, wrath and terror. He was the legacy of Naruwakiru, her child in spirit, and she hovered in the back of his mind, whispering thoughts to him.

No one could resist him. Anything he desired could be his.

"Sobei?" Iniru whispered. "Are you all right?"

Turesobei heard her but couldn't see her. He saw the cabins below, from far above in the storm clouds where his consciousness now resided. He saw the mountains behind them and the lake below. He thought of the shaidera, and instantly an enormous lightning bolt struck down from the sky and blasted the lake. Thunder followed a moment later, booming so loud that it shook the cabin.

With a rueful smile, he looked up past the lake to the stricken lands of the Gawo. He could rid his clan of their enemies.

Then he looked beyond Gawo Province to the lands of the Chonda, the home of his forefathers and of all the people he loved. The people who suffered most from this storm, whose homes and crops were ruined, who might starve come winter.

It couldn't go on. The storm had to stop. Turesobei refused to let Naruwakiru's ghost dominate him. With a burst of determination, Turesobei sent his consciousness back into his body and commanded the heart to end the storm. Immediately the storm weakened. It did not die, however. The orb resisted his will and raged against him, sending lightning pulses through his bones, generating excruciating pain.

"You will obey me," he hissed through clenched teeth.

Pain lanced through him with stronger pulses, but he resisted. The heart wouldn't kill him. It had no other bearer now but him. And he knew the heart wanted him more than any other. For whatever reason, the orb desired a baojendari, specifically a Chonda.

It wanted him. Maybe he had always been its true target.

Turesobei struggled on. The energies relented and drained from the sky back into the heart. The pain ceased. He took a deep breath and nodded to Iniru, trying to smile but failing.

The storm was over.

But the heart had not finished. It had only gathered its strength to use against him alone. While he was relaxed, with his defenses down, Naruwakiru's jade heart struck again, through his body and deep into his mind. Turesobei collapsed to his knees. He could see nothing but dark, menacing clouds laced with thunder and lightning. No matter how hard he tried, he couldn't release the orb. Somehow it was fused into his hands.

"Turesobei, you must fight it," Iniru said, crouching next to him. "We have to get out of here. I can hear cultists coming."

But he couldn't move or respond. Hesitantly, she reached down and touched his shoulder. Only the slightest contact was made, but the heart lashed out against Iniru with a jolt of lightning. She staggered back against the wall with a web of static buzzing across her body. She cried out and then fell unconscious.

Her fur was singed, and smoke rose from her bodysuit. Turesobei's fear for her only weakened him further. He fell into a haze, just barely conscious.

The heart couldn't conquer him. He wouldn't give in.

Their standstill continued until Sotenda burst into the room with a half-dozen cultists at his side. The nazaboko high priest furiously stomped over and heel-kicked Turesobei on the side of the head. Turesobei's jaw cracked, a tooth broke off, and blood spilled onto the mats.

Chapter Fifty-One

An electric shock, burning his jaw, jolted Turesobei awake. "Ow!"

He tried to touch his face, but his arm couldn't move. He opened his matter-filled eyes, blinked them clear, and found himself within a sparse dojo located inside the manse. His feet and hands were bound together behind him, and the binding had been tied to a crude hook nailed into the wall. He was leaning forward, staring at the shining wood floor below him. Or rather at the moment, staring into Haisero's gleaming, sinister eyes.

Haisero lifted a finger and touched Turesobei's cheek, on the side without the blood-magic sigil. Another shock followed, and a spot of skin melted. A numb ache sunk down into Turesobei's cheekbone.

"Now that you're awake," Haisero said calmly, "I wish for you to tell me about your tattoo. When I try to burn you on that cheek, the energy disperses. Nothing at all like this."

Haisero shocked him again. Turesobei flinched and tried to wriggle free, but all he could do was sway from side to side. Haisero laughed, as did Sotenda and the four cultists who stood just beyond him.

"If you don't tell, I will keep burning you." He frowned and touched the right side of his face, which had been ruined by Turesobei's dark-fire. "Oh, I forgot. I'm going to burn all of your face anyway. Well then, perhaps we'll make another deal. I'll give you water and food, and I won't burn your girlfriend's face."

"Niru!" Turesobei looked beside him and saw that she dangled from a hook just as he did. She looked terrible. Her face was swollen, with bruises visible beneath singed fur. She was unmasked but otherwise still dressed in her uniform. Her eyes met his. They were glazed and unfocused. She somehow managed a smile.

"A lovely reunion," Sotenda said. "But we will have to beat her some more if you don't answer our questions."

"I would like that," added Haisero. "I haven't even shocked her yet."

Turesobei snarled and wrenched forward.

"I am afraid," said Sotenda, "that you won't be able to tear free. Your bindings are anchored into a support beam."

"And do try to use magic," Haisero said. "I'd love to see the result."

Turesobei painfully activated his kenja-sight and saw the binding spells Haisero had placed on him. The kenja from any casting Turesobei made would transform into a layer of dark-fire that would engulf both him and Iniru.

"You see what I mean," Haisero said, noticing that Turesobei's eyes had glazed over white with the activation of his kenja-sight. He glanced to Iniru. "Tenda, give me your knife, please."

"Wait!" Turesobei said. "Give her some water and I'll talk."

"Talk first," Haisero said.

"The tattoo is blood magic. My father traced it onto my cheek when I made a vow to avenge his death and reclaim Yomifano."

"Yomifano?"

"My grandfather's sword."

"Oh." Haisero drew the blade from the scabbard at his waist. "You mean my sword, don't you?" He angled it back and forth and then sheathed it proudly. "Yomifano. I think I like that name. Yomifano." He let the name roll off his tongue several more times, savoring it.

Sotenda gave them each two sips from a wooden bowl then splashed the remainder into their faces. Turesobei bore the insult because he knew the water would keep them alive for a while longer. Of course, that was probably what the cultists wanted. Sotenda might tire of this, Turesobei reckoned, but Haisero wouldn't stop until Turesobei had suffered at least twice as much as he had.

A cultist rushed into the room and bowed. "My lords, Garizu has returned."

"Send him in at once," Sotenda commanded.

Moments later, a baojendari in garb almost identical to Iniru's sauntered into the room. Turesobei recognized the eyes at once. Garizu bowed to Sotenda and Haisero then approached Turesobei.

"I thought I killed you months ago."

"Not hardly," Turesobei spat.

A knife suddenly appeared in the man's hand, and he danced the tip of it lightly across Turesobei's throat.

"Don't hurt him," Haisero said. "He's mine."

"Of course." Garizu looked over Haisero critically then said, "Is he the one that ruined your face?"

Haisero's unmarred cheek reddened, and he turned away.

"I meant no offense," Garizu said with a shrug.

"None taken," Haisero hissed. "Did you get the book?"

"Of course." Garizu drew a satchel from his backpack and handed it to Haisero. Sotenda placed a hand on his companion's shoulder, and they gazed at the satchel's contents with awe.

"You found the other volume, too!" Sotenda exclaimed. "I wasn't sure it existed."

"They had them both all right. Stealing it wasn't easy, though. The West Tagana Imperial Library is more like a prison than a place of learning."

"Well, you will be rewarded greatly by seeing the return of Naruwakiru!" Sotenda exclaimed.

"Lovely," Garizu said sarcastically. "What about money and power?"

"You will have those things in plenty when our goddess returns."

"I would like to be paid now."

Sotenda finally looked up from the books, though Haisero continued to brush them longingly with his fingers. "Of course, Garizu. You have done better than I expected, though you are late."

"I couldn't penetrate the storm you put up. I waited outside for several days until it dissipated. I killed a denekon getting here before you put it back up. As it was, I still spent several hours struggling through wind and hail."

"We had to use the storm to pin down our enemies. The Gawo have not yet given in and the Chonda are not yet destroyed."

Haisero lifted the books toward Turesobei. "Now I shall learn greater command of the powers within Naruwakiru's heart. Soon we will restore her! This second text will teach me rituals that can reconstruct Naruwakiru using her heart."

"The heart will destroy you," Turesobei said. "You are nothing more than a second-rate sorcerer."

Haisero fumed and stuffed the books into Sotenda's hands. He stormed over to Turesobei and lifted the orb, which throbbed menacingly. The heat from it began to blister Turesobei's face, and he thought Haisero was about to consume him with lightning.

But Haisero withdrew. "You will not trick me into killing you so soon. I have many hours of vengeance to meet upon you." He laughed. "You should have known, Chonda dog, that the orb would not respond to you. Naruwakiru would only entertain a high priest or a wizard of quality like me. You don't know the least about the rituals and prayers needed to calm her raging spirit. Besides, the heart hates you. I can sense that well enough."

"Soon," announced Sotenda, "you will see the full and awesome power of our goddess. And you will know firsthand what happens to the fools who resist her."

Laughing, Haisero and Sotenda exited the dojo with Garizu. Two cultists remained behind to watch Turesobei and Iniru. Two more stood right outside the door.

"Are you all right?" Turesobei asked Iniru.

"I've felt better," she muttered through her swollen, cut lips. "At least they didn't beat you."

"I think they're saving me for worse pleasures than that. I was afraid the heart had killed you when you touched me."

"I still feel numb. Every time they hit me at first, sparks flew, like touching metal in the winter. I think your grandfather's lightning charm saved me. If we make it out of this, we must thank him for keeping us alive."

"Any chance of winning free?" he whispered, noticing the guards didn't seem to actually be paying them any attention as they knelt at a table and shared a bowl of tea.

"Not in the state I'm in, if at all."

Turesobei sighed. "That assassin, Garizu. Is he a qengai?"

"No. He's from Okonuji. They're not prophecy-bearers. They use similar fighting techniques, though."

Turesobei groaned. "What should we do?"

"Rest and bide our time until an opportunity presents itself. That's all we can hope for at this point."

"I can try Lu Bei." He whispered the fetch's name several times, but he didn't appear. Turesobei could only assume that wherever they had placed his satchel and the diary, it was too far away, given his strength right now, for him to summon Lu Bei.

Despite the uncomfortable positions they were in, Iniru drifted off into sleep immediately. Turesobei tried to think of ways to win free from the binding spell on him, but he couldn't see any way he to do it without killing himself.

He cursed Naruwakiru's evil heart. He was certain it would kill Haisero eventually, unless their rituals succeeded in resurrecting her into her true dragon form. But Turesobei had doubts about whether such a thing was possible. He guessed it was more likely that her lingering spirit wanted to possess a human host. But only a suitable one.

Haisero's talent for handling raw power and his knowledge of the Storm Cult rituals had kept him alive this long. But Turesobei could see the strain in Haisero's face and knew his enemy couldn't last forever this way. Naruwakiru would burn through him to get the host she really wanted. And Turesobei knew the heart wanted him more than Haisero, for whatever reason. The heart only had to break his will first, so that it could gain a hold in his mind and dominate him forever.

Twice more during the first day, Haisero woke Turesobei and Iniru and tortured them. Turesobei grew angry each time, especially when Haisero shocked Iniru. He refused to show it, though. Haisero didn't spend nearly as much time on her, and Turesobei knew that if he let Haisero see how much it bothered him, Haisero would only treat her worse.

Iniru spent most of her time sleeping. How she could do it, Turesobei didn't know, but he suspected that it had something to do with her training. Pain and discomfort didn't bother her as much. She would begin to breathe deeply, and soon she would be fast asleep.

Turesobei's arms felt as if they were going to rip out of the shoulder sockets. He would twist his hands and feet as much as he could to loosen them. His muscles ached, the ropes chafed his skin, and his hands and feet had fallen asleep and were now consistently numb. His chest wound was an entirely different realm of pain, and it was starting to burn. He feared infection would soon set in.

He fell into shallow sleeps filled with dreams of loved ones followed by sudden nightmares. He would see his father paint the sigil on his cheek. The blood burned like the shocks Haisero gave him, and he would scream as the blood turned to acid and ate through his flesh down to his bones.

Turesobei dreamt of Awasa. She stood naked under a cherry tree. Tender blossoms rained down upon her. They got caught in her lustrous black hair and stuck to her ivory skin. She laughed softly, with a glint in her eyes. She spoke, but he couldn't hear her. She became distressed that he didn't answer, and then she disappeared.

And he dreamed of many past times and people long dead—daring enemies, beautiful women, exotic lands, dazzling treasures, endless hours of spell casting, and searching through musty tomes. These were, he knew, memories within the kavaru. Most likely they were those of Chonda Lu and not the later owners of the channeling stone. Yet he felt they were his memories, and he felt that he was Chonda Lu. And he could hear Lu Bei telling him, "Master, you and the stone, you and Chonda Lu, are one and the same."

Suddenly, he was awake, and Iniru was whispering harshly at him. The glint in her dark-rimmed, swollen eyes was nothing like the glint that had been in Awasa's, though he'd seen Iniru's eyes filled with love for him before. Or he guessed it was love. Something like it at least. Right now, a qengai's intensity filled them.

"Stop dreaming and pay attention," she said. "Something's going on."

"Sorry." He looked around but saw nothing out of the ordinary. One guard napped with his back against the wall. The other was shaping a rock. "I don't see anything," he whispered.

"Can't you feel it? Something's happening, or something's about to happen."

Turesobei opened up his kenja-sight. He began to shake his head and say no, but then he glimpsed a tiny current of air kenja. It seemed familiar somehow, but he couldn't figure it out. Footsteps sounded in the hallway. Turesobei hoped for a rescue as the doors flew open. But Garizu, Sotenda, Haisero, and six guards strolled in laughing. Even Garizu was chuckling. Judging from his mood, Turesobei guessed that they'd paid the Okonuji assassin.

Haisero closed on Turesobei, shooting sparks at him as he went. The cultists continued to laugh as Haisero grasped Turesobei around the neck and shot electricity directly into his body so that he jerked and flailed.

Haisero pulled back with a look of pure ecstasy twisting his face into a maniacal grin. Then, suddenly, one of the cultists standing guard in the doorway stood painfully erect with his mouth locked open in a silent scream. The body toppled forward with a steel spike embedded in the throat, sparkling amongst the crimson blood. A moment later, the other guard fell.

Chapter Fifty-Two

Haisero, Sotenda, Garizu, and the remaining cultists fell back from the doorway and drew their weapons. Six Chonda soldiers in mud-covered lamellar armor and a bedraggled Onudaka burst into the hall. Grandfather Kahenan strolled in behind them. He looked worn and weary. Water dripped from his tattered robes. One hand rested on the hilt of a borrowed white-steel short sword. The other was tucked into his spell pouch. His kavaru was alight with power. A headband was wrapped across his brow, holding aloft a strange gemstone with a glowing rune Turesobei didn't recognize. Whatever it was, it wasn't another kavaru.

Turesobei had never before been happier to see his grandfather. Their eyes met for a moment, and then Kahenan turned his gaze to Haisero. "So, it comes to this, twisted spawn of the Gawo."

Standing below Turesobei, Haisero cackled and raised the orb. Lightning blasted forth. At the same moment, Kahenan, with a bamboo strip clutched between his fingers, swiped his hand diagonally across his body and spoke a spell command.

The thunderbolt fired to within an inch of Kahenan's chest and struck an invisible barrier. Crackling webs of electricity sparked all along the invisible shield. The talisman on Kahenan's forehead glowed a brilliant azure. As the electric web faded, the talisman grew brighter, then...

Whoosh! The electricity and the talisman's glow disappeared. Kahenan collapsed to the ground, unconscious or worse.

"Grandfather!"

Even as he yelled, Turesobei realized the talisman had worked automatically to protect Kahenan. The spell he had cast, however, did something else entirely, and Turesobei had less than a heartbeat to prepare. The ropes binding him and Iniru disintegrated. Turesobei painfully extended his cramped, bruised muscles as he fell and tackled Haisero.

The jade orb thunked against the bare wood floor, but it didn't leave Haisero's relaxed hand. The skin of his palm had melted onto the heart's surface. With horror, Turesobei realized Haisero must have done it intentionally so that no one could easily take the orb from him again. Now that he thought about it, he hadn't seen Haisero's left hand leave the heart since he had awoken as their prisoner.

Despite her injuries, Iniru tucked into a ball, hit the floor shoulder first, and rolled to her feet. The others rushed into action, and the dojo erupted into a chaotic frenzy.

The Chonda soldiers engaged Garizu and the cultists, while Sotenda conquered his fear and faced his older brother.

"We will end our quarrel today, Daka."

Onudaka hefted his quarterstaff and rolled his shoulders. "Fine. But it would go easier if you'd just give up. You are not stable, Tenda. You need to return to the priests. They can care for you, help you."

"Never again!"

Sotenda lunged forward. Onudaka parried the attack, sidestepped, and redirected Sotenda's energy. Sotenda stumbled past, and Onudaka slapped the quarterstaff into Sotenda's lower back. Sotenda tumbled to the floor but rolled back up to his feet before Onudaka could strike again. His face reddened with humiliation. Then his eyes narrowed and all the emotion drained from his face.

"I won't make that mistake again. You have always angered me when we fight, always made me lose control. But no more. I think you were the one who made me overreact to things in the first place. You twisted me and sent me to the priests to make it worse, all because you wanted to be father's only child, because you hated my mother, because you hated me for being what I am."

"I never hated you, Tenda. I loved you. And if you will recall, you killed our father and your mother before I sent you there."

"It was their fault I was born nazaboko! Not even a noble baojendari's son, but a pitiful bastard of society."

Sotenda leapt forward, swords whirring, chipping away at Onudaka's quarterstaff as he parried the blows. Sotenda's confidence increased and Onudaka grew tired. His step faltered, and a sword stroke cut deep across his thigh. Sotenda shouldered into him and knocked him down. The back of Onudaka's head struck hard. He tried to climb to his feet, but only got up to his knees as Sotenda hammered away at his defenses.

Meanwhile, the Chonda soldiers and the cultist guards fought, but they were not evenly matched. Kahenan had brought the best men available to him. Swiftly, they killed the first four cultists who stood against them. Then they faced Garizu, whose skill they had no hope of matching. Garizu fought with movements so fast that only a qengai could have noticed the subtleties. Within moments, two Chonda soldiers lay clutching fatal wounds.

Turesobei thought about rushing to Kahenan, but he knew he had to deal with the Storm Dragon's Heart first. Haisero tried to squirm out from under him for several moments before he remembered the power he commanded.

"Get off me!"

Electricity flared down his body and shocked Turesobei, who screamed and tried to let go, but couldn't. The current locked their bodies together. Turesobei would have died within heartbeats, but Iniru appeared out of nowhere and kicked Haisero in the jaw.

The electricity discharged to her instead with a tremendous boom that knocked her back against the wall. Turesobei didn't waste another moment. He reached out and took hold of the orb.

At the same moment, he said to Iniru, "Help the others!"

As she picked herself up, again saved only by the lightning wards Kahenan had placed on her uniform, Iniru gave Turesobei a look of admiration, then darted away.

The energies of the Storm Dragon's Heart poured into Turesobei like liquid fire and tried again to enthrall him. He stood, tugging the heart and trying to exert his will over it. Haisero rose with him and added his other hand to the jade orb. Neither could wrest it away from the other.

Turesobei's mind expanded as before, becoming one with the storm clouds above. But as he fought to stay with the orb, somehow his awareness ended up hovering above the room, not in his body and yet not in the clouds, either.

Haisero remained himself, and Turesobei knew at least one reason why the heart wanted him. Haisero couldn't do this. Either he lacked the talent or his cult rituals protected him. And Turesobei was now more than certain that Naruwakiru still wanted him and was only using Haisero to weaken him first.

Sotenda had Onudaka backed up against the wall. Several cuts on his arms and the gash on his leg bled profusely. Sotenda attacked, and his brother blocked the strikes slowly. Sotenda feinted with a lunge, slapping his foot down on the floor. Onudaka fell for the trick and raised his quarterstaff to block the high cut. But the cut never came. Sotenda leapt in and with his off-hand sword stabbed Onudaka deep in the stomach.

Onudaka gasped, dropped his staff, and slid down the wall. He looked up into his brother's gleaming, hateful eyes. "Finish it then."

Iniru had rushed in to help the Chonda soldiers. Despite being injured and exhausted, she was still a qengai. Garizu, on the other hand, was well rested. He was also stronger and more experienced. While Garizu engaged the two remaining Chonda soldiers, she lunged in. He dodged her attack, and elbowed her on the base of the skull. She fell limp.

The two soldiers attacked when Garizu spun and put his back to them. Garizu parried the sword of one without looking, but the other slashed him across the back. Garizu turned, slowed just barely by the wound, defended against three more attacks, and then disposed of the soldiers in successive maneuvers.

Turesobei saw, heard, and somehow sensed all of this from where he hovered above the room. Soldiers were dying or dead already. Kahenan and Iniru might be dead as well. Onudaka would soon be murdered. Already, Garizu had turned and eyed Turesobei. The assassin's hand dipped into his vest, to a place Iniru kept throwing blades.

But Turesobei wouldn't let them win. He wouldn't let Haisero and Naruwakiru get the best of him. He was a Chonda, and for the moment, he was their high wizard. The fate of his entire clan and the people he loved most in the world rested in his hands. Self-doubt left him—worries, anxieties, and fear as well. The crimson goshawk sigil on his cheek burned more intensely than any lightning strike of Haisero's. The sigil burned down into his soul, connecting to who he was.

"Naruwakiru!" he yelled. "You will answer to me! You will obey me! Me and no one else!"

Turesobei's consciousness slammed back into his body so hard that he staggered and nearly lost his grip on the heart.

Haisero sneered at him. "The heart is mine."

So many lives had already been destroyed for this one jade orb, for the power of Naruwakiru. But no more innocents would die. Turesobei knew his will was stronger, that he would not give in, despite the odds against him, despite Haisero and Naruwakiru, despite Garizu with his throwing blade in hand.

"Blade!" Turesobei thought, and he remembered the other half of his vow. His eyes fell upon the hilt of Yomifano hanging in its scabbard from Haisero's belt. Then, with sheer force of will, he did what Haisero could not do. He relinquished the Storm Dragon's Heart. His hands slipped away and Haisero exulted in glee.

But even as Haisero fell back from him, Turesobei dropped his hand to Yomifano's hilt and pulled the blade free.

"Sobei!" Iniru cried out weakly.

Turesobei ducked. Garizu's throwing spike whistled overhead, missing its mark. The assassin charged toward him. But Garizu wouldn't make it in time.

Lightning-fire enshrouded Haisero as the heart, jilted by Turesobei, at last gave to him its full power. His mouth opened in a scream of both agony and ecstasy. "I am Naruwakiru!" he screamed, no longer conscious even of himself. Haisero had talent for wielding power, but this was too much. He began to scream and rave incoherently.

The screams made Sotenda spin around before his final strike against his brother. His companion's name issued softly through his lips, and yet everyone could hear it over the roaring of the heart. "Sero. What have you done?"

Turesobei lifted Yomifano and lunged forward. He yelled as he brought Yomifano's edge down onto the orb. The white-steel blade cut into the jade heart with a piercing crack. He drew the sword back for another strike, but it wasn't necessary.

Fault lines appeared on the heart, glowing crimson and brilliant white. Flailing lightning tendrils shot out from the cleft and lashed everything within twenty feet, scoring cuts into the wood floor, burning holes into the ceiling, filling the air with the stench of ozone. The building shook with thunder. Rain and fog appeared within the training hall and swirled around in a growing vortex.

Garizu halted his charge and backpedaled, but too late. A random tendril struck him in the chest, burned through his ribs, and seared his heart.

The Storm Dragon's Heart began to consume Haisero, sucking out every bit of kenja within him as it tried to repair itself. Smoke rose from his simmering hair. His clothes burst into flame. His screams turned shrill and inhuman and then faded into the sizzling of burned flesh as his body became a blackened hull. Screaming and maddened, Sotenda blindly rushed forward to aid his friend.

Two tendrils locked onto Obu Sotenda and within moments burned him into a smoldering lump of charred flesh. His screams echoed long after his body was no longer recognizable.

The tendrils didn't strike Turesobei. He held Yomifano forward and warded them away. Haisero's body collapsed into ashes and charred bones, but the orb didn't fall. The heart hovered in the air and expanded with larger and larger cracks in its surface. The lashing tentacles of lightning grew longer and multiplied in number.

Turesobei glanced at his fallen grandfather, to Iniru who was pulling herself up to her knees, to Onudaka who was breathing heavily and clenching his hands over the wound to his stomach. He couldn't get them out of the room before the tendrils reached them. It was only a matter of moments. And the imminent explosion he now sensed would probably level everything for miles around anyway.

A tendril lashed out toward Turesobei, and he dispersed it with Yomifano. At that moment, through some mental connection he still had with the heart, he understood how it had been made so powerful. Hundreds of storm spirits had been bound into the heart and were now seeking to escape. That was what had so greatly increased her power millennia ago. And to rebind the spirits would require a new, unbroken vessel. It would require dozens of wizards and powerful blood magic. Years of preparation would be necessary.

And Turesobei had only Yomifano. The sword could disrupt much of the energy, but it could never cut through all of it. But there was something he could do.

He waded toward the heart, slashing tendrils of lightning with the white-steel blade, killing storm spirits with every sweep of Yomifano.

"Sobei!" Iniru called. "Don't take it."

"There's no other way to save everyone." He smiled and almost said, "I love you." But what he was doing said it better than words ever could.

Turesobei drew Yomifano back and reached out his free hand. Lightning struck him and alternating waves of numbness and pain shot up through his arm, through his shoulder and into his chest and head. But he remained confident, and the lightning didn't kill him.

Because the heart wouldn't kill him. It wanted to be saved.

He kept the image of Iniru's worried face in his mind. For her and for Kahenan and for Onudaka and for all the Chonda, he willed the hateful orb to obey him and called on the blood-magic sigil Noboro had drawn onto his cheek. It was all he had to call upon, so it would have to do.

The goshawk sigil flared, the amber kavaru of Chonda Lu glowed like the sun, and Turesobei screamed as kenja from the Storm Dragon's Heart poured into him at full strength, as he became the vessel for the heart's power. His flesh did not burn as Haisero's had, so he knew in part that it was working, though his body did glow as if he were made of lightning. He dropped Yomifano. Tendrils of lightning wrapped around him and lashed him across the back.

Time meant nothing to him anymore. His only thoughts were of what he must do. The orb emptied, and the jade fragments clinked and clattered onto the floor.

Turesobei staggered out of the manse and down to the lakeshore. His insides began to boil. His skin began to bubble. Pure glowing kenja seeped from his eyes and from in between his fingers where the skin had split open. But he willed the energies to stay within. Just a few moments more, that was all he needed.

Envisioning the magic runes of banishment, Turesobei commanded the storm spirits to go far out into the upper reaches of the atmosphere where he hoped they would dissipate. Then he fell to his knees and unleashed a primal scream.

A bolt of lightning, the size of a hundred of the largest bolts ever seen on Okoro combined, shot out from his mouth. The bolt pierced the sky for twelve agonizing heartbeats. A thunder blast rocked the land for hundreds of miles with the force of an earthquake.

Turesobei's burned-out body collapsed onto the cold shore with a final breath wheezing out from between his lips. His heart stopped beating, and with it faded his last pain-filled thoughts.

Chapter Fifty-Three

Turesobei glided along on the currents high above Okoro. The land scrolled beneath him, a patchwork of valleys and plains, forests and rivers, all dominated by hills and mountains. Large cities like anthills dotted the coasts. Towns were motes of dust. Coiling reefs wrapped around the shores, and the ocean stretched out endlessly beyond. Turesobei felt omnipotent and eternal, free without the least restraint. Was this an afterlife? The path to the heavens? Perhaps this would soon end and his soul would be reborn into a new body. Perhaps he would ascend into a realm of bliss. Of course, he hadn't attained perfection in life, but maybe the gods would reward him for the sacrifice he had made for his friends and family.

For days he lived like this, as a cloud above Okoro. Sometimes he flew high and nearly froze. Other times he swooped down low and dropped rain onto the land. Never once did he rage and storm.

And then one day, Turesobei rolled across his homeland. Below him, zaboko farmers struggled to rebuild homes and gather food stores for the coming winter. Their fields lay in ruin. Rice paddies had been washed away to the ocean, livestock had drowned, fruit had been torn away by the winds. Townspeople fared no better. Things were worse for them. Farming supported them, and the farmers had no food to share. Ekaran was half ruins. Soldiers worked in the fields all around and were helping to rebuild homes. Repairs to the palaces would have to wait for winter. The people had to come first.

Turesobei's pride in his lineage swelled, and his heart ached that so many had been hurt by the Storm Dragon's Heart. And then he felt his body, his actual physical form below. He wasn't dead. Not yet. He was a cloud, and yet he was like a kite in the wind with a kenja string tethering his soul to the earth. He could let go and fly away with perfect freedom. But his people needed him. Loved ones surely missed him, and there would be endless labors for a high wizard's apprentice at a time like this.

I may even be the High Wizard now.

Turesobei knew he must return.

The dream that was more than a dream ended. Turesobei's lungs pulled at Cloud-Turesobei, drawing his spirit back in. He opened his eyes to daylight streaming through his bedroom window. He was alive. And strangely enough, he felt good. His muscles were cramped as if he hadn't moved them in days, but that was all. Over the last weeks he had endured wounds and complete exhaustion, even torture, and the effects had lingered and plagued him. But now, he felt good. Perhaps better than ever before. Something or someone had healed him entirely. How many days had he been asleep, recovering? Weeks? Months?

Turesobei sat up, and immediately his sister tackled him.

"Sobei! You're awake!"

Turesobei laughed as he fell back onto his sleeping mat. "I am, Shoma." He hugged his sister tightly and his eyes began to tear up. "I'm awake and I'm alive."

"Of course you're alive. Nothing could kill my big brother. Not even Naruwakiru."

He pulled back and looked into her bright, admiring eyes. Tears streaked down her face. She dabbed at them and smiled. "I've got to go tell the others."

"Wait, Shoma. Grandfather..."

The smile drained from her face. "He's alive, but we don't think he's going to make it."

"Did he wake up?"

"Only once, they said, after you broke the orb and then released the lightning into the sky—we saw it all the way here—then he fell into a coma."

Turesobei's heart sunk. "What about Onudaka and Iniru?"

"Onudaka's recovering. It'll take him a few more weeks, but he'll be fine. He's been downcast, what with his brother's death and all, and he's been worried about you. Iniru is recovered, too. She's already practicing her martial arts again. She checks on you all the time."

He smiled all the way down into his belly. "Shoma, how long has it been?"

"Two weeks."

"And I just lay here asleep the whole time?"

"You glowed sometimes."

"What?!"

"You'd better let one of the wizards tell you about it. I think it's just some of the excess energy discharging from you." She touched his cheek. "There's also the ... well, I should let someone else tell you about that."

Turesobei frowned, but he had so many questions that he decided not to pursue it. "Besides you, who's been—"

"Master!" cried a voice from the hallway and Lu Bei, bearing a tray with a steaming— and now sloshing—cup of tea, zoomed into the room. "Master, you're awake. You've returned to us!"

Lu Bei was a good six inches taller than before and there was an indigo lightning bolt sigil emblazoned on his chest. Turesobei was stunned. "Lu Bei, what happened to you? You've grown! And that symbol..."

Lu Bei carefully set down the tray. Then he shot into Turesobei's arms. "Much to tell, master. Oh, there's so much to tell you."

"Lu Bei has been helping me," said Enashoma. "He's very dedicated, and he doesn't have to sleep. And he is so incredibly awesome!"

"But he's not supposed to be seen ..."

"Oh, well," said Lu Bei, sitting back, "I wasn't having any of that. Master needed me. Besides, I never left the house. Only Enashoma knows about me. Not your mother or the servants. I am careful not to be seen."

"Wait, how could you be in your fetch form while I was asleep? And travel so far from me? And —"

"The storm energies, master. They affected us both."

"Because we are linked by the kavaru?"

"You absorbed so much energy. In turn, the kavaru and myself took on some of that power. That is why I am changed now. I'm bigger, faster, and I even have a few magic tricks I can do now." The amber fetch lifted his hand and sparks shot out from his palm. "See?"

"That's very impressive, Lu Bei."

Enashoma was bouncing up and down on the balls of her feet. "Please let me go tell everyone the news. Lu Bei can answer your questions."

"Go on then."

Enashoma skipped out of the room. Turesobei touched his cheek. It felt tender, like a bruise, where the Sigil of the Chonda Goshawk sigil had been. Kenja still gathered there. With the vow complete, it should have left him, but if anything it had grown twice as intense. Yet he had used the blood magic to contain and release the heart's power, so anything was possible. He really shouldn't be alive, and he didn't doubt strange things had happened to his body over the last week.

"Lu Bei, how did I survive the blast?"

"I'm not certain, master. All I know is that the energies healed instead of killing you. I mean, your heart did stop. Iniru had to resuscitate you, but after that you were fine. One of the wizards who checked on you said you had the kenja of a newborn babe, only a hundred times more of it. You're still charged with energy from the heart."

"Do you know how Grandfather found us?"

"He had secretly placed a tracking charm in your armor, and they rode a team of denekon to death to reach you while the storm was down. After the fight, the remaining cultists fled."

Soft footsteps pattered down the hallway. He recognized them immediately and said, "Niru," as soon as she walked into the room.

"Sobei," she replied in a warm, smiling whisper.

Iniru took his hands, and he drew her toward him. She held back at first, until he assured her she wouldn't hurt him.

"I don't know how you're all right," she said. "Honestly, you should be dead."

"I know. Lu Bei says you revived me."

"That should not have worked."

"But it did," he said cheerfully.

"You're not worried about it? That seems unlike you."

He shrugged. "I'll worry about it later. Right now I'm just happy to see you again."

Their eyes met, and then their lips.

"Ahem!" said a woman.

They drew apart as Wenari, her face painted with disgust, marched into the room. Iniru backed away, as if cowed, though Turesobei knew that was only an act to keep things civil. Lu Bei was suddenly a diary, an inch thicker than he used to be, sitting on the table. Wenari's expression threatened an outburst, but then she exhaled and relaxed. She gracefully bent, hugged her son, and kissed him on the forehead.

He hugged his mother and assured her he felt fine. After a few moments of having her coddle him, he asked for food and water. He was absolutely starving. "Cold things only, please. I don't want anything hot."

"I'll see to it, my poor darling."

Wenari left, and Iniru knelt beside him.

"You don't have many friends," Iniru said.

Turesobei groaned. "Thanks. That's just what I needed to pick up my spirits. I almost die and that's what you have to say to me?"

Iniru shrugged. "You seem well enough for some criticism. Besides, it's true. No one has come to check on you except the two of us, Imi and Shurada, and a bunch of adults. Lu Bei, of course. And the ones who weren't your instructors were all nobles whose well-being depends on your well-being."

"I don't have time for friends. And I don't get along well with people, either."

Iniru agreed. "Shoma and I have decided you need more friends. A few male associates your own age would be good for you. Sobei, you just don't even try to get along with people."

"What about Awasa? Did she even bother to ask how I was?"

"Oh, I forgot. She checked up on you."

"Yes, she did," Enashoma said, returning to the room. She handed him something from the table beside his sleeping mat. "She brought this letter here for you and actually sat with you for several hours."

"You're kidding, right?"

"Nope."

"What does the letter say?"

"How would I know? I didn't open it."

"Are you sure?"

"Check the seal. See? No one touched it."

"I don't believe it, as nosy as you are."

"Niru wouldn't let me open it."

"Ah. Well, I'll read it later." He set the letter on his pillow. "Niru, what's this about my cheek? Shoma wouldn't tell me, and I didn't get the chance to ask Lu Bei."

Iniru and Enashoma exchanged glances. There was a puff of smoke and Lu Bei joined them.

"Well," Iniru said, "the goshawk is gone and a new sigil has replaced it."

"Bring me a mirror."

Lu Bei returned with one. Turesobei stared into it. The crimson goshawk sigil was gone, and in its place rose the storm-blue and black sigil of Naruwakiru, reminiscent of a jagged lightning bolt within a cloud, all contained by a black circle.

"It won't wash off," Enashoma said. "We tried."

"I'm cursed," Turesobei muttered.

"The wizards were concerned about it," said Iniru.

"They should be. I used the blood magic my father started to bind the storm kenja within me. I had hoped only long enough to release it. It seems not all of it left. Lu Bei and I are carrying quite a bit of it."

"The clan wizards," Enashoma said, "are still puzzled by how all of this worked out. They kept mumbling that none of what happened out there should've been possible. We really need grandfather to figure it out, but he may not..." She couldn't finish her statement.

"After I eat," Turesobei said, "I'll go visit him."

"Are you up to that?" Iniru asked.

"Except that I'm a little light-headed from hunger, I think I could conquer the world."

Sunlight and a fresh breeze filtered through the open window into the tower's bedroom. Grandfather Kahenan was lying on his plush sleeping mat. The skin was drawn tight around his mouth and eyes. His complexion was pallid. His grey hair hung limp and some had fallen out.

Turesobei took one of his grandfather's withered hands in his and shuddered. "He's going to die."

"The other wizards have cast healing spells on him," Iniru said. "They did everything they could think of. But that seems to just barely keep him alive."

"Enashoma, summon King Ugara for me, please. Tell him I must speak with him immediately."

His sister wiped a tear from her cheek. "Sobei, you can't. I mean, you're not supposed to summon the king that way."

"I am the acting High Wizard, as far as I'm concerned, and I need to speak with him now. It's important."

She rushed off. Turesobei gathered various objects of wizardry: ink and brushes, papyrus, gemstones, a compass.

"Lu Bei, can you go up into the workshop and retrieve some things for me? We must hurry. He's going to die soon. We have a few more hours at best."

"Are you sure?" asked Iniru.

"Grandfather sensed my presence when I touched his hand. He was waiting to see that I would succeed him. Now that he knows I'm well, he's ready to give up fighting for life. I have no doubt about this. I don't know how I know. I just do."

Turesobei described what he needed as he drew the sheets back. Iniru cleared the room of everything non-essential and then ran to the workshop to help Lu Bei retrieve the instruments Turesobei needed.

On his grandfather's bare skin, Turesobei drew lines in Zhura-ink, marking the energy channels within the body. Then he drew runes on Kahenan's forehead and on his chest above the heart. Lu Bei watched him paint the complex glyphs. Anytime a stroke wasn't perfect, Lu Bei would grumble, and Turesobei would correct it.

At last, King Ugara entered with Prince Chien and two guards. Iniru bowed and spoke with them a few moments while Turesobei finished the rune he was drawing. Turesobei glanced to Lu Bei but discovered that he was lying on the floor in book form.

He stood up and bowed to King Chonda Ugara. "Your majesty, thank you for coming so quickly."

"What is it, Turesobei?"

"Grandfather is going to die unless I act quickly."

"Then by the gods, do it," Prince Chien said. "You don't need permission."

"Actually, I do. Grandfather would not approve of what I am going to do. But we need him. My training is not complete. I have talent, but there is much that I need to learn from him. The clan needs him, as well. I am too young to fulfill all the duties of a high wizard, and the other wizards of the clan..."

"Are ultimately not suitable for the task," replied the king. "I understand. So you want me to order him brought back?"

"Yes, your majesty."

Ugara scratched his cheek and frowned. "I have been friends with Kahenan all our lives. We speak every day. It is easy to bring back a friend, but it is hard to defy a friend's wishes." He took a deep breath and nodded. "Turesobei, I order you to revive High Wizard Kahenan. He is not allowed to die today."

"Thank you, your majesty."

"Will this take long?"

"Many hours."

"Notify us when you are finished. May the gods be with you tonight, Turesobei."

Bows were exchanged and the king and the prince departed. Turesobei breathed a sigh of relief and placed a hand on Kahenan's chest.

"There's no risk to you in this, is there?" Iniru asked.

"Only a little."

"You didn't tell them that."

"If they had known, they would never have allowed me to try it. But I'll be fine."

"Master will be fine," said a returned Lu Bei, "because he says so."

"I know," said Iniru, smiling. "It's wizardry. I trust him."

Chapter Fifty-Four

Turesobei worked long into the night, chanting and drawing the runes again, this time using his own blood. Just before dawn, when the kenja tides were strongest for this day, he performed the *ritual of complete restoration*. It was a healing designed specifically for restoring someone who had suffered from massive shock, blood loss, and other injuries. Or for wizards depleted of kenja and on the verge of dying. For the latter, there was little hope for an elder wizard who had spent years damaging his organs through the overuse of magic. And Grandfather Kahenan was decades past his prime.

But Turesobei had more than enough storm energy within him. He reasoned that if the storm energies had rejuvenated and healed him, then they might have a similar effect on his grandfather. He figured it was worth trying. He was also using risky blood magic to make it work. He believed this would have an increased effect on his own grandfather. If any of the runes were not drawn precisely, or if any of his chants were off, he would die. But he felt confident in his efforts.

He gave the final commands. A warm, blue glow emanated from his hands. He touched Kahenan's brow. Kenja flared along the meridians Turesobei had marked and down into Kahenan's heart. Turesobei's tired mind ached and energy drained from him, but there was more than enough to cast even a spell this difficult.

The glow surrounded Kahenan and remained for several minutes before it seeped into him. Kahenan opened his eyes. He smiled at Turesobei. Then he looked at the markings on his body, drawn with blood, and the storm sigil on Turesobei's cheek.

Kahenan frowned. "You are ... an evil, evil child. You should not have brought me back like this."

Turesobei grinned. "I know, but you have more to teach me."

Coughing, Kahenan asked, "Is that Naruwakiru's mark upon you?"

"I destroyed the orb and had to take in the energies long enough to banish them."

"Not all of it left you. Much remains."

"I know. There's plenty more than what I just used on you."

"Do not heal anyone else with it, no matter how minor the healing spell. You will kill them."

"It did not kill you, master."

"That is because you shocked my heart back to life. Trust me. My body needed that

226

much strength."

"Yes, master."

"I am proud of you. Your father ... would be proud, too. I knew you would come through. You did what I could never have done."

"It marked me, though."

"Aye, it is part of you now. But we ... we will have time to figure that out later. I suppose maybe you do still need me."

"I know, master. Now rest. I will have someone keep watch."

Turesobei informed King Ugara of Kahenan's recovery. Then he slept until the next morning. After that, he spent nearly all of his waking time for the next three days with Iniru. Those three days were like heaven. He didn't even think about them ending until the evening they sat together on a lakeshore outside Ekaran and watched the sun fall toward the horizon.

"As far as raw capability, I'm probably the most powerful wizard in Okoro now," Turesobei said. "My energy levels are ten times normal, but I don't seem to have any adverse reaction. Still, I can't help but think that I'm going to have a heavy price to pay."

Iniru stroked her hand across his face. "I wish I could help you through it." She sighed. "But you know that I cannot stay."

Turesobei looked away, stunned. He felt as if his soul was being ripped apart. "I'll be lost without you."

She laughed. "You'll be fine. You have Enashoma and Kahenan. Onudaka is going to retire here. You can visit him anytime. And you have Awasa."

"Oh, yes. Wonderful."

"You know, she really does like you. That note she left was sweet."

"You weren't supposed to read it."

"I think I have every right to read love notes sent to you."

He stared into her soft eyes and chuckled. "I supposed you do." He sighed. "The letter was kind?"

"She apologized for how she's treated you. That's a start."

"She's just doing it because she's jealous of you."

"Of course, but she really does like you."

"Oh come on, Niru."

"I'm serious, Sobei. Give her a chance. You have a bad habit of not thinking about what other people are going through. Like all the other girls here, Awasa has been pressured to become a certain type of person when she grows up. Just as you're being forced to become a high wizard, she's being forced to become a lady of Chonda society. A high wizard's wife at that. She has fewer options and less freedom than you do."

"I never really thought about it that way."

"She didn't get to pick out who'd be her husband anymore than you got to pick out who'd be your wife. How do you think that makes her feel? She's frustrated, and she's trying to get power the only way she knows how, by bossing you and everyone else around, by trying to force you away from her. You were happy about the betrothal, so she took it out on you.

"Don't get me wrong. Awasa is arrogant. She's headstrong, proud, and absolutely spoiled. But those things can improve over time. Too many people have molded her into that form, and if you don't give her room to break out of the mold, who will?"

"Maybe you're right," Turesobei said darkly, staring off at the hills beyond the city. "But I don't want to think about it. I don't want to spend my life with anyone else but you."

"That's just not possible, and you know it."

"But it has to be."

Turesobei stood and took her hands in his. He kissed each finger and then brought her hands to his chest. "I promise I will find a way. I vow to you this day, that I will come and join you. Then we'll live the rest of our lives together."

Iniru kissed him tenderly, then passionately. Sometime later, she drew his head into her hands and said, "You're sweet. And I love you. But I won't hold you to that vow. You will never be able to keep it."

"But I will!"

"No, you won't. You'll never escape this place. You're a good man, and your people need you. They rely on you. You know that. And you really do enjoy being a wizard. Admit it."

"Now that I feel like it's useful and I know what I can do, yes. And they do need me here. But maybe you could join me here instead."

"I took a vow before I ever knew you, and I won't forsake it. I have a place in life that I must fill, too."

Turesobei rested his forehead against hers and strained back the tears in his eyes. "When are you leaving?"

"I have fulfilled the prophecy given to me. I can feel that it is so in my heart. And so I cannot waste any more time. I will leave as soon as the sun sets."

He shook his head. "Three days isn't long enough!"

"It will take weeks for me to get back home. I have duties to fulfill. And sooner or later, I will have a new prophecy mission."

"But you haven't told everyone goodbye."

"Actually, I did that this morning before you woke up."

Turesobei cringed. "That's why Enashoma was so sullen at breakfast. You must have made her promise not to tell."

"I thought it would be easier this way."

"Nothing could make it easier."

Turesobei and Iniru clung to each other until the sun fell below the hills. Stray clouds glowed pink and orange and purple in the pale blue sky above. Tears fell and Iniru kissed him one last time.

She stepped away, her fingers lingering in his for just a moment. Then she took a deep breath and let go. She recovered her pack from behind a shrub where she'd hidden it earlier.

"I love you," he said.

Iniru smiled, lifted a hand to wave goodbye, spun around, and walked away solemnly. Every so often she would turn and look back. He would wave to her, and she would walk on.

"Sobei?" a voice called from behind him.

He turned and saw three figures. One was Awasa walking toward him. The other two were her attendant Marumi and her bodyguard Zaiporo, both of whom stood uphill, just within sight. He wasn't sure how they had found him out here. He didn't really care. Turesobei turned back and watched Iniru walking away.

Awasa stopped just behind him. "I'm not intruding am I?"

He shook his head, and she stepped forward and held out a string of bright yellow flowers wound together. "I hadn't heard from you the last several days, but Enashoma said you were doing fine. Did you get my letter?"

Turesobei took the flowers and looked at them in confusion, as if he didn't really know what they were. "It was very kind."

He held the flower-chain absently and stared back at the distant figure, nothing more than a shadow cast by the setting sun. Awasa seemed to just then realize why he was standing here.

"Who is —"

"Iniru. She's going home."

"Well, good —" Awasa drew in a deep breath. "I — I'm sorry, Sobei. I ... I know you will miss her."

He twisted the flowers in his hands then looked up at her and strained a smile. "Terribly," he said. "But this is the way things must be."

Epilogue

Iniru walked as far as she could before she slumped down beside a gnarled oak and hunkered over—body shaking, tears streaming from her eyes.

Leaving Turesobei was the hardest thing she had ever done. And the thought of never seeing him again was unbearable. But she had to return to her clan. She had a vow to fulfill, and giving up her life as a qengai for a boy was *not* an option. Duty was more important than love. It had to be.

Still, to never see Turesobei again....

Heart aching, she glanced back toward Ekaran. It would be so easy to turn around and go back. Turesobei and happiness were so close, while her clan and her qengai obligations were so far away.

Iniru took a deep breath and shook her head. No. She couldn't.

She had spent ten years training to be a qengai. She'd promised herself she'd become the best, and then she had set out to prove it to everyone in Yasei-maka who doubted her. Most importantly, she had vowed to make her mother proud, no matter what it took.

From a pocket, Iniru drew the pebble with her mother's name etched into it. She kissed the pebble and clenched it tight. She had to go home. She had to give up on Turesobei. That was the way it had to be.

It just wasn't their destiny to....

Iniru perked up. Her destiny!

Through the whirlwind of adventures, she had completely forgotten about her vision in the Cavern of the Prophet. She pocketed the pebble then fumbled through the hidden compartments of her uniform until she found the stack of twelve sketches she'd made, wrapped up tight within an oiled-leather pouch.

Despite several desperate battles, a tremendous rainstorm, and her traipsing along the bottom of a lake, the paper squares had remained in good condition. She thumbed through the eleven featuring Turesobei and found the one with the exact look on his face the moment she'd first seen him on the rope bridge.

She glanced at the other ten squares featuring him, ignoring the one of her alone with the stone arch, the one that made her sad and uncomfortable. For a few moments, the intense feelings she had experienced in the visions rushed through her again. She laughed through her tears, then wiped them from her cheeks.

Like the Prophet and the Acolyte with their destinies tied to their cavern, hers was tied to Turesobei. If one of the visions could come true, then all of them could. She nodded. Yes, unless something terrible happened, she and Sobei would meet again. They had to. She was certain of it.

Iniru kissed the stack of images, wrapped them up, and tucked them safely back into her uniform. She stood and gazed back toward Ekaran. She smiled into the twilit horizon.

"We'll meet again soon."

Afterword

Thank you for purchasing this book. If you enjoyed this tale, please leave a review at your favorite online retailer. All it takes is a sentence or two!

For a full list of all my books available, or to sign up for my newsletter, please visit dahayden.com or typingcatpress.com.

More Stories In ...

The Storm Phase Series

THE MAKER'S BRUSH
Storm Phase Interlude One

LAIR OF THE DEADLY TWELVE
Storm Phase Book Two

THE FORBIDDEN LIBRARY
Storm Phase Book Three

THE BLOOD KING'S APPRENTICE
Storm Phase Book Four

THE FIRST KAIARU
Storm Phase Book Five

Made in the USA
Middletown, DE
08 August 2020

14745663R10130